Inge's War

A great war leaves the country with three arm
cripples, an army of mourners, and an ar
Proverb

Sieglinde P. Young

This book is a coming of age novel about the horrors of war as seen through the eyes of a young girl. It is based on historical facts. All characters are fictitious. The resemblance of any characters (except historical figures) to actual persons living or dead is purely coincidental. The dialogue and specific incidents described in the novel are products of the author's imagination and creativity. She has written two sequel novels to this work entitled: "Inge's Unexpected Guest" and "Inge, Revolution and Witchcraft".

ISBN: 1452838798 EAN
Library of Congress

Printed

Acknowledgments:

I want to thank my dear husband Jim for his patience, encouragement and technical assistance. Special thanks to my daughter Dannielle for her diligent review of my manuscript. I also want to thank my daughters Shavon and Charmain and my cousin Elsbeth for their interest and reinforcement of my efforts. Thanks to Andrew and Bill for designing the cover of this book, and to the Cocoa Beach Writers Critique Group for their input and support.

A word of clarification

The pronunciation of the names of two of the main characters is:

Inge – In-gee

Hamdi – Hahm-dee

Chapter One

Egypt 1984

Allah u Akbar, Allah u Akbar Mohammed rasoul - Allah!

Happy to be back in Egypt, Dena and I listened with pleasure to afternoon prayers coming from Mersa Matruh's minarets. Not paying attention to where we were going as we shuffled along the soft, sandy beach, we nearly bumped into two men speaking French. We performed a little impromptu dance act and mumbled apologies. The older man smiled, doffed his straw hat and gave a small bow.

I knew that smile.

"How gallant." Dena giggled and looked after them.

My heart skipped a beat and a torrent of emotions shot through me. Could it be? I grabbed Dena's arm and almost ducked when an Egyptian military jet roared overhead. Don't be stupid I scolded myself and glared first at the plane, already a dot on the horizon, then at the man, for both brought back memories of World War II.

"Handsome men," Dena said, "what do you think, father and son?"

Was this a special or a cursed day? I climbed onto an outcrop and stared at the shimmering water of the Mediterranean Sea.

"Do you know them?" Dena settled herself in an indent in the limestone, leaned back on her elbows and tilted her face toward the sun.

I contemplated my daughter and wondered, could it be after all these years? What if that man really was Paul-Emile Diderot? He had wanted to become an archaeologist. Was he too at Mersa Matruh for the excavation at Umm Rakham?

I sat next to Dena and chuckled. "Dena my love, if the older man is who I think he is, he's in for a surprise, for Inge Lyndt Boag has not forgotten the past."

"You sound positively ferocious. Are you going to tell me about him?"

I ran my fingers through her shock of auburn hair that reminded me of an autumn forest. We smiled at each other. "Since you are all grown up and famous, and won't be influenced any longer by a mother's impulsive and thoughtless character flaws, maybe I will. I hope you won't judge me too harshly."

When she didn't respond, I threw a few pebbles in the direction of the water and lost myself briefly in a maze of visions. Dena always had patience, whereas my other two daughters were more like me, full of sublime imaginations and adventures. I'd never bared my soul before and took a deep breath.

"I gave your Grandma much grief when I was small. I don't blame her for preferring your Uncle Edward. But in a way she brought it on herself, because for some reason she couldn't stand me from the minute I was born."

"Oh come on, all babies are sweet and loveable. Weren't we?"

"Of course you were, but maybe I was different. Maybe I was born wicked."

"Nobody is born wicked. And what does Grandma have to do with that man?"

I tossed another pebble, almost hitting Dena's foot. She didn't stir. "Nothing really, except ... I ... I felt she didn't love me anymore after Edward was born. I was so angry with her I ran away twice. Once I took him with me in his baby carriage, and the other time I left alone. I couldn't stand his constant screaming."

"Maybe he had cholic."

"For a whole year or longer?" I lit a cigarette and took a few puffs. "Instead of loving my mother, I transferred my love to Paul-Emile and I'd like to believe that he once loved me too."

"How romantic."

"It started before Edward was born, when the Nazi Reich instigated *Kinderlandverschickung*."

Dena bolted upright. "Huh, what on earth does that mean?"

I laughed. "Quite a mouthful isn't it. It means sending

children to the country. Germans love long words."

"Is that what happened to you?" She resumed her sun-worshiping position.

"Grandma was desperate to get rid of me, at least so I thought for years."

Chapter Two

"**The morning dawned** crisp and sunny that winter day of 1941 when I was five years old. When Mother turned on the radio shaped like a church window, Wagnerian fanfares announced Propaganda Minister Goebbels. His hypnotic voice praised the troops, touted their victories and promised Germany would soon rule the world.

"Happy and carefree, I sailed through our small flat in Hannover. I dipped my arms first right and then left and pretended I could fly like a swallow. After Goebbels' voice faded, Mother joined in with a men's chorus singing the Horst Wessel song. I stopped flying. This song called for marching as I'd seen the soldiers in their jackboots do on the broad boulevards of our city.

"I stood rigid with my right leg stiffly stretched forward then clomped it on the floor, my left leg followed. I stretched my right hand out in front of me and marched through the apartment to the soaring voices and Mother's singing.

"When the song ended, she scooped me up and carried me into our bedroom. I snuggled against her bosom, loving the fresh scent of the 4711 Cologne she favored.

" 'Time to get dressed, Inge, we need to leave in a few minutes or we'll be late.'

"After she helped me on with long wool stockings held up by a garter belt, warm pants, a shirt, sweater, a coat, mittens and a wool cap with a pompon on top, I scrambled down the stairs and ran out on the sidewalk covered with glistening snow. I grasped a handful and formed a snowball, but she waved a finger in front of my face and shook her head.

" 'Not now, we don't have time, maybe you can play with the other children later.'

"Hand in hand we walked to the factory where my father worked as a mechanical engineer. In the big yard, in front of the administration building, several ladies helped other children my age climb onto a bus. When my turn came, Mother tried to lift me up, but I braced my legs and held onto the handrail. One of the strange ladies smiled, pried my fingers loose, and helped swing me onto the bus.

"I kicked and screamed. 'I don't want to go, Mutti, I don't want to go.'

"But Mother turned her back and the lady pulled me to a seat. The door closed, gears clanked and the bus moved slowly toward the gate.

"I banged on the window with my fists and sobbed. 'Mutti, I want my Mutti, Mutti.'

"She waved but made no attempt to help me. They took us to a *Lager*, a camp, run by the Hitler Youth. What better age for indoctrination into National Socialism. I cried, the other children cried. Bedlam. The bus rolled on. I cried all the way to Braunlage in the Harz Mountains, a trip of several hours.

"When we arrived, we had to form ranks of two and march up a steep hill. Still crying, we slogged through the slush on the street, my shoes were soaked and my feet wet and cold. Out of nowhere something solid connected with my face. My voice froze into silence, then, with renewed indignation and rage I howled even louder. A teenage girl shook me by my skinny arms and threatened me with more punishment, but nothing worked. They finally left me alone. Still crying, I climbed the hill with the others toward our camp.

"We slept in a dormitory on cots low to the floor. Most of us cried ourselves to sleep that night and many other nights. When I did stop crying, I chewed my finger and toe nails to the quick and into the flesh. But good German girls are heroic, they don't cry and chew their nails. Consequently they made me stand for hours in a corner of a room with a plaster over my mouth. Not until painful cold sores festered on my lips did they bundle me in a blanket, hustle me into a car and drive me home.

"Mother waited for me on the sidewalk. She took my hand and led me upstairs to our flat. She told me to sit on my little white chair and handed me a baby-sized celluloid doll.

" 'This is a gift from your brother, come and have a look.'

"I followed her into the bedroom and found a baby sleeping in my crib. I loved Edward, but I could never forgive Mother for sending me away.

"In July 1941 the air raids began. The RAF always bombed at night. The USAF, once they entered the war, bombed during the day. The RAF's first target in Hannover was the railway. Several more raids followed and we spent many hours in the cellar or the bunker at Father's factory.

"Late fall that year my parents packed several suitcases, locked the door to our flat, and moved us to the industrial city of Litzmannstadt(Lodz), where Father was to teach at a technical school. We had become part of the *Germanization* of Poland, the new frontier for the Aryan race.

"I hated Litzmannstadt, a dirty, dreary city. It was bitterly cold and the snow black with grime. One day Father took me to see the movie "Snow White and the Seven Dwarfs". When the wicked stepmother appeared on the scene I screamed, terrified of her evil intentions. Embarrassed, Father hustled me out of the theater. He never took me anywhere again.

"Another petrifying incident occurred the evening Mother and Father left us alone in the flat. Edward cried. Unable to comfort him, I sat on the floor, leaned against a wall and took him on my lap. 'Don't cry, please don't cry.'

"I kissed him and wiped his tears, but he was inconsolable. Suddenly the wall behind me collapsed and fell into the courtyard two stories below. We screamed and didn't stop until our parents returned."

I stopped talking for a few minutes and wondered if these happenings had left an indelible mark on my psyche after all. Had they, and other circumstances, contributed to shaping my personality which definitely had shortcomings at times? No need to dwell on what happened eons ago. I couldn't reverse them and certainly wasn't about to justify and defend myself.

I continued. "When out shopping, we always had to walk

along a fence that separated us from the ghetto and 160,000 Jews who lived there in an overcrowded area. They wore a yellow star on their backs. Any Jew who approached the barbed wire fence was to be shot.

"The German Army drafted my father three months later. He had to present himself in Posen (Poznan) for induction. After we'd dropped him off, Mother, Edward and I traveled by train to Marienburg, West Prussia, to visit my maternal grandmother on the ancestral estate in Tessensdorf, three kilometers away.

"I loved everything about Tessensdorf except my cousins. They made fun of my speech. I complained to Mother. She said to ignore them, 'Hannoveranians speak the best German. Don't ever let anybody tell you differently.'

"I stuck out my tongue and laughed when they tried but couldn't imitate me correctly. To show them I had courage, I climbed the windmill ladder almost to the top. Apparently this was strictly forbidden for they screamed for Grandmother, their mother, my mother. Everyone shouted to hold on tight. Not afraid, I laughed and waved at them. One of the stable boys climbed up to get me.

"Besides German farm laborers, we also had three newly arrived French prisoners of war working on the estate. Grandmother assembled us children and gave instructions.

" 'Don't talk to the foreign workers, ever, do you hear?'

" 'Why not?' I asked her.

"She scowled and gave me a stern look. I don't think she was used to being questioned, especially by her grandchildren, but she answered.

" 'Government directives. They are to be treated as nonentities. Any more questions?'

" 'What does non ... non...?' I asked.

"My cousins giggled. Hilde whispered in my ear, 'You are going to get whipped.'

"I glared at her. 'I am not.'

" 'Silence,' Grandmother said, 'now run along.' We scattered. She called after us, 'Remember, stay away from the prisoners.'

"For a few days they were a curiosity, then we ignored them. My cousins in the meantime accepted me, for I brought with me new ideas of having fun. I quickly established myself the leader of our little group, a boy and a girl my age and four younger ones. When I climbed the tall ladder in the barn, jumped onto the haystack and slid down to the bottom, they followed. We plucked wiggly, pink, mud-streaked piglets with small blue eyes from the pigsty, scrubbed them, then took them for a stroll in a doll carriage. I suggested we harness their father's Labrador Retrievers to a small wooden wagon to pull us all over the yard. Every day I thought up different games.

"In the evenings we often sang rounds, our children's voices interwoven with those of the adults, and when we messed up, which resulted in confusion, we would double over with laughter and start all over again.

"New experiences abounded in Tessensdorf. I realized over the years one frequently received stronger impressions through the senses than through words. The cows, the horses, sheep, goats, chickens, geese, every animal on the farm emitted its own scent, and everything intermingled made me feel warm, cozy and content.

"Besides the animals I also treasured the elegant wedding coach stored in a barn filled with straw. Although we'd been forbidden to play in the coach, nobody supervised our activities much once we'd finished our assigned tasks. After school we did our homework, then we took turns practicing the piano. We had knitting, crocheting and embroidery projects, finally we were allowed to play outside weather permitting.

"A couple of months after our arrival, Mother took off for Hannover without me. She kissed me goodbye and said she'd see me for Christmas. Thank God she took Edward with her. This time I didn't cry, although at first I felt a little lonely without them. I often sat in the coach in the barn and pretended to be a princess. I talked to my doll and wished she would answer me. I asked her if she thought Mutti still loved me now that she had Edward. But my doll just smiled sweetly as if she knew a secret.

"I kissed and rocked her and whispered through tears, 'Sh,

don't cry, don't cry. I love you, you know I do.'

"On one memorable day in 1942, I skipped, with my doll in my arms, across the farmyard toward the barn and peered around the partly open door. After I checked behind me to see if anybody of consequence was watching, I slipped inside and followed the dust-laden sunbeam toward the coach.

"A strange noise stopped me. I clutched my doll to my pounding heart and thought about the field mice I had seen in the barn. Pooh, I wasn't afraid of them any longer and relaxed. Then came the mournful wail again. Not mice, a ghost. I shivered and listened for a moment longer then gritted my teeth and snuck cautiously in its direction.

"I found him. He lay in a nest of straw with his hands over his face. His body shook with wrenching sobs. I gaped at the wiry adolescent with unkempt hair. He must have sensed my presence, for he tried to burrow deeper in the straw.

"I realized at once he was one of the French prisoners. Although Grandmother had forbidden us children to speak to them, I didn't always follow her rules. He stared at me with frightened eyes. 'I won't tell,' I said, 'I promise. Don't be scared, I won't get you in trouble.'

"When I climbed in next to him he cringed. I stretched out my hand. 'My name is Inge Lyndt. What is yours?'

"He tried to rise, but his hands slipped in the loose straw and he fell back. I scooted closer, 'Can't you talk? My name is Inge and I'm almost seven years old. Do you have a name?'

"His adam's apple bobbed when he cleared his throat. 'Paul-Emile Diderot,' he croaked in a toneless voice. I repeated his name. He corrected me with an expression of misery and an unsuccessful effort at a smile.

" 'Why are you a prisoner? My Grandmother said you come from France. Is that a long way? Did you do something bad?' When he just looked at me with a frown, I patted his cheek. 'Please don't cry anymore. You don't have to worry, I won't tell anybody we spoke. Are you hungry?' I scrambled out of his nest. 'Wait here, I'll be right back.'

"I couldn't find him when I returned and softly called his name. He appeared before me like magic. I held my present for him behind my back. He sniffed with his nose in the air. I giggled. 'You smell something good?'

"His eyes twinkled and he spoke in French. I handed him the sausage sandwich. He gulped it down in a few bites.

" '*Merci, merci*, Inge.'

"When he bent forward and kissed my cheek, I wrinkled my nose for he smelled of straw, horse stable and cow manure.

" 'Don't you ever bathe? I have to take a bath every evening.' I walked to the wedding coach, climbed in and waved to him. 'You want to be my prince? I'm Cinderella. Do you know that story?' "

I laughed, jumped to my feet, stretched and rubbed my backside. "Sorry, but my bum is getting tired." I extended my hand and pulled Dena up.

She looked at me dubiously, "I think you are telling me a fairy tale as you did when the girls and I were little."

"Here I am revealing a deep secret and you don't take me seriously?" I gave her a playful scowl.

She kissed my cheek. "You are the greatest Mommy in the world.... Hey, don't cry.... Of course I take you seriously. It's just that you've never talked about your childhood and this sounds so ... well unreal."

I had myself under control again. "World War II was in many ways unreal. It was the most destructive war in human history. You won't find too many people who experienced the devastation talk about it because no one wants to talk about their own failures. Let's have dinner, Hamdi is probably wondering what happened to us. I'll tell you the rest later if you want to hear."

"Of course I want to hear. You think one of the men we saw a while ago is that same individual? What if he recognizes you?"

"It's been thirty-five years since we saw each other, he'll probably have forgotten all about me." I'd almost succeeded dismissing Paul-Emile completely from my thoughts over the years and now he was within arm's reach. I took a deep breath.

"Are you nervous?"

"I came to Mersa Matruh to participate in a dig, not to spend my days steeped in nostalgia. Let's go eat."

The hotel consisted of a collection of buildings along the beach. When we found the dining room we saw Hamdi talking to the men who'd passed us on the beach. He excused himself and walked over to us.

"I'm starving," Dena said, "what do you recommend?"

Hamdi led us to a table and helped us into our chairs. "Are those the French archaeologists you were talking to?" I asked.

Hamdi nodded, "They are eager to start. I'll introduce you later. Maybe we can invite them to your room for a cognac. You did bring a bottle?"

"We brought two," Dena said, "after all I am on vacation."

I hoped Paul-Emile wouldn't have a heart attack when he recognized me, if he recognized me. Served him right, that traitor. I glowered at the men who had taken a seat across the room from us and were studying the menu.

Hamdi recommended the large grilled shrimp with lemon butter and *roz bel khalta*, fried rice mixed with currants, nuts, beef and chicken liver, the cucumber salad and melon for dessert. I brought Hamdi up to date on Magda's chosen career as a botanist at the University of Florida, and Stephanie's relentless quest for the Ladies Open golf title. Dena talked about her upcoming concert tour in Australia.

"Three beautiful, talented daughters." Hamdi smiled.

"My life savers and my friends," I said and gave Dena a proud look.

After we'd finished our meal, Hamdi suggested a walk on the beach. We joined the other strolling guests who appeared to share our delight in the stiff, cool breeze blowing in off the sea. Hamdi kissed my hand. "Habibi (my darling), I am so happy you are here."

From the inside of his shirt he pulled the gold chain to which he'd attached my amber necklace I had given him many years ago, each bead imprisoning an insect.

"See, I still wear it, it is part of my life. I touch it a hundred times a day or more, wishing for the time when I can touch you when I wake every morning." He smiled. "When you want it back, tell me, that's all you need to do and I will understand."

I squeezed his hand then let go.

Dena turned, "Hey you two, maybe a cognac will put a smile on your faces. Come on, I'll race you back to our room."

"I am too old for such games, but I agree," Hamdi said. "Maybe we can invite the French." He winked, "One of them is beautiful, just right for you, tall, athletic, rich and unmarried, not too young ... Camille and his father Paul-Emile are a team ... Camille is the beautiful one."

"Uncle Hamdi, men aren't beautiful, they are handsome."

"Of course ... come, let's find them so I can introduce you."

Dena and I exchanged glances. My heart did a flip flop – to talk to him after all this time. Stop this nonsense, heart. Give him the cold shoulder, said my brain. I had to be sure.

"What did you say the men's names are?"

"Diderot. Didn't I tell you about the French financing this part of the excavation?"

Time, I needed time. Feeling slightly breathless I said, "I once knew a Paul-Emile Diderot when I was a child and he a prisoner of war. He would be fifty-eight or nine by now."

"That seems about right. When did you last see him?" Hamdi looked at me. "Are you all right, habibi?"

I nodded. "I'm fine." My moment of weakness passed. But when I tried to laugh I almost choked. Hamdi reached for my hand. I liked the way he gripped my hand, strong, warm, friendly and reassuring.

I gave him a grateful look. "Can't this meeting wait until morning?"

Someone shouted, "Hullo Dr. Gamal, wait up."

I tensed with a surge of emotion at hearing Paul-Emile's

voice that made me nearly dizzy. For a second, the white swirling clouds of snow began to close all around me and I shivered in the heat of the Libyan Desert. I breathed deeply trying to master myself, then turned with the others and watched the two men plow their way toward us through the white sand. The older was about five feet eleven, the younger slightly taller.

Paul-Emile looked elegant and aristocratic in his impeccably creased, gray trousers and white polo shirt over which he wore a dark gray vest with numerous pockets. His aquiline nose had grown more patrician with age and his thick, wavy, dark brown hair only slightly grizzled, but receding, gave him added distinction. Still a good looking man.

"Paul-Emile, Camille," Hamdi said, "I want you to meet Inge Boag and her daughter Dena. Inge is joining us at Umm Rakham. Dena is taking a break from her concert tour and unfortunately is leaving again in a week."

We shook hands.

"I knew an Inge once." Paul-Emile's eyes fixed me with a stare. He had an expression I could not read. It wasn't surprise, or love, or anger, he simply stared for several seconds then said, "You wouldn't be the same one would you? No, that would be too much of a coincidence."

Paul-Emile barely looked at him when Hamdi said, "Would you care to join us for a glass of excellent cognac? We were about to have a drink."

Camille and Dena chatted animatedly and led the way back to our room. After we'd toasted each other, Paul-Emile said in his thick French accent, "Madame Boag, this is your first excavation?"

"Dr. Gamal and I have been friends for many years. When I finally received my MA in archaeology, he promised to let me come and work with him. So here I am, looking forward to finding exquisite treasures in the sand."

"Much tedious work is involved, one has to have a lot of patience. Do you have patience, Madame?"

"We'll find out, won't we?"

"Mommy," Dena said and winked. "Camille and I are going for a walk. See you in a bit."

After they left, Paul-Emile studied my face carefully. "Madame, you remind me of my little Inge. Where were you during the last big war?"

Hamdi reached for my hand. "You mean World War II of course." I dabbed the pearls of sweat on my upper lip with my handkerchief. "Well, the way I remember, I traveled with some crazy Frenchman with whom I almost froze to death." The words came out thick and intense, not at all like the frivolity I'd aimed for.

Paul-Emile stared at me then leaned forward in his chair. Oh my God, I thought, he is going to embrace me, but he sat back again.

"Do you mind if I smoke?"

I shook my head. He fumbled in his vest pockets and withdrew a pipe and a pouch of tobacco. Fascinated, I watched him fill the bowl, tamp, then light it. After he'd taken a few puffs he said, "Madame Boag, Inge, when I first saw you, I had the most extraordinary sensation in the pit of my stomach ... your eyes ... I'll always remember your eyes."

He couldn't have seen my eyes for I wore sunglasses. I smiled. Men were such fibbers.

"Inge, you will allow me to call you by your first name? I must have said your name to myself a thousand times over the years, always accompanied by a sigh, and now I say it aloud ... I am talking to you ... really talking to you." He gazed at me. "Do you remember when you discovered me in the barn crying?"

I wanted to say, why did you come back into my life? Of course it was too late, we were sitting in the same room. I stuck a cigarette into my ivory holder. Paul-Emile jumped forward with his gold lighter. I took a few quick puffs then turned to Hamdi, "I found Paul-Emile crying in my grandmother's barn. He was one of the French prisoners working on the farm."

"You stood in front of me and stared," Paul-Emile said. "You wore some kind of sweat pants underneath a dark blue dress with white polka dots, and over that an open jacket with a hood. You also had a big, white bow in your hair and a missing tooth, making you look rather comical. I knew we weren't allowed to speak to each other. I was scared and anxious about what you would do next."

I nodded. "I remember that dress, one of my favorites and that bow, rather goofy, I agree ... I still have a picture of me in that outfit." I turned to Hamdi, "I told him not to cry, I wouldn't snitch on him."

"You remember...." Paul-Emile said with a broad smile.

"I remember everything about you, Monsieur."

"Why were you sent east, weren't you a bit young to be a prisoner?" Hamdi asked Paul-Emile.

"I was sixteen. My parents and I lived in Paris. Determined to somehow help my country, I volunteered to be a runner for the underground. I didn't tell my parents what I had done. On my first job I got caught. The Gestapo interrogated me then sent me to a camp where we were made to sleep in dog kennels. We had no water, no toilets and the fleas...." His lips trembled.

I wanted to comfort him but sat frozen in my chair. Thoughts of Freudenstadt where the French II Army Corps committed three days of killing, plunder, arson and rape flitted through my mind. I also thought of Stuttgart where French soldiers overstepped their boundaries at the end of the war by raping more than 3,000 women. I hugged myself. When would we be able to put the misery of World War II to rest? I glared at him, not feeling very kindly.

When he had himself under control he said, "I am sorry ... I will spare you the pain the Boches inflicted on us. After weeks of this inhumane treatment they sent me and hundreds of my countrymen east. The trip was brutal, hardly any food, little to drink, but the most devastating experience came when I had to listen to fellow prisoners die. Some went quietly, some screamed, some sobbed, some retched their guts out from being bludgeoned."

He glared at me accusingly. Feeling guilty, I lowered my eyes and played with my ring wishing he would stop talking.

He continued, "The vilest event of all occurred when the train stopped and we had to collect the dead, dig a grave and unceremoniously dump them one on top of the other...." He stared at his shaking hands, put down his pipe, then shoved them into his trouser pockets.

Hamdi squeezed my fingers. No one spoke. After a long moment Paul-Emile broke the silence. "When we arrived at our destination we were given all sorts of rules ... no use of railroads, no buses, no other public transport.... No visits to churches, no theaters, no motion pictures, no other cultural entertainment ... everything was strictly prohibited.

"Most of us were assigned to farms and told to work the hours the employer demanded. If we refused or loafed we were threatened with *special* treatment." His voice shook. "The *special* treatment ... hanging.

"I am sorry. I haven't spoken about this for a long time. I shed many tears, but always in secret, ashamed to show anyone I was scared of death which to me lurked around every corner. If it hadn't been for little Inge befriending me, I might not have survived the first year."

"And you haven't seen each other since the end of the war?" Hamdi asked.

Glad his revelation of his ordeals was over, I smiled and pursed my lips, "1949 to be exact."

Camille and Dena, laughing and chatting, burst into the room.

"Ready *mon père*?" Camille said. "We want an early start tomorrow morning."

Paul-Emile rose slowly and contemplated me with a fervent smile. He turned to Camille, "This has been an exceptional day my boy. Your Father has been reborn."

He gave me a small formal bow. "We'll see you at the site tomorrow?"

"Of course," I said, "that's what we are here for."

He nodded and bowed toward Dena. "*Bon soir* Mademoiselle, Dr. Gamal. Until tomorrow, Inge." He placed a hand on his son's shoulder and guided him outside.

I rose and let out a long breath. We looked after them until their voices faded and they disappeared in the darkness. Once back in our room I poured an ounce of cognac into my glass, downed it, and poured again.

"Hey Mommy, take it easy."

"Your Mother had a shock," Hamdi said. "She knew Dr. Diderot as a child, can you imagine? They haven't seen each other since 1949."

"So it is the right Diderot. All the time I chatted with Camille, a nice chap by the way, I wondered." Dena turned to Hamdi. "Mommy told me earlier about their first meeting, but she wasn't sure he was the right man. She also said all contact with the prisoners was forbidden."

"Yes, except for work instructions, we were not permitted to fraternize with the slave laborers."

"Why do you call them slave laborers?"

"That's what they were considered. This fellow Sauckel, hung after the Nuremberg trials, was in charge of the allocation of labor. He directed that 'the foreign workers were to be treated in such a way as to exploit them to the highest possible extent at the lowest conceivable degree of expenditure'."

"You didn't know that then, surely."

"Of course not, not until years later."

"How old were you when you met Monsieur Diderot?"

I took a sip of my drink and sat down again. "1942, I was six. I remember everything, at least everything different, scary and important."

Hamdi rinsed his glass. "I'll go now and let you two talk. Don't stay up too late. Like Camille said, we want to get an early start." He kissed my cheek and left. We looked after Hamdi.

"You think he's jealous?"

"Don't be silly. He has no reason."

Wide awake with my brain racing, I wondered whom Paul-Emile had married. Not a Boche, I knew that for certain. He was an attractive man, what if? No, I could never forgive him, and the way he had looked at me – I doubted he'd forgiven the Germans for his abominable experiences. His Mother would have made sure.

I kissed Dena on the cheek. "Let's go to bed."

I lay on my clean, white sheets and thought about the column of prisoners, barely living men, trudging with bowed heads as if in a dream or fog, past our street. Some had no shoes only rags wrapped around their feet. Their whole demeanor should have told us of their misery and pain, yet, some neighborhood kids and I threw stones at them. I don't know what happened to them but I, for one, would never forget them.

Dena sat next to me and stroked my hair. "Why are you crying?"

"I was thinking of an incident ... in that war nothing was normal. The most important aspect was not to be afraid."

"Were you afraid?"

"At first. Later the war seemed to obliterate fear the way smoke or a blizzard erases the horizon. Everybody who values life gets hysterical in a war and does things one would never dream of doing in ordinary times."

"I would like to hear more."

"Everything seems as if it happened yesterday. Although Paul-Emile was a stranger and the enemy, I was convinced I had found a true friend."

"**Once I met** Paul-Emile I no longer had time to be a princess. I had a new purpose in life, caring for the boy. After I brought him the sausage sandwich and saw how he'd devoured it, I snatched whatever food I could, sometimes a boiled egg, an apple or a slice of bread. It wasn't easy, because Grandmother had an upstairs maid, a downstairs maid, a milkmaid and a cook. Grandmother oversaw everything and knew exactly what the pantry contained.

"When fall turned the leaves into beautiful colors and the first frost silvered the earth, I slung a blanket over my shoulders early one evening and walked into the yard. Grandmother shouted for me to come back, but I ignored her and headed for the barn. I had it all planned. If she asked me later, I would tell her I left the blanket in the coach. She'd scold me for playing there at night, however, she had so much on her mind all the time, I knew she wouldn't think about it after a while.

"I pushed the creaking barn door open and stared into the black interior. I hesitated a moment, unsure whether I should enter, but the thought of Paul-Emile freezing emboldened me to squeeze through the small opening. The flapping wings of bats roosting in the rafters nearly panicked me into turning back.

"I made myself as small as possible, tiptoed in the direction of the coach and whispered, 'Paul-Emile, it's Inge, are you here?'

"The straw rustled, he touched my arm. I jumped and gasped, 'Don't scare me like that. I brought you a blanket.' "

" '*Qu'est-ce que ma petite?*'

"I groped for his hand and laid it on the blanket, 'To keep you warm.'

"I pulled the blanket from my neck and handed it to him. He said something, then, when he realized I wanted him to have it, he kissed my cheeks, first one side then the other. He smelled even worse than before.

"I pinched my nose, 'Don't you ever take a bath?'

"Of course he didn't know what I said. I wished we could talk to each other and told him to learn German. I pulled on the blanket he'd slung across his arm, '*Decke*, this is a *Decke*.'

"He repeated the word, then said in French, 'couverture.'

I imitated him, soon we laughed and practiced our new words over and over until he whispered, 'Hush.'

"I opened the door of the coach and climbed in. When he didn't follow, I hopped back out. He was gone. I knew he had to be careful. Uncle Peter, in whose house I lived, and Uncle Ludwig, the elder who lived next door, were members of the SD (*Sicherheitsdienst* - security service of the SS - Schutzstaffel or Blackshirts). Hardly anyone dared trifle with the older, arrogant brother because of his strong belief in Hitler and Nazism. I always felt sorry for my three cousins, two boys and a little girl, the older, my age, and the others a little younger, because he was very strict. Even Mother was afraid of him.

"The barn door squeaked. Grandmother, carrying a lantern, stood framed in the doorway calling my name. I walked hesitatingly toward her knowing I was in trouble.

" 'What are you doing here in the dark?' She grabbed my arm, shook me and pulled me out into the yard. 'Can't you behave yourself? You are more trouble than all the other children put together.'

"She was tall and lean like a string bean. Her gray hair was cut in a mannish style. She mostly wore black, long sleeved, three-quarter length dresses and black stockings, winter and summer. The only touches of softness were white cuffs and white lacy collars coming clear up under her chin. Her movements were quick, precise and energetic.

"Even though Uncle Peter owned the estate and his wife Gunhilde was first lady, Grandmother had never relinquished her role as grande dame after Grandfather's death. Everybody obeyed. Her word was law.

"She shoved me into the kitchen and said to Louise, the cook, 'Clean her up, feed her and put her to bed. No story for her tonight.'

"I slept in an iron double bed in a small, windowless, musty smelling room with a sloped ceiling and faded flowered wallpaper. A crib stood next to the bed and a narrow, curtained-off alcove held a chamber pot, a wash stand with a bowl and an ewer filled with water. My family always used this room, although father seldom visited here.

"I lay in the dark and thought about Paul-Emile. He looked so thin and had no gloves. Before I met him I always thought about my mother and my brother in Hannover, sometimes my father and wondered what they were doing, but now Paul-Emile dominated my whole life.

"A trunk in the attic was filled with one of my dead uncle's clothes. Under cover of darkness I brought Paul-Emile warm trousers, suspenders, a pullover and a jacket, socks and shoes. I had to be careful and worried about getting him into trouble. Every time I was cold, I pondered what to take him next.

"It was almost Christmas 1942 when Mother arrived from Hannover with Edward, along with her four sisters from various parts of the country. The house smelled of baked goods. My cousins and I fought over who would lick the dough bowl or the spatula.

"Louise lifted a big wooden spoon. 'Enough, get out of here, all of you.' We scattered and ran, for we knew she wouldn't hesitate to use it.

"Grandmother, Mother and my aunts sat at the long dining room table sipping from dainty cups. A cozy covered the china coffeepot. My aunts laughed and bantered. I snuck behind Mother's chair and was about to tickle her when Grandmother said, 'Inge is so preoccupied, willful, wild and disobedient. She's become a problem. What's going on with her?'

"Mother shrugged. 'Blame it on the war. We never get a decent night's sleep with all the bombing and the false alarms, one of the reasons I left her here with you.'

"Grandmother knitted her brows, 'The next time I catch her hiding in the barn I'll give her a whipping. I give you fair warning. I don't need her disobedience, I have enough on my mind.'

" 'Do what you have to do,' Mother said and took a bite of the apple cake.

"I snuck into the kitchen. A wave of warm air and appetizing vapors enveloped me as I sat quietly in a corner next to the tile stove. Louise and the other three maids stirred pots, polished silver and chatted. At first I didn't pay attention, then Louise said, 'I can't imagine why he hung himself.'

" 'Those frogs are kind of cute,' one of the girls said, 'wish we were allowed to talk to them. I feel sorry for the young kid, he couldn't be more than sixteen or seventeen. I wonder how come he's a prisoner.'

" 'Was he the one who hung himself?' Louise said.

" 'I don't know who.'

"I jumped up and shouted. 'Who hung himself?' and burst into tears.

" 'Oh shut up,' the maid polishing the silver said, 'what are you doing here anyways, always eavesdropping. If I had my way I'd have belted you by now.'

"I howled.

" 'Inge shut up,' Louise said, 'what are you bawling about?'

"I sobbed and stuttered, 'You said he hung himself.'

"She wiped my tears. 'I don't think it was the young one. Here,' she piled cookies on a plate, 'take him some of these.'

"I clutched the plate to my chest and ran across the yard to the barn. 'Paul-Emile, are you here? I brought you cookies.' I waited and shivered.

" 'Boo!'

"I jumped. The cookies flew off the plate and landed in the straw. I cried, 'Now look what you've done.' We bent down at the same time and banged heads. He laughed. He didn't know. I threw my arms around his neck. 'Promise you won't ever hang yourself, promise, you must promise.'

"He unclasped my hands, held me at arms length and spoke in French. A noise at the door caused Paul-Emile to melt into a corner; the straw rustled then all was quiet. I climbed into the coach, held the plate with three cookies on my lap then bit into one.

'I knew I'd find you here,' my cousin Hilde said. 'Your Mother wants you.'

"Mother took me to our room and told me to sit on the bed. She talked. I didn't listen to anything she said because images of Paul-Emile hanging himself had invaded my mind. I cried. She wiped my tears.

" 'What am I going to do with you?'

"I wanted to spend more time with Paul-Emile but I couldn't get away. Three of Mother's sisters behaved like leeches toward us children, clinging, cuddling, fondling and kissing. Being single and childless, they didn't understand when to quit.

"On Christmas Eve, after we sang carols and my cousins and I acted out a Christmas play, Grandmother allowed us to open our presents. She gave each of us four girls an amber necklace and a matching bracelet with an insect imbedded in each bead."

Dena interrupted, "Is that the same necklace Uncle Hamdi has worn for so many years?"

"The same." I smiled, knowing what she was going to ask next.

"Why did you give it to him and not to Daddy?"

"I gave him the greatest treasure I possessed, a piece of my childhood, because I didn't want Hamdi to ever forget me."

"And Daddy?"

"Your Daddy was not a sentimentalist. It would have meant nothing to him. Shall I go on now?"

"On Christmas Day things became hectic and complicated. I couldn't get away so easily because every relative living in the area and good friends of the family arrived to celebrate with us, about twenty adults and eighteen children in all. I can't imagine where everyone slept that night.

"The long dining table was laden with food. I had never seen such a sumptuous *Tafel*. Three roasted hares, deboned and stuffed with spiced chicken, lay on a bed of cabbage on huge white and blue platters. Two geese, a pork roast, herring salad, mousses, potato salad, vegetables, mashed potatoes, gravy, preserved fruits, punches, lemonade, and more were offered to the guests. Later the maids served coffee, an assortment of cakes and delicious cookies.

"Afterward, as cigar and cigarette smoke eddied around the chandelier, and different kinds of liqueurs sparkled in tiny crystal glasses, the servants pushed aside the dining table and chairs to make room for dancing and games. The feasting, dancing, piano-playing and shrieks of laughter went on until deep into the night. Grandmother shooed us children to bed, but who could sleep with that ruckus. Giggling, we snuck one by one back into the dining room to watch the adults' relaxed hilarities. After a hearty brunch the next day most of the guests left.

"A couple of days later Mother whisked me away without discussing any of her plans. Unable to say goodbye to Paul-Emile, I screamed all the way to the railway station. 'I don't want to go. Why are you making me go?'

"We visited Father in Posen for a week, then took the train to Hannover. All the compartments and the narrow corridors were jammed with people. They completely ignored German politeness and correctness and shoved and jostled for position. No one wanted to be left behind. Troop trains passed us going east. We'd be pulled onto sidings so trains loaded with wounded could move past. Sometimes the troop trains stopped, men carried out bodies on stretchers and laid them beside the tracks. Tanks, trucks, motorcycles, clogged the roads. All of Germany appeared to be on the move.

"When we reached Hannover and walked toward the streetcar stop, we passed marching soldiers. They sang and the cobblestones resounded under their jack boots and rhythmic steps. Further down the street a crowd stood gathered near a platform. Someone screamed words I couldn't understand. I jumped up and down and craned my neck for a look at the orator.

" 'It's a loudspeaker,' Mother said with a disgusted grimace on her face.

" 'What's he saying?'

" 'Gibberish. Nothing worthwhile listening to.'

"The audience applauded Hitler's recorded voice. Soon after we arrived at our apartment, the warning sirens howled throughout the city. First came the *Kleinalarm* (small alarm), then, if an attack was imminent, came the second alarm or *Fliegeralarm* (airplane alarm), fifteen rapid, four-second wails. They penetrated the walls, our skins and our veins. The house and our bones vibrated, we couldn't escape them. Whoever invented those sirens knew what evil was all about, because the sound itself instilled terror in our hearts.

"Mother had just peeled potatoes for our lunch and set them on the stove to boil. She grabbed Edward and the ever ready packed suitcase and scrambled down the two flights of stairs into the street where smoke pots had already been activated. People tumbled out of their buildings as though they were starving rats on the scent of food. I raced after Mother shouting, 'Wait for me!'

"The entrance to the public shelter, a domed, silo-like structure called *Hochbunker,* was two and a half blocks away. An excited mob milled around the air raid wardens who shouted, 'Mothers and small children first, mothers and small children first'. Mother showed her *Platzkarte* which entitled us to the shelter and they let us in.

"Soon the thunderous drone of many airplane propellers almost drowned out the wardens. Frantically we climbed the steps that still smelled of damp concrete. Up, up, we panted, then came to a room with space for us. Each room contained benches and pails filled with sand and water.

"Only moments later the thunder of exploding bombs shook the earth and our silo. Wave after wave of planes emptied their wombs of their deadly cargo and sent it screaming toward their targets.

"There we sat, petrified, steeped in lies and fear, hunted and at war. My eyes followed the noise, the flickering bulb in its cage and the racket of the exploding bombs falling above and around us. I scented danger and held Mother's hand in a death grip. When dust permeated our room and the bulb extinguished, my stomach cramped. She lightly covered Edward's face with a damp handkerchief then pressed a wet cloth in my fist and told me to cover my face. People prayed and howled as the silo once more whipped back and forth.

"When, a couple of hours later, the *all clear* sirens sounded, the tenseness relaxed. Although the air was still thick with dust and fear, we dared breathe again and thanked God for sparing our lives.

"The sky loomed black with acrid smoke and the air appeared turbid and smelled of explosives when we emerged that afternoon. A snowstorm of ashes, rubble and ruins greeted us, and a once familiar scene was unrecognizable. I briefly wondered if we'd been transported onto a barren, unfriendly planet. Dead horses, dead people, and dead dogs all grotesquely mutilated lay on the street among shattered roof tiles, bricks, broken glass, fallen chimneys and bomb shrapnel. A groaning man with blood streaming down his face crawled along the curb.

"Mother told me not to look, but I couldn't help but gawk at the man and the scarlet puddles in the gutter. Hardly daring to breathe, we picked our way through the rubble toward our apartment. We peeked around an undamaged corner building at our street.

"Our apartment house stood between two wrecked ones. Of the other apartment houses only part of the foundation walls were intact. Bent girders hung between them like a jungle of liana vines. Air raid wardens, firemen and civilians shouted and milled about, unsure of how to attack the enormous problems facing them.

"Stretchers stood by the side of the road. Because my eyes burned and teared from the acids in the vapor from the bombs, I couldn't tell if the persons on the stretchers were dead or alive. In the dull glow that hung over the area, people dug frantically with pickaxes and their hands for strangers or loved ones still presumed under the debris.

"Relieved we still had a home, we shuffled past them ignoring their misery. Once we entered our building, we ran up the stairs to our apartment. Mother tried to push the door to our flat open but it wouldn't budge. We shoved and shoved again until we managed to squeeze through the crack. Several feet of earth had taken up residence inside and the glass in all the windows was gone.

"Mother all of a sudden shouted, 'Oh my God, I didn't turn off the stove!'

"She rushed into the kitchen, but her pot had been saved by the bombs that cut electricity to the whole city. The potatoes were just nicely done and sitting unspoiled on the stove.

"After a quick lunch we attacked the mountain of debris. I helped Mother fill buckets which she dumped through the broken window back into the bomb crater from which it came. We marveled at our luck, just a few yards over and our house too would have been gone.

"The park-like area behind our apartment building, littered with uprooted trees, their trunks split open, resembled a haunted and enchanted wasteland. For the still burning trees were covered with silver tinfoil that the Allies had tossed in bundles out of airplanes to interfere with radar by distorting the radio waves. The foil fluttered and sparkled in different colors resembling angel's hair on Christmas trees.

"Many times during our night scrambles for the bunker the sky was lit up with what we nicknamed "Christmas trees". These were actually target markers attached to small parachutes resembling pyrotechnic candles, yellow, red and green. While they floated gently to earth, the planes made their bombing runs. The Germans in turn sent up decoy flares and with their overlapping searchlights cutting across the sky, it made for a spectacular fireworks display.

"Hannover burned that day. On the horizon an occasional wind gust parted the billowing, black plumes of smoke revealing a sea of licking flames that sprouted higher and higher into the sky. We had no electricity, no water. The Germans were either prepared for such events or ultra efficient. Before long they set up soup kitchens and supplied water at various locations throughout the city. A week later we found glass for the windows and tiles for the roof neatly stacked at the entrance to our short street.

"In August 1943, Mother bundled us up again, packed many suitcases and took us to Prussia via Posen. Again we had to fight our way onto the train and push through the crowds. Most of the time we sat on our suitcases in the corridor.

"Although the German people were changing, the steeples, rivers, hillsides, trees and the brown, black and white cows peacefully grazing on the meadows, remained the same. From the train I saw ordinary people, few military this time. Each station master had a tiny garden in which grew dahlias, irises, or roses.

"Posen was an attractive, clean city with wide avenues lined with blooming beechnut trees. We stayed in housing especially provided for families visiting the soldiers. Father took us to a botanical garden with a huge solarium full of tropical plants and flowers, and an aviary with colorful birds. We rode in a pony cart; listened to German bands play gay music; sat at round tables and drank lemonade and watched all the soldiers pass by in their different uniforms representing various branches of service.

"I adored the bands that played selections from operettas.

Most Germans loved music. Daily concerts in band shells, zoos and parks kept people's minds off the ever worsening catastrophe rapidly engulfing them. Everything about German National Socialism was orchestrated to music. When soldiers marched, they sang. When the Hitler Youth went on outings or whatever they did, they sang. We children sang. Mothers worked and sang. Glorious!

"I drove Mother crazy asking her when we could leave, when are we returning to Tessensdorf. What if Paul-Emile was dead? Just thinking of the possibility made me cry. I knew Mother was at her wit's end. I had become such a problem that she often lost her temper and beat me with her hairbrush. The more she beat me, the more defiant I became.

"I wandered away into a crowd of wounded, haggard-looking soldiers with expressionless faces. Many hobbled on crutches, others had arms in slings or heads wrapped in bandages. Yet, like marionettes controlled by strings, their good arms flew in the air as they saluted and shouted, '*Heil Hitler*' every time someone of a higher rank passed by.

"When Mother called my name I hid behind a tree. Of course she found me. She grabbed my arm and dragged me back to our table where Father, dressed in his Private's uniform sat with Edward. Tears rolled down her cheeks and I could tell she was angry enough to murder me.

"Father accompanied us to the train. After we'd hugged and kissed goodbye, he helped us push our way aboard, handing Mother the heavy suitcases one after the other through the window.

"Upon our arrival in Marienburg, I hopped off the train and ran toward the street to look for Uncle Peter's rig. Mother, surrounded by her five suitcases and holding my brother in her arms yelled for me to come back. When I saw Uncle Ludwig marching in our direction, I ran back and obediently stood next to her.

"He clicked his heels, touched his peaked cap with his right hand and said, '*Heil Hitler.*'

" '*Bist Du verrückt?*' (Have you gone mad?) Mother asked with a contemptuous laugh.

"He scowled and snapped, 'Respect, I want your respect.' He kicked one of the suitcases, 'You expect me to carry those?'

"Mother looked forlornly around her, 'Would you rather carry Edward? I'll take care of the bags.'

"And that's what happened. She had to make three trips while he sat impatiently in the carriage. When everything and everybody was aboard he whipped the horse and it took off like a flying machine. Soon the three kilometer trip was over and we stopped smartly in front of Grandmother's house.

"After a servant had taken care of our luggage, Mother asked Grandmother why she'd sent Ludwig to pick us up from the railway station. Grandmother frowned, 'Didn't he tell you? Your brother Peter drowned while hunting last month.' She looked angry. 'He shot a duck and instead of sending the dog in training, he swam out himself.'

"Mother sat on the bench by the front door and buried her head in her hands. I hated to see her cry. It always made me angry. I hugged one of my uncle's beautiful black Labrador Retrievers, held on to his collar and led him slowly toward the stables. I checked once to see if Mother and Grandmother were watching me, but they were still in deep conversation and finally walked into the house.

"Then I saw him. Paul-Emile leaned on a pitchfork in the middle of a pile of cow manure. We stared at each other. He smiled, then bent over and lifted a fork-full of the stinking, dripping, brown goo and pitched it onto the steaming dunghill.

"I wrinkled my nose hoping he'd take a bath and change his clothes. What if he didn't have clean clothes? I trotted back to the house. Grandmother stopped me as I was about to run upstairs.

" 'No greetings?' She bent down and I gave her a quick peck on the cheek.

" 'May I go now?'

" 'You are in a hurry?'

" 'My doll needs me. I haven't seen my baby for weeks.'

"She nodded. 'Run along. I think I hear her crying.'

" 'You do?' I stared at her. She smiled and walked toward the kitchen.

"After the swing door shut behind her, I scrambled upstairs to the attic. I flipped open the trunk lid and rifled through the clothes. A shirt and a pair of pants would do for now. I rolled everything up, tucked it under my arm, and was about to sneak back down, when I saw Mother coming toward me. I pushed the bundle of clothes under the bed and washed my hands in the bowl, knowing this would please her.

"I fidgeted all through dinner, gulped my food and was ready to run off, but this didn't work at Grandmother's house. We children, who sat at our own small table next to the long dining table, were not allowed to leave until everybody had finished eating.

"That evening I couldn't get away from my cousins. Uncle Ludwig's three children also ate with us. Soon after dinner Mother decided we had to go to bed because we'd had a long day. I gritted my teeth and climbed into the bed she and I shared. She settled my brother in the crib, said good night, and left us to join the other adults. I waited until I heard my brother's light snore. Then I laced my high-top shoes, belted my overcoat, stuck the bundle of clothes under my arm and stole across the hall into Grandmother's room.

"She slept in the best and largest room in the house. French doors led to a balcony entwined with old, gnarly wisteria. I threw the bundle to the ground and climbed down. My cousins and I had done this numerous times before, so I knew just what to do. I picked up the bundle and headed for the barn.

"He was waiting for me. 'Paul-Emile, did you take a bath? I brought you fresh clothes.'

" 'Bath,' he laughed and pressed a book into my hands '*Votre grand mère . . . une dictionnaire....*' He found my hand and pulled me closer, '*Viel Wasser*, much water.'

"But he still stank. I groped for the buttons on his shirt and unbuttoned it. He pulled it off and threw it away. I sniffed, he sniffed, he still carried the faint aroma of cow dung.

'Your pants, take off your pants.' I tugged at them. 'I can't see you, go ahead.'

"I heard a rustle, '*Voilà!*' His hands found my face, he hardly smelled at all when he planted a fat kiss on my forehead. I sat next to him in the straw and holding tight to my hand, he talked to me in whispers. It didn't matter what he said. My heavy eyelids drooped and his voice faded. He shook me awake only minutes later, walked me to the door and pushed me outside.

"I climbed the wisteria, over the wall and onto the balcony just as Grandmother entered her room. She found me curled up in a chair and called to Mother, 'I found her.'

"Mother nudged me gently. I rubbed my tired eyes and followed her to our room. 'You stink ... never mind, you can bathe tomorrow.'

"Two weeks later Mother knelt in front of me. She told me she was leaving me with Grandmother again because of the bombing in Hannover. It was safer for me to stay, and I could play with my cousins. This suited me perfectly. I didn't complain."

"Why didn't Grandma stay in Tessensdorf?" Dena asked.

"I didn't learn until later that Mother's sister-in-law Gunhilde disliked her visiting so often. She had the gall to ask Mother to pay for her keep. This request made Mother angry, so she went back to Hannover. I never did find out exactly what went on between those two.

"Paul-Emile learned German. When we had a few moments together, he taught me his new words in French. Grandmother had mellowed toward the young man. When Uncle Ludwig was gone, which happened often, she used Paul-Emile to take her to Marienburg in her horse and buggy and us children to school. Happy to be near him, I frequently sat on the coachman's seat.

"Mother returned for Christmas 1943. We didn't celebrate much that year. The army had requisitioned our beautiful thoroughbreds as well as four of the work horses. Only two work horses and Grandmother's carriage horse remained. They also took some of the cows, pigs and sheep to feed the starving soldiers fighting on the eastern front. All the German stable boys were soldiers now. We had, besides Paul-Emile and René, three Polish prisoners working the land and tending what was left of the animals. Uncle Ludwig still had all his horses."

I yawned.

"You are not going to stop now, are you?" Dena said covering her mouth trying to suppress a yawn.

I looked at my watch. "It's after one. We have all week."

"All right."

I kissed her cheek and tucked the sheet around her shoulders. "Sleep well."

I'd just dozed off. However, being a light sleeper, a faint tapping at the window woke me. I smiled, Hamdi or Paul-Emile? No, not Hamdi. I slipped into shorts and a tee shirt, softly released the safety chain from the door and stepped onto the lit stoop. The cool air and a vague excitement made me shiver. The thrill of the unknown, missing since Kane's death and my youth, set my blood to racing. I descended the four steps, stood on the sand and listened for a moment. When I didn't hear anything, I strolled in the direction of the sea.

He clasped me from behind, suddenly, without warning. I slipped out of his grip, spun around and punched him in the throat.

He grabbed my fist and rasped, "Inge, *c'est moi*."

I laughed at the hurt and indignant tone in his voice. "Monsieur, you have grown arrogant in your old age. You tried to kiss me. How dare you. We've just met ... and you a married man. You have a son so I assume you have a wife."

"I do, but...."

"She doesn't understand you." I pushed the hair out of my face then tucked in my shirt. "Paul-Emile, I've blamed you for many things that went wrong in my life ... and you want me to disregard everything and allow you to kiss me?"

"I never stopped loving you, never ... I want our skins to touch. I want to kiss every inch of your body ... I've dreamed of this moment all these years. It's a miracle we found each other again."

I headed toward my room. Liar, why were men such liars?

"Inge...." He reached for me. But I stepped back and his arms dropped by his side. "I apologize for being presumptuous. Images of a sexy, fourteen year old climbing all over me without a stitch on her gorgeous body still dance before my eyes."

"I was rather nubile back then, wasn't I?"

Oh my, what would my daughters think if they knew of their mother's exploits? I broke into laughter and sat on the sand. He lowered himself a couple of feet away and drew a pack of cigarettes out of one pocket of his robe and a small flask out of the other. He handed me the flask. I took a sip of the excellent Napoleon, handed it back and contemplated the black horizon. "Why did you never come looking for me?"

"I had no resources. My parents blocked all funds my grandparents had left me. They didn't relinquish them until I married the woman they decided would be good for me. Of course then it was too late. Looking for you after I married would have been useless. So I tucked you away deep in my heart. I wrote you several letters at first, then later, I allowed myself only to think of you on your birthdays."

"You wrote letters. I don't remember receiving any."

"I burnt them."

"Better you than me."

He stared into the distance for a moment, "I ... I should have behaved differently, paid attention to you ... instead I was selfish, thoughtless ... I regret that now."

"Forget it. Regret is the most useless emotion in the world. Besides, regrets cannot be recalled and cannot be fixed. We were not meant to be perfect, for many times we act on our feelings of the moment." I laughed. "Can you imagine a world full of saints?"

"I never regretted sending you birthday cards though. Did you receive any?"

"You actually sent cards?"

"I sent them to every big city in the world, every year a different one."

I leaned over and kissed his cheek. "Thank you. I never sent you a single one. I could never forgive you."

"And now you do?"

"I should, just like that?" I snapped my fingers. "Your wife is waiting for your return?"

He reached for my hand and tried to kiss my palm, but before he could, I pulled it away.

"Why are you so touchy?"

"I dislike being handled by strange men." I scooted further away from him so he couldn't reach me.

"I am not a strange man."

"Never mind. What about your wife?"

"She is waiting. My parents told her about what they called, 'a young man's folly', and when we have a fight, which is often, she brings you up. Her names for you are quite colorful."

"All these years?"

"She is a haughty, wealthy and controlling woman. I loved her once, or thought I did, not now, not for a long time." He shrugged.

"What about your son, what if he finds out about us here tonight?"

"I love him very much, he is a fine son. He loves his mother's money, so, alas, he is in her pocketbook. Is this the right expression?"

"I think it's in her pocket. Dena and Camille seem to have hit it off."

"He is charming, however I wouldn't recommend him as a husband. So, will you give me your address?"

"I'll think about it."

"Dr. Gamal stands in our way?"

"What do you have in mind?"

"A little wayward love now and then?"

"I don't think so, Monsieur, for that you can engage a mistress." I rose. "Good night, Paul-Emile."

He jumped to his feet. "Please don't be offended. You must promise never to leave me again. Will you promise?" He leaned over as if to kiss me then didn't.

I gazed at him for a moment, smiled and walked back to my room.

"You've been gone a long time." Dena said.

"I walked on the beach and did some thinking. Do you mind if I take a quick shower?"

She mumbled something. I lay awake and felt young and vibrant, ready for an adventure, but sex? The last time I had sex was with Kane just before he died. My God, I was probably all shriveled up. I chuckled inwardly, why did my heart throb just at the thought of having sex with Paul-Emile?

I decided growing old was just a physical phenomenon and had nothing whatever to do with how one felt inside. 'Don't ever leave me again,' he'd said. I smiled. He certainly knew the words to a middle aged woman's heart. Maybe this new adventure would lift me out of my doldrums. Whoever said, 'getting used to things is death - it is ennui', was right, Paul-Emile came along at just the perfect moment.

What was I thinking? I bolted upright and whispered, "Hamdi." By God, I was an evil woman even thinking about a liaison with Paul-Emile. I was grateful Hamdi couldn't read my rotten mind. Hamdi, so gentle, kind and loving. I lay back and sighed. He loved me – so I was worth something, if I weren't he wouldn't love me. And Kane had loved me too. Maybe I wasn't so evil after all. What to do? I loved Hamdi, my best friend, had for years and years. How could I possibly lust after another man? Lusting, I wasn't lusting, Paul-Emile was. Oh for crying out loud, Inge, go to sleep. I closed my eyes and rocked for a while longer on the waves of duplicity toward my faithful friend.

After breakfast the next day Hamdi picked us up in his Land Rover. "I see you've done your research, smart ladies." Dena and I looked at our hiking boots and socks into which we'd tucked our trousers.

"We'll have a look at the excavation site first," Hamdi said. "It's a few miles west from Umm Rakham, next to the Ramses II monument. Unfortunately Ramses, built of limestone, is in bad shape. During the winter rainy season we have frequent floods here, bad for limestone. We are unconcerned with the temple at present, only what might be buried nearby. After I show you the site we'll drive to Siwa Oasis."

When I sat next to him, Hamdi leaned over and kissed my cheek. "Did you sleep well, habibi?" I waved my hand in the air. "Lots on your mind?"

"Lots."

The road to Umm Rakham paralleled the stark white sand dunes alongside the blue-green waters of the Mediterranean Sea. The temple stood in an olive-fig grove overgrown with thistles. Three local men in *gallabiehs* wielded pickaxes, while several others scooped the debris into baskets and dumped it through a screen beyond the limits of the site. We watched them for a few minutes, then walked to a deeper trench out of which only a hat was visible.

"Good morning, Paul-Emile," Hamdi said, "anything of interest?"

Paul-Emile looked up, smiled and shook his head. "Good morning Inge, *comment allez-vous ma chérie?*"

"*Tout va bien.*" I continued to speak to him haltingly in French, then reverted to English. "I haven't spoken French for ages, it's a bit rusty."

"A few hours with me will bring it all back."

I stole a sidelong glance at Hamdi who watched us with a wrinkled brow, then mumbled in Arabic and stomped off in the direction of a third trench. Dena followed him and tucked her arm in his. She leaned into him and said something. Hamdi nodded.

Paul-Emile, too, looked after them. "Dr. Gamal is in love with you?"

"For many years."

"And your husband?"

"Kane is dead." I was glad he couldn't see the tears behind my sunglasses.

"I am sorry ... you loved him very much?" When I didn't answer he continued, "We must talk."

I stared at him for a long time. When I had myself under control, I said, "I am uncertain what talking will accomplish."

I adjusted my straw hat and followed Dena and Hamdi. Dena's throaty laughter wafted toward me. She knelt next to the trench. Two arms reached for her and drew her into the channel. "What is she doing down there?" I said when I stood next to Hamdi.

"Camille found a small stone statue imbedded in the limestone, he is showing her how to dislodge it. So, what have you decided about Paul-Emile?"

"Nothing. Don't worry, he's unimportant." Was I lying? I wished I hadn't come, then things would have progressed normally. After Kane's death, Hamdi had been up to this point the only man of consideration in my life. Damn. I kicked a stone and watched it drop into the ditch. "If you brought me to your room tonight would we have any privacy?"

He studied me intently. "And Kane?"

"He could watch."

"I think we should leave now." He called Dena whose head popped up out of the trench.

She waved. "Give us a few more minutes, almost done."

I walked away in the direction of Ramses. Poor Ramses all by himself in this lonely place.

"If we don't leave soon," Hamdi said, "it'll be dark before we get to Siwa. They are still working on the road it might be slow going. I hate to drive in the dark."

"Are the French coming?"

"You want them to? I can ask them."

"Might be nice for Dena, she doesn't have much time for male companionship."

"And the father, you are curious about the father after all this time."

I turned to look at him, "Do you mind?"

"I'll go ask, then see if I can get a permit for them."

I followed him slowly back to the dig. Dena rushed toward me. "Look what Camille found," she stretched out her arm and handed me the small stone statue of a young girl. "He thinks she might be a little princess. What do you think?"

I examined the statue. "It's possible. It will need more research on my part. Hamdi and the Diderots are the Egyptologists, ask Hamdi." I handed back the relic. "Are you ready to go?"

Hamdi strode toward us, "Paul-Emile said they'd love to come if we wait until tomorrow. They have to pack a few things and catalogue today's find."

Dena and I looked at each other, "Tomorrow sounds great," I said.

That evening after dinner with the French, we all strolled on the beach for a while, then the French invited us for a cognac in their room. The men talked about the dig, while Dena and I listened. Paul-Emile kept gazing at me while Hamdi glowered at him, and Camille and Dena exchanged smiles. It had been thirty-five years since his parents kicked me out of their house. Hamdi loved me – why dwell on the past – I was so young – who determined at what age a girl could fall in love, real love, love that lasted a lifetime?

"Inge, what do you think?"

I smiled. "I'm afraid I wasn't listening. What was the question?"

"We were talking about the soldiers who came through here during the Africa campaign." Hamdi said. "They probably did a little digging themselves."

"Wouldn't surprise me a bit. I've seen tourists pick up little pieces of colored rocks from underneath frescoes in the tombs. If it's lying there why not? They don't consider this stealing antiquities. I am sure the soldiers didn't think twice about using their shovels during a lull either." I rose, "I think I'll turn in."

"Me too," Dena said.

Hamdi escorted us to our room. Dena excused herself, went inside and left us standing on the stoop. "Hamdi darling, when my two months are over, I want you to take me on a Mediterranean cruise, somewhere only travelers go. No tourists. I hate swarms of tourists. You think about it. When you have it all planned out present me with your agenda."

"Somewhere remote ... you have a place in mind?"

"I'd love to visit some of Salah El Din Yusuf's castles and fortresses."

"You want to go to Syria?"

"We could start at Latakia. What do you think?"

"Just you and me? And you will love me in the mountains?"

"If Kane doesn't object." He hugged me, then found my mouth. We clung to each other.

He released me and clasped my shoulders, "Habibi, I love you. I will arrange everything the way you want."

When I entered our hotel room Dena smiled. "He kissed you." I nodded.

"He loves you so much."

"Yes, he does."

Last night you said your Uncle Ludwig still had all his horses. Why?"

I plumped my pillows behind my back and sipped on a glass of cognac. "He was buddies with the *Gauleiter*, the political head for a district."

"What happened next?"

"In June1944 mother returned to Tessensdorf. Although bombs still fell on Hannover almost daily, she came to fetch me. When Grandmother questioned the wisdom of her decision Mother said, 'If she stays here, she is stuck. In my opinion the war is lost. I would rather risk bombs than Russians.'

"Mother was either brave or stupid when she said the war was lost. If anyone who mattered had overheard her, she could have been shot or hung. She talked defeatism, strictly forbidden.

"All my temper tantrums didn't sway her. Even though the front was only about a hundred miles east of Tessensdorf, everything was still tranquil. We hardly knew a war raged nearby.

"The next time Paul-Emile and I sat in the grass splendid with blooming buttercups in the evening sun I said, 'I'll never see you again.' I sobbed till I couldn't speak any longer.

" 'Stop crying, I can't stand crybabies, I've told you that often enough.' He urged me to go with Mother and promised to find me later no matter what. When he saw he couldn't pacify me, he became angry. 'What do you expect me to do? I am a prisoner here, a prisoner, do you hear?' He threw his arms in the air and stalked off.

"I ran after him and pulled at his sleeve. 'I won't cry anymore, don't be angry.'

" 'Remember, I hate tears.'

"Only a few days later we prepared for our journey back to Hannover. Mother had a dated special travel permit engineered by my father's boss. Summer had arrived early and the sun filtered warmly through the heart-shaped leaves of the mighty linden trees surrounding the yard. They were laden with small, yellowish-white, drooping clusters of flowers and scented the air with an indescribably enchanting aroma.

"I sat on the threshold of the doorstep, yawned and watched Paul-Emile cross the farmyard. A dog barked and danced around him. He'd grown in the last two years. Now eighteen, he was lean and hard and instead of pimples his face sprouted brown peach-fuzz. I blinked into the sun and the surrounding white puffy clouds swimming on the horizon. He lowered himself on the stoop.

" 'I have to leave with my mother.' My voice broke, but I was determined not to cry.

"He nodded. Edward sat next to us, his pudgy fists grasped a sausage sandwich. My stomach grumbled. I asked for a bite, he handed me the sandwich. I broke off a piece and shared it with Paul-Emile.

"A joyous cacophony erupted when Grandmother strode proudly across the yard with her feed pail. The dogs barked and wagged their tails, geese, ducks and chickens cackled, quacked and clucked excitedly and flocked toward her. The routine never varied, everything here appeared so steady, so sure. Paul-Emile rose and said he had to go to work.

"In the afternoon, my great-aunt Lena, my two aunts,

Mother's sisters-in-law, Grandmother, Mother and we eight children sat on the large terrace at the back of the house sipping hot chocolate and eating cookies. The adults talked about the war and wondered what would happen if the Russians came.

"I sipped my cocoa and looked at the beautiful rock garden brilliant with flowers, golden in the sunshine, and a luminous white in the shade. Quiet – so quiet and peaceful, a wonderful peace, full of safety and security. Beyond the garden on a soft incline stood a copse of birch trees, their leaves fresh and green. I gazed at the deep blue sky above and at the tall beechnut trees that grew on either side of the house. I didn't want to leave here.

"Mother stood on the edge of the terrace with Edward in her arms and looked forlornly into the distance. She appeared sad and preoccupied, probably thinking about her dead father and brothers whom she'd loved so much. Everything had changed, one great love lost after the other. Life would never be the same.

"She stepped lightly down into the garden, put Edward on the path and slowly they walked hand in hand toward the wisteria entwined gazebo. Her fingertips slid over the moss covered sundial. I guessed she was saying good-bye to her ancestral home.

"She walked every corner of the garden, with Edward toddling after her on his short, chubby legs. She fed a last few cookie crumbs to the strutting peacock who wouldn't let her forget his beauty, then resolutely returned to the veranda. Tears dripped from the tip of her nose.

"Grandmother hugged her and patted her back. Neither spoke a word. They just held each other for a moment. Then Grandmother pushed her away. 'It's time you left.'

"Mother nodded. We climbed the stairs to our room. Our one suitcase for traveling was packed. She knelt on the floor and looked beneath the bed at the other suitcases holding her prized possessions she'd brought to Prussia for safe-keeping. I crouched next to her.

" 'Maybe we should have left everything in Hannover.' I climbed on the bed and cradled my doll.

" 'Maybe,' she said, 'but who knows, perhaps the Russians

won't come after all.'

" 'I don't want to go with you. Why can't I stay here? The others are all staying. Why can't I?' I kicked Mother's shin as hard as I could and gave her the meanest look I could muster. Her large hand lashed out and hit me on my swinging legs. I cried.

"She sat next to me and hugged me. 'They have to stay. They aren't allowed to leave.'

" 'Why not?'

" 'Inge, don't argue, it's all too complicated to explain.' She helped me on with my coat, 'The train leaves at five.'

" 'May I say goodbye to Paul-Emile ... may he drive us to the station?'

" 'We'll see what your Grandmother says. Come on, let's go.'

"My mind worked feverishly. I would hide so we'd miss the train. But Mother knew me too well, she'd never let me out of her sight. I tucked my doll under the sheets and smiled. We would have to return for my doll, surely she wouldn't let me leave without my doll. We would miss the train. I almost laughed, happy I devised a way to stay.

"We descended the stairs. Grandmother stood at the bottom along with the servants, Aunt Gunhilde and my three cousins. They crowded around us and we said goodbye.

" 'Paul-Emile may drive you,' Grandmother said. 'He's over at Ludwig's picking up the rig.'

"Mother instructed my brother and me to sit on the bench by the front door. Our three cousins squealed with shrill laughter while they chased each other.

" 'I'm going to say goodbye to *Tante* Lena, Ludwig, Margo and the kids,' Mother said. 'It may be ages before we see each other again. You children wait here, don't move.' She turned to Grandmother, 'Keep an eye on Inge, I don't want her to run off somewhere.'

"Mother took the garden path to Uncle Ludwig's house. Suddenly raised voices, shouting and screaming disturbed the peace. I recognized Paul-Emile's voice, 'Get in, get in, Madame.'

"A shot rang out. Horses hoofs and wagon wheels clattered over the cobblestones. Another shot and another. I stopped swinging my legs. Edward cried. I was frightened, though I didn't know why and held his hand.

"Grandmother stiffened and muttered, 'What is going on over there?'

"A child's scream. 'Noooo, Daddy.'

"A fourth shot and a fifth."

"Oh my God!" Dena clapped a hand over her mouth. "How horrible!"

So steeped was I in the events of long ago that I hardly heard her.

"Great Aunt Lena, out of breath and holding her chest, emerged from the garden path. The horse, pulling the carriage with Mother aboard, rounded the corner into the yard. Paul-Emile pulled in the reins and the horse skidded to a stop. Grandmother ran toward Great Aunt Lena and held onto her arm. Mother jumped out of the carriage, grabbed the suitcase and Edward and climbed back aboard.

" 'Come on Inge, get in ... Mother, Ludwig's gone crazy ... he shot Margot and Kurt ... I am leaving. Let's go.'

"Then she saw Great Aunt Lena leaning heavily on Grandmother's arm. Mother rushed over and held on to her other arm.

"Auntie tried to catch her breath then blurted out, 'He shot them all. He said he had an extra bullet ... I ran and shouted, I'll take my chances with the Russians. Without saying a word, he turned aside, stuck the gun in his mouth and ... and....'

"She slid out of their arms onto the cobblestones.

" 'You better leave or the train will take off without you,' Grandmother said.

"Mother sobbed. Edward screamed. I sat rigid wondering what had happened. Mother tried to soothe my brother.

" 'Why are you crying Mutti?'

" 'We must bury them....'

" 'Go already,' Grandmother said, 'we'll take care of that

later.'

    "Mother climbed into the carriage. We passed through the high, wide, iron gate, curved smoothly to the left and soon reached the tarmac. The horse's hoofs rhythmically beat the road and the carriage swayed as we headed at a gentle trot for Marienburg, three kilometers away."

Chapter Three

" **'What happened, *Mutti*?'**
"She looked at me through a veil of tears and shook her head.
" 'Your uncle shot his family,' Paul-Emile said.
" 'Are they dead?'
" 'Yes, all dead.' "
My voice broke. Dena climbed on my bed and stroked my back. We held each other until I calmed. I blew my nose, wiped my eyes and continued.

"When we arrived at the Marienburg Hauptbahnhof, (main railway station) and I saw a huge crowd of people milling about, I felt rather subdued, thinking, we'll never get on that train. Paul-Emile tied the horse to a hitching post and helped Mother with the suitcase. She thanked him and told him to stay with the horse, she could manage on her own. Without a backward glance she marched toward the station. Paul-Emile hugged me and slipped a piece of paper in my hand.

" 'Will you mail this for me please? It is for my parents telling them I am alive and well.'

" 'I want to stay with you,' I sobbed. 'Will you wait until the train leaves? Maybe it won't and you will have to take us back home.'

"Paul-Emile promised to wait. Mother shouted for me to hurry and ordered me to hold onto the handle of the suitcase. 'Don't let go.'

"With all the excitement I had completely forgotten my doll. I let go of the handle and stood still. 'My doll, I forgot my doll.'

"She turned and gave me an angry look. 'You should have thought about that before we left. No more dawdling, now hold on, or else....'

"I knew what else meant. So with me in tow, she charged the platform like a cornered rhino, the suitcase her battering ram.

"Dressed in their brown uniforms and black boots, members of the SD guarded the doors to the train. 'Papers.' The man impatiently snapped his fingers. Mother shoved her travel papers under his nose. He examined them carefully then initialed them.

"A soldier with a bandaged head leaned out of a window closest to the door. '*Gnädige Frau* (gracious Madam), hand me your suitcase.' She handed him screaming Edward instead. Another soldier with one arm in a sling stretched out his good hand for her suitcase.

"She grabbed my hand and waved her papers at the SD man at the door once more. While we climbed the three steps onto the train, I tried to get one more glimpse of Paul-Emile. All I saw were three men and a woman, their coattails flapping, elbowing their way through the crowd toward the train. They tried to push past us. The SD man screamed in a high pitched voice for them to stop.

"The train lurched forward. Mother struggled to get up the last step, suddenly my hand slipped out of hers. 'Inge," she screeched, 'my daughter ... somebody help ... Inge....'

"The shoving men propelled her forward. '*Mutti*....'

" 'Inge....' Her voice sounded muffled and far away.

"The SD man flung his arms around the woman's waist and tried to pull her off the train step. Her arms flailed looking for something to hold onto. She grabbed me, pulled me off balance, and I landed on top of her on the platform.

"My eyes stung as white, billowing steam clouds enveloped us and the train chugged slowly out of the station. The woman thrust me aside, scrambled to her feet and took off after the train. Sobbing, I tried to get back on my feet but a boot came down on my hand. I screamed. My hand was free. I shoved and kicked and tried to scramble away from the forward surging crowd. Like a miracle I suddenly found myself standing alone next to a *Litfasssäule*, a large, round advertisement pillar plastered with 'Strength through Joy' posters, while the heaving, wild-eyed throng congregated next to the empty tracks once more.

"I wiped my tears with my coat sleeves and stared after the train now only a small dot on the horizon. Then I remembered Paul-Emile and looked frantically to where we had left him. He still sat on the same spot and stared after the train looking truly sad.

"I climbed into the carriage, sat next to him and kissed his cheek.

" 'Inge, what are you doing here? *Mon Dieu*, what will your grandmother say and your mother?' He stared at me as if I was a ghost.

"On the way back to Tessensdorf I said, 'Why don't we run away. We have the horse and the carriage. Uncle Ludwig is dead, he won't miss them, and Grandmother won't worry about it because she likes you. She'll understand you want to go home.'

"Paul-Emile slapped his forehead and puffed out his cheeks. 'Your *grand-mère* is going to have my head for this.' He slid a finger across his throat and gave me a dark look. He sat up straight and flicked the reins. 'Running away sounds great, but we have no food for us or the horse, no water and above all, no money. We don't have a penny. I am taking you back to your grandmother. She will trust me even more after I do this. We need her, she is the only one who can help us. With your uncles dead, your grandmother and aunt will need a man they can trust. It will help both of us in the long run.'

"An idea popped into my mind. I jumped up and stood in front of him hopping from one foot to the other. 'I know where we can get money,' I sang. 'I bet you can never guess where it is.' I sat down, picked up the whip and waved it in the air. The horse took off and I laughed. I felt so happy I could have soared.

"Paul-Emile grabbed the whip. When the horse slowed he said, 'What do you know about money?'

" 'You and everybody else think I am a little girl, but I'm not. I see and hear everything, Mother said so herself.' I leaned close, 'We must get it tonight before someone else finds it.'

" 'Where is the money?'

" 'I'll show you when it's dark. We must wait until everybody is asleep. You think of a hiding place. It's lots of money, you'll see. Meet me at the back door of my uncle's house.'

"The horse's hoofs clattered and the wagon wheels rattled over the cobblestones in our yard. Paul-Emile jumped off his seat and helped me down. I skulked behind him as he marched to the front door. He was about to knock when Grandmother confronted us.

" 'I saw you coming. Don't hide behind him child. Why are you here?'

" 'People shoved and fought,' Paul-Emile demonstrated, 'everybody wanted to leave with the train. Someone pushed Inge aside and madame lost contact and the train moved and....'

" 'Your mother will be frantic. I will try to contact her. Now go into the house and take off your good coat. Your cousin will give you an apron. I am glad you are back Paul-Emile. We must bury everybody come along.'

"Grandmother had taken control. She tucked me in herself that night. 'You poor child, don't cry. I will see what I can do to send you to Hannover, but with the Russians rattling on our door I'm not quite sure how we will accomplish that.'

" 'The Russians are here?'

" 'Not yet, but it won't be long.' She kissed my brow and left.

It seemed to take forever before her slow, tired footsteps trudged up the stairs and her squeaking bedroom door closed. After a while I crept into the hallway and listened. The house was silent.

"Dressed in my cousin's nightgown, I laced my high-tops and tiptoed down the stairs. The third step from the bottom always creaked, so I held on to the railing and skipped to the next one. Spooky shadows loomed in every corner. I gritted my teeth and slowly opened the front door. My heart hammered in my ears as I ran past the tall iron windmill, along the garden path to my uncle's house. With a shiver I wondered where they'd buried my cousins.

"When I arrived at the back of Uncle Ludwig's house someone said, 'Psst, Inge.'

"I jumped. 'Paul-Emile?'

" 'No the bogeyman. Now what?'

"I opened the back door and led the way through the mud room, through the mess hall for the field workers and servants, past the butler's pantry and into the marble floored foyer. I stopped and listened, 'Follow me.'

" 'Where are we going?'

"I took his hand. 'Every time my uncle went away we played hide and seek in the house. I know it from top to bottom. Come with me. Did I ever tell you about my uncle's dining table? When he takes off the top it becomes a billiard table. Have you ever seen such a clever idea?'

" 'No never, is that where we are going?'

"I opened the door to the dining room. The heavy, brown velvet draperies were always drawn and it was pitch dark. 'You'll find candles on the buffet and matches in a bowl next to it.' Glass tinkled against glass. 'Careful, the candle holders have bangles.'

"He struck a match and lit the five candles. 'How do you know there is money here?'

" 'I was hiding under that long tablecloth over there,' I pointed, 'when my uncle came into the room. I watched him stash away a big bundle of money. You want to see the billiard table? It's beautiful. You have to move half of the table top, just push it over to the side then lift it off.'

"Paul-Emile did so. 'It is beautiful.' He traced his fingers over the ivory and mother of pearl inlay. 'Now what?'

" 'Uncle Ludwig crawled underneath the table. I almost laughed because he banged his head and said some nasty words. He fiddled near the right leg, then took money out of his pocket, laid it on the floor and flipped through the bundle. He tucked it into the table leg, crawled out, brushed off his uniform and inspected his shiny black boots. He took out his handkerchief, spit on it, and polished the tip of one boot. Then he examined his teeth in the mirror, saluted and marched stiff-legged out of the room.'

" 'You do see everything.' Paul-Emile chuckled, set the candelabra on the floor next to the table and crawled underneath. I followed close behind. He searched for a couple of minutes. 'Found it.' A faint click and a narrow panel sprung open in the thick round, elaborately carved table leg. He stuck his hand in the opening and pulled out bundles of money. 'How many shall I take?'

" 'We'll take them all. You don't want to leave it for the Russians do you?' He drew out ten bundles and a small velvet pouch. I grabbed it out of his hand and opened it. 'Glass, why would anybody want to hide glass?'

" 'Let me see.' He scooted on his bottom next to the candelabra, shook a piece into his hand and held it up to the candles. 'Diamonds. *Maman* loves diamonds. She told me all about them when I was little. They are worth a lot of money, probably more than the *Reichsmarks*. What do you want me to do?'

" 'We'll take everything.'

" 'Haven't you been taught that stealing is a crime?'

"I looked at my muddy shoes. Had to clean them before Grandmother saw them. Stealing? Stealing was bad, but this was different. I looked around the familiar room and heard my cousins squealing with laughter.

" 'Well, what did you decide?'

" 'Do you think my cousins can see what we are doing?'

" 'Your dead cousins?' Paul-Emile pushed his cap back and scratched his head.

" 'Yes. I thought I heard them.'

" 'Inge! *Mon Dieu*, they are dead.'

" 'What if they are ghosts now?'

" 'Too soon.'

" 'What do you mean.'

" 'Inge, what do you want to do?' He puffed out his cheeks and exhaled noisily.

" 'Are you sure they aren't ghosts?' He threw up his hands and walked toward the door. 'Okay, okay, no ghosts.' I scanned the room once more to make sure nobody lurked in the corners. 'We are borrowing everything. Besides, my uncle doesn't need them anymore. Put them in your pocket.'

"He inspected his pants pocket. 'No holes. You sure you want me to keep them?'

" 'Of course.' I opened a drawer in the buffet and pulled out a tablecloth. We wrapped the money and replaced everything the way it had been.

" 'I'll see you in the morning when I take you to school.'

" 'Would you walk me back to the house please?'

" 'I thought you were fearless. Remember, there are no ghosts.'

"I ran all the way without stopping to breathe back to Grandmother's house. One of the dogs barked suddenly. I stood still, panting. He came closer and sniffed then stuck his cold nose in my hand. 'Sh, no more barking.'

"I felt suddenly very sleepy, sat on the bench next to the front door and scratched the dog's ears. Was Mother crying too? I wiped my tears then tiptoed to my room, turned on the light in the alcove and peeked under the bed. Nothing there only Mother's suitcases. I climbed into bed, pulled the covers over my head and hoped Grandmother wouldn't notice the light burning all night.

"The next morning, July 21st 1944, the maids chattered excitedly in the kitchen about an attempt on Hitler's life at Rastenburg only eighty miles east of Tessensdorf.

" 'Is he dead?' I asked. They shooed me out of the kitchen.

"After we'd all assembled at the dining table, I said, 'Louise said someone tried to kill Hitler. Is he dead? Maybe the Russians won't come now.'

" 'Won't make much difference,' Aunt Gunhilde said, 'they are coming. Nobody can stop them.'

"Grandmother pursed her thin lips. 'We don't talk about such things at the breakfast table. Are you children ready for school? Homework done?'

" 'Yes Grandmother,' Hilde and Gretchen said in unison.

" 'I will give you a note for the teacher, Inge. Now eat your breakfast, it's almost time to go.'

"I climbed next to Paul-Emile on the driver's seat. 'Did you find a good hiding place?'

"He nodded, 'I'll tell you later.'

"Since it stayed light so late I slipped out of my room almost every evening. Paul-Emile and I usually met in a meadow on the other side of a pond in an apple orchard. He stretched out on the grass and I sat next to him. Being eight years old had its advantages sometimes. Nobody paid much attention to what I was doing as long as I was in bed by the time Grandmother went to her room. She always stopped by now and gave me a little kiss on the cheek before she went to bed.

"I'd brought Paul-Emile a piece of sugar and butter cake and as he nibbled, I asked him about his parents. Haltingly, often rifling for a word through the dictionary, his constant companion, he said, '*Maman* is a beautiful woman. She loves to dress up. In 1939, when I was thirteen, she took me to the salons of Schiaparelli and Lanvin. She always needed new dresses for the parties she loved, for the *Comedie-Francaise* and *L'Opera* and for the *Théâtre de l'Athénée.*'

" 'Who are Schiaparelli and Lanvin?'

" 'Dressmakers, but not the ordinary type, very fancy ... you sit in a salon and are served *petit fours* and coffee or tea, or champagne, whatever you want. Then mannequins, wearing beautiful gowns, glide past so that the buyer can see how they look on a person.'

" 'When we get to Paris, will you take me?'

" 'If they are still in business, *naturellement*. Nobody in our household ever talked about the war. My mother ignored it completely. Life was wonderful and she only wanted to sing and have fun. *Maman* looked radiant when she and *Papa* left to attend a *soirée* at the Polish Embassy gardens. She told me all about it later when I sat on her bed and watched her take off her jewelry and make-up.

" 'She said the Bengal torches, and the electric lights in the Chinese lanterns, turned the garden into a fairy-tale land, and the great white marble sphinx took on the colors of the rainbow. She said she danced the mazurka with a crazy Pole who danced faster and faster until she had to sit down completely dizzy.'

" 'What's a mazurka?'

" 'Some kind of a dance, probably invented by the Poles, after all they were at the Polish Embassy. After that party, she and *Papa* talked more and more about the approaching war. They were confident France would be able to resist Germany. When Germany invaded Poland, France had to fulfill her promise to fight with Poland.

" 'In November 1939 life was still good in Paris even though we had to black out our windows. *Maman* brought home gas masks for everyone in our household.'

" 'We had to do the same. Mother also brought us gas masks.' I giggled. 'I really scared my little brother when I put mine on. Did you ever use yours?'

" 'No, we waited for the air raids, but they never came. *Maman* and *Papa* attended the opera again and Maurice Chevalier and Josephine Baker were back at the Casino de Paris. Except for two meatless days a week, starting in January 1940, everything was almost back to normal and she was happy again. We also still had plenty of gasoline and spent weekends in the country.

" 'At the beginning of May, when the chestnut trees were in bloom along the broad avenues and the Seine, the Germans struck our airfields. And a month later your country demanded the surrender of our city. *Maman* cried and swore she'd never leave Paris.'

" 'What will happen if the Russians come?'

" 'Bad things. Maybe we'll leave with your grandmother and your aunt before they come.'

" 'What if they don't want to leave?'

" 'Don't worry, I'll take care of you, I promise. You better go home now.'

" 'Do I have to?'

" 'You have to.' He tickled my nose with a blade of grass. I laughed, shoved him on his back and sat on his stomach. He lifted me by my waist, hoisted me in the air and before I knew it, he turned me back and forth with the soles of his feet.

" 'Let me down, let me down,' I screamed and laughed.

"He bent his knees and our faces were only inches apart, then he straightened his knees and I landed in an arc back on the grass. He jumped to his feet, 'You better go now.' He lightly kicked my rear end. 'I am the boss, you must obey.'

" 'No you are not, no you are not, you are just a prisoner, just a prisoner. Catch me if you can, prisoner.' I giggled and ran home.

"At the end of July, Grandmother received a cable from Mother in Hannover acknowledging Grandmother's cable that I was safe with her.

"In the last days of that month soldiers of the Second Army packed most schools and assembly halls in our area. The order to entrench Marienburg had come. Marienburg had been designated a defensive bridgehead crucial to keeping the Russians from crossing the Vistula River.

"And in an efficient German way, they organized six thousand men and women to build tank ditches ten kilometers long, as well as walking trenches, and about 180 bunkers. The workers slaved from August until December, Paul-Emile, and other prisoners of war who worked on estates, included.

"He came home exhausted, thirsty, hungry and dirty. 'The overseers worked us like the pyramid slaves of old Egypt.'

" 'What is a pyramid?'

" 'Bring me a piece of paper and I'll draw you a picture.' Paul-Emile drew a pyramid and several figures reminiscent of the Egyptian style.

"I hopped up and down and yelled, 'I saw this at the Berlin Museum. I also saw a beautiful lady ... the head only ... her name was Nefertiti.'

" 'You saw her? She was a very famous find. I wish I could see her because I plan to study archaeology some day.'

" 'What is that?'

" 'It's the study of ancient cultures through remains. I am tired, no more questions please.'

Chapter Four

"Grandmother by now had taken a total liking to Paul-Emile. This made things so much easier for us. His German vocabulary grew, however, his accent was atrocious.

"More and more fleeing refugees from East Prussia streamed into Marienburg. Many lingered on our doorstep and three families made themselves at home in Uncle Ludwig's house. So they wouldn't take off with the livestock, we'd moved everything into our barns, including the feed.

"One winter evening Paul-Emile whispered to meet him at the barn with the wedding coach. When I arrived, he placed a finger over his lips and motioned me to follow him. We walked along the pond away from the refugees in the barn, who sat on little islands of uncertain existence, not knowing where to go.

"Together with a chilly breeze the mournful strains of a harmonica wafted melodiously in and out of hearing. Paul-Emile squatted in front of me. 'Inge, I think your grandmother will not leave, because your aunt won't. They plan to take their chances with the Russians. I think they are foolish. Even if they want to leave, they can't, because your stupid *Gauleiter* (political head of an area) hasn't given them permission. He gave strict instructions that he be notified of anyone making flight preparations. Defeatism is punishable by death.'

"He grimaced. 'Me ... I don't have to abide by his rules ... of course if I get caught....' He slit a finger across his throat. 'Will you forgive me if I leave? We'll split the money and the diamonds I'll take a third and you will take the rest. With my accent I will need to buy my way to the West and freedom.'

" 'I am going where you go. You need me to speak for you.

I thought hard about this. You are unable to talk at all and I will speak for you. Everybody will be sorry for you and me and will be helpful. What do you think? I am a good actress.' "

A smile played about Dena's lips. "You've always had the glorious gift of imagination. I think all of us girls inherited a touch of theatrics from you, especially Stephanie. I'm sorry I interrupted, please go on."

I laughed. "Theatrics never got you girls very far with me, did they? Fortunately, the circumstances were different so I could more or less ignore them. During the war one had to use every available ruse to survive.

" 'Your grandmother will be angry if I take you with me,' Paul-Emile said.

" 'So she is angry, she can't do anything about it. She'll probably be glad to get rid of me. She always tells me I am a lot of trouble.'

" 'Winter is coming. I am strong. You are just a little girl.'

"I told him about an old fur blanket and my uncle's fur boots I found in the attic. I had them hidden in my room. Then I had another idea. 'We could take one or two carpets from my uncle's living room, they should keep the wind out.' I reached for his hand, 'Come on, we better get them now before they walk away with the refugees.'

"He held me back. 'Before you run off, listen to Paradsky for a moment ... that Pole is a musician with his mouth organ. I just wish he'd play something lively sometimes. Every time I hear him, I want to cry ... he makes me so homesick.'

"Some of the weary refugees slumped on the straw and listened to Paradsky perched on a milking stool inside the open barn door, play his harmonica.

" 'His music makes people forget they are enemies.'

" 'Are you going to cry now?'

"He pulled one of my long, thick braids. 'Not when I am with you, you are my happiness.' We stood for a few more moments and listened, then walked quickly to Uncle Ludwig's house.

"Weary heads lifted when we stormed inside. Someone had rolled up the living room rug and pushed it against the wall. An old man and woman sat on the carpet, their suitcase stood in front of them. '*Entschuldigen Sie bitte (*excuse me please*),*' I said, 'my grandmother wants us to bring the carpet to her house.'

" 'Yeah, and she sent a little girl to do that,' the man growled, 'this belongs to us now.'

"I stomped my foot and glowered at them. 'My Uncle Ludwig is coming home in two hours. He wears black boots, a brown uniform and is bad tempered. He probably won't mind you staying in his house for a little while, but he would be angry if you took his carpet.'

"The man sneered.

"Paul-Emile nodded, 'SD ... I am a French prisoner here ... those are my orders. He must be obeyed. I don't want to lose my head over this.'

" '*Schweinehunde!*' (Pigs- dogs)

"He and his wife rose. Paul-Emile shouldered the heavy rug and walked out. We took the garden path to Grandmother's house. When we were out of sight of the couple who'd followed us to the door, he slid the rug into the gazebo to retrieve later after dark.

" 'I'll have to watch out for your imagination. Hope you'll always be on my side.' Paul-Emile chuckled, planted a kiss on my forehead, then told me to go to bed.

"We baked cookies and cake for Christmas. Paul-Emile chopped down a small tree which we decorated with candles, colorful balls and silver icicles. We sang Christmas songs with little enthusiasm, because we knew the Russians were only a few miles away.

"All was still quiet on New Year's Eve. Only the thousands of refugees from East Prussia who clogged the main road past our estate gave a glimmer of a desperate situation. Even then we were unaware of the torching of bunkers and shelters with flame-throwers, and the raping, beatings and robbing of women and hospitalized patients, nuns and the old. The Russians showed no mercy, they were out for revenge.

"By January 14th and 15th, 1945 the citizens from or surrounding Marienburg still had not received permission to leave. Grandmother went about her business as usual. Her face revealed none of her internal emotions.

"Aunt Gunhilde sat next to the tile stove and cried all day. The maids talked about the seven Russian tanks that pushed into Elbing. Rumor had it that the Germans had disabled four of them, while the other three were on their way to Tessensdorf. Nobody knew for sure what the Russian situation was.

"On January 22nd, a snowy day, Paul-Emile warmed his red, chapped hands over the kitchen stove. Louise, the cook, a well developed blond with lively blue eyes, handed him a steaming cup of tea. I knew she was sweet on him and watched them laugh and banter. I frowned and glared at Paul-Emile.

" 'Don't frown, you'll get wrinkles.'

"Aunt Gunhilde called Louise's name. Louise grumbled but obediently went to do her bidding. Paul-Emile leaned close, 'I am leaving tomorrow morning. Are you coming?'

" 'Tomorrow morning?' I polished an apple with my apron until it shone, took a bite and chewed slowly. 'So soon?' A cobweb in the corner of the wall and the ceiling caught my eye. I wondered if Grandmother knew about it and looked for more. Leave this warm house and everything familiar? I took another noisy bite.

" 'Well, are you coming?' For a split second he glared at me with an expression of contempt I had never seen before. Then he smiled, seemingly the old Paul-Emile again. 'Are you scared?'

" 'Where are you going?'

" 'You know where I'm going ... to Paris, home.' Tears glistened in his eyes. 'If you are not coming, I will take a third of the money and the diamonds and leave you the rest.'

"I walked close and whispered, 'You better take it all, because it will cost more if I come with you. You promised to take me to Schiaparello, remember?'

" 'Schiaparelli. Okay, if you are sure. You'll have to get up early, before it's light and while everybody is still asleep. Wear all your warmest clothes, your wool stockings, several pairs of socks over them, all the long pants you have, long sleeved shirts, pullovers, sweaters, your warmest jacket or coat and your mittens and scarves.'

" 'I won't be able to move.'

" 'At least you'll be warm. Pile on all the clothes you can and wear your uncle's fur boots because your shoes won't fit. Be sure you bring them though, don't forget. I've equipped the chaise with everything I think we'll need. I stole food from your grandmother. She will be very disappointed in me.'

" 'She's fond of you, she'll forgive you.'

" 'But not when she discovers you've come with me.' He poured more tea into his cup and clasped it with both hands.

" 'Did you think of food for the horse?'

" 'Yes, but we are taking two horses, your Uncle Ludwig's best two Trakehners. They are young, strong and fast. I've spent as much time with them as I could, they trust me, they will take us home.'

" 'May I bring my doll?'

" 'You play with dolls?'

" 'I've had her since Edward was born. She's my child.'

" 'No doll.' Paul-Emile sighed.

" 'She doesn't take up much room. I can't leave her.' I sobbed.

"Paul-Emile furrowed his brows. 'Stop that, you are not a baby any longer. I can't stand crybabies.' He rolled his eyes, '*Mon Dieu, quelle enfant difficile.*'

"I was glad when Louise returned to the kitchen. Still mumbling, she prepared a platter of sausage and cheese sandwiches. I watched her return the unused butter, sausage and bread to the pantry, then she locked the door and slipped the key into her apron pocket. I winked at Paul-Emile and nodded my head slightly in Louise's direction. He smiled and sipped his tea.

"When Louise took the platter into the dining room, I said, 'Grandmother takes control of the keys when she goes to bed. I will try ... Louise always loses things.'

    " 'I will plan a diversion, just listen.'

    "After dinner and the dishes were put away, Louise hung her apron on a peg behind the door. She sighed, sat at the kitchen table and poured herself a glass of hot milk. I watched through a crack in the door as she slurped contentedly. The other three maids joined her and they chattered about the Russian advances. Suddenly a loud crash and dogs barking brought them to their feet. After they'd rushed out the door, I snatched the pantry key from Louise's apron pocket. I stuck it into my own apron pocket and ran up the stairs to prepare for the next day.

    "When everyone in the house was asleep, I stole downstairs and emptied everything I found appetizing into a pillow case. I debated what to do with it and thought about the cats and the mice if I left it by the back door. I lugged it into the dining room, hid it under the table and decided to worry about getting it out of the house in the morning.

    "I couldn't fall asleep at first, then I did, at least for a little while. The urge to use the chamber pot woke me. My wintery room was completely dark. I felt my way to the closet, groped for the light switch and emptied my bulging bladder. I shivered and looked longingly at my warm featherbed. Was it time to go yet? All at once, excitement over the upcoming adventure set me in motion. I pulled my nightgown over my head and climbed into everything I could find in the dresser drawer, most of which belonged to my cousin.

    "When I finished I could barely move. I slipped into my uncle's fur boots, but tripped on the way to the door. I took them off again and stuck them into the pillow case with my high-tops. A sob escaped me when I kissed my doll and told her to be good. One more furtive look around, then as quietly as I could, I tiptoed down the stairs dragging the bear skin behind me.

    "After I'd retrieved my food sack I tried to open the front door. It was locked. Before all the refugees arrived the door was never locked.

    "Tears rolled down my cheeks. I sat on the floor, laid my two sacks and the bear skin next to me and sobbed, trying hard not to make a noise. I wiped a sleeve across my dripping nose and surveyed my surroundings. Then I remembered the nail with the key next to the door. I jumped up but couldn't reach it. Still crying I wrestled a child's chair out of the dining room into the foyer and climbed on. I took the chair back into the dining room then unlocked the door.

"Paul-Emile waited for me. 'What took you so long? I was about to leave without you.'

"I sniffled and sobbed. 'I couldn't get out.' He hugged me briefly, grabbed the two pillow cases and the bear skin and strode across the yard.

" 'Wait, I don't have my shoes on.'

"He ran back, dug out the fur boots and helped me put them on. 'Come on, we have to hurry before someone wakes up.'

"I tried to run and fell on my nose. He rushed back and squatted, 'Climb on my back.' He carried me to Uncle Ludwig's horse stable. His two huge, black, prized Trakehners shuffled and snorted uneasily. When Paul-Emile talked to them softly in French they soon quieted again.

"Both horses wore their dressage finery and the looser night clothing on top. Over that Paul-Emile had tied a piece of the oriental carpet. He'd hidden the chaise behind a pile of straw and now led Donner forward revealing the two-wheeled open carriage with its pair of curved shafts and a collapsible leather hood.

"The third carpet piece he'd fitted inside so it protected our backs from the wind. It also covered the seat and the small platform for our feet. Three blankets lay on top of the carpet.

" 'Jump in, *ma petite.*'

"He tethered Amsel to the back of the carriage, then climbed in next to me. We muffled our mouths and noses with woolen scarfs, wrapped the blankets round our shoulders and across our laps and covered all with the bear skin. I felt delightfully snug and warm.

" 'All set?'

"I smiled and nodded. I was ready for this adventure. Paul-Emile clicked his tongue and the horse walked out of the stable."

I stopped talking. Silence lay between Dena and me as I drained the last drop of cognac in my glass.

"You really did it, you went with him," Dena said.

I nodded. "I loved to ride in the carriage and looked forward to the adventure. If he had stayed I would have too, of course, but I couldn't bear the idea of him going off without me. I had no choice. Good night my love."

"I am not sure I can sleep. Why did you never talk about this?"

I smiled, snuggled under my covers and lay there for the longest time thinking about that horrible time and my later regrets at ever having undertaken that journey. Finally I said, "Most people are not interested in other people's hardships. It makes them uncomfortable."

"Will you tell Magda and Stephanie?"

"Maybe some day, when the time is right. Now go to sleep."

Chapter Five

The next morning Dena and I breakfasted with the Diderots. Dena and Camille bantered and smiled at each other while Paul-Emile and I played with our food. When we stood outside waiting for Hamdi, Paul-Emile whispered, "I couldn't sleep. I haven't felt this alive in years."

"Because I refused to kiss you?"

"Because I found the woman I love. I want to live with you, wake up with you...."

I gaped at him, wondering if he'd taken leave of his senses and turned away with impatience. Coming to Mersa Matruh had been a dreadful mistake.

When Hamdi arrived, Dena sat between the two men in the back and I climbed in next to Hamdi. I kissed his cheek.

"You all right?" he asked in Arabic.

I nodded. His eyes lingered on my face. Could he detect my conflicts?

"Siwa is about one hundred seventy miles and the trip usually takes anywhere from five to eight hours," Hamdi said. "When you think about it, that's not bad, considering it probably took Alexander the Great as many days to cover the distance."

The road, covered by blown sand and barely visible at times, dropped steadily south among rolling sand dunes and large limestone formations. Siwa lies some sixty feet below sea level and is sandwiched between the Qattara Depression and the Egyptian Sand Sea. Hamdi stopped to show us the ancient cisterns built before the Greeks conquered Egypt and still used by the Bedouin today.

When we drove over a small rise a dark horizon lay before us. "Not long now," Hamdi said. "The governor told me they have three hundred thousand date palms and seventy thousand olive trees and enough water for all. It's a miracle, nothing but sand then all this water. They claim to have a thousand springs."

When we drew closer, the beautiful, weaving palm plumes became visible and we all sighed with relief to finally have escaped the dull, tan desert. Hamdi drove us to the Government Rest House where the staff greeted us with great enthusiasm, for only a handful of tourists took the time to visit this far, out-of-the-way place.

After refreshing glasses of tea and a plate of delicious dates, we visited the crumbling site of the famous Oracle Jupiter-Amon located in the old capital of Shali, or Siwa, as it was called now. It has been a Berber community since the thirteenth century and is located on the old date caravan route.

We climbed over the ancient ruins. Hamdi pointed out the secret passage leading to three niches, and, near the ceiling, to two small entrances to crypts.

"The stone between these niches and the inner chamber of the temple is very thin," Hamdi said. "So when a priest, hidden in one of these niches spoke, his words sounded as if they came from far away and all those inside the temple, except the priests in the know, believed it was the voice of the God."

"What did the priests get out of these deceptions?" Dena asked.

"Power." Paul-Emile said. "Their powers rivaled those of the pharaohs, provoking political problems similar to modern church - state rivalry. So, using the oracle, they could make predictions suiting their own agendas."

After we left the ruins Hamdi drove us to the northern edge of the Qattara Depression composed of sand-encrusted saline lakes and marshes punctuated by small table-topped hills and weird sand sculptures several hundred feet tall.

"Surreal ... awesome," gasped Dena.

I hugged her as we stared at these phenomenal natural works of art.

"What's in the Sand Sea, Uncle Hamdi?"

"Lots of danger. Dry quicksand and World War II land mines."

We spent the night at the Government Rest House, then early the next morning readied for our return trip. A cloud of dust trailed after us as we drove through the narrow streets. Three women, wearing long, embroidered, blue cloaks they clasped shut with their teeth, scurried in front of us. Their produce-filled baskets sat firmly ensconced on their heads. Hamdi explained that most girls married at age fourteen and afterward had very little communication with the outside world.

"Aren't they curious?" Dena said. "I wonder if they ever rebel? Have you ever been in one of their houses, Uncle Hamdi? They look so forbidding from the outside, small windows, a small door...."

"Most houses are built of mud bricks and the inside consists of one room that serves for everything. Some houses have beautiful secluded gardens and if they are lucky, even a spring bubbling up inside."

"I wouldn't mind staying here a few days," I said, "everything seems so tranquil and relaxing. It's not as hot as I expected."

"It gets cold in the winter," Hamdi said, "the summer is hot, but spring and autumn are very nice."

Paul-Emile offered to drive. Hamdi shook his head, "I will drive, sometimes there comes the unexpected."

Camille said something to Dena I couldn't understand. She gasped. "Oh look Mommy what Camille bought me. How beautiful!" She handed me a Bedouin necklace crafted of silver.

Camille smiled. "A beautiful necklace for a beautiful lady. For your next concert I will sit in the front row ... *Papa*, Dena has stolen my heart."

"You better watch out." Paul-Emile chuckled. "He will sweep you off your feet with flowers. He buys out all the flower shops when he is in love."

"Does this happen often?" I asked.

"About once a week usually," Camille said, "but this time it's for real. I have never met someone so matter of fact ... Dena isn't at all frilly, yet she is so feminine."

"Being matter of fact saves me from being devoured by my fans." Dena smiled. "I just sweep them away with one wave of my arm and knowing me, they sigh and slink away muttering to themselves, what a bitch. My life, alas, belongs to my music, Monsieur Camille. I give you fair warning."

I glanced at her and knew she was smitten. I promised myself to have a talk with her after we returned to Matruh. Later, after we had showered, I told Dena what Paul-Emile had revealed about his son.

She smiled. "Don't worry, I meet men similar to him all the time. In the meantime it's flattering and fun, so let me enjoy my stay here. But you, Mommy dearest, better watch out for the father ... like father, like son. I'm sure you are familiar with that saying."

I stretched out on the bed – she had a point.

"What are you going to do about Paul-Emile, Mommy?"

"Perhaps I shouldn't tell you this, but I will. This is the first time since your daddy died that I feel alive, challenged and adventurous."

"Two men are vying for you."

"That's not true. Hamdi doesn't have to compete for me, he's got me, for Pete's sake."

I gave Dena a thoughtful look. Maybe she did have a point. I realized suddenly that Paul-Emile's appearance had caused in me a lightness and elation that I hadn't experienced since my husband died. Could I trust her to understand what I was about to reveal? She waited patiently for me to continue.

"All the years with your daddy, a mixture of joy and despair, mostly joy once I learned how to master him, died with him. I miss him dreadfully.... And Hamdi, though I love him, have always loved him, is not Kane. No one can replace him, his humor, his mischievousness, his deviousness, his selfishness ... even...."

I paused, though he betrayed our love, he still loved me, he couldn't live without me. I sighed. "And now there is Paul-Emile. I don't know what it is that draws me to him, nostalgia? I don't know."

"Mommy, I know what you were going to say about Daddy. The girls and I weren't blind, but we still loved him."

I blew my nose and wiped my tears.

"And now here is Paul-Emile," Dena said. "You shared something special, unique, death and destruction and for you a hopeless dream."

I laughed. "A dream that went up in smoke." I thought for a moment. "He probably still blames us Germans for his misery, his suffering."

"Aren't you exaggerating?" Dena smiled.

"I didn't suffer as he did during the war. Yet I never forgot, why should he? I bet meeting me brought back his bad memories."

"Mommy, you were a child, innocent...."

"I was born German, his enemy, his enslaver, the reason for his nightmares...."

"You are feeling guilty."

I nodded, "... complicity, where does it begin and end?"

"You are too hard on yourself. So tell me, was M. Diderot brave?"

"Hmm ... once Paul-Emile overcame his fear of dying he became more decisive. At the time I adored him, he was my hero. In retrospect ... he wasn't the most courageous person, although he did protect me from harm. I have to give him credit for that."

"And now you find him once more attractive?"

I frowned. "Somewhat, I'm afraid. Therefore I am coming with you when you leave. I don't want to hurt Hamdi. Now I am going to take a nap."

I awoke to whispering voices and listened for a few minutes. At first they talked about Stephanie and Magda, then Hamdi said, "I think your mother is in love with Paul-Emile."

"Nah," Dena said, "he just brings back old memories. You should know by now she dwells on the past a lot."

"Maybe you are right."

"What are you two whispering about?" I raised myself on my

elbows and searched their faces.

"You of course." Hamdi smiled. "I am curious about your history with Paul-Emile."

"I'll tell you about that when we are old and gray and have nothing better to talk about."

"So you expect we'll grow old together?"

"Absolutely."

"That's a pleasant revelation." Hamdi fingered my amber beads hanging from his neck and gave me a scrutinizing look.

He didn't trust me. Maybe I was a rotten apple. Why wasn't I born with a smile instead of a scream? I looked at him, feeling miserable. He knew me too well. I closed my eyes and wished I were a thousand miles away.

He sat next to me on the bed, smiled and stroked my brow. "Don't frown, it doesn't become you."

I wanted to cry.

Dena gave us both a hug then removed her violin from its case. "I think I'll practice a bit."

She played scales, then enchanted us with Sibelius' Violin Concerto in D minor. Hamdi kissed my cheek. Tears shimmered in his eyes as we listened to her play. When she finished her piece someone knocked on the door. It was Madame Madwak, the hotel's owner, complimenting Dena and wondering if she would play for her guests after dinner. Dena frowned, then agreed.

Dena said after Madame Madwak left, "I knew this would happen." She smiled. "I guess it doesn't really matter where I practice."

After Dena and I returned to our room that evening she said, "All I thought about today was your story. I couldn't wait for bedtime."

I lit a cigarette.

"What was Hitler doing during this time?"

"Hitler." I shrugged. "He ruled from his headquarters called the Wolfsschanze at Rastenburg, about ninety miles east of

Marienburg, until the fall of 1944. He declared that as long as he stayed in East Prussia it would be held, but if he left, it would fall to the Russians. So he left and returned to Berlin."

"And East Prussia fell to the Russians."

"With or without him." I laughed.

"Back to my story. On the morning of our departure Paul-Emile circumnavigated the farm to avoid the clatter from our iron-bound wheels on the cobblestones in the yard. When we reached the entrance to the main *Chaussee,* we joined a convoy of about forty other horse-drawn wagons heading in the direction of Marienburg.

" 'Where did you find the horse covers?' I asked Paul-Emile.

" 'In a wooden box in the stable. Your uncle took good care of his horses. Even though they are tough, they get cold the same as we do.'

"My feet were already numb and we'd barely gone half a kilometer. Stop and go, stop and go, something always went wrong with either the horses or the overloaded wagons in front of us.

" 'Damn this snow,' Paul-Emile said, 'it'll take forever at this pace. I'd love to turn off onto a field path but I'm afraid we'd get lost or stuck.'

"Five hours – three kilometers. Women pushed baby carriages. Old men and women carried heavy-looking suitcases, or pulled wooden hand wagons or sleds piled high with possessions, children and the elderly. All converged on Marienburg hoping for a train to take them to safety. The railway station was clogged with people burdened with luggage.

" 'Is it possible to get on a train?' I asked a man standing next to our carriage while we waited in the convoy.

"He shook his head. 'Not even the sick and wounded from the hospital are being picked up. They lie on their stretchers ... and all the women and children, half frozen ... it must be eighteen or twenty below zero ... what a catastrophe! They say trains are standing ready at Dirschau but so far, nothing. That your brother?'

"I nodded. 'He can't talk.'

" 'Well good luck to the two of you, you'll need it.'

"I had to go to the bathroom so badly I couldn't stand it any longer. Paul-Emile glared at me, 'Can't you sit still for just a moment?'

"I sniffled, 'I have to go.'

" 'We are stuck here. Go behind one of those houses.'

"I jumped down and ran across the manure-splattered, snowy street dodging horses, wagons and people and squatted behind a house. Feeling much better, I wrestled with my clothes. Once everything was back in place, I looked around and gasped. Across the street a man hung from a flagpole. His head lolled to its side as he swung gently to and fro in the sharp east wind.

"A piercing whistle tore me away from the grisly picture. I dodged back across the street. Paul-Emile sat in exactly the same place where I'd left him, while other wagons drove past him, the drivers cursing. I hopped back into the carriage, huddled against him and snuggled into the blankets and the fur.

" 'I saw a man hanging from a pole with his tongue drooping out of his mouth.' I demonstrated.

" 'Inge, don't make up stories.'

" 'Really, he scared me half to death. A cardboard sign hung from his neck saying: 'I am a traitor and a defeatist'. What does that mean?'

" 'Next time don't look.'

" 'Don't you have to pee?' He gave me a stern look and pointed next to the carriage. I saw a yellow hole in the snow and giggled.

"Paul-Emile swore under his breath. 'If I could only get out of this mess and reach a side street. Staying in the wagon train is going to do us in.' He climbed down, took Donner by the halter, and tried to lead him toward the left, but nobody allowed him through.

"I joined him and shouted, '*Achtung, Achtung,* attention, attention, can nobody see that my brother is deaf and dumb, he is almost blind too. Please, I have to take care of him. Please let us through.' I dabbed at my eyes and took Paul-Emile's hand and placed it on my shoulder. 'Please let us through.'

"When the convoy progressed a few feet the ones behind us allowed us to turn off. Soon we left the congestion and found ourselves in a *Gasse*, one of the narrow lanes abounding in this old city. Traffic was light, mostly pedestrians pulling or pushing small wagons and sleds piled high with their possessions. All headed in the direction of the Nogat River. Paul-Emile and I climbed back into the carriage.

" 'Now what, *ma petite*?'

" 'I am hungry and thirsty.'

" 'There must be many empty houses. I bet not everyone obeyed the *Gauleiter's* orders. We'll find one with a door large enough for the horses and the carriage then spend the night. We'd be crazy to go out into this madness at night.'

"We found a house with a large wooden door that led into an interior courtyard. We unhitched Donner and led him and Amsel carefully into a high-ceilinged vestibule with terrazzo-type, marbled floors. Their hoofs slipped and slid and clanked.

"Paul-Emile said, 'Go see if you can find a carpet or some blankets before they break their legs. I'll try to keep them still.'

"The beastly cold even here out of the wind penetrated my clothes. The kitchen was immaculate and everything appeared in its place as if the owners were returning shortly. I walked into the next room expecting someone to stop me. The house was empty. Carpets covered the living room floor, but the furniture was too heavy for me to push aside. I ran back into the vestibule and told Paul-Emile what I'd found.

" 'Can you keep them quiet?'

"I looked at the towering horses. 'I'll try.' My teeth chattered as I took the leather reins into my half-frozen hands. One of the horses nibbled on the pompom of my knitted cap. 'Hey, stop that.' I covered the pompom with my gloved hand. He nibbled on my glove. 'I know you are hungry. Can't you just wait a few more minutes? My stomach is growling too, don't you hear it?'

"Paul-Emile led the horses onto the carpet. We fed them, then tried the pump in the yard. Not a drop of water. He built a fire in the kitchen stove, then melted enough snow to water the horses. I complained about being hungry and thirsty too. He sighed and warmed his hands. 'Horses come first. What would we do without them?'

"He pulled on his mittens, stomped outside again and returned with more snow. 'Let's warm you up and then we'll eat. I think you should stick your feet in warm water.'

" 'Take off all these socks?'

" 'You want warm feet?'

"I did as he ordered. Even though the water was only lukewarm it felt too hot. He rubbed my feet, splashed a little warm water over them, dipped in a toe, then all my toes. Little by little he immersed my whole foot and added a little more hot water. Soon the tingling stopped and my feet felt like they belonged to me again.

" 'Your turn,' I said.

"We ate sparingly of our stash of food and opened a jar of raspberries we found in the cellar.

" 'Can't we stay here?'

" 'And the Russians ... did you think we were doing all this for fun?'

"We explored the upstairs bedrooms. Ice boxes. All the bedding was gone. 'I guess we better sleep in the kitchen, it'll be warm soon.'

"We pulled two chairs next to the stove and wrapped ourselves in our blankets and the bear skin. I dreamt the hanging man was laughing at me. He kicked his legs and tried to jump on my shoulders. My screams woke me. Where was I? Then I saw the dying embers in the stove and remembered. The seat next to me was empty.

" 'Paul-Emile!'

"Several loud booms suddenly shook the house. Something heavy fell and broke. I ran to the window. Pale lightning whipped through the windows. The sound of mortars came amid the pauses in the flak and red flashes illuminated the trees across the street.

" 'Paul-Emile,' this time I screamed. When he didn't answer I climbed back on the bench and drew the blankets over my head.

Boom, boom. I couldn't breathe. My body trembled. Everything inside of me seemed in motion, I had the curious sensation that death was approaching. In the momentary silence someone groaned or laughed, I couldn't be sure.

"The door blew open. Paul-Emile panted, 'The Russians.'

"His face appeared pale in the glow of the candle. Bright flickers danced on the walls, our shadows trembled. 'We have to get out of here.'

"I grabbed the blankets and the fur and tried to hurry but stumbled, entangled in the blankets and fell. He helped me. A crash. We ducked. The candle sputtered and died.

" 'What happened, are you hurt?'

"He grunted, then in the flash of an additional fireball I saw blood running down his forehead. The horses neighed and stomped their hoofs. Paul-Emile grabbed me by the waist and bundled me into the carriage.

" 'Don't move.'

" 'Your forehead is bleeding.'

"He wiped his hand over his face. 'Just a flying stone, it's nothing, don't worry.'

"Soothing the terrified horses with soft words, he backed Amsel between the two shafts of the carriage, then took up the reins and led him toward the dark part of the city and the Nogat River, away from the thuds of rattling, whining high explosives and the blazing sky.

"For a while we followed long columns of troops who appeared to be heading out of the city. Paul-Emile soon became impatient and turned once more into another side street and climbed into the carriage.

" 'They are all heading for the two bridges. It will take days before everyone gets across ... and guess what the Russians are going to shoot at.'

" 'Uncle Peter took everybody swimming on the river beach two years ago. The only road, he called it the promenade, I know that leads to the beach, is through the city ... at least I think we went through the city ... I'm not sure. Maybe we can get down to the river ... there are some grassy banks on either side. Do you think the horses can make it? Maybe we could cross the ice ... just walk across.'

" 'I've never seen the banks but the horses are strong. If it isn't too slippery we could maybe do it. Is it very high?'

" 'Very high, I couldn't see across.'

"He laughed softly and hugged me. 'When you are small everything looks big ... let's try it.' He flicked the reins and Amsel took off at a trot. When his right front hoof slipped Paul-Emile reined him in. 'There must be ice under the snow.'

" 'I could have told you that. Can't you hear the way the snow crunches?'

"We came to a dead end street and had to make a decision, right or left. I saw a horse-drawn wagon and some pedestrians further down the street to the left. 'Follow them, I think they are familiar with the area.'

"We soon caught up to a heavily loaded covered wagon. A woman stared at us out of the back. Her pale, austere face looked unreal in the cold light of early morning. I waved. She kept staring. A man walked next to the team of two horses.

" 'Shall I ask him where they are going?'

"Before Paul-Emile could object, I threw aside the covers and jumped down. I almost fell on my nose in my uncle's fur boots, but recovered quickly and pretended they were snowshoes. I asked the man where he was going.

" 'To the river,' he said.

" 'May we follow you? We are thinking of crossing the ice. What are you going to do?'

"He nodded, 'Cross the ice if I can get the wagon to the river.'

"I studied the bulky, wooden vehicle. Could his team handle the hard work? Maybe Donner and Amsel could help. 'Do you know the way? We thought maybe the bathing beach might be a good place. Have you ever been there?'

"A smile crossed his weathered face. 'Many times, that's where we are going.'

"I returned to Paul-Emile and reported what I had learned. 'Just listen, don't speak.' The woman was still staring at us with her dead eyes.

"When I told him about maybe letting them use our horses, he vigorously shook his head and mumbled under his breath, 'Are you crazy, don't offer.'

" 'They might get hurt?' He nodded. 'I understand, but the man won't be happy.'

" 'Don't worry about that now.'

"Even though it was a sunny winter day, the boom boom in the distance and driving along the almost deserted street past the empty-looking houses, made me jittery. I frequently leaned out and looked back to see if the Russians were in sight. We suddenly dead-ended at a snow-covered field. The woman disappeared inside her wagon and the man reined in his horses.

" 'Is this the riverbank?' Paul-Emile asked, 'You said it was high.'

" 'On the other side ... I can't remember. I think they grow wheat here because I remember the cornflowers and the poppies. *Mutti* pointed them out when we went swimming ... it all looks so different now.'

" 'Never mind, we'll just go slowly.'

"The wind was much stronger here. The snow blew across the stubbles and our tracks were instantly obliterated. He untied Donner from the back of the carriage and secured him on the right shaft next to Amsel. He told me to stay in the carriage and to hold tight while he guided the horses across the field that merged with the sky.

"Suddenly he shouted, 'Whoa.'

"I hopped off the carriage and ran to see what he was staring at. We'd reached the edge of the bank and the river lay below us. The horses snorted as the wind blew their manes across their powerful necks. Paul-Emile took off his glove, dipped one hand in his coat pocket and stretched out his palm. Each horse nibbled his oats delicately, pricked up his ears and swished his tail back and forth. Paul-Emile smiled and patted their muzzles.

"The man and his team pulled alongside. He grumbled to himself, stared at the river, then at his two horses and the wagon then shook his head. He looked at our horses. Before he could say anything, Paul-Emile took Donner and Amsel by their bridles and led them slowly over the edge and at an angle to the slope toward the Nogat River. The horses almost sat on their haunches as they slipped and slid down the steep, snow covered decline to the road below. I stumbled and slithered after them.

" 'Hop in,' Paul-Emile said, 'I'm going to walk them across.'

"Slowly, slowly he led them onto the pristine, snow-covered ice. The horses' ears stood straight up. I gathered Paul-Emile was talking to them again telling them not to be afraid.

"A humming noise, which soon grew into a roar, caused us to look up. Terrified, we watched as the plane flew directly over our heads. Then flames spit from its machine guns followed by a staccato rat-tat-tat as it dived toward the wagon train crossing the river downstream from us. Amsel and Donner reared and neighed. Paul-Emile calmed them while I watched the carnage.

"He urged the horses toward shore. Our breath mingled with the freezing air, and the wheels of our carriage creaked. When we reached the opposite side of the river, he walked the horses as close to the bank as possible. I couldn't stop looking at the chaos near the bridges.

"The thunder of the low-flying plane with its red hammer and sickle markings returned. The machine gunner appeared poised for the *coup de grâce*. He sprayed the ice with bullets and dropped small bombs which disappeared in the river along with several wagons. Then the plane left, leaving a ghostly silence behind. Mercifully a large snow-covered bush finally obscured my view.

" 'You all right?' Paul-Emile asked.

"I nodded, too numb to talk. He stroked our horses's heads and spoke to them soothingly. 'We'll have to stay here until nightfall. If we go up on the road above we'll be sitting targets. Are you warm enough?'

"I shivered and whined, 'I think my fingers and toes are dead.

I can't feel them.' I took off my mittens and stuck my fingers in my mouth, one hand at a time. They tingled painfully.

"Paul-Emile did the same, then he did jumping jacks. '*Eins, zwei, drei, eins, zwei, drei*, come on, Inge, jump. *Un, deux, trois, un, deux, trois.*'

"I followed suit, but was soon out of breath and quit while he kept jumping. 'I'm hungry and thirsty.' I ate a handful of snow. Paul-Emile handed me a piece of bread and stuck a bite in his mouth. 'No sausage?'

" 'Not now. I promise sausage when we are on the other side of the levee.'

"The horses nibbled on the snow and scratched the ground with their hoofs. '*Mon Dieu*,' Paul-Emile gasped, 'he's going to try it. Hope he has brakes and lightened his wagon.'

"We watched the empty-eyed woman and her three children, who stood across the river silhouetted against the flames, climb back into the wagon.

" 'What fools!' Paul-Emile said.

"The man stood next to his horses and appeared to encourage them to cross over the edge. The front wheels of the heavy wagon rolled over the lip. When one of the horses slipped, I covered my eyes. Peeking between my fingers I saw the horse struggle to regain its footing. The other horse had been pulled off balance and crashed sideways into the shaft. The shaft broke. The wagon rolled on top of the horses and everything somersaulted to the bottom.

"The man surveyed the carnage. Two shots stilled the screaming horses and the third stilled his agony. The short day came to an end as the pale winter sun set illuminating the burning city of Marienburg across the river."

Chapter Six

"**Paul-Emile guided** the horses underneath two sparse trees close to the up-slope of the levee. A fierce north wind penetrated every pore in my body. I shivered uncontrollably and shouted tearfully, 'Do something ... I want my mother ... it's all your fault ... you are just a stupid frog, frog, a prisoner frog.' I punched his chest with my fists.

" 'A frog, did you call me a frog?' Paul-Emile wrinkled his brow and pursed his lips. 'This mean frog is going to eat you if you don't run over to that bush this very minute.' He opened and closed his mouth and leaned toward me.

"I jumped out of the carriage and ran. He followed me and I didn't stop until he caught me, held me close and wrapped me in his large overcoat. He kissed my forehead. 'See if you can beat me back to the horses.' I ran and stood panting, waiting for him to catch me.

"I shrieked with laughter when he reached me and ran back down the road. 'Come and get me if you can.'

"With his arms flung wide, jumping from one leg to the other, he made funny faces pretending to be a monster. I ran back to the carriage and he followed me still clowning. I found I was warm and had feet again. After I climbed back into the carriage, he joined me and said with his face close to mine, 'Now I will kiss you and turn into a prince.'

"He kissed both cheeks. 'Is the frog gone?'

" 'My prince, I shall never call you a frog again.'

" 'Okay. Let's go, it's almost sausage time.'

"For a moment we glanced back at the dancing fires on the horizon, then Paul-Emile flicked the reins and the horses fell into a light trot. A few minutes later he said, 'Now we will try to get to the top of the embankment. You stay in the carriage and hold tight.'

"Once more the lumbering horses dug their hoofs into the snow-covered grass, lunged forward and pulled the carriage up. When we reached the top, flat land lay before us. Paul-Emile stood next to the carriage and panted, 'I hope I wake in the morning. I am exhausted.' He hopped in, leaned back against the seat and closed his eyes.

"As I watched him, the heavenly aroma of freshly baked, black bread and a slice topped with lots of newly churned butter and golden honey from the comb tormented my growling stomach. Plump, ripe strawberries in cream danced in circles about me. I almost smacked my lips, when I saw the blue bowls filled with cream-topped curds sprinkled with cinnamon sugar sitting on the windowsill.

"Saliva welled helplessly and tantalizingly from the ducts under my tongue. I wailed, 'I am hungry. You promised sausage and bread and the horses are hungry too.'

"He sighed and jumped down again. A few minutes later he was back after rummaging in the luggage rack which held our wooden food box and handed me a small piece of sausage and a chunk of hard bread. I wanted to stuff it all into my mouth at once, but instead nibbled daintily, because we'd discussed earlier that it lasted longer this way. Then he fed the shivering horses.

" 'We'll have to look for a barn. If they don't get warm they'll be no good to us tomorrow.'

"I tried to penetrate the darkness as we moved slowly forward on the barely visible road. Not a single tree was in sight, only the white, glistening desert of snow. Fires burned on the other side of the river and barrages of gunfire boomed. Twenty minutes later a black hulk loomed to the right of us.

" 'An estate,' Paul-Emile said, 'let's see if anybody's home.'

"The pitiful sound of lowing cows tore at my heart. They

quieted for a moment when Paul-Emile guided the horses and the carriage into the stinking stable, then, one after the other began to complain again. A single light bulb hung from the ceiling leaving the corners in eery shadows.

" 'Are you going to be okay here by yourself?' Paul-Emile said, 'I am going to check out the house.'

"I wondered what hid in the shadows. 'I want to come too.'

" 'No. If somebody shows up at least you can scream for help. By now it's cow eat cow. I don't want someone to take off with our horses.'

" 'Cows don't eat cows and besides, you'd never hear me over this noise.'

" 'True, but one of us has to stay here and that is you, *ma petite.*'

"I knew he was right. 'Why don't you lift me onto one of the horses. We can warm each other, and I can see who's coming and take off at a moment's notice. Give me the whip.'

" 'You'll get wet.' He removed the rug piece then swung me onto Donner's broad warm back and handed me the blankets and the bear skin from the carriage. I lay on my stomach and he covered me. Paul-Emile had situated Donner so he faced the large barn door ready for a fast exit. Amsel was tethered to the back of the carriage once more.

"We'd been on the road two days and had covered only about eight or ten kilometers. Thirty-five more to go if we were still heading for Danzig. Paul-Emile returned with two pillows, a sack full of apples and two bottles of liqueur. He lifted the bottles in the air. 'Have you ever tasted egg liqueur?'

" 'I cleaned out a glass or two with my tongue. It's delicious. May I have some now?'

" 'Only when we are on death's door or our stomachs are frozen.'

" 'Did you find food?'

" 'No, but I found beautiful books, a grand piano and a sack full of oats someone probably overlooked. I'll get it in a little while.' He fed an apple to each horse.

"Suddenly the stable door flew open. Two men in brown uniforms entered with drawn pistols. We stared at each other. 'You there' one of them pointed at Paul-Emile, 'give me those bottles.' He waved his arm with the pistol.

"Before Paul-Emile could react, I shouted, 'Don't shoot, he can't hear you.' They seemed to notice me for the first time. 'He can't talk either and is almost blind, don't hurt him, please.'

" 'These horses look in excellent condition.' One of the men elbowed his companion in the side. 'I'm not about to shoot a fellow German, but we are taking the horses and your wagon.'

" 'My Uncle Ludwig will be angry. He wears a uniform just like yours, perhaps you've heard of him? He is very important.'

" 'Is he here with you?'

" 'He's in the house.'

"They lowered their pistols, turned and mumbled something to each other. They stood with their backs to me, on the spot where they had entered and appeared to contemplate their situation.

"Take our horses – oh no, you won't. I held on to Donner's mane and hit him with the whip as hard as I could. Donner charged into the men and didn't stop until the carriage crashed into the closed side of the double door. The men lay unmoving underneath the carriage."

Dena said in an appalled whisper, "You really did that?" She looked at me with disbelief.

"I'd learned by then that one acted and asked questions later. What would we have done without our horses?

"Paul-Emile took hold of the restless horse's bridle and backed him into the stable. Then he removed the men's pistols, dragged them into one of the stalls and shut the door. He contemplated the pistols in his hands for a moment then threw one into the stall.

" 'Might come in handy. Here, you hold it until I see if the buggy is still usable. Don't play with it.'

"I was surprised at the weight of the pistol. Paul-Emile inspected Donner and didn't seem to find any damage, but the right wheel of the carriage had sustained three broken spokes. 'We'll be okay for now. Inge, you were magnificent ... why are you crying?'

" 'I didn't mean to kill them.'

"He pulled me off the horse and held me in his arms. '*Ma petite chérie*, you saved our lives with your quick action. It was either them or us. We have to be bold and brave during these terrible times. I would have done exactly the same. To reward your bravery I'll let you take one swig of the egg liqueur.'

" 'Two.'

" 'You want to get drunk?'

" 'Two.' I stomped my foot and glared at him.

" 'Two small ones.' He uncorked the bottle and handed it to me. I sipped once, twice and handed it back. He did likewise and corked the bottle. 'Very nice. Now what do you want to do, stay here till morning or leave?'

" 'I feel so sad for the cows. Do you know how to milk a cow?'

" 'Of course, I learned a lot on your grandmother's farm. My mother and father will be proud of me when I tell them about all the things I learned as a prisoner of war.' He chuckled and untied the pail.

" 'I wonder if Donner and Amsel would like warm milk?'

"Paul-Emile crouched on a milking stool and from under his fingers ran the lukewarm, foaming milk into the pail, smelling of the cow who provided it. After we'd drunk as much as we wanted, he milked some for the horses who had no second thoughts about slurping it up.

" 'I think we should stay here for the night,' I said.

"A groan and a shot rendered us momentarily rigid. I clamped my hand over my mouth and hid behind Paul-Emile. He jerked the pistol out of his pocket and deliberately emptied it into the stall door. We listened – silence.

" 'Stay here,' he whispered, 'I am going to check if they have more bullets.'

" 'What if they are just pretending to be dead?' The cows lowed again. 'I think we should leave now.'

" 'We need bullets.'

"He climbed on the box wall at the end of the run and walked from beam to beam. When he reached the one with the two SD men inside, he leaned cautiously forward, hesitated a moment, then jumped down. Shortly he rejoined me holding his hand over his mouth. He ran outside and bent over double.

"I ran after him. 'Are you sick?'

" 'Go back inside,' he gasped, 'leave me alone.'

"When I didn't move, he yelled, 'Go inside, right now. *Va t'an.'*

"He looked pale and shaky when he returned. He waved three full clips in the air, 'Let's get out of here before we have more surprises. We are not safe from anybody. You better pee before we go.'

" 'Are they dead?'

" 'Of course. Now do as I asked.'

"I squatted behind the carriage and decided this wasn't fun any longer, this was getting to be hard work. When I'd rearranged all my clothes, I asked Paul-Emile, 'Couldn't we take a cow with us?'

" 'Good idea, but it'll slow us down. Now let's get out of here.'

"Paul-Emile decided to use both horses to pull the carriage, everybody needed company he said. We soon reached a crossroad. This road sign, like most others, had been painted over. We asked the lone guardsman with a rifle over his shoulder whether this was the road to Danzig. He professed ignorance.

"The land in front of us was barren, dreary and looked treacherous. Nothing was familiar. Everything was penetrated by the chill loneliness of the unknown and nothing offered warmth.

I shivered. What was to become of us?

"We rounded a bend in the road and found ourselves in a stream of pedestrians. Most carried one suitcase, a blanket, a backpack, some pulled a small wooden hand wagon. Children and old grandmothers sat on sleds pulled by the mothers. I asked a woman where they came from. She examined our horses and carriage with a pinched mouth then said, "Elbing (Elblag)."

" 'Where are you headed?'

"She looked at me wearily and pointed her chin at Paul-Emile, 'Shouldn't he be asking the questions? You are just a child. He doesn't look much older. Why are you out here alone?'

" 'We are running away from the Russians just like you. Is this the road to Danzig?'

"She nodded. I could see she wasn't sure what to make of us. I wished we could give her a ride, 'You can stand on the step for a while.'

"She shook her head, 'You aren't going any faster than I am. You better walk too otherwise you'll freeze sitting in your coach.'

"Paul-Emile nodded and leaned close, 'She is right of course, good advice, but not right now.'

"We were stuck in the middle of this swarm of people because we needed to cross the Vistula via a bridge. The Vistula wasn't as tame as the Nogat had been and the ice was unreliable we were told. Also, low flying bombers had blasted the ice.

"Someone shouted, 'Soldiers are taking explosives to the bridge.'

"Our column suddenly took on a sense of urgency and picked up speed. Paul-Emile mumbled under his breath, 'If we could only get out of this beastly humanity.' He took the horses by their bridles and pushed into the crowd. Our horses looked impressive and dangerous. Nobody wanted to get trampled, and miraculously they stepped aside. Then I saw the bridge. Soldiers were tying something to the girders. I couldn't see what it was.

"Paul-Emile and the horses pressed forward while I

shouted, 'Achtung, Achtung, watch out, if they get loose they go wild, *Achtung, Achtung.*' I waved the whip in the air and tried to make it crack, but it wouldn't. The horses' ears perked up and their pace quickened. Paul-Emile had difficulty keeping up and I realized what I had done. I pulled on the reins and shouted, 'Whoa, whoa.'

"They slowed. Paul-Emile jumped to the side and climbed panting into the carriage. He punched my arm and shouted in French. I placed my gloved hand over his mouth. His eyebrows furrowed and I knew he was angry enough to wack me.

" 'I am sorry, I am sorry.' I cried.

"He leaned back, slapped his forehead and laughed. '*Ma petite diable*, you will kill me yet.'

"We waited hours to cross. Besides the bridge, two ferries were also in use. However, the Army coming from behind came first, then the walkers and last the vehicles. After we finally crossed the bridge dawn was breaking. We had become part of the trek that choked the road with vehicles, horses, soldiers and refugees, all headed for Danzig.

"Because the sea of snow raged from above and below, Paul-Emile decided to shelter behind a barn that evening. The snow flew off the roof past the moaning, bending and whistling willows. The refugees tried to squeeze inside the overflowing barn for a trifle of warmth. We didn't dare leave the carriage and the horses, so we huddled together on the seat and tried to keep from freezing to death. Our teeth chattered and our feet and hands were no longer part of us.

"Even though the wind pushed us sideways, Paul-Emile decided to move on. I trudged next to him as we joined others who had also decided movement was safer than rest. Only the creaking wagon wheels and occasionally barking dogs penetrated the train of silence, as we plodded through the clouds of drifting snow, guided by a dim lantern hanging from one of the lead wagons.

"An eerie shuffling noise closed in on us from the darkness behind, horses, shadowy in the moonlight, accompanied by men with bundles, rifles and cardboard boxes. No one sang. Hardly anyone spoke. They moved silently, columns of gloom, on the right side of the road to leave space for the vehicles. The road throbbed like a vein. We didn't hear a rifle shot, nor the boom of a cannon, only the constant rustle of the moving crowd similar to an army of moles digging their tunnels. One moment they were there then the next they were gone, swallowed by the blanket of snow.

"We arrived in Danzig with its ancient, peaked rooftops three days later, on January 27th. After asking for directions many times, we found my Grandmother Slavitzky's house in the warren of narrow, crooked alleys. It was really Uncle Werner's house, my father's brother, who lived there with his wife Karen and their two sons. One was about fourteen and the other nine, my age. My grandmother had moved in with them at the beginning of the war after my grandfather, who had been a blacksmith, died from injuries sustained while shoeing a horse.

"My parents, brother and I had visited here sometimes in 1942 for a few days. Now that I saw their house again, I was dismayed at its primitive and simple appearance. It stood in the middle of a small yard covered with sooty snow and was surrounded by a four-foot high, thick, brick and cement wall with glass splinters sticking out of a rounded top.

" 'This is it?'

"I nodded. 'They are not rich, but Grandmother is very nice. You'll like her, wait until you meet her.'

" 'Where are we going to keep the horses?'

" 'In the house of course. They have a cow and a few pigs and chickens. See that door, it opens on the top. It's big enough for the horses.'

" 'And the carriage?'

"I shrugged. Paul-Emile pushed the double gate open then led the horses into the small yard. I ran to the door. The familiar odor of an animal stable and cooking cabbage greeted me. A crowing cock strutted on a beam above my head. I wrinkled my nose, banged on the kitchen door with my fist and shouted, 'Omchen, where are you?'

"I flung the door open and almost collided with her. She stood in the doorway wiping her hands on her apron and gawked at me with her watery, pale blue eyes.

" 'Omchen, Omchen it's me....' I bawled and couldn't stop.

"She spread her arms, hugged me and patted my back. 'Hush, Kindchen (little child), hush, Kindchen, don't cry.'

"When I was able to pull myself together, I took her hand and pulled her along toward the front of the vestibule. She stuck her head out the door and was confronted by our two huge, black Trakehners and Paul-Emile, who stood between them. She raised her eyebrows.

" 'They are freezing, may they come in?'

"Without a word she grabbed a metal pole sitting in the corner and pushed the bolt of the top door to the side. Half of the wooden door swung open, she gave the other half a nudge and stood aside. 'Put them in with Dellchen. Hope they don't eat each other.'

"The vestibule was chilly but much warmer than outside. Paul-Emile brought our blankets, carpet, and the leather seat cushion from the carriage inside and dumped it on the smooth dirt floor of the vestibule. After he'd also retrieved the wooden box with our remaining food supplies, he bowed in front of my tiny grandmother. He stretched out his hand and when she gave him hers, he raised it to his lips and kissed it lightly. '*Enchanté de vous voir*, Madame.'

"Grandmother pulled her hand out of his and hid it under her apron. 'Who is that Inge?'

" 'Paul-Emile, my special friend.'

" 'What are you doing here ... where is your mother?' She had many questions.

"I asked her if we could come into the house, we were cold and tired.

" 'Come, come,' she said and we followed her into the

snug low-pitched kitchen.

"A green *Kachelofen* (a large stove made of Dutch tiles), with a bench next to it stood in one corner. An old-fashioned iron, wood burning cook stove, a deep sink and a china cabinet occupied the opposite wall. Under the single window, covered with lace curtains, stood a square table with four chairs with lyre-shaped backs. In a dark frame, hung next to the window and surrounded by bunches of dried herbs, was a large portrait of my grandfather. Attached to the cord of a single-bulb bowl lamp hanging from the low ceiling swung a strip of sticky fly paper covered with dead flies. I wrinkled my nose. Grandmother in Tessensdorf would never have allowed something so unsightly to remain.

" 'Sit, sit.' Omchen chuckled. 'They are going to be surprised when they come home and find your big beasts in there with Dellchen.'

"I was glad we had come. I'd only met my aunt and cousins once before. But Omchen had stayed with us twice for several weeks in Hannover. I felt certain of her love for me.

"When my aunt returned from scrounging for food, she stormed into the kitchen, the boys close behind her, and yelled, 'What are those horses doing in our house?'

"Then she spied me and Paul-Emile sitting close to the *Kachelofen* with our feet in a basin. 'Who are these people?' She frowned and squinted at me. 'What are you doing here? Where is your mother?' She banged her string shopping bag on the table and pulled off her mittens and kerchief.

"Omchen explained while my aunt busied herself emptying her bag. I placed my finger over my lips. Paul-Emile nodded. My aunt shouted that they didn't need more mouths to feed. Hans asked if the horses belonged to us.

" 'Aren't they beautiful?' I said proudly.

"He turned to his mother. 'We can sell them, or maybe even butcher them ... Mr. Rostovsky will take care of that for some of the meat.' He held out his arm and pointed a finger, 'Bang, bang and they are dead meat.' He doubled over amid shrill laughter.

"Aunt Karen, a chunky woman, leaned on her fist and gave him a thoughtful look. She had ruddy cheeks, one of them was blemished by a large brown mole. She sucked in her breath, accentuating her high Slavic cheekbones, let it out with a smack and nodded.

"I leaped to my feet, almost upsetting the washbasin, reached into Paul-Emile's coat pocket and pulled out the Luger. Omchen gasped and said in a quavering voice, 'Kindchen, Kindchen, put that gun away.'

"Aunt Karen looked at me startled.

" 'If you harm Donner and Amsel I will kill you. They are our friends. I will shoot anybody who tries to take them.' I burst into tears. Paul-Emile reached over and grabbed the gun out of my hand.

"Omchen drew me into her arms. 'Kindchen, Kindchen don't talk about killing, we have enough of that already.'

"Aunt Karen lowered herself slowly onto a kitchen chair and pointed at Paul-Emile. 'Who is that man ... we don't have any extra food ... you have a tongue, can you speak?'

"I disengaged myself from Omchen and placed my arm on Paul-Emile's shoulder, 'He can't talk. I am taking care of him.'

"Aunt Karen snorted. I didn't like her much. Erwin, my smaller cousin said, 'May I ride your horses? I have never ridden a horse before.'

"He grabbed a carrot from the table, broke it in half and bolted out into the vestibule. Before he could offer the carrot to the horses, who had stuck their heads over the Dutch door, Aunt Karen grabbed him by his collar with one hand and slapped him across the face with the other. Erwin howled and tried to kick her. She shoved him back into the kitchen and told him to sit down. She laid the retrieved carrot halves carefully on the table next to the other three, the four potatoes and the cabbage.

" 'You better leave,' Hans said.

"My tiny grandmother's hand flashed out and gave him a

glancing blow to the head. 'Keep your big mouth shut.'

"Paul-Emile had his shoes back on. They all watched us. I pulled at his jacket collar and when he bent forward I whispered, 'One sausage?' He nodded. I dried my feet, pulled on two pairs of socks and slipped into my fur boots.

"Without saying a word I shuffled with Paul-Emile into the vestibule and slammed the door shut behind us. 'I bet they'll let us stay the night if we give them a sausage.' He agreed, but slashed his finger in half. 'Okay.'

"We checked to see if the horses had stopped shivering. They stomped their hoofs, snorted and shook their manes. Their muscles rippled.

" 'Their clothes are wet,' Paul-Emile whispered, 'I wonder if I should take them off and let them dry.'

" 'Then they'll be naked and get sick. Uncle Peter always rubbed his horse after he rode it. Maybe we should rub them too?'

" 'With what?'

" 'The blankets.'

" 'I am going to remove their clothing,' Paul-Emile said. 'Maybe we can dry them inside on top of the *Kachelofen*.'

"We led the horses into the vestibule, untied the carpets, then grappled with the ties of the damp covers. My cousin Erwin asked if he could help. As if the horses knew we were trying to do our best for them, they held perfectly still and just snorted off and on. Dellchen the cow, looked on chewing peacefully.

"Hans watched and sneered. Omchen looked at the damp horse clothing and shook her head. 'Too big but I'll see what I can do.' She took them into the kitchen and slung them across the top of the large stove. She returned with several old, mended sheets. 'You can use these to dry the horses.'

"Erwin asked to be lifted onto Donner and I sat on Amsel and we rubbed until we were worn out. Paul-Emile worked on their flanks. Soon I found that the bottom of my pants and my pants legs were damp and wondered how I would get them dry again.

"Paul-Emile tapped my leg, held out his arms and said as he pulled me off Amsel, 'That's enough.'

"We covered the horses with our blankets, the fur and the carpet from the carriage, gave them each three cups of oats, an apple and water to drink and returned them to Dellchen's stall.

"I hid the sausage behind my back and stood in front of my aunt. Feeling important, I said, 'We will pay you with this, if you let us stay two nights.' I waggled the sausage in front of her nose. She swallowed and regarded it with longing, then tried to snatch it out of my hand. I jumped back. 'Two nights.'

"She squished her lips together and nodded. After we had eaten her meager fare, she and the boys soon went to bed. Omchen offered us her bed and I was about to accept, when Paul-Emile dug his elbow into my ribs. He leaned close, 'The horses, the food ... we must be on guard.'

" 'I want to sleep in a bed....'

"Omchen hugged me. 'I'll stay here with your friend, you climb into bed. I'll bring you a hot water bottle in a few minutes.' She pushed me in the direction of her room.

"I looked back at Paul-Emile who sat next to the stove with his eyes closed. He looked so tired I felt sorry for him. 'I'll stay here with him. He may need me.'

"Omchen tousled my hair. 'I'll bring you some covers. You also better change your pants.'

" 'I don't have any dry ones.'

" 'I'll be right back.' She handed me boy's underwear and long pants.

" 'I can't wear this.' I held them up and tried to hand them back to her.

" 'Sure you can, they are nice and warm. Come, I'll help you change.'

"I felt better and warmer. She added a shovel of coal to the dying embers and left us. Paul-Emile and I sat on the bench next to the stove and snuggled together under a feather comforter. Two seconds later he was snoring and I realized it was up to me to guard our possessions. However, the heat from the stove made my ears buzz and my eyelids grew heavy. A wonderful calm settled over my body as I hugged the hot water bottle to my belly and before I knew it, I too had slipped into unconsciousness.

"A rustling noise and a blast of icy air tore me back into cognizance. I slipped from under Paul-Emile's heavy arm on my shoulder, reached for the gun in his coat pocket and tip-toed to the door that led into the vestibule. In the dim light coming from a flashlight I saw Aunt Karen and Hans rummaging through our food supply. I shoved the door to with my foot and it shut with a click.

" 'That's our food, put it back.' I waved the gun.

"Hans sneered, 'What does a little kid know about guns. I bet it isn't even loaded.'

" 'Oh yeah? You want to find out? I already killed two SD men with this. You stand in my way, I'll kill you too.'

" 'You are lying ... your mother said you always tell lies ... I heard her tell Omchen.' "

"Did you lie a lot?" Dena asked with a grin.

I shrugged, "Sometimes. Tell me you never told a lie."

"Sometimes." We laughed.

"Aunt Karen stretched out her hand. 'Give me that gun.'

"She stood almost in front of me. I raised the gun. Someone snatched it out of my hands. Paul-Emile broke into rapid French. They gaped at him.

"Omchen stood next to him in her long nightgown. Her thin gray hair, plaited into a braid, lay over her shoulder. 'You want to invite all the neighbors to a feast, is that what you want,' she almost screeched.

"I had never seen this tender soul grow angry before. 'They stole our food.'

"Omchen grabbed the gun from Paul-Emile and said in a soft, low voice, 'Put it back, all of it.'

"I think Aunt Karen and Hans had never seen her exert herself before. They emptied their pockets and returned what they had taken to our wooden box.

" 'Now go to bed. You promised them two nights. You will stand by your word.'

"Aunt Karen hung her head, clutched Hans by his arm and dragged him back into the kitchen. At the door he turned and screamed at the top of his voice, 'I'll get you for this ... harboring an enemy ... they will hang you and I will spit on you ... you are a traitor.'

"We followed them inside.

" 'Please forgive them,' Omchen said, 'we haven't had much to eat lately. Everything is difficult and it will only get worse. Hans' brain has been polluted by the Hitler Youth. Even now we have to be careful. Many children denounced their parents.' She slumped into a chair and placed her folded hands on the kitchen table. 'I don't know what will become of us.' She wiped her sleeve across her forehead.

" 'We will leave in the morning.' Paul-Emile said.

"Suddenly the horses snorted. Someone was banging on the outside door. Omchen wrung her hands, 'Oh my God ... the Gestapo ... quick, hide under the bed. She shoved Paul-Emile toward her bedroom door. He grabbed the gun off the table and hurried out of the room. She smoothed her nightgown, grasped one of the blankets off the bench and wrapped it over her shoulders. 'Kindchen, stay here.'

"Voices, then the door swung open and in strode a soldier followed by Omchen. 'Kindchen, look who has come back from the war.' Her pale eyes brimmed with tears as she grasped the soldier's hand and brought it against her wrinkled cheek.

"To me he was a stranger. 'Kindchen, it is your Uncle Werner, your dear father's brother. The Lord saved him from the clutches of the Russians. Give your uncle a kiss.'

"He stretched out his hand. 'Where are your parents?'

" 'Father is in Posen and Mother in Hannover ... we are trying to get home.' I wiped angrily at my tears.

" 'Those are your horses? They are beauties.' He collapsed

on a chair at the kitchen table, pulled a long-stemmed calabash pipe out of his uniform pocket and filled it with tobacco. He scratched a match with his thumbnail, lit up, and a few puffs later smiled. 'I've been waiting for this all day.'

"Omchen brought him a glass of water. I studied him closely for I had a hunch he would be our savior.

"I tugged at Omchen's apron. 'What is it, Kindchen?'

" 'Is he a good soldier?' I whispered. 'Is my friend safe?'

"Omchen placed a hand on either side of my face and kissed my forehead. 'He is a good man. None of that Hitler stuff for him. Your friend is safe, believe me.'

"I opened the door to Omchen's room and found Paul-Emile standing ready with our big gun in his hands. 'Omchen says he is a good man, you can talk to him.' Paul-Emile followed me into the kitchen and I introduced him to my uncle.

"They shook hands. 'I'll be right back.' Paul-Emile said.

"He returned shortly with a bottle of egg liqueur and the other half sausage. They were about to toast each other when Aunt Karen entered the room. She and Uncle Werner gazed at one another for a moment then embraced. Aunt Karen was a different woman all of a sudden. She sobbed and kissed her husband, sobbed and laughed and held him at arms length as if to make sure he was not a mirage. Maybe she wasn't such a bad lady after all.

"The children ran into the room and hugged their father. Everyone was smiling except Hans, who pointed at Paul-Emile and me and said in a shrill voice, 'Father, you must report those two immediately to the Gestapo. They are traitors.'

" 'Quiet,' Uncle Werner hissed, 'all that garbage is finished ... finished, do you hear ... not another word or I'll throw you out into the snow.'

"Hans stood behind his mother and said to her, 'Tell him ... they have all that food and won't share it.'

" 'One more word and out you go. I only have a few hours, so let's have a pleasant visit during that time.'

" 'You have to go back?' Aunt Karen wailed. 'Why? There

is no front left. Inge said the Russians are in Marienburg ... why do you have to go back?' She clung to her husband who wiped her tears with his thumbs.

" 'I promised to come back. We have to keep the Russians from entering Danzig because this city is full of refugees and we want to get as many as we can out of here before they shell us and kill us all. Ships are still leaving Gotenhafen (Sopot).'

"Paul-Emile and I looked at each other and nodded. He said, 'Monsieur, may I speak privately with you please for a moment?'

"They stepped into the vestibule. I followed close behind. 'We have money, lots of money,' I said before Paul-Emile could open his mouth. 'Can you help us get tickets for a ship?'

" 'She is exaggerating. We have a little money ... will you help us please?'

" 'In the morning, let's talk about it in the morning. I'm exhausted.'

Chapter Seven

"**The next afternoon** Uncle Werner stomped into the kitchen waving two tickets in the air. 'The Gustloff leaves in three days from Gotenhafen. If you want to be on it, you better leave tomorrow at the latest. I'll draw you a map, you can't miss it.'

" 'What about us?' whined Hans, 'why can't we leave?'

" 'You leave when I say you can,' Uncle Werner waved his finger in front of Hans's nose, 'now shut up.'

"The next day Paul-Emile and I cleaned the horses' mess the best we could. Although their covers were still damp, Paul-Emile decided to redress them. When we left the warm kitchen a couple of hours later the wind creaked the doors in the entrance hall and drove the snow in at the chinks. I shivered uncontrollably knowing we'd be going out in that blizzard momentarily. We waved goodbye and embarked on our twelve kilometer trip to Gotenhafen. Our horses acted frisky and refreshed, but it wasn't long before the cold wind pinched my face, brought tears to my eyes and froze them on my cheeks.

"After we left the narrow alley where my relatives lived, we once more encountered hordes of people, vehicles and animals who appeared to have no particular destination other than finding shelter from the arctic blast. Paul-Emile maneuvered our horses slowly forward.

"Signs posted in some of the shop windows ordered soldiers to report to the nearest recruiting station. They warned: 'Whoever hides in civilian clothes or shirks their duty will be considered a deserter'. Another sign read: 'Danzigers keep discipline! Panic and rumormongers are the best companions of the Bolsheviks'.

"Cannon thunder from the front accompanied us as we traveled past the railway station. A train almost hidden by desperate people who hung from the steps, from the roofs and between the cars, pulled into the station. When it came slowly to a halt, men dressed in heavy overcoats boarded and returned carrying stiff bundles, which they laid side by side on the edge of the road.

" 'I wonder what those are.'

" 'Don't look, just watch the road.'

"But our progress was so slow I had nothing else to look at. Further on more bundles lay in the snow and abandoned baby carriages had been pushed into ditches. An Army truck convoy, their horns blaring, forced the pedestrians, horse-drawn wagon traffic, a few tractors and cars close to the edge of the road. Many slid into the snow covered ditches and were unable to get out again. Some people climbed out of their wagons and sat in the snow, their heads buried in their hands until all movement ceased and they too became part of the roadside bundles.

"We followed Uncle Werner's map and when we reached Gotenhafen, the harbor was wrapped in white clouds of thick, whirling snow. A sharp, northeast wind swept unhindered over the bare, flat terrain. Refugees who'd arrived by train trudged through the snowdrifts trying to find shelter in schools, barracks or in the harbor sheds. Despite the storm, long lines formed to receive a piece of bread and soup from the kitchens in the harbor sheds operated by the Navy.

"When we arrived at the eight and a half mile long wharf along the Baltic Sea, it too was packed with an indescribable litter of baggage on which feverish owners, quaking with fear and hopelessness, sat or sprawled. Everyone was waiting to board the Wilhelm Gustloff or any other ship that would take them to safety.

"The Gustloff, at 685 feet long and 184 feet high, towered over the masses. Hundreds of abandoned baby carriages, sleds, and hand-drawn wooden wagons littered the wharf.

"I reproached Paul-Emile in a weepy voice, 'You don't

care what happens to Donner and Amsel. You don't love them anymore.' I sobbed hysterically. 'I don't want to leave them. I don't want to go on that ship.'

"He sighed, bent close and said in an angry whisper, 'Of course I care, don't say stupid things like that and stop bawling. We'll set them free, they'll be fine. They can take care of themselves.'

"A man climbed on our step. 'Hey you,' he pointed at Paul-Emile, 'climb down ... shirking your duty, will you?' He waved the gun in his hand.

"I wiped angrily at my tears and screamed, 'He's not, he can't hear you and he can't speak either. I have to take care of him ... what do you want with him?'

"Another man shouted, 'Go pick on a healthy pig. We don't need nitwits in the people's army.'

"The man poked his gun in Paul-Emile's chest, 'If I had my way you'd be dead ... it's your lucky day.'

"He jumped off and faded into the crowd. The man who had intervened said, 'If you have tickets for that boat you better get aboard. You might not be so lucky the next time.'

"Paul-Emile took a deep breath and let it out slowly. He rubbed his chest and groaned.

" 'Did he hurt you? Don't answer ... don't say a word.'

"We watched the panicked people assault the ship trying to gain access. They shouted and shoved. An old woman with a red bandana on her head and lugging a heavy suitcase, pulled herself step by step up the gangplank by holding on to the manrope. Suddenly she stumbled. She tried to regain her footing and let go of the rope to push herself up, but the crowd behind her marched right over her. The woman, her red kerchief a vivid spot of color against the drab background, slid under the rope, over the side and plunged into the arctic water below.

" 'Did you see that?' I stared at the running people, the mayhem – another person jumped or fell into the water. I clutched at Paul-Emile's arm, 'I don't want to go on that ship, I don't want to, I'm scared ... you can't make me.'

" 'Inge, this may be our last chance. We have tickets ... I'll take care of you, we won't go anywhere near the edge of the ramp, I promise.'

"I kicked his leg. 'I'm not going ... I'm not going ... I'm scared.'

"He hugged me. 'Okay, okay we won't go ... now stop crying.'

"A woman standing next to our carriage said, 'Permission papers to leave, but no tickets. Isn't that a laugh. I'm not even sure I want to try to get aboard. It looks like an insane asylum.'

"She was young and pretty. Her face glowed from the frost and her hair was spangled with rime. She was talking to an identical lady. Sure I'd won this round, I poked Paul-Emile in the ribs. 'Shall I give them our tickets?'

" 'Why not, no use wasting them.'

" 'Hey you, pretty lady, I have a gift for you.'

"Startled, she looked at me. 'Why you poor child, you've been crying. It's so beastly out here. Sometimes I just want to sit on the curb and never get up.'

"I leaned over the side of the carriage and reached for her gloved hand. 'For you and your sister.'

"She gasped. 'Tickets for the Gustloff ... thank you, thank you ... you precious child ... are you sure?'

"We watched the sisters push their way through the crowd for a few moments then lost them. Paul-Emile sat still for several minutes staring at the ship, then climbed down, took the horses by their bridles and turned them back in the direction from which we came.

"Omchen was happy to see us, whereas Aunt Karen grumbled when we brought the horses back into her smelly vestibule. Hans grinned and rubbed his hands but kept his mouth shut. I didn't trust him for one minute and promised myself to watch him carefully. Erwin asked to sit on one of the horses and wouldn't come down even for lunch. Paul-Emile brought him a hard boiled egg, a slice of bread, a glass of hot milk and a blanket.

"Uncle Werner had gone back to his unit. Paul-Emile gave me a handful of *Reichsmarks* and told me to give them to Aunt Karen. When I handed her two hundred Marks she squinted first at the money then at me. A smile cracked her face. 'I won't ask where you got this. It will allow me to buy food. Danzig is still well supplied and I have rationing cards, but I didn't have any money. Thank you.' She bent over and kissed my cheek.

" 'Maybe you shouldn't say anything to Hans.' I tilted my head.

"She nodded, shrugged into her coat, tied a kerchief over her fur cap and pulled on her gloves.

"I knelt on a chair next to Paul-Emile at the kitchen table and watched him pore over a map. 'If only we knew exactly where the Russians are. I tried to listen to the radio but all I hear is propaganda telling everyone to stay calm the lines are holding. How can your people believe this nonsense?'

" 'We've been taught over and over, that's what,' Omchen said. '*Onkel* Goebbelchen has it all figured, out how to keep us trembling in our boots with his stories. We are still told today to believe in the Führer, that we could never lose the war, that he still has something up his sleeves and will use it at the last moment. The turning point will come. It is only a trap that he allows the enemy to come so far into our country.'

" 'And you believe him?' Paul-Emile asked.

"She cackled, 'Goebbelchen lost me years ago but I had to keep it to myself ... didn't dare voice my opinions ... especially with a Hitler Youth in our midst. Can't trust anyone anymore. How is your food supply for the horses?'

" 'Running low, three more days of meager meals.'

" 'So, what are you going to do?'

"Paul-Emile contemplated Omchen. 'What do you suggest?'

"She thought for a moment rubbing her forehead. 'You have to get out of this city. You won't find food here. The countryside is your best bet ... abandoned farm houses ... get off the beaten path, cross country.... You must find hay. Without hay the horses can't stay warm and they'll get weak.'

"Paul-Emile nodded. 'But the snow is too deep, what if we leave the carriage behind?'

" 'You'll be without shelter,' Omchen said, 'and if you find food, you won't have a way to carry it. Take the carriage is my advice, although it might be easier to travel without.'

" 'Why did we see so many baby carriages by the side of the road?' I asked her. 'Didn't the people need them for their babies?'

"Tears filled Omchen's eyes. 'Kindchen, you are too young to understand all the terrible consequences of this war.'

" 'I am not too young. I have seen many dead people.'

"Omchen shook her head sadly. 'I've heard that many babies died because of the cold. Wet diapers....' She buried her head in her arms resting on the kitchen table. Her body shook.

"I stroked her hair. 'Don't cry. Paul-Emile hates tears. We must be brave ... no tears.' I wiped my eyes and looked at Paul-Emile who's head was bent over the map.

" 'Where do you suggest we go, Omchen?'

"She dried her tears with her apron. 'West of course.' She tried to smile and picked up her darning.

" 'Of course. Where specifically?'

" 'How should I know? I took the train twice to Hannover ... I lived all my life in a small town, now I live in Danzig ... how should I know?'

" 'How come your name is Slavitsky and Inge's name is Lyndt?' Paul-Emile asked.

"Omchen looked up from her darning. 'How should I know? So many questions. Slavitsky sounded too Polish for her father, so he changed it, Werner too. My maiden name was Kraschevsky ... so now you will ask me more questions ... we are not Polish. We are German, although it might not be a bad idea to be Polish right now.' She brushed her hand across her brow and I saw she tried hard to keep from crying.

" 'Are you worried?' Paul-Emile asked.

" 'All these questions. Of course I am worried. I might lose all I have. I still care for my life, don't you?'

"I climbed on her lap, hugged her and kissed her cheek. She laid the sock with the darning needle on the table next to her chair. 'Kindchen, Kindchen, careful.' She smiled. 'Don't be so sentimental. Tell that Frenchman to use his head. You still have money? Go find a ship, go, go, before the Russians come.'

" 'She is right,' Paul-Emile said, 'we must go back to Gotenhafen, maybe even further up the coast, until we find someone to take us.'

"The door banged open. Aunt Karen unknotted her kerchief and shook off the snow. She pulled off her gloves with her teeth and blew on her fingers. 'Didn't you have tickets for the Gustloff? It sank last night. Torpedoed by the Russians. They say at least nine thousand people drowned, half of them children.' "

Dena gasped. "How could this happen? Didn't the Russians know it was full of refugees?"

"This was war, my darling," I said. "The weather was so bad and the waves so high that the smaller *Torpedoboote* accompanying the Gustloff had to return to Gotenhafen. The captain of the Gustloff asked for other protection, but word came that the only boat able to do so had engine problems. So the captain had to decide, to go on, or wait and risk an uprising on the overfilled ship where the majority of people were already seasick. The captain decided to go on with only one *Torpedoboot* still in position.

"Russian Captain Alexander Marinesco's U-Boot S13 managed three direct hits which raised the Gustloff out of the water. Only 1239 people were later registered as survivors."

"How could they stay alive in the freezing water?"

"Minus 18 degrees centigrade."

"You consider yourself lucky, Mommy?"

"Luck's been my middle name for most of my life."

"What happened next?"

"Paul-Emile and I looked at each other. I jumped off Omchen's lap and hugged him. 'Aren't you glad I was scared. The ship looked so big and the people shoved, I was afraid I would lose you.'

"He pulled my braids, 'I'll never doubt you again, you shall be my inspiration. Where do you want to go?'

"I stuck my finger on the map. He read the name under my finger. 'Wejherow, what kind of name is that?'

" 'It isn't far from Gdynia, hilly, very beautiful, very old.' Aunt Karen said. 'I suggest you find a boat though and you won't find one in Wejherow.' She dumped the contents of her string bag on the kitchen table. 'Bortsch tonight.'

"Early the next morning Paul-Emile rearranged ours and the horses's diminished food supplies. Our clothes could have stood a wash, but it would take too long for them to dry. I suspected we smelled a bit gamy. He laid out the clothes he wanted me to wear. I dreaded going outside again, but kept it to myself. I was convinced he needed me. I had a job to do.

"Paul-Emile handed me five hundred *Reichsmark* to give Omchen, buttoned the carriage seat pillow again and replaced it. I whispered, 'Where are the diamonds?'

" 'In Donner's collar. I cut a slit into the padding and stuffed them inside. It's risky if we should lose him or get separated, however, it is safer for us this way.'

"The outside door flew open and crashed against the wall. Erwin, out of breath, shouted, 'You must leave. I followed Hans to Gestapo Headquarters. When I saw where he was heading I turned around to warn you. You better leave right now.'

"Paul-Emile patted him on the back and thanked him. 'Inge, get dressed.'

"Omchen gathered together our blankets and pillows while I dressed, and Paul-Emile loaded the carriage and hitched up Donner. Fifteen minutes later we waved good-bye and followed Omchen's instruction on the quickest way out of the city.

"She'd suggested we circumvent the city rather than go through it. Good advice to a degree, now instead of being part of the treks we traveled against them. The roads were still jammed with incoming refugees.

" 'At least they won't look for us going this way.' Paul-Emile said. 'Your cousin knew we were headed for Gdynia ... if they are even looking for us.'

"Though Omchen had given us an old feather comforter, my feet were already clods of ice. It stopped snowing. We reached the top of a small hill relatively quickly and came to a fork in the road. Below us, in the white, misty veil of the weak morning sun stretched a trek resembling a never-ending black, giant, undulating serpent.

"Soon we joined this drove of people, most on foot and many dressed in quilted winter coats and sheepskin hats. Some traveled in four-wheeled, wooden wagons pulled by teams of horses who leaned into their harnesses and strained to pull them along the icy and snowy road. I asked a woman where they were headed.

" 'Kolberg (Kolobrzeg),' she said.

"I told Paul-Emile. He shook his head. 'That's a hundred twenty kilometers. I wonder why they are going that way? Sure it's west, but....' His shoulders drooped. 'I guess they have to have some kind of a destination. It's on the coast, maybe we can catch a boat.'

" 'With all these people going in the same direction, how can we find food for us and the horses?'

"Paul-Emile bent forward and studied the landscape. 'When we run out of food for the horses, we'll drop the carriage and go across the fields. We'll find a homestead somewhere I am sure. What do you say?'

"Before I could answer someone screamed, 'Planes....' Then I heard them. Paul-Emile jumped off the carriage and urged Donner to the side of the road into the forest of snow-laden firs. We almost got stuck in a shallow ditch. He cracked the whip and when the shells whizzed, screamed and crashed into the wagon train on the road, Donner lunged forward and pulled us among the trees.

"In only seconds the planes zoomed off into the gray sky leaving behind moaning people and screaming horses. Paul-Emile secured the exposed Amsel from the back of our carriage next to Donner under the trees.

" 'Make them stop, make them stop, make them stop.' I sobbed, pulled the feather comforter, reeking of the sour smell of wood smoke, over my head and clamped my hands over my ears. I still heard them.

" 'Stop the tears and stay here.' Paul-Emile said.

"Shortly after two shots rang out and the screaming stopped. He returned carrying a heavy sack on his shoulder, dropped it on the frozen ground and left again. A few minutes later a second sack joined the first. Paul-Emile puffed, 'Food for the horses. You wouldn't believe how the people stormed the bombed wagons and searched for food. Thank goodness I was the only one looking for horse food, at least in this particular wagon. Three were hit and everybody is dead. We'll wait a bit to make sure the planes don't return.'

"All remained quiet. It was pretty here in the forest as the thin sun shimmered on the glistening snow on the tree limbs. After Paul-Emile fed the horses, they nibbled daintily on the snow and scratched with their hoofs for a blade of grass.

"Paul-Emile handed me an icicle. 'Your lollipop, *Mademoiselle*.'

"I threw it away. 'You want my blood to freeze too?'

"He stowed the two sacks on top of our storage box. 'When we get back on the road don't look.'

"Of course I did look and the snow was red and the side of the road was strewn with corpses. We joined a few walking stragglers, passed them, and soon overtook the main trek again. 'I'm going to turn into the next crossroad," Paul-Emile said, "there's bound to be a farm somewhere.'

"It snowed again. All I saw were the tracks behind us, no horizon, no sky, no ground, only the shifting quarters of the horses with their tails blowing in the direction of the wind. Beyond was the harness of the shafts and the horses's rocking heads and necks with their floating manes.

"Slowly we journeyed across the monotonous sea of white. It seemed that our world had somehow been suspended in a time warp. We traveled for days across this endless landscape broken only here and there by a lonely wind-blown grove of trees, or a farmhouse abandoned with all its contents waiting for a new owner who might call it home.

"Ten days later we arrived in a town named Bülow (Bytow), we and thousands of others. Paul-Emile and I had been quite lucky, if you could call it lucky. The Russians continued to attack the wagon trains. Most homesteads off the beaten path were abandoned. We plundered and survived as did our horses. Only once did we come across a farmer who greeted us with a volley from his shotgun.

"When we arrived in Köslin (Koszalin), about the 25th of February, the story was the same. The city overflowed with refugees. Paul-Emile and I continued our charade of his disabilities, although he doubted it was necessary any longer. However, we still found soldiers and men in civilian clothing hanging from trees with shields across their breasts reading: 'I hang here because I refused to obey my transport leader. I am a deserter – I am too cowardly to fight'. So we knew bloodthirsty man-hunters still searched for soldiers who'd mixed in with the civilians.

"We also discovered that many refugees were returning to their homes in the east because rumor had it the Russians were encircling our position and cutting off all routes of escape.

"Staying in the city was out of the question, there was no food. We left immediately and continued our foraging through small villages without names. Some were completely deserted. We and the horses ate what we found in cellars and grain silos. A glass of preserved plums or peas – we dug for potatoes and boiled them in someone's kitchen. On many occasions I didn't want to leave because of the cozy fire. But leave we did, always heading west.

"Donner and Amsel's ribs protruded and they weren't nearly as peppy as they had been. The weather had moderated somewhat and the roads turned first slushy then muddy. By now the flat land slowly disappeared and we entered rolling, hilly countryside.

"Paul-Emile decided to abandon the carriage. We kept our fur rug, our pillows, blankets, the comforter and the rug pieces, because we knew winter was not yet finished with us. On March 2nd, 1945, we stood on a hill and looked down at the city of Kolberg."

My mouth was dry from talking. I drank some water, then closed my eyes.

"Are you going to sleep?" Dena said.

"If I can."

"Did you ever have counseling?"

I sat up and stared at her. "Why would I need counseling? Do I appear deranged?"

"No, but you experienced so much trauma...."

"It made me strong. Don't you think I'm strong?"

"I'm glad you are my mommy," Dena smiled.

I sighed. I hadn't thought about Paul-Emile for years. Now he once more occupied my mind. I longed to rehash our experiences, to laugh and cry with him as we had long ago. I decided to cancel the trip I'd told Hamdi to organize for us, it could wait, a meeting with Paul-Emile could not. I definitely would leave with Dena. Now everything was clear in my mind, I soon drifted off.

Chapter Eight

The next morning when Hamdi came by to pick us up I told him of my decision.

"Do you want your bugs back?"

"Why would I want those old things? You can't get rid of me that easily. We'll reschedule." When he didn't say anything, I knew I'd hurt him. "Darling, please understand, I need to sort out this situation I suddenly find myself in. Paul-Emile coming back into the picture has been quite a surprise." I stroked his cheek. "Please don't be angry." I hoped my words sounded gentle and kind, something I wasn't particularly good at.

He simply nodded and strode toward the excavation site. The French were already hard at work. I too was soon caught up in sifting through the debris the workers brought to the sieve. Paul-Emile kept his distance, while Camille and Dena flirted outrageously.

We all had a farewell drink in our room. Hamdi appeared distracted. I had to pacify him somehow. After the French left, I took Hamdi's hand. "Let's walk shall we?"

We listened for a while to the dark sea lapping at the shore. "What happened to us?" he said.

I kissed him. "Darling, Kane's death is what happened."

"But we love each other, we have always loved each other. Our love should be strong enough to overcome that tragedy."

"Hamdi, my darling, we still love each other. Please, be patient for just a little longer. Paul-Emile and I have a little bit of unfinished business between us. When it's settled ... darling please, just a few weeks longer."

He took me in his arms and we kissed. "Don't worry, I'll

be waiting for you ... for always ... as long as it takes ... I have no other love but you."

He took my hand and walked me back to my room. I invited him in but he shook his head. I slumped on my bed. I hated myself at times. I knew though that I had to get rid of those butterflies Paul-Emile elicited in my stomach. Damn him.

I woke when Dena returned. I smiled and hoped she'd had a good time. I told her of my plan to return with her to Cairo.

"You are running away. One of these days soon you have to decide about Uncle Hamdi. You can't keep him waiting forever."

"Darling, this unexpected meeting with Paul-Emile has brought new excitement into my life. I also still have a score to settle with him. When it is all finished ... never mind ... you'll see ... you've heard about a woman scorned?" I kissed her cheek.

"From what you told me, he tried his best to take care of you. Although I think he was wrong and selfish taking a child along on that dangerous trip."

"I insisted on coming."

"Mommy, come on, he was an adult or almost, nineteen, he should have gone to your grandmother and told her what you intended to do."

"Well he didn't. Be quiet if you want to hear the rest. You'll understand when I am finished with my story."

"In our wandering Paul-Emile and I came across a deserted farm. We had shared it with two other families for the past three days. To our surprise we found potatoes and apples still stored in bins in the cellar of the grain silo and in the barn, hay for the horses.

"At first we enacted our scenario of the past weeks, but the two women, their old mothers, an old father and four children ages seven to twelve were so kind, that we revealed that Paul-Emile was a French prisoner of war trying to get home and get me to safety.

"Paul-Emile chopped down small trees and fed the fire in the kitchen stove day and night. Finally the warmth seeped into our icy veins and made our feet, hands and fingers tingle. The children's cheeks were cracked from the raw weather. The exhausted women, each having pulled a heavily loaded sled for many miles, didn't have the strength to bring in snow to boil for potable water. Paul-Emile took over most of the chores.

"I was warm for the first time in weeks and insisted we visit the town. We sat on our horses and stared at the city below and the Baltic Sea beyond. I kicked Amsel lightly and he clambered down the snowy slope toward the crowded road. People streamed into Kolberg, an old, oft repeated picture by now. We trotted past them. It was Danzig all over again.

"A lone soldier pushing a bicycle with a flat front tire and a rifle slung over his shoulder, stopped to light the butt of a cigarette. I asked him if he knew anything about ships still leaving the harbor. He nodded. 'If you have a thousand *Marks* each,' he said in a hoarse, gravelly voice, 'that's the going rate.'

"He squinted at Paul-Emile, 'You should help secure this city instead of sitting on your horse. Hitler ordered this town defended to the last man because he read somewhere that Kolberg withstood Napoleon's army for six months.' He mused, 'Six months, we don't have six days and he wants us to protect the city. With what, our bare hands? So, why aren't you fighting?'

" 'He can't speak or hear and is almost blind. My brother is all I have left. My parents are dead ... my brother and our two horses. You see, they aren't healthy either.' I was crying real tears for I totally believed in my now oft repeated story.

" 'They are trying to evacuate the city of all civilians by ship. Who knows what will happen....' He drew one last puff deep into his lungs then threw the centimeter long butt onto the sooty snow. It hissed briefly and went out. I reached for Amsel's reins and we returned to the farm.

"That night we all huddled in the kitchen as we did every night. Donner and Amsel resided in the attached stable.

'Inge, *ma petite*, wake up.' Paul-Emile shook me gently. 'I think the Russians are here.'

"The vibrations of heavy, rumbling engines shook the house. 'What about them?' I pointed at the sleeping people.

" 'They don't have a chance on foot. I'll wake the old man, he can make his own decision.' Paul-Emile shook him awake and told him what he suspected.

"The man nodded, 'You better leave while you can.'

"Ever ready, we gathered our covers, led the horses out of the stable and slipped into the dense fir forest a couple hundred yards behind the house. The ground trembled. A cannon thundered and the sky lit up with crackling, sizzling fire. I quivered with fear and clutched Paul-Emile's hand. Another flash, followed by a boom, reverberated and shook the earth and the snow off the pine needles. I buried my head inside his coat. Suddenly an eery silence.

" 'I bet they've entrenched themselves on top where we stood yesterday. It's a perfect spot for a shot into the city.'

" 'How are we going to get past them?'

" 'Carefully ... we'll have to leave the horses behind. Can you walk to the beach? It's a long way but our only chance now.'

" 'We can't leave them,' I sobbed. 'I love them ... if we go now ... it's still dark, they won't see us.'

"He sighed. 'Not for long.'

"I pulled on Amsel's halter and walked deeper into the forest. When I sank to my knees into the virginal snow, I stopped and looked back. Paul-Emile hoisted me on Amsel's back and without saying a word, walked the horses to the edge of the clearing.

"Suddenly he groaned and dropped like a felled tree. Evil laughter was followed by a corrosive voice mumbling in a foreign language, '*Urri, urri*' (*Uhr* - watch).

"I gaped at the soldier wearing a green tunic, felt boots and trousers bagging at the knees. A fur cap with ear flaps sticking out on either side sat jauntily on his head. He knelt next to Paul-Emile and searched his pockets.

" '*Urri, Urri*'.

"I wasn't at all sure he knew I was even there. As soon as I saw Paul-Emile lying on the ground, I'd leaned forward on the horse's neck trying to make myself as small as possible. I was so scared that it hurt all over my body. The soldier clambered to his feet and swaggered up to Donner. We stared at each other. He gently stroked first Donner's then Amsel's muzzle. I could see he admired horses and felt a little less frightened.

"Suddenly his hand lashed out and with one swift movement he yanked me off the horse. I landed at his feet and lay in the snow staring up at him. He chuckled, pulled his bayonet out of its scabbard and with one quick slash slit my pants leg. I kicked him and tried to scoot away, but he held me down and laughed at my feeble efforts. His sour, rancid breath almost suffocated me when he leaned close and patted my face.

"I screamed for Paul-Emile. The louder I yelled, the louder the man roared with laughter. He knelt over me and fumbled with his belt. His pants dropped below his knees. I kicked and squirmed and let loose a piercing scream before he clamped his big hand over my mouth. I tried to bite him, but couldn't get a grip. Then the crack of a pistol reverberated in my ears and the soldier's heavy body crushed the breath out of me."

Dena sucked in her breath.

I'd never talked about this to anyone and was glad it was dark in the room.

"I thought I was going to drown in the sticky substance that smelled oddly of wet, rusty iron and tasted warm and salty. I twisted my head trying to get away from the cloying fountain and saw a boot raised about to strike. I cringed.

"The weight was gone and I could breathe again. A soldier holding a pistol in his hand inspected me. He grabbed a handful of snow and rubbed it gently over my face.

"Paul-Emile groaned. '*Mon Dieu*, what happened?'

" 'Paul-Emile!' I screeched. I scrambled on all fours over

to him and threw my arms around his neck.

"He grunted and said in French, 'My head, something cracked my head open.'

"The soldier examined Paul-Emile's head then pulled him to his feet. He spoke at length in French. Paul-Emile nodded.

" 'Inge, shake hands with an officer and a gentleman, he saved your life.'

" 'Is he a Russian?'

" 'A Russian.'

"I stretched out my hand. 'Thank you for saving my life.'

"Paul-Emile translated. I washed my face and hands in the snow and examined my torn pants leg. 'Why did he cut my pants? I'll never get warm again.'

"Paul-Emile wrapped me in a blanket and lifted me on Amsel's back. The Russian officer pointed in a westerly direction. They spoke for a few more minutes then the Russian handed Paul-Emile our *Reichsmarks*. They shook hands.

"We rode just inside the outer edge of the forest on a ridge leading down into the city. Someone from nearby shouted through a megaphone, 'Comrades, surrender the city. Today we are serving goulash with noodles. Our soldiers send you greetings. We will now present you with Stalin's organ concert. Listen....'

"A whistling hiss swooshed over our heads followed by a dry, sharp report. I ducked, squeezed my eyes shut and gritted my teeth. When I opened them again, I saw a high fountain of dirt and debris spew into the air. Seconds later more detonations followed and we became spectators to an action-packed movie on a theater screen. The roof of a house rose leisurely into the air then settled back on its walls. Then, as if in slow motion, the walls crumbled, the house exploded and white clouds of dust enveloped the ruin as it disintegrated in a heap.

"Tiny people ran among the houses and threw themselves to the ground as shots and salvoes smacked, thudded and plopped among them and the high dirt fountains. Red bricks flew through the air, beams tumbled after and licking flames and black smoke surrounded everything.

"We slid off our skittish horses and hunkered behind a large pile of logs. The horses whinnied and strained against their reins with ears lying flat and nostrils flaring. Amsel reared, his front legs and pawed the air. Suddenly there was a howling buzz and Amsel's head was gone. His legs buckled and he crumpled to the ground.

"I tried to scream. My lips moved, but nothing emerged as I stared at Amsel's twitching body. Paul-Emile grabbed me, swung me onto the dancing Donner and climbed on behind me. I held on to Donner's mane as we careened along the street as if chased by the devil.

"Riderless horses galloped through the streets. Black smoke and flames belched out of the ruins, spitting glowing embers into the air which then gradually extinguished as they fell back to earth. Explosions surrounded us. The Russians and their Polish allies shot from the hill into the city and answering German naval armament from destroyers lying offshore, roared over our heads.

"Donner raced past the burning houses. He dodged bomb craters and galloped past disorganized soldiers who didn't seem to have a clue of what to do or where to defend the city. As if the horse had a sixth sense, he headed straight for the beach.

"A man waved his arms and shouted something. Donner slowed then reared and slashed the air. The man said, 'Whoa fellow, whoa, easy does it.' His sides heaving, Donner snorted, shook his head, pawed the sand and stood still. I loosened my death-grip from his mane and stared at the smiling, middle-aged German sailor.

" 'He gave you a wild ride. Now you have to let him find his own way home ... come, we are about ready to go.'

"Paul-Emile jumped off the horse, then lowered me to the ground. The sailor took my hand and walked in the direction of a rubber dinghy bobbing in the surf. I held back. 'We have to wait for my brother, he needs me, he is deaf and dumb.'

" 'We'll wait.'

"Paul-Emile removed Donner's collar, the halter and bit and slapped him on the rump. The horse just stood there for a moment, then turned and looked at us with his large friendly eyes. He blinked once and trotted off. I tore my hand out of the sailor's, ran to Paul-Emile, struck him with my fists and sobbed, 'I don't want to go in that boat. I want Donner, I want Donner.' I threw myself down and lashed at the sand. 'Donner, come back, come back....'

"Paul-Emile lifted me up and wiped my tears with his scarf. 'He'll be fine, come on, we have a boat to catch.'

"The sailor shouted for us to hurry as a salvo of *Stalin Orgeln* (rockets) hit the edge of the beach. 'They'll have the range before long.'

"Paul-Emile carried me to the dinghy, handed me to reaching hands and climbed aboard. The sailor shoved us off the sand, jumped in, and together with the other sailor leaned into his oar.

"I wiped my tears, rose and looked for Donner. A woman pushed me down, 'Sit, you want to capsize us?'

"Paul-Emile wrapped me in his arms and held me tight. He whispered, 'He'll find a good home, now sit still.'

"We bobbed on the gray water and seemed to be standing still even though the sailors strained at their task. Three women and two children shared our space. Arctic water sloshed over the sides and the bitter air, keen as frozen steel, burned my face until it cracked and my feet and fingers were only memories of bygone days. But the lice on my head didn't seem to mind, for they chewed away until I was ready to tear my hair out strand by strand.

"Paul-Emile opened his large overcoat and pulled me inside. His heat engulfed me like a hot water bottle. He wrapped us in our fur rug, our only possession. I studied the two girls, one my age, the other a bit younger as they lay quietly in their mother's arms.

"I'd just dozed off when I felt Paul-Emile's arms tighten.

Reading his tension, I struggled out of my somnolence and looked around. The two sailors used their oars to stave off the huge black hull hovering above us in the heaving sea. I shrank into myself and tried to fuse with Paul-Emile's body.

"A small boat maneuvered next to ours. It was packed with silent people all staring upward. A cargo net slapped against the hulk. The sailors shouted, '*Los, macht schnell*, get going, hurry.'

"I watched two women from the other boat climb up. Suddenly one slipped. She tried to get a grip on the net, but she either didn't have the strength or her hands were frozen. Screaming, she plunged into the sea. They tried to reach the gasping woman but couldn't. She emitted one last feeble shriek and was gone. I stared at the spot where she'd gone under and wondered how long she could hold her breath. I waited and waited.

" 'Where did she go?'

" 'To heaven,' Paul-Emile said.

"The boat next to ours was almost empty now except for a handful of children who whimpered for their mothers. A bosun's chair carried two of the children at a time. I watched until they disappeared from view.

" 'Don't look down.' Paul-Emile whispered.

"It was my turn. I clung to him and sobbed, 'No, I can't leave you.'

"Paul-Emile strapped me kicking and screaming into the chair. 'I'll see you up top. Here, hold onto our fur, don't lose it.' He leaned close, 'The diamonds, you are in charge of the diamonds.'

"After we landed in Copenhagen a truck transported us to a school in town. The German Red Cross people tried to separate us. Women and children in one section and the men in another. I cried and clung to Paul-Emile. We'd agreed to continue playing our mute game until we felt it was safe to do otherwise. The Red Cross ladies took pity and assigned us straw mattresses on the edge between the women's and men's section. Most of the men were wounded German soldiers.

"We dropped exhausted on our pallets. Holding hands, and still rocking gently from our sea journey, I fell into a deep sleep. I awoke in the late afternoon. My stomach grumbled and my head itched. I couldn't stop scratching. A woman lying next to me called over a Red Cross lady and asked her to check my hair, she didn't want to get infected. My hair was infested. The Red Cross worker said the best and quickest way to get rid of them was to shave off all my hair.

" 'No, no.' I screamed and covered my head with my hands.

"Paul-Emile shook me by my arm and gave a slight nod. With tears streaming down my face, the Red Cross lady sheared off every single hair, then tied a scarf over my bald head. I hadn't felt this good in days.

"We stood in line for food, but didn't have any bowls or plates. A woman gave us one of her bowls and two spoons. The school was warm and for the first time since leaving Omchen I pulled off my ripped outer pants. I wore long woolen stockings and clothes that hadn't been washed for weeks.

"I asked Paul-Emile, 'Do I smell bad?'

" 'Maybe a little.'

"The following day the Red Cross workers told us we were being moved, nobody knew where. A train took us to a ferry for transport to Jutland.

"In Jutland, German soldiers drove us via truck to Kolding and dropped us off at another school. All we possessed at this time was our fur, some *Reichsmarks* and of course the ten small diamonds. We collected our straw mattresses and bedded down on the assigned three-story bunk beds in a gymnasium. Authorities wanted to separate us. I hollered and screamed and stomped my feet until people felt sorry for me and let Paul-Emile stay.

"About a hundred people shared the room. The lights stayed on day and night. Some infants, barely alive, whimpered because their mothers had no milk. Others screamed and older children sniveled and whined. Mothers tried to soothe them. Many children suffered from ear and intestinal infections, diarrhea and delirium from dehydration and high fever. The elderly groaned and sat with their heads in their hands apparently totally exhausted and broken in spirit and body.

"Paul-Emile and I sprawled on our mattresses and watched the listless yet intense activities surrounding us.

" 'I need to get us some new clothes, a bath and food. Judging by their jeering and catcalls when we rode into town, I have a feeling the locals aren't too happy with the German refugees. I think my being French will come in handy now. I want you to stay here and guard our fur and my mattress. I'll be back when I can.'

" 'You promise?'

" 'I promise.'

"I don't think I ever felt so abandoned, but when Paul-Emile returned, he had to shake me awake. I climbed from my third level bunk bed onto his. We huddled underneath our fur.

" 'The Germans are still in control here, so I had to be careful. I did find out that the *Reichsmark* buys things and that we will receive the same food given the German Army, so that shouldn't be too bad. Let's go for a little stroll now shall we?'

" 'What about our fur?'

" 'Ask the grandfather on the bottom bunk to take care of it.'

" 'What if he doesn't give it back?'

" 'Promise him extra food and a Schnaps if he makes sure nobody takes over our bunks.'

" 'You can get some?' He nodded.

"So I asked the old man who gave me a strange look. I pressed a fifty *Mark* bill into his hand and smiled my sweetest smile. 'Please.'

"He nodded and lay back. I covered him with our fur and told him we'd be back soon. Paul-Emile and I walked hand in hand out of the school. He looked like he knew where he was going so I followed him without questions.

"Fifteen minutes later we entered a patisserie. The heavenly aroma of mixed fragrances of chocolate, baked goods and whipped cream made my mouth water like a spring. Was this a fairy tale or a dream? I gazed at the eclairs, the napoleons and the colorful meringue swirls, the cookies and the Schwarzwälder tortes.

"I tugged at Paul-Emile's coat, 'May I have an eclair please?'

" 'Shsh.'

"I stuck my nose against the glass case separating me from the delicacies. The lady behind the counter finished with a customer and after the woman left she said, '*Vite*, Monsieur.'

"Paul-Emile grabbed my arm and whisked me behind the counter and through a door into a back room. We climbed a staircase and walked into a living room. An elderly woman sat by the window knitting. She laid the needles on her lap and beckoned me closer. As I neared, she said something in French and wrinkled her nose. Paul-Emile nodded and spoke to her at length.

"She rose, smiled and stretched out a hand. Paul-Emile pushed me forward, 'She will help you with your bath.'

"I stomped my foot. 'I don't need help.'

" 'You'll need help peeling off your clothes. I bet they have grown to your skin. After your bath I will buy you an eclair. Is it a deal?'

"Saliva collected in my mouth again. I swallowed, took the lady's hand, and allowed her to lead me into a bathroom with a large tub on claw feet. She turned on the faucet and helped me off with my many layers of clothes. For the first time I smelled the rank odor of sweat and dirt. She tucked at my kerchief but I held on tight. '*Nein, nein, non, non*, Madame.'

"She smiled and spoke soothingly in French. She dried my tears with a corner of her apron and gave me a little kiss on the cheek. I pulled the kerchief off my head and she gasped. But she had her emotions quickly under control again, because without further ado she bade me climb into the tub. When the warm water embraced me I relaxed and hoped I'd never have to leave again.

"I watched as she wrapped all my clothes in newspaper and laid the bundle on the floor in a corner. 'What are you going to do with my clothes?'

"She smiled and showed me a pretty, long-sleeved sweater with a Scandinavian design on the front.

" *'C'est à vous, ma pauvre enfant.'*

" *'C'est beau, merci,* Madame.' She was delighted with my French, and I was rather proud of myself and felt happy for the first time in weeks. She talked to me while she washed my back and my head. I felt the soft downy hair covering my scalp when she took my hand and brushed it over my head.

"After my bath she rubbed lotion all over my rough skin, helped me dress and tied a pretty new scarf over my head. Then she led me to a mirror. I didn't recognize myself. She smoothed my furrowed brow, kissed me on the cheek and led me back to the living room. Paul-Emile picked me up and swung me in a circle.

"I wrinkled my nose, 'You stink.' We all laughed.

"He too looked clean and his straggly whiskers were gone when he reentered the living room. The woman from downstairs brought us each an eclair and hot chocolate. We thanked her and took tiny bites savoring the familiar taste of long ago. When we finished, Paul-Emile spoke at length with the lady, wrote something on a piece of paper and handed it to her. He dug in his pocket, handed her two diamonds, bowed deeply and kissed her hand.

"We walked back downstairs and waited until the patisserie was empty. Paul-Emile picked up a valise standing by the door, gave me the paper bag full of cookies to carry, took my hand and led me out into the street.

" 'What's in the suitcase?'

" 'A change of clothes for you and me and a bottle of Schnaps. I asked her to contact my parents. She said she'd try.'

" 'You gave her two diamonds. Why two?'

" 'To keep her happy ... we want her happy ... because we need her to want to help us.'

" 'What happens to me when you find your parents?'

" 'They will become your parents until we find your real parents again. Will that satisfy you?'

" 'I will tell you later.'

"Paul-Emile and I stomped through the city most days just to get away from the noise in the gymnasium. The grandfather on the bottom bunk guarded our few possessions. For that we rewarded him with a piece of cake from the patisserie and a generous shot of Schnaps.

"We usually visited the bake shop for our afternoon cake and tea with the owner in her living room. She told us that she had contacted the Danish Underground who'd promised to send a message to the French.

" 'Is your father important?'

" 'No, but my mother is famous.'

" 'Why?'

" 'Because, *ma petite*, she can sing. She has a range many divas only dream of. She can start low like a basso and soar to a high C that will shatter a glass.' He tried to demonstrate. When he came to high C it came out in a screech. We doubled over with laughter.

" 'She sings opera. Do you know what opera is?'

" 'Wagner.'

" 'Hey, you are a smart kid.' He kissed my cheek.

" 'I heard it on the radio all the time when we lived in Hannover. My mother told me Hitler loved Wagner.'

" 'Do you like Wagner?'

" 'I like the ride of the *Valkyries*.' I sang, 'Hoyotoho, hoyotoho ...' ran through the living room and pretended to fly. Madame and Paul-Emile smiled and clapped when I finished my wild ride.

" 'Almost as good as my mother.' Paul-Emile said. 'I'll ask her to give you singing lessons. You'll be a great singer some day when you are grown up.'

" 'You really think so? I love to sing.'

" 'Now sit down and eat your eclair. Madame and I need to talk.'

"They talked in French. I'd learned a number of words from Paul-Emile by now, but didn't understand a word they said. Instead I concentrated on my eclair and dreamed about going to Paris. He told me later we had to be patient.

"The weather had turned cold again. An infant next to our bunk screamed incessantly for twenty-four hours. The mother tried to feed it. All it did was scream louder. Other women tried to help. Nothing worked. Suddenly the screaming stopped and the mother's smothered sobs were the only sound.

" 'Is the baby dead?'

"Paul Emile nodded. A tear dribbled down his cheek.

" 'It won't hurt any longer?'

"Paul-Emile blew his nose and said in a choked voice, 'Angels don't have pain. It will be happy now.'

" 'How do you know?'

" 'Inge, have you ever seen an unhappy angel?' He wiped his sleeve across his face and looked at me with red-rimmed eyes.

"I frowned. 'I don't think I've ever seen an angel, have you?'

" 'Stop asking stupid questions. Angels are in heaven. How could I have seen one.'

" 'You said you've never seen an unhappy angel.'

" 'Inge.' Paul-Emile threw up his hands and stalked out of the gymnasium.

"I ran after him. 'I'm glad the baby is an angel now. I don't think angels cry. Do they?'

" 'No. You are glad it stopped crying?'

" 'Yes. It made me so sad.'

"He nodded, took my hand and led me through the city until it was nearly dark and I was very tired. I slept well that night.

"A few nights later my ear hurt. I shook Paul-Emile awake.

He asked if I could hold out until morning he'd try to get somebody to help. My ear was on fire, my head pounded and felt like it would explode. I tried to be brave and bit my lip trying hard not to moan. In the morning he brought me two Aspirins. That helped some. He asked if I could walk to the patisserie.

"When we arrived at Madame Blanchard's she was sympathetic and said she'd try to find a Danish doctor. She returned half an hour later, shook her head and mumbled something under her breath. We waited for her to explain her downcast demeanor. She just kept shaking her head and sat in her favorite chair by the window.

" 'Madame?'

"A tear fell on her hand. She cleared her throat then spoke to Paul-Emile at length.

"When we stood outside once more, I asked why the lady was crying and what she'd said. Paul-Emile stuck his hands in his overcoat pocket and walked swiftly away. I ran after him and pulled at his sleeve, 'Tell me.' He grimaced, took my hand and looked at me with a frown. 'Tell me, or I won't walk another step.'

" 'Inge, it's not important.' He sounded impatient and annoyed. 'Okay I'll tell you.' He sighed deeply then squatted in front of me. 'She told me her Danish doctor refused to treat you because you are a German refugee. He also warned her against further contact with you, reminding her that Danish civilians were strictly forbidden to have any contact with German refugees. They are considered enemies regardless of age.'

"I stomped my foot. 'Pigs, I knew they didn't like us the moment we came here.'

" 'Don't call them pigs, that's not nice. Madame Blanchard gave me eardrops for you. I'll dose you when we get home. Come on, let's get going.' He rose and pulled me after him.

" 'Home, that's no home.' I kicked at a clump of sooty snow. 'When are we going to Paris?'

" 'I am working on that. Don't be so impatient.'

" 'I can't wait. I hate this place.'

" 'That's all we have right now.' He grabbed my hand and pulled me after him.

"The next day my ear felt much better. Paul-Emile decided to go into the city again to find someone to contact his family. He returned late that afternoon with flushed cheeks and out of breath. 'I've been so stupid. Come outside, I'll tell you.'   "We walked hand in hand along the snow-covered sidewalk. 'Why I didn't think about the International Red Cross before ... well, never mind. It will cost at least two of our diamonds, maybe three, it doesn't matter does it?' He looked at me and raised his eyebrows. 'We want results, right?'

"I nodded, not at all sure what he meant.

" 'I promised the lady at the Red Cross two diamonds, one for each ear if she contacted my parents. So all we have to do now, is wait.'

" 'How long? I want to go to Paris now.'

" 'Patience, you should have learned patience by now. Nothing in this war happens overnight.'

" 'Except bombs.'

" 'Not any longer, the bombs are finished.'

"I sighed, not quite believing him. Paul-Emile visited the Red Cross every day with no results. On the fourth day he showed the Red Cross lady in charge two of our diamonds. Paul-Emile told me later that she reached for the diamonds, then thought better of it and asked him if he was trying to bribe her. Paul-Emile grinned and concurred. He told her they were hers and that his mother, the opera singer Yolande Diderot, would make sure the Red Cross lady would receive tickets to the opera when she visited Paris.

"She promised to do her best and asked for one week's time. She stretched out her hand but Paul-Emile returned the diamonds to his pocket.

" 'Let me see them,' I said.

" 'Not here. This place is getting more dangerous every day, especially for you. I've heard rumors that the Germans are leaving Denmark and that the Danes are preparing refugee camps with barbed wire fences and guards. Once you lose your freedom it will be difficult to get you out. I want you to listen to me and not make any scenes, do you promise? You must blend in and be very good until I can get us out of here.'

" 'You wouldn't leave me?' I tried to suppress a sob because I knew he hated tears.

" 'Never.' He hugged me. 'You have to be good though.'

" 'I promise.'

"A week later a messenger asked Paul-Emile to return to the International Red Cross. Paul-Emile told me later about everything that occurred. He said the lady handed him a wire. It was from his mother and father telling him they were arranging transportation. Then he told the woman about his Polish charge, the little deserted girl he'd picked up while fleeing through the Polish corridor between Marienburg and Danzig. He told me she shook her head and said it was impossible.

"He showed her the two diamonds and added one for a necklace pendant. He said for her anything was possible. To please inform his parents of the situation and to tell them that he would not leave without the little girl. If they didn't leave together the diamonds would remain in his pocket.

"She wasn't happy with his request. She asked for my name and age, where I came from, who my parents were, and where they might be now. He told her there was little chance my parents were alive, because it had been shortly after bombs hit the area that he found me alone and crying.

" 'That woman wants our diamonds,' I said after Paul-Emile finished telling me about his meeting. 'Are you going to give them to her?'

" 'Only if she comes through, of course.'

"She did. I ran around the gymnasium, waved my arms and sang '*hoyotoho, hoyotoho*'. At first people smiled, then they looked at me strangely and told me to stop that nonsense. How could anybody be so happy in this miserable place."

"**Did you get** to Paris?" Dena asked.

"I'll tell you the rest tomorrow. Go to sleep. I'm exhausted from all this mental activity. Too bad you didn't have a recorder."

"You are planning to write everything down?"

"I think I should, don't you?"

"For the girls, definitely and Uncle Hamdi."

I laughed softly. "I'll fill his ears when we are old and gray, it will give us something to talk about while we sit in our rocking chairs. Sleep well. Don't dwell on this too much, it's all in the past."

"Yet it won't go away." Dena whispered.

"No, never."

Paul-Emile and Camille joined us for breakfast the next morning. "So, you are leaving us." Paul-Emile said.

"I have decided spending the next two months with three attractive men is too much of a temptation for mischief, besides, I find this dig rather boring. Call me when you find something exciting."

"Most digs are boring. You must have patience." Paul-Emile smiled.

"Excuse me for interrupting," Dena turned to Camille, "how about helping me with our luggage?"

As soon as they were out of sight, Paul-Emile leaned close, "Your address, please."

I gave him my card. He studied it briefly and tucked it into his pocket. "Where shall we meet?"

"Marrakech, La Mamounia Hotel on the first of December. Separate rooms."

He raised an eyebrow, then nodded. "Done." He rose and walked out without looking back.

Tall, lanky Hamdi strolled in shortly after. I told him we were ready. I'd wanted to take the bus back to Alexandria. Hamdi wouldn't hear of it. He insisted on taking us all the way to Cairo, commenting, he didn't want to miss a moment, never knowing if I would change my mind.

On our arrival in Cairo, Dena and I wanted to spend our last night together at the Nile Hilton. Hamdi tried to persuade us to stay with him at his beautiful house near the pyramids. We vetoed him, arguing that it was more practical to stay in town because it would add another hour or more to our trip to the airport in the morning. We dined together then said goodbye to Hamdi.

That night I told Dena about the rest of my association with Paul-Emile.

"Two weeks after arrangements for our trip to Paris had been completed, we took a bumpy two hour ride in the back of a truck, between bales of hay, to Esbjerg on the western coast of Jutland. I smelled the sea, so fresh and clean. We had to wait a long hour before two men finally asked us to come out of hiding. One of the men picked me up and ran toward a freighter being readied for departure. Once aboard, the screws vibrated under us and the ship slipped into the rolling fog of the North Sea.

"Now it was my turn to keep my mouth shut, for I had become a Polish refugee. Although many people living in the Polish corridor spoke German, it didn't hurt to be on the safe side, especially when we discovered that we shared passage with several Poles, English and French men and women. They tried to make a fuss over me and the Poles coaxed me to talk, but I shied into Paul-Emile's arms and buried my head under his coat.

"The approximately three hundred mile trip to Harwich took thirty-six hours. Thirty-six hours of warmth and food. I ate ravenously everything they set in front of me until I became sick and threw everything up again. Everybody felt sorry for me. I clung to Paul-Emile's hand and allowed the strange languages to lull me to sleep.

"Paul-Emile warned me, 'Don't speak German. Pretend you lost your voice.'

"Unable to talk was one of the hardest things I had ever done. I frowned constantly because I had so many questions and couldn't ask them. English, French, Polish, all was gibberish to my ears.

"When we arrived in Harwich, I clasped Paul-Emile's hand as we lurched down the gangplank. All at once his steps quickened. He let go of my hand and ran toward the couple searching the disembarking crowd of tired men and women. I knew immediately that the woman swathed from head to toe in mink was his mother.

" '*Maman, Papa.*' Paul-Emile shouted.

"They didn't appear to recognize him for they kept looking and searching. The woman grasped the man's arm and stared at the running man.

" 'It's me, Paul-Emile.' He shouted.

"I stood alone and watched the scene. They fell into each others arms and kissed and hugged, and the woman talked and kissed him again and again. The man slapped Paul-Emile on the back, embraced him too and kissed both cheeks.

"He had forgotten me. Tears trickled into the corner of my mouth. I felt very small and alone and it was my mother standing there instead. I wiped my tears, marched angrily toward them and pulled on Paul-Emile's coat sleeve.

"He turned, spoke in French, then took my hand and introduced me to his parents. His mother's diamonds sparkled on her ears and neck, and her perfume ... heavenly clouds of it, made me sneeze when she bent down to give me a brief hug.

"She wrinkled her nose, stepped away and spoke to Paul-Emile. His father offered his hand. When I gave him mine, he kissed it lightly. A charming man his *papa*.

"They hustled us into a limousine and drove us to London to the Claridge Hotel. I sat with the chauffeur in front while Paul-Emile sat with his parents in the back seat. His mother kept murmuring endearments and every once in a while I heard a kiss. They laughed and giggled and I grew angrier by the minute.

"I looked straight ahead but saw nothing because of my veil of tears. They were stealing him away from me right under my nose. It took all my restraint not to burst out and tell them to keep their hands off him. He belonged to me. Every time his mother kissed him, I wanted to pull out her hair by the fist full.

"But I forgave her when I entered the hotel with its Art Deco decor. I'd never seen such a beautiful place. And when I saw the gorgeous dress, the warm coat and stockings and the new shoes she'd brought with her from Paris, I practically drooled. Madame Diderot smiled and called me quite pretty for a Pollack when her maid presented me to Paul-Emile's *maman*.

"Not being allowed to talk was very hard on me. When we arrived in Paris and entered his parents' flat, I forgot everything bad, for I'd walked into a palace.

"I clasped my hands behind my back and examined every figurine, every picture, photograph and book. Without asking if it was allowed, I sat at the grand piano and played a simple little tune from Donizetti's opera La Figlia del Reggimento. I loved the melody of that aria and had practiced it every day at Grandmother's house. It was the only one I knew by heart. Paul-Emile's mother walked over to the piano and looked at me a little closer, then hummed along while I played.

" '*Encore*,' she said and applauded when I finished. She sang. I almost gave myself away when I heard her beautiful voice, so full-throated and rich. From that moment on I decided to become an opera singer.

"When Paul-Emile tucked me into bed that night, so soft and clean, the sheets smelled of sunshine, he told me his mother had decided to engage a teacher to teach me French and a music teacher to give piano and singing lessons. He kissed my forehead. Without preamble, feeling happy, I pulled his head forward and kissed his lips.

"He jerked away as if my lips had shocked him and rubbed his sleeve across his mouth. 'Don't ever do that again,' he said in a frosty voice. He switched off the lamp next to my bed and sidled toward the door.

" 'You don't love me anymore,' I whispered, wishing desperately somebody would hug and stroke me.

"As if he heard the tears in my voice, he said softly, 'Can't you remember anything? I hate tears. Now stop crying.'

" 'Do you still love me?'

" 'Of course I love you.' He sighed deeply.

" 'When may I talk again?'

" 'Soon. Don't be so impatient. I'll tell you when. Now go to sleep.' The door closed with a snap. I wept until sleep released me from sorrow.

"The next morning Emma, the housekeeper, woke me and showed me what I was to wear after my bath. I was starving, but she stood firm, 'Madame's orders.'

"I studied myself in the mirror and decided I looked pretty. My hair had grown back and framed my face with short auburn curls.

"The Diderots were already at breakfast and said good morning. I curtsied like Mother had taught me and took my seat. I think I must have impressed Madame Diderot because she leaned over and patted my cheek. Paul-Emile winked at me and I found myself smiling shyly.

"They watched while I ate. Grandmother had been strict when it came to good manners. I think she would have been proud of me. When they addressed me I gave them my most innocent look and smiled sweetly.

"After breakfast Madame Diderot led me to the piano. She rummaged through her sheet music and pulled out a book with scales. She asked me to play. Scales I knew. She pointed to a simple little etude. That too was easy. A satisfied smile crossed her lips. She stood, with her right arm crossed under her diaphragm and her left arm stretched out, she sang scales. She nodded and I followed her example. I loved to sing and tried to imitate her exactly. She patted my head and spoke to Paul-Emile and her husband who had been listening to us.

"Then Madame and Monsieur left. Paul-Emile said, '*Maman* likes you, that is very important. I am proud of you. Now don't spoil it. Keep your mouth shut until I tell you to speak.'

" 'But I may sing?'

" 'Just scales, I don't want you to give yourself away.'

"I sat at the piano and practiced the etude. 'You are lucky,' he said, 'school for you won't start until August, while I have to work hard already trying to catch up. Behave yourself and all will go well.'

"I nodded and concentrated on the ivory keys. A week passed without incident. Emma was kind. The man servant cum chauffeur was a snob and the Diderots were gone a lot. I played the piano and practiced singing scales.

"One day Madame sat next to me and asked me to play for her. When I made the same mistake twice over I shouted, '*Verdammt nochmal* (damn it all).'

"I started at the beginning and when I made the same mistake, I became really upset and banged on the keys with my fist, '*Verdammt.*' Awareness of what I had done came with a gasp. I slapped a hand over my mouth and gave Madame a sideways glance.

"Her face turned ugly. She glared at me, rose and said in an icy whisper through gritted teeth, 'You are a German child.'

" 'Polish, I am Polish,' I said in French, 'but I speak a little German.' My heart sat in my mouth.

"Shouting for Paul-Emile, she stormed out of the room. I leaned my arms on the keys, cradled my head and wept.

"Paul-Emile's *maman* raged. I couldn't understand what was so bad about being German. In a way I was relieved. It was very hard playing at being Polish.

"Madame Diderot yelled at Paul-Emile. They argued in angry voices. He came to my room that night and told me his *maman* agreed I could stay for now. He warned me to be on my best behavior and not to speak German, just French. If I didn't know the French words to keep silent. No German. I promised I'd try my best.

"One teacher came to the flat three times a week to teach me French and another once a week to teach piano and singing.

After the summer holidays Paul-Emile went away to boarding school. From that time on I was always angry at him. His mother and father's calendar overflowed with engagements, that left me with the maid and the butler.

"The good cook Emma took pity on me and I gained twenty pounds and looked like a blimp. I blamed it all on Paul-Emile. When he came home for Christmas and asked, 'Is that you Inge?' He didn't add, under that blubber, but I could tell he thought it."

Chapter Nine

"**The next two** years passed as if in a dream. While I attended school, did my homework or practiced the piano, I thought of Paul-Emile. Many evenings I waited impatiently for Emma's and my visit to the opera. Even Paul-Emile was sidelined while she and I sat in the loge and listened to Madame sing Lucia di Lammermoor or Mimi, or Madame Butterfly.

"When the orchestra opened with the overture, enchantment embraced me and I was carried away on wings of pure joy. I wept and lost myself in Lucia's sorrow when she sang 'Oh, dire misfortune', followed by the mad scene in which she sang first of her joy and her lover, and then of her miserable marriage.

"At the end, when the bells tolled and the lovers were dead, silence reigned over the audience. Then a thunderous explosion, fireworks and cheers erupted. Flowers and crowns of glory rained upon the performers. Weeping uncontrollably I wondered, would I too go mad from sorrow? The arias filled me with longing, for what, I didn't have a clue.

"Emma wiped my tears and we rode home in silence, each steeped in our own fantasy world. I learned that night and every night I attended the opera that beauty could indeed pierce the heart with pain.

"Thoughts of the next performance and the one after that distracted me in school and I listened with disinterest to everyone jabbering in French. I was eleven when someone found my parents living in a small village just eighteen kilometers from Hannover. When my parents discovered with whom I was living they gave me a choice, I could come home or stay.

"I chose to stay. The opera, tragedy, love, music and the piano and singing lessons, how could I possibly do without? It was easy pretending to be a princess, or an opera singer, or an actress in this palace I lived in. I had visions of becoming famous like Paul-Emile's *maman*.

"For my thirteenth birthday Paul-Emile convinced his mother to allow me to accompany her to Schiaparelli. I studied the models' every move, their make-up, their coiffeurs, their smiles and of course their attire.

"After this I always walked around the flat with a book on my head. I spent hours in front of the mirror and practiced smiling and gesturing. I slowed all my actions, quit climbing trees and ate like a pixie, daintily instead of ravenously. I waved my perfumed handkerchief at the piano teacher, sang with it pressed to my vibrating throat and rolled my eyes at him until he shouted, 'Mademoiselle, pay attention.'

"And of course I waited for Paul-Emile to come home. But he was changing. I felt he didn't really love me any longer the way he did when I was nine. When I confronted him he said, 'Inge, you can't believe how hard I have to work. I am so far behind, I wonder if I'll ever catch up. I am exhausted, leave me alone.'

"One day he exploded and shouted, 'Shut your mouth. I don't want to listen to your worthless chatter, nor do I want to watch you prancing in my mother's dresses and high heels.'

"I unfurled my fan and held it in front of my face so only my eyes were visible. I batted my lashes and said in a haughty tone, 'Men don't understand how a woman feels when she is shrouded in silks, satins, pearls, diamonds and high heels. She feels desirable, seductive and enchanting ... irresistible.'

" 'You are thirteen years old, a child ... what have you been reading?' He stared at me then broke into laughter.

"I lowered my fan to my chin and rolled the tip of my tongue over my lips. 'Reading and observing, Monsieur. I am no dummy.'

" 'No dummy, you speak the truth. I do love you like a

brother, an adoring brother. Now behave yourself.'

"I'll always remember the Christmas after my fourteenth birthday. Determined to make him change his mind about my juvenile status, I decided to absent myself from home when he arrived for the holidays. Before this I always watched and waited and assaulted him the minute he stepped through the door. He practically had to pry my hands loose when I embraced him. Not this time.

"His parents weren't due home for two more days. Prodded by the little devils slumbering in me, I made plans. The flat must have felt quiet to him when he returned from school. Usually, when his parents weren't at home I always did something noisy, pound the piano, sing, or play the record player and dance on my toes.

"When I entered the flat that evening I slammed the door, stood in front of the hall mirror and carefully wiped the smeared lipstick from my lips. I slowly applied new lipstick and slithered my tongue seductively over my lips to moisten them.

"I watched Paul-Emile in the mirror and saw anger gathering on his brow. He didn't know what to make of little tomboy Inge. I'd lost weight and my hair lay in soft waves across my shoulders. Emma had helped me with make-up. I wore high heels and an elegant dress I'd borrowed from his mother's trunk. It accented my tiny waist, I knew I looked pretty. In fact I felt beautiful.

"Suddenly he took three great strides, grabbed my arms and swung me around to face him. He glared at me with a dark, smoldering look. Confident my plan had worked, I smiled. Before he could speak or come to his senses, I pulled down his head and kissed him.

"He crushed me against his pounding heart and explored my mouth with his tongue. When our tongues touched I knew this was a grown-up kiss. I marveled over the wonder of this kiss, almost drowning in my passion and the glory of my triumph. We didn't stop until we were out of breath. I felt dizzy. He loved me.

Now he would never leave me again. We would get married and have babies and live in a beautiful house.

"He pushed me away, pulled out his handkerchief and wiped his mouth. My heart sank. He glared at me with compressed lips. I tilted my head and said in a small voice, 'Don't you like to kiss me?'

"He turned his back on me and strode in the direction of his room. My mind worked feverishly on what I could do next to get him to come back. He stopped and whirled toward me, 'Who kissed you?'

"I crossed my arms. 'I'm not telling you anything.' I grinned then stuck out my tongue.

"He glared at me. I loved it when he became angry because he always did something impulsive. I was right. He grabbed my hand and pulled me along the corridor into the living room and slammed the door shut. He pinched my cheeks together until my mouth puckered and hissed, 'Who did you kiss?'

"I couldn't stop laughing, but it came out all funny and I doubled over and sputtered, 'I can't talk when you pinch my mouth.' He released me and I laughed and laughed and he stood before me totally perplexed.

"He raised his hand. I ducked. He groaned and dropped his hand. I saw my opportunity and lunged. I clasped him in my arms, wound my legs around his waist, pressed myself into him and kissed his mouth. At first his arms hung by his side, then he grasped my waist and engulfed in Emma's perfume, we devoured each other. He lowered himself onto the divan and I lay in his arms and he caressed my breasts. He was mine forever.

"Someone pounded on the door. Damn Emma. Paul-Emile pushed me off his lap. He ran his fingers through his hair and paced. Finally he stopped in front of me and said in a husky voice, 'Don't ever do that again, do you hear me, never. I am sorry I touched you. I don't know what came over me.'

" 'But we love each other ... you can touch me all you want.'

" 'Inge, we don't love each other. We are just very fond of each other. Besides, you are way too young to think about love. Now behave yourself, no more theatrics.'

" 'You don't love me.'

" 'Of course I love you, but kissing like this is improper. You are just a little girl. Behave yourself.'

"I smoothed my dress, slipped on the pumps and wiped my tears. 'Why are you so mean to me? I'm not a little girl any longer. See,' I stood before him, 'I am all grown up.'

"He patted my cheek. 'You'll always be my little Inge.' He turned and left the room.

"I looked after him and chewed my lip. My stomach churned, sure I was going to be sick, I stormed into the kitchen.

"Emma sat at the kitchen table drinking tea. I slumped on a chair and glared at her. She studied me silently for a moment, then she smiled.

" 'Passion can lead to dangerous consequences. I found that out the hard way. He doesn't see you as the woman you are growing into. He just sees the child and he loves the child.'

" 'How can I make him see the real me?'

" 'Paul-Emile has many problems. Even though he was strong during your time together, he has now caved in and reverted to the sixteen year old adolescent he was when the Boche caught him. He has much work to do with growing up and until he does, he cannot love you like a woman. He is a boy in a man's body. Give him time, he will come to you.'

" 'I can't wait. I love him now. I want him to be my husband. I want us to have children ... I love him so.'

"She clasped me into her arms and I cried. 'He loves you too, *ma petite*, because he was disappointed when you didn't greet him.'

" 'He was?' I wiped my tears.

"She nodded and told me that Paul-Emile came into the kitchen and asked where I was. She told him I was out. Out where, he asked. Out with the young gentleman from next door.

"He gaped at her. She told him to close his mouth, after all beautiful young ladies did have gentlemen callers. He grimaced and said, little, chubby Inge out on a date? He began to pace, then stopped and poured himself a shot of liqueur from the bottle standing on a tray on the entrance hall table. After he took a sip, he looked at his glass, picked up the bottle and read the label. He swivelled on his toes and glared at her. She said she had a hard time keeping a straight face. He asked what the egg liqueur was doing there.

"Then he saw the photograph of two beautiful, black horses galloping across a snowy terrain. He picked it up and stared at it for a long time. He looked at Emma and asked what this was all about. She told him that Mademoiselle Inge liked to decorate, that she was thinking of becoming a decorator. Did he like the picture and the bottle? She was about to break into laughter when she saw the look on his face. She left him standing there with his thoughts.

"When the clock chimed eight he confronted her again, and once more asked her where I was. When she just smiled, he stormed into my room. He looked under every bed into every armoire. He shook her and shouted, 'Where is she?'

"Emma smiled and repeated that I was out on a date. When the front door slammed, he ran into the foyer. She said she followed him and they watched me reapply new lipstick. Emma said 'I would dearly have loved to know his thoughts.'

"After she finished telling me this, I hugged her and thanked her for playing along and being such a good friend. When Paul-Emile didn't show up for dinner that night, I banged on his door. He didn't answer.

"I yelled, 'Bull frog, once a frog, always a frog, a slimy, fearful frog.' I rattled the door handle. Suddenly the door popped open and I almost fell into the room and let out a loud whoop.

"Emma came running from the kitchen. 'Monsieur Paul-Emile has gone out.'

" 'Where did he go?' I twisted a strand of hair round my

finger. 'Emma, I can't stand this awful gnawing in my stomach. I think I am going to be sick.'

"She placed an arm about my shoulders and led me to my room. I'll bring you an eclair and hot chocolate, it'll calm your stomach.'

"I couldn't eat a bite. I had to act before his parents came home and convince him that I would take care of him. He had to love me. I took a sip of the hot chocolate and smiled. It might work. I undressed, slipped into my nightgown and tiptoed to his room, removed the key from the lock, returned to my room and waited.

"The front door softly clicked shut. He had to walk past my door. He stopped for a moment, then the squeak of his door hinges and all was quiet once more.

"I waited an eternal hour. A distant church bell tolled. Someone giggled under my window which faced the street. I tiptoed to his room, listened through the door to his soft snores and slipped inside. I pulled off my nightgown and rained little kisses on his closed eyes, his cheeks, his nose, his bare arm and his hairy chest.

"Slowly, slowly I pulled down the duvet, he wore pyjama bottoms, lay on top of him and kissed his lips. He sucked in his breath, his hands roamed and heat engulfed us. We panted and wrestled and kissed. The light came on.

"Paul-Emile's mother gasped and collapsed in his father's arms.

"When we were alone, Paul-Emile groaned. '*Mon Dieu*, Inge, what have you done?'

"I sat up and glared at him through the strands of hair hanging over my face. 'What have I done?' I combed the hair away from my face with my fingers. 'You kissed me back, you ... you frog. No wonder they call you French, frogs, ice water in your veins instead of blood. You never loved me.'

"I sobbed and hit him again and again on the head with a pillow. 'You never loved me, *je te détester*, I hate you!' I wrapped myself in my nightgown, slammed the door and ran to my room.

"I threw myself on the bed, sobbed and thought about death. Not my death, but death to all those who didn't love me. Someone knocked on my door. I didn't answer. Emma sat on my bed and rubbed my back.

" 'Emma, I am doomed. Nobody loves me. Will I ever find love?'

" 'Of course you will, you have to have patience. Love can't be rushed, it develops over time. Paul-Emile will love you with time. I think you should stay in your room for now. I have never seen Madame so angry. Did you do something bad?'

" 'Is sex bad when you love each other?'

" 'Of course not, but there is always the right time. You didn't, did you?'

" 'Sex? I don't know about sex. We kissed, is that sex?'

"She hugged me. 'You still are a little girl and have much to learn. Tomorrow I will tell you, now you must sleep.' She kissed my hair and softly closed the door behind her.

"Surprisingly, the next day was uneventful. I stayed in my room and Emma brought me food. In the afternoon she served an eclair. 'Now I will tell you about sex.'

" 'We didn't do that.' I said when she finished.

" 'I am glad. You may kiss. What is life without kissing. However, that also can lead to trouble. You just have to use your best judgement. Always stop before you get too carried away, because sex must wait ... you will know when it's right.' She smiled. 'You will know.'

"I felt calmer that night and dreamt about sex with a faceless stranger. In the morning when Emma brought me breakfast I asked her to fetch Paul-Emile. I wanted to share my new understanding with him and tell him that I was willing to wait. She informed me that he'd returned to university.

" 'But he's on holiday.'

"She patted my cheek, 'He'll be back.'

"When his parents returned two days later they invited me

into their parlor. His mother told me to pack my things we were going on a trip. When I asked where, she said Germany. Of course I knew what they had in mind. It was his father who took me back to my parents. His mother refused to set foot in Germany."

"You returned to Grandma and Grandpa and Uncle Edward. How did that turn out?" Dena asked.

"I went from relative luxury to relative poverty. It was a comedown and a disappointment. I'll tell you that part of the story next time we meet."

"At Christmas I hope."

"Yes, I hope so too. Now go to sleep, it'll be a strenuous trip for both of us tomorrow."

Dena stretched. "Australia here I come." She giggled. "Camille promised to sit in the front row when I perform in Sydney. What do you bet he'll be there?"

I laughed. "You are a beautiful, talented woman. I wouldn't be at all surprised if he showed up."

The next day, while Dena and I stood in line for luggage check-in at the Cairo Airport, an arm slid under mine. Hamdi. I stood on my toes and kissed his cheek.

"Darling Hamdi."

Dena laughed. "I should have known you would show up." She looked at her watch. "Sorry, but I have to move on." We hugged and kissed her and stepped out of line. We waved, then she was gone.

"I've got another hour, where shall we go?"

The Cairo airport didn't have many amenities, so we sat on a couple of chairs alongside the large, dirty windows in the reception area. A smile crossed his lips. I smiled too knowing what he was thinking about.

"Twenty-seven years ago I stood on one of these chairs and saw you for the first time. Did you know it was love at first sight?"

I clasped his hand and held it to my cheek. "So much has happened since then."

"And it is not finished yet, is it?"
"Almost my love, almost."

Chapter Ten

Hamdi called me in Miami in November telling me he was back in Cairo, the dig had relinquished little of value. Stephanie had invited him for Christmas. What did I think of his coming to Miami? I told him we'd love to have him, he could look over Magda's new interest. Dena too was going to be at home.

"Please do come."

I flew to Casablanca at the end of November, and on the spur of the moment took the train rather than a plane to Marrakech. First class was filled. I told the ticket agent to give me what he had available. When he found I was traveling by myself, he cautioned me. I rebuffed him and climbed aboard alongside the women with their lacy patterned hennaed hands and feet, the men with their fezzes, their bundles and chickens in slatted, wooden crates.

The train whistled its way through the brown, rolling countryside. Occasionally a farmer trudged across the arid landscape next to his camel or donkey pulling a primitive plough. Aside from one or two people using long poles to dip water from the infrequent covered wells, I seldom saw another human being. It appeared to be a world of emptiness with no visible crops. I imagined though that even this emptiness throbbed with a rich pulse, why else would these families toil for their daily existence in this barren-looking region?

Occasional flat-roofed houses surrounded by mud walls and a tree or two broke the monotony. Dangerous-looking cacti and thorn bush fences divided plots of land. Eventually we crossed the Djebilet Hills down into the flat plain of Marrakech. The Atlas Mountains loomed in the distance.

Taxi drivers bombarded me. I ignored them when I spotted a surrey. The ancient-looking horse and driver drooped, both appeared asleep. I hailed the man in French. His lips cracked with a faint smile and the roan pricked up its ears. Before I knew it, he'd lifted my bag onto the luggage rack. He bowed, stretched out his arm and bade me climb aboard. I told him to take me to the La Mamounia Hotel which was situated within the ramparts of the old *medina*.

When we reached the hotel, the driver told me he was not allowed to enter the hotel complex. I smiled, handed him the fare and told him to drop my suitcase at the entrance of the driveway.

A big turbaned Moor watched us closely. I waved him over. He ignored me. What an arrogant son of a turkey. I left my suitcase where it sat and walked toward the hotel. In a hushed, icy voice I told him in French that his father was a dog and his mother a bitch. It was no wonder they raised such an ugly cur. If he didn't fetch my suitcase in the next minute, I would make sure the ugly cur would end up in the street with my suitcase.

I placed my hands on my hips, glared at him and waited. He gave me the once over and I could see the wheels in his head turning for I knew I looked elegant in my black, tailored silk pantsuit. I made as if to enter the hotel, but was afraid someone would snatch my bag if I didn't keep an eye on it. The doorman grunted, then decided he better follow my request. I smiled and entered the fabulous hotel decorated in the traditional Moorish style.

I gave my name to the desk clerk who raised his eyebrows. "Madame, we sent a limousine to the airport, but the driver came back without you. How did you get here?"

"In a surrey."

"You weren't afraid?"

"Monsieur, you are talking to a traveler, not a tourist. Has Monsieur Diderot arrived?"

"He was worried when you didn't appear at the airport. He turned red in the face and shouted at everybody. I am so glad you are here Madame Boag. I will ring his suite immediately."

"Don't, I want to surprise him. His room number please?" I turned to the doorman and fixed him with a level stare. "Your doorman here will accompany me and carry my suitcase. You can spare him for a few minutes?"

"Of course, Madame, but this is not his duty ... the bellhop...."

"He needs the exercise, it will only take a few moments."

The desk clerk gave the doorman instructions. When we entered the elevator I said, "I will give you a generous tip if you promise to always treat guests arriving in that carriage with courtesy."

He bowed deeply, "Please forgive this ugly cur, he does not deserve a tip, but...." He spread his hands.

We'd arrived at my room. I gave him my key to open the door. He placed the suitcase inside and withdrew.

I took a quick shower, perfumed myself and dressed in a black chiffon cocktail dress. One more look in the mirror and I was out of the door. My heart galloped in my throat as I neared Paul-Emile's suite. I took a deep breath and knocked.

"*Un moment s'il vous plâit.*" He opened the door still knotting the belt of his black silk smoking jacket,.

A spasm of irritation crossed his face, then he grasped my wrist and pulled me into the room. He slammed the door shut with his foot and crushed me in his arms.

"Where have you been? I was frantic when you didn't arrive at the airport. I ranted, I raved ... you must find her ... I notified the police ... everybody is looking for you. I couldn't lose you again ... *mon Dieu* ... you are giving me a heart attack." He shook me lightly. "Where did you come from?"

"Casablanca of course." I laughed and wriggled out of his arms.

"Inge ... you are beautiful ... do you mind if I smear your lipstick?"

I leaned forward and proffered my cheek. He barely

touched it with his lips, then sat on the edge of the sofa, crossed his legs and stuck his pipe between his lips. "You have become decorous, Madame." He lit his pipe, took several quick puffs then set it in an ashtray.

"We are practically strangers. And just because I am a widow doesn't make me merry or promiscuous. Have you ever been unfaithful before?"

"Never."

I sang softly, "Never say never," and glided through the room turning off one lamp after the other except one small one on the desk. "There, much cozier. Now my faithful swain...."

I clasped his face between my hands and kissed him lightly. When I tried to step away, he seized me with the frenzy of a starving vulture. Yes, I would allow this now, this once, because I wanted it, needed it – oh Kane, I miss you so. When one of his hands started to roam, I drew away.

"Wow."

I took a deep breath, picked up my purse, withdrew a lipstick and looked for a mirror. I repaired my lips and hoped it gave him a hint that our kissing was over. After I ran a comb through my hair, I smiled at him.

"I haven't been kissed like that since ... well, it's been a while."

Paul-Emile got the hint. He turned his back on me and switched on all the lights again. We stared at each other for a moment then he said. "You have changed."

"Of course. So have you Paul-Emile. All sorts of lascivious ideas pervaded my mind when I first saw you in Mersa Matruh. You caused in me a lightness and an elation...." I sighed. "Perhaps it was only nostalgia."

I ambled around the room as though I were in a cage. I shouldn't have come. I sat on the edge of an easy chair and looked up at him as he stood there with his pipe in his hand.

"I don't know why I agreed to this tryst," I said. "Perhaps I came because we shared something special and unique ... death, destruction and prayers for survival. I thought it would be nice to talk about it. But you came because you wanted to make love to me. Although our adventures bind us, love no longer does."

He shook his head and smiled. "I don't think much about the war any longer. My wife drilled it out of me. For years she said, 'You must forget that period of your life, it never happened'. So I did what she said, except for you."

I ignored what he said. "You don't remember the howling Stukas over your homeland, and your arrest, your transport to Prussia and the rest? And you don't blame me, us, the Germans for your lost youth and misery during the war? Are you happy about forgetting?"

I laughed briefly, thinking, why am I pursuing this topic? Damn, I came here to talk about it, to lay it to rest. I said, "It did happen. Certain smells keep reminding me." I nodded, "Mostly smells and old bombers winging their way to air shows. You can't tell me this doesn't happen to you? I slumped in my chair. Don't make fun of the poor man, Inge. I smiled at him.

"What do you want me to do about that?"

I stared at him, "Do? Nothing."

"Tell me, what would have happened if my parents hadn't interfered and we'd made love?"

"You might have become a very young Papa." I laughed.

His mouth quirked in annoyance, "You don't care about me at all."

"Oh, but I do, otherwise I wouldn't be here. Besides, you have a wife and I have Hamdi, and ... we just met."

"He means a lot to you?"

"Yes, everything"

"Is he your lover?"

"No. I haven't had a lover since my husband Kane. Can you imagine, we were married for twenty-three years and every time he touched me in certain ways I couldn't resist him.... Before I came here I toyed with the idea of making you my new lover, I really did, but then I thought about Hamdi. I couldn't do that to him. Hamdi is my comfort." I watched Paul-Emile closely, "We were lovers as long as Kane was my husband. Hamdi and Kane loved me together and each other."

Paul-Emile stared at me.

"Do I shock you? Or maybe it even excites you?" I raised an eyebrow.

"Inge...."

"Have you ever been with a man?"

He cleared his throat. "I've had visions but never pursued it. Hamdi doesn't strike me as being gay at all."

"Oh, he isn't. He was just misguided at one time. Never mind."

Paul-Emile uncorked the bottle of champagne sitting in a cooler. After we'd toasted each other, he said, "This chance meeting has changed my whole life. Even though you won't allow me to love you, I feel like I have been let out of prison. How can I ever let you go again?"

"Why do you say prison?"

"I shouldn't have said that."

"Oh, come on, I want to hear all about your dark secrets. Tell me about your escape from prison."

Paul-Emile took a deep breath. "Ever since I married Celeste, I have been trapped in an unbearably, dominating relationship out of which I'm unable to extricate myself. It's like a symbiotic union, the equivalent of a mother with her fetus. She's made me submissive, she directs and guides me and...."

"And now you've run away."

"Yes. I dared and lied."

I drained my glass and rose. "I'm tired." I felt a little guilty leaving him so abruptly then shrugged, I didn't owe him anything. "I'll see you in the morning."

When I opened the drapes the next day, a cold sun streamed into the room. For fifteen minutes the Atlas Mountains soared vividly in the distance then disappeared in a sea of clouds.

I should let the girls know where I was – in a couple of

days I decided – I wasn't quite ready to answer any questions. I turned away from the window and started the shower. Memories were kind of sad at times because the past could never be brought back. I wondered what the day would bring.

We met for breakfast. His trousers, blazer with leather elbow patches and shoes had the look of London, whereas the shirt I decided, was French. His nails were beautifully manicured and his cologne smelled expensive. I proffered my cheek.

"We have so much to talk about." Paul-Emile said after our food arrived.

His gaze rested on my face as I took a bite of the crepe filled with baby oysters in a wine, cheese and mushroom sauce.

"Hmm, delicious." I closed my eyes momentarily savoring the delicate combination. Ready for my next fork full, I watched him taste his cereal mixed with fruit. "Do you ever indulge in decadent delicacies like this omelet I'm eating? I am so lucky ... never gain a pound. Do you want a taste? Poor baby oysters, never got a chance to grow up and make a pearl."

He looked sharply at me then said without preliminary, "You arrived at your grandmother's estate only a few days after I did. I saw the carriage draw up in front of the house. You hopped out and skipped from one leg to the other all the way to the front door. I said to myself, there goes a happy little girl, I wonder who she is."

"I was happy when we arrived in Tessensdorf."

Paul-Emile chuckled softly. "I watched you when you and your cousins and friends skated on the brown, frozen run-off juices from the cow and horse dung pile. I prayed with all my heart the ice would crack and all of you would land in the goo and you would run howling, dripping and stinking to your precious mommies, and they in turn would get it all over their Christmas dresses and...."

"Did you really?" I doubled over with laughter. "Even frozen over it stank and when we came home, everybody wrinkled their noses and we were sent for a bath in the washroom and a clothes change." I gave a wistful sigh, all these memories. "And then came the day François hung himself. I was so upset and worried about you doing the same. I wanted you to promise me never to hang yourself, but you didn't understand what I was talking about and didn't know yet."

"I have René to thank for that. He kept me from seeing François swing."

I shuddered, "I wonder what possessed François."

"He was a melancholy fellow, always talking about his girl and wondering if she was still waiting for him. He hadn't seen her in three years. When I asked him what she looked like, he couldn't remember. He cried every night and said her name like a mantra. Finally he'd fall asleep and René and I would sigh with relief."

"Were you ever mistreated by my uncles?"

"No, but we felt so terribly isolated from the rest of society. We were nonentities. We didn't count. We were considered sub-humans, deprived of all social comforts and intercourse. If I hadn't had you...." His lip quivered slightly. "And it being Christmas made everything worse."

"I am sorry, I should have been more considerate. Did it ever occur to you to harm any of us especially later when Grandmother relaxed her vigilance toward the prisoners?"

"No. I never knew when I might need her protection. Why harm someone on whom I was totally dependent. As to your other question, you did the best you could under the circumstances and given your age. Soon after you left to return to Hannover I found René hanging from the rafters. If it hadn't been for you I might have been the third."

"Did you ever figure out why he hung himself?"

"No, he never said a thing, just mostly sat and brooded. Once I heard him cry. When I approached, he had himself under control again. Sometimes I think it might have been François's death that had overwhelmed him so." Paul-Emile squeezed his eyes shut for a moment and I saw a look of pain cross his brow. He regarded me wearily, "I don't know."

I rose. "Shall we go for a walk in the garden or return to our rooms?"

"It's chilly, let's go to your room."

He sat in one of the comfortable easy chairs and twirled his pipe. I stepped behind him and massaged his shoulders. "Do you want to stop talking about the war?"

He was silent for a few minutes. "You were right, one doesn't forget. There are still moments when everything overwhelms me and then I wish ... I wish for oblivion."

I wondered what he meant. I sat down again. "Remember the day I was pulled off the train?"

Paul-Emile smiled. "I was so happy to see you. I wanted to wrap you in my arms, to hold you and keep you safe ... I knew I loved you. I told myself I was crazy, she is just an eight year old kid, but I loved you."

"And you love me now?"

"All over again."

I studied his face and felt a little sorry for him, for he seemed so sincere. And here I was torturing him by rehashing the past. Perhaps he had a miserable marriage. If he'd married me – no, it wasn't meant to be.

"You know, Inge, you were a mean kid at times. I almost hated you when you called me 'just a prisoner'. However, then I thought, she's just a little girl, she doesn't realize what she is saying."

"I was rather nasty, wasn't I. My cousins always teased me about fraternizing with that French prisoner. I am sorry I offended you."

"It doesn't matter now."

"I wanted to kiss you, just a little kiss on the lips. I dreamed about it when I lay in bed at night. I'd seen my parents kiss and how the kiss did something to them ... I wanted for you to love me, to hug me, to cuddle me. I didn't know about sex."

"But I knew about sex. I came across lovers all the time in the barn."

"Oh *ja*, who?"

"The maids and the Poles, almost every night. Sometimes I watched them until they left."

"And you, did you indulge in a bit of autoerotic diversion yourself?"

"Inge, what kind of a question is that." He gave me a stern look.

"You are blushing."

"Sometimes."

"And when I sat on your tummy, I did things to you?"

"Sometimes."

"What self-control, you pervert!" I laughed.

"What else did you expect."

"Do you remember my ninth birthday?"

"Of course, you reminded me for days before and after, that you were a year older."

"No, I don't mean that. I'm referring to what we heard on the radio that day. October 16th, 1944, my birthday, it was a major event." I paused, "You don't remember."

He shook his head.

"You men are so amnesic. The Russians began their offensive on the East Prussian border that day, barely a hundred kilometers from Tessensdorf."

"Inge, it doesn't matter any longer what happened on that day."

"Of course it matters. It was my birthday for crying out loud. I'll always remember ... besides, somebody has to think about all those pour souls who died because of that offensive."

His face grew sullen and he said with a grim smile, "So, what do you want me to do, fly flags, take out an advertisement in every newspaper announcing the great historical event?"

"No need to get sarcastic. I'm going to take a hot bath. Just thinking about that time makes me shiver with cold." I headed for the bathroom.

After I'd climbed into the tub, he leaned against the

doorpost and watched me lounge in the steaming water. "Inge, I want you to marry me. I'll divorce my wife. I want to spend the rest of my life with you."

I smiled and paddled the water gently with my hands, sending up puffs of suds and whiffs of Kane's spicy cologne I continued to use. I inhaled deeply. "I've had a husband." I clutched a fistful of the perfumed water and when I opened it, it was empty – like my life without Kane. I wondered if he was laughing down at me, or was it up at me, ridiculing my wistfulness.

"Inge?"

Definitely up at me. I smiled. How passionately we love everything that cannot last. I looked through Paul-Emile.

"Have I turned into the invisible man already?" Paul-Emile watched me with a smile that did not reach his eyes.

I cleared my throat and wondered what we had been talking about. I said, "I like my way of life and enjoy my freedom. I can come and go as I wish. I think that's probably why I don't commit myself to Hamdi. When I married Kane, I needed security. He offered me that and a comfortable life. I have three beautiful, talented daughters and enough money to live moderately well. I am flattered of course at your offer, but it comes about forty years too late."

"You always went your own way, even as a child, stubborn like a mule, slippery like an eel and cunning like an otter."

"Until that one day when I miscalculated. I am glad I can laugh now, for the nightmares have not appeared for years and years. I hope now that we are talking about that horrible time they don't return. When we reached Marienburg, I must admit, I was ready to go back home."

He took the washcloth, lathered it and washed my back. "Me too, but I worried mostly about you. I knew I'd done you a disservice by taking you along, but I couldn't bear to leave you to the Russians."

"And then we did meet the Russians." I shivered and wept.

"Why are you sad, *ma petite*?"

"I don't know." I reached for the towel on the edge of the bathtub. "Please give me a moment, I'll be right out." I dressed, walked into the sitting room and lit a cigarette. Then I poured myself a shot of brandy and slumped on the sofa with my feet propped on the coffee table. "Did you have any idea where you were going when we left Tessensdorf?"

"Talk, talk, talk ... I came here to make love to you not to reminisce about every little detail."

"Don't pout Paul-Emile. I dislike men who pout when they don't get their way."

"I am not pouting."

"Then answer my question."

He lit his pipe and paced the room. "Danzig. Definitely Danzig. Look Inge, give me a break let's go out. I'll arrange for a tour of the town. I don't want to think about that time."

"Okay. Let's eat first though. I'll meet you in an hour in the Bahja Restaurant.

"What are you going to do between now and then?"

"Read."

My heels sank into the thick oriental carpets lying on top of Berber carpets throughout most of the public areas of the La Mamounia Hotel. The gorgeous crystal and metal filigreed chandeliers and the Moorish tile decorations on the walls and the stairs made it easy to believe one had entered the opulent palace of a Moroccan Prince.

Paul-Emile had hired a guide and a car to take us into the city. "I want to buy you something. What would you like?"

"Are you rich?" I tucked my arm through his and stopped him in front of one of the huge, ornate, gold mirrors in the lobby. "I think you should shave off that thing on your lip ... I'll do it when we get back ... or will your wife object?"

"My wife, my wife, who cares about my wife ... it's you I will try to please. Are you sure you won't marry me?"

"I'll decide after we shave off your mustache." I laughed and kissed his cheek.

We waited for our guide on the steps of the hotel. An Arab six and a half feet tall, who weighed at least three hundred pounds and wore a red fez, baggy, gray trousers and a white, blousy shirt presented himself to us. We climbed into his equally big Chrysler and told him to drive around for a while.

We'd both been to Marrakech before so weren't really interested in the tourist bit, although I couldn't ignore the twelfth century, two hundred twenty foot Kotubia Mineret with the stork's nest on top. I also admired the amazing skill of our chauffeur as he maneuvered the car through crowds of people in the small alleyways without getting stuck or running someone down.

Our impressive guardian angel persuaded us to take a stroll across the great square of the Djemaa el Fna, where we stopped to watch snake charmers and the man who told a *small story*, by pouring water from one tiny receptacle into another.

We watched a woman with a vase on her shoulder cross the square. She had the poise and grace of a figure on an ancient frieze. Next to her walked a man holding two squawking chickens by the legs and behind them limped a donkey laden with clay jars.

A man squatted next to the entrance of the souk, a dark mouth of a covered alley, playing a weird melody on his flute. It sounded like sheer improvisation, music of the hills, wild notes of a solitary man, fierce, sad, obsessive, yearning and defiant. He played with his eyes closed, seemingly hypnotized by his own composition.

After I'd dropped a few dirhams into his box, we wandered among the tented booths of doctors, barbers and letter writers. We passed shops hung with silver, leather and crafts made by the Berber in the mountains, and cafés, where the faithful sat counting their amber beads and the idle smoked tasseled *hukkas*. Also among the throng of people wandered water boys dressed in colorful costumes festooned with brass cups. Their bells ringing with insistent jingling and tinkling notes.

Our driver took us to large, marble floored shops. Their walls were covered with Moroccan rugs and finely stamped leather poufs. Silver shops abounded. Men sat cross-legged in workshops, no bigger than cubby holes, stamping out intricate designs on bracelets and pouring the inlay from little iron pots of molten metal.

"I am rich enough," Paul-Emile smiled. "What can I buy you?"

I led him to a jewelry counter and studied the heavy silver bracelets, anklets and bulky Berber necklaces. "How about a hand of Fatima?"

"Do you need protection from evil spirits?"

"One never knows what may lurk around the next corner ... it could be your wife." I looked at him and grinned. He ignored me. I pointed at an inch long hand, "That one will do nicely. I'll put it in my wallet. I'm never without my wallet."

Paul-Emile spoke to the clerk behind the counter, handed over a few dirhams and presented the silver hand with a small bow. "You are too modest, but if you are happy ... I want to see you happy. Now what do you want to do?"

I tucked my arm under his and pulled him out of the shop. "I have this devilish urge to do something outlandish. We have a few more days before I must return to Miami. I promised the girls and Hamdi we'd spend Christmas together. Tell me, do you by any chance play golf?"

"I play tennis."

"Too bad, I don't. Let's go back to the hotel. I must call my girls and Hamdi."

"Hamdi, why him?"

"Because I must, he'll be worried about me. Don't you have to call your wife?"

"Inge, what are you trying to do? I thought we were going to talk about our flight."

"Maybe later, after we call our families."

"I don't need to talk to my family. They don't care what I

do with my time. Besides, only my wife is at home now. Camille is off in Aruba or maybe even Australia, somewhere where it's warm."

I told the driver to take us back to the hotel. When we stood in front of my door, I kissed Paul-Emile lightly on the cheek and told him I'd see him later.

"What do you mean later, you don't want me to come in?"

I pushed him gently away from the door, "Darling, I must talk to Hamdi privately. Please now be a good man, I'll call you when I am through with my calls." I slipped into my room and closed the door on him.

I called Magda and Stephanie and told them where I was and how they could reach me. They had all sort of questions, but I cut them short and told them I'd tell them everything when I returned home. I didn't call Hamdi, no need to, Stephanie would do it for me.

I took another long bath, perfumed myself, poured a shot of Napoleon Brandy and climbed into bed. Before long I dozed and dreamt of Kane. The telephone interrupted our kiss. Annoyed, I let the phone ring – eight, nine, ten. I stretched, then concentrated on my lost dream and tried to recapture Kane's kiss, but he eluded me as he did so often these days.

Chapter Eleven

Bang, bang, the door shook, well not quite, but it did sound urgent. "Inge, open up *tout de suite* or I shall break it down."

I pursed my lips, just a few seconds more and he'll be good and angry. I wanted to see him angry, for it seemed he'd been cleansed of all hostile emotions.

When I opened the door he shoved me back and slammed the door shut. "You ... you *enfant terrible*." He grabbed and kissed me all the while moving toward the bed. He pulled me over his knees and wacked my rear end until it smarted. I tried to get away, but he held me and poured all his anger out on my bottom.

"You have stalked me all my life, all my life ... I could never get rid of you ... you...." He let go and I slid to the carpet and huddled at his feet.

"Inge," he lifted me and crushed me in his arms. "Inge, I love you." He kissed my eyelids, my lips, my throat and fed on his hunger for Inge the child of his past and his dreams. "Why are you torturing me?"

"Am I?" I pushed him away, lit a cigarette and waved my long ivory cigarette holder at him. "If you'd stood up for your rights and mine, you would be the father of my children now, and I wouldn't have had to spend several miserable years in poverty. You and your family gave, then took everything I'd grown to like and admire away from me. I had to start all over again. Do you have any idea how that felt? No you don't. In fact you don't know anything about me.

"Because of your family I was able to taste the delights of haute couture and after they sent me away, I couldn't even afford to shop at Sears and Roebuck. I bet you haven't even heard about that sensational high fashion establishment. You have no idea what that did to my self esteem. It was embarrassing and left me extremely depressed.

"I shouldn't really be complaining. I'd only tasted Schiaparelli for a few years whereas quite a few refugees never knew anything else from the moment of birth. Now, for them it must have been a catastrophe and a come-down. I once met a Comtessa and her brother, I guess he'd be an Earl or Comte or Baron, whatever, who worked for my girlfriend's family as a scullery maid and a farmhand, mucking out stables and such ... of course you did the same ... did it embarrass you?"

He sat on the side of the bed. His shoulders slumped. "Are you trying to pick a fight?"

"I'm not sure, maybe ... but I am smart enough to realize that my fate had been determined long before I met you. So tell me, what did you think when I refused to go on the *Gustloff?*"

Paul-Emile sighed, "You want to throw the last half hour onto next year's compost pile without clarifying your emotions ... just overlook it happened?"

"I didn't realize you were a gardener."

"I'm not, but I figured you might be able to relate to it."

"It's quite immaterial." I shrugged. "I wanted to let you know what was on my mind ... however, it's no longer important ... so tell me what did you think?"

It was his turn to wander the room, his ever present pipe twirling in his fingers. "I ... I am not as mercurial as you are in your thought processes. How can I go back forty years in the blink of an eye?"

"Easy, you simply concentrate on that point in your life and don't think about now."

"Now is important. The past is the past, it doesn't matter any longer."

"It's made us, at least me, what I am today ... mean, selfish and demanding, ready to punish you for your sins. Come on, let's get down to business, but let's get rid of that fuzz on your lip first."

We examined his clean shaven face in the mirror. "Now you look like my young Paul-Emile. I didn't realize that something so small could change a person's feature so drastically."

I poured us each an ounce of brandy and made myself comfortable on the sofa. He sat in an easy chair by the window and took a sip.

"At first I was terribly annoyed with you for giving away the tickets and wasting our money, but then I realized I too had grown quite fond of the horses and letting them fall into all sorts of nasty hands should not be their destiny. They'd brought us this far, I knew they'd take us all the way. I decided to return to Danzig. With a roof over our heads, I could make plans, for I knew we needed a plan."

Paul-Emile rose and stretched. "One thing I'll never understand is why we went to Kolberg. That place was a disaster. Are you sure you want to talk about it?"

"Did you know the Germans made a film called 'Kolberg'? Its first showing was in January 1945. To shoot some of the scenes they used 187,000 soldiers, specially withdrawn from active service for this project. The film told of the triumph of the defenders in the besieged Port of Kolberg in 1807. While the film was shown in Germany, the real Kolberg was overrun by the Russians. And we were there. How lucky could we get.

"Kolberg, how could I ever forget Kolberg." I knew I was getting emotional, took a sip of my drink and walked to the window. The rose garden down below looked unkempt. When I had myself under control again I said, "I learned to be hard and distrustful toward people, however animals had and still have my deepest sympathy. A wounded or mistreated animal tears at my heartstrings and I get weepy-eyed. I'd grown extremely fond of Donner and Amsel and couldn't bare to see them suffer. I was sure they needed us as much as we needed them."

"Inge, are you crying?"

"I loved the horses." I blew my nose. "I hope Donner found a good home and poor Amsel, he never knew what hit him, I hope."

I answered the ringing phone at my elbow and handed Paul-Emile the receiver. "For you Monsieur Diderot, the front desk."

He listened for a moment. "Yes, please. With his hand over the mouthpiece he said softly, "Clarice. *Qui, Clarice, qui ... ma secrétaire, elle est très douée.* She speaks French, Arabic and English, all very useful with the work we are doing on the Prince's old documents." He nodded, "I love you too. See you in two weeks ... I'll call you if it takes longer. *Noël? Je ne sais pas.*" He listened for a couple more minutes then hung up gently.

We looked at each other.

"Your secretary," I sputtered, "you told her you loved her. Oh this is all *zu köstlich.*" I doubled over with laughter.

"Inge, stop laughing. What else did you expect. I couldn't tell her I was with you, be sensible."

"You said she didn't care where you went or what you did."

"She enjoys being in control, so I humor her. It makes life easier. You know how it is, a woman likes to hear she is loved. They are after all just words, they don't cost anything."

"You lied. Do you do that often?"

He smiled. "Only when it comes in handy."

I studied him for a moment, there was definitely more to this man than I had first realized. Surely, in the meantime – what did it matter. He was rather charming. Who cared what was, or was not between him and his wife.

Paul-Emile waved a finger in my face. "I don't like that brooding look. This phone call changes nothing." He hugged me. "You changed my life so long ago and now you are about to do it again."

"I am?" He tried to kiss me, but I turned my head and his kiss landed on my ear. I said, "Let's talk about Denmark. You promised me a warm bed, lots of food and new clothes and shoes

... all lies. Denmark, how could people be so cruel to us poor refugees who had been through hell. The Danish Red Cross, the Geneva Convention ... that's one thing I've dwelt on more than any other part of our flight."

"Why don't you allow me to kiss you? And why do you want to rehash everything? I'd rather not think about it."

"Because I don't kiss strange men, and the answer to your second question, I can't forget. I am planning to write my memoirs. Every parent should do that. Did you ever discuss the war with Camille?"

"I'm not a stranger ... oh never mind." Paul-Emile's fingers worked deftly in the tobacco pouch refilling his pipe. Then he paced the room from end to end and gave me an annoyed look. "Discuss the war with Camille? Not much. I never had anything to say I was really proud of. Did you tell Hamdi about our association?"

"Just that we met on my grandmother's farm. I haven't talked to him about our flight together, or about me falling in love. I was so in love with you ... I worshiped you."

Paul-Emile stopped pacing and looked out the window. He lit his pipe, turned back and sat down.

"My parents had their hands full when I rejoined them," I said. "I couldn't understand why you let everything happen ... how could you?" I sounded like a petulant child and almost grinned at my inadvertent regression.

"Inge, I explained it to you already. When I returned from the university you were gone."

"You knew I was born in Hannover ... oh never mind. I don't want to get angry at you all over again, but I'd sure like to punish you. How can I punish you?"

"If you want to punish me," Paul-Emile said, "you must leave me now, this very moment and never come back. My heart would wither and die a slow agonizing death."

All at once I felt a great anger rising inside of me. "Everything changed between us when you saw your parents. You allowed it to happen. Why didn't you protect me?"

He rose and paced again. "Don't be unreasonable. I did protect you when you needed protection. When we reached Paris I felt relieved not to be in charge of you any longer. I just wanted to collapse and let my parents take over and make all my decisions. Being strong had sapped all my energy. Now I could relax. I just wanted to totally disregard the past few years. I wanted to be a boy again without any responsibilities.

"My mother's perfume made me feel small and helpless and safe. Oh Inge, can't you understand how difficult it was to have to be strong all the time, fear for my life and protect you from harm?"

I glared at him. Was I unreasonable? Why get mad now. He was right, it was all so long ago. I grasped his hand and pulled him down next to me. To change the subject I said, "Upon entering your parents' flat I thought I'd walked into a palace."

"Mother liked to be surrounded by comfort and beauty, one of the reasons she didn't spit in the Boches faces when they asked her to entertain."

"What happened to the flat when your parents died?"

"I live there now. My wife wanted to rearrange the furniture, but for once I told her no. So she bought her own apartment where she could do what she wanted. She stays with me when the mood strikes her or when she wants to impress someone. Camille comes and goes, mostly goes."

"Aren't you lonely?"

"Sometimes.... Did you bring long pants ... some comfortable shoes ... I have arranged a jaunt for the two of us."

I clapped. "Where are we going?"

"It's a surprise, don't ask. We leave at dusk. Pack your things, we are moving out. Now run along, I'll see you in an hour."

He was treating me like a child. What the hell, if it made him happy, no harm done. I wondered where we were going. He knocked on my door an hour later. He'd brought along a porter who loaded my suitcase onto his trolley.

"Where are you taking me?"

"You wanted to do something special so I made the arrangements. Will you trust me?"

"I am not sure. The last time I trusted you, you let me down."

"Can't you let it be?" He sounded angry.

He ushered me into the back seat of a Mercedes and after our luggage was stowed, the chauffeur drove us to the airport. We boarded a small plane and thirty-five minutes later landed in Casablanca. When I tried to press him to reveal his plans, he just said to trust him and held my hand, lifting it to his lips every so often to give me a lingering kiss.

He hurried me to the international flights and stopped at the Lot Airline counter. "Warsaw!"

"I am taking you to Marienburg. It's all arranged. We can visit Tessensdorf ... everything you want to see and we can finish our conversation. After that you can ignore everything, go on with your life and be my bride. What do you say."

"I can't."

"You can't."

He sighed deeply. "You are still playing with me. I am serious. I'll set the wheels in motion as soon as I return to Paris."

"Please, I can't do that to Hamdi, I can't. Now let's enjoy ourselves. I wonder if things have changed a lot? I shivered. "I dread the cold."

Chapter Twelve

We spent two days in Warsaw. Paul-Emile wanted to show me through Lazienki Park. We strolled arm in arm down an *allée* of bare trees. Suddenly, before us, reflected in the stillness of an ornamental pool, stood the romantic eighteenth-century White Cottage, a wood-and-stone wedding cake type building built for Stanislaw II, the last king of Poland.

"He died in exile in Saint Petersburg writing his memoirs," Paul-Emile said.

"I wonder why. I'd much rather have stayed here in this beautiful place, peaceful and tranquil, surrounded by water. I bet swans add to the beauty in spring."

"He abdicated when he saw Poland disappearing from the map as an independent nation. I believe he was a great friend of Catherine the Great. Maybe that's why he chose Russia."

"Why did you bring me here?" I said shivering in my macintosh.

"I thought you'd appreciate the history and its beauty." He hugged my shoulders, "Come on, I'll take you back to the hotel. You need something warmer than what you are wearing."

I wasn't sure whether I shivered from apprehension, excitement or memories. He told me to rest, take a bath, whatever, he'd be back as soon as he could. He was gone three hours and carried a large bundle wrapped in newspapers under his arm. He ripped off the paper revealing a sable coat. He hung it over my shoulders and perched the matching hat jauntily on my head. "No use for you to freeze this time."

He had rented a car and drove us the approximately hundred-fifty miles to Malbork, or Marienburg the way I thought of it still. We checked in at the Zamek Hotel next to the Marienburg (castle). For the first time I appreciated the enormous structure built so long ago by the Teutonic Knights in 1280. The Poles were in the process of restoration, so we were unable to enter, but we admired it from the promenade alongside the Nogat River.

Our hotel was adequate, most of the food mediocre. The bread however, the fresh butter, the bortsch and the herring tasted heavenly. We traveled the countryside and retraced our route of long ago. Everything appeared close together now. Back then we'd spent hours traveling the short distance from Tessensdorf to Marienburg. My grandmother's house no longer existed and the large iron windmill was also gone. My uncle's house still stood. We didn't stop.

Our drive to Danzig the next day was easy although snow covered the countryside. Had our flight been a figment of my imagination? When we returned to the hotel in Marienburg I flopped on Paul-Emile's creaking bed.

"Aside from the fur coat, I didn't get much out of this trip. How about you? I didn't even buy you anything."

I lit a cigarette, walked to the window and watched the snow whipping past. It almost obscured the medieval castle from view. "We've come to a no-man's land, let's go for a walk."

"Now?"

"Now." I donned my London Fog and hung the sable on a hanger.

"You'll be cold."

"I want to be cold. Come on, we are going into the city." I wrapped a shawl over my head and pulled on my leather gloves. As far as I could see we were the only ones out in this blizzard. As we strode, with our heads bent, through the fast accumulating snow, we almost bumped into an old man. He said something I couldn't understand. I asked him if he spoke German. He grinned showing off his bare gums except for three crooked stumps. "*Ja, natürlich, ich bin doch ein Deutscher* (Yes of course, I am after all a German)."

I told him briefly about our pilgrimage.

He nodded, "I'll always remember that winter. Terrible ... the winters are still terrible. I should have gone west." He patted his pockets, smiled and shrugged. I gave him my pack of cigarettes. He looked at them, "American."

"Enjoy." I couldn't resist. "Did you by any chance know the farmer Ludwig Weber?"

"*Ja, natürlich, ich bin doch ein Deutscher.*" He stowed the cigarettes carefully in the inside pocket of his jacket and mumbled, "*Ich bin doch ein Deutscher.*"

We looked after his stooped form.

"I am ready to leave here," I said. "Where are we going next?"

"To Paris." Paul-Emile laughed when he saw my mouth fly open.

"You must be crazy. I am never ever setting foot in Paris. I vowed this on ... on.... I don't know what, but I mean it."

He tucked my arm under his, and we strode back to the hotel. I shook the snow off my coat as we entered the lobby, shivered and rubbed my hands.

"I can't imagine how we stood the cold. I swear to you, this is my last excursion to anywhere below seventy degrees."

Paul-Emile talked to the waitress in the restaurant. "I ordered *Glühwein*, that should warm you."

"Not too sweet, please."

"I'll tell her."

We climbed the stairs and I wondered what we were doing here in this place that had no resemblance to the beautiful medieval city of old. Aside from the castle, two thick, rounded stone gates, and a few cobblestone streets, nothing remained. The narrow, high gabled houses with the tastefully sculptured entrances and their jutting upper stories and the round towers in the walls were gone. The loggia bookshops, the cartographer's, and the tobacco shop beneath the houses, all gone. The small café, its front doors flanked by two gaslights in round frosted globes in massive brackets, gone too.

Everything had been replaced by ugly, square blocks of apartment houses built by the Russians. The once tree-studded street, lined with shrubs and flowers in season, had been denuded by the fighting and nearly remained so to this day. Depressed by this dismal picture, I decided it was time to go home.

When the waitress arrived with our *Glühwein*, she poured us each a glass of the hot spiced wine and we toasted each other. I told him of my decision. "Our flight together is finished. The rest of my story has nothing to do with you."

"Oh but it does. You still hold a grudge and until that disappears you cannot forgive me. And if you don't forgive me, you will never agree to marry me. So I am taking you to Paris. I own a small flat on the Left Bank."

"I'm not setting foot in Paris." I glared at him and held out my glass. He refilled it and sat on the bed.

"This is a rather dreary hotel. Shall we drive to Danzig or back to Warsaw?"

"Warsaw, because I am flying home." I stretched out on the bed. "When I entered your parent's flat in Paris, I felt I had to tiptoe everywhere for fear I'd get something dirty, or break something."

"You blew it when you spoke German."

I nodded, "Your *maman* raged. I couldn't understand what was so bad about being a German child."

"Mother felt totally humiliated during the German occupation. To perform exclusively for their elite forces was repugnant, but she and Father needed the extra rations their compliance brought. That first night I was home she ranted and raved until she fell exhausted onto the divan and wept into her handkerchief.

"Mother was determined that she could make you talk by teaching you the piano and singing, and you took to it like you were a natural. And then you blew it. You were quick, but you didn't fool her much."

"No, I didn't, and in a way I was relieved. It was very hard playing at being Polish."

"Mother confronted me, she shouted and called me a collaborator. I pleaded with her to be compassionate, and again reminded her that without you I might not have returned home at all. After she calmed, Father and I convinced her to give you a chance. She reluctantly agreed, but insisted on looking for your parents. I was glad for you that the deception was at an end."

"Do you think they have Russian caviar in this town?"

"I'll find out, be back in a minute."

I returned to my room, undressed, stepped into the shower and sang the aria from 'La Figlia del Reggimento' I'd played on the piano at the Diderot's. After I was dressed and had revamped my make-up I returned to Paul-Emile's room.

"Inge, be mine." He handed me my glass with the wine.

"Don't pressure me, don't ever pressure me. I've told you what I want from you. Please accept my decision gracefully."

"You haven't changed much Inge, and that attracts me so. Forgive me I can't help myself."

I spread home-made butter on the delicious bread with its crunchy crust, topped it with caviar and took a big bite. "What we need is some chilled Russian vodka."

"On top of the *Glühwein*? You'll be sick."

I munched. "You are probably right."

"Let me see if they have chilled Russian vodka." He returned with two martini glasses and a bucket of ice holding a bottle of vodka. After he'd poured, we toasted each other.

"Your Emma told me, 'He'll come back to you'. It took you thirty-five years and then we met by accident. Hilarious." I giggled.

"Are you getting looped?"

"Don't be silly. Don't you think it's funny? You are lucky I am a forgiving soul."

"My parents didn't say a word about what they'd seen. After breakfast they asked me to accompany them to our country home. I asked about you. Father said they had something to discuss with me and would prefer to do it in private. I was sure we'd be back that afternoon so I went with them. They drove me to Switzerland. I protested, knowing that you'd be upset if we didn't discuss the incident. I also knew that in their way they were punishing us. And I believe I deserved to be punished, after all, I was the adult and adults are not supposed to get carried away.

"I decided to write you a letter, hoping you'd understand. As soon as I entered my room I sat at the desk and wrote what was in my heart."

"What did you write?"

"That I loved you."

"Why didn't I ever receive your letter? Never mind, it's immaterial now. I am ready to pack and leave. You are history for the next thirty odd years."

Paul-Emile frowned. "What do you mean."

"I am going home to write my memoirs. I have decided to become a writer. My whole life has been a fantastic saga. It's time to reveal everything. I have lots of secrets, are you surprised at that?"

"You mean your relationship with your husband and Hamdi?"

"That's only one of them, darling. I haven't talked about Canada yet. Canada." I sang, 'O Canada, our home and native land'. I went somewhat wild there."

"Are you going to tell me about Canada?"

I looked at him askance. "You are just trying to keep me from leaving. Well, I do have a few more days, let me think about that a bit. What are we going to do for the rest of the day?"

The telephone rang. It was the hotel manager saying a man wanted to talk to us, could we come downstairs. When we walked into the lobby, a man dressed in coveralls and a sheepskin-lined jacket pushed himself off a chair. He twirled a flat oilcloth cap in his gnarled hands as he walked toward us.

His breath wheezed and rattled when he said in accented German, "I am sure you don't remember me, especially you lady, but you and I," he pointed at Paul-Emile, "were prisoners together on the Weber farm." He wrinkled his brow and looked quizzically at Paul-Emile. "I watched you prepare the horses and the carriage for flight and hoped you made it home. I prayed for you."

"Paradsky, the man with the mournful harmonica." They clasped hands. "When I asked you to play something gay, you shook your head and said, this is only a time for sadness. My heart is heavy, all I see is death."

"You want to hear happy harmonica?"

Paul-Emile and I looked at each other then nodded. "You have warm coat?" Paradsky asked.

Paul-Emile collected our coats, helped me into the sable and we followed the Pole into the cold winter afternoon. Great ragged flakes of snow drifted lazily through the pearly air and quickly dissolved on the steaming horse hitched to a sleigh.

Paradsky covered our laps with a fur, clicked his tongue and the horse took off at a trot. Only the swish of the sleigh gliders and the muffled clop, clop of hoofs disturbed the peaceful silence. I wondered briefly where he was taking us then sat back and enjoyed the white winter scene.

I drew up the wide collar of my coat, tucked my fur hat over my ears and hoped we didn't have too far to go. Suddenly I knew where we were. I clutched Paul-Emile's hand. "The trees, do you see those mighty linden trees? We pulled into a yard and stopped in front of a house. Uncle Ludwig's house.

"You recognize this place?" Paradsky turned and smiled.

"You live here now?" I asked.

"My home. I take good care of everything, you will see, everything is beautiful, even the dining table." He coughed, then shook a finger in our faces. "I follow you into the house and watch you take the money. I check later, all was gone."

Paul-Emile and I looked at him in disbelief. "And you let us get away?"

"I know you want to go home. I saw your tears."

I gave him a kiss on the cheek. "That's for not telling on us."

"Come in, come in, my wife is waiting."

A pleasant aroma of pipe tobacco pervaded the house. It was as if time had stood still here. Paradsky took my hand and led me into the dining room. He removed the *Advent* star with the four candles and slid the table top to the side to reveal the billiard table underneath, "See, like new. Can you play this game?"

"I sure can."

"We go see my wife now, she has trouble walking. Come, she is waiting in the kitchen."

His wife sat in an upholstered rocking chair. Her thin gray hair was combed straight back from her forehead and twisted into a knot in the nape of her neck. She wore a black, long-sleeved three quarter length dress and over it a flowery apron. Deep wrinkles ridged her cheeks, but they almost disappeared when her face lit up like sun sparkling on the frost. She laid her darning mushroom, over which she'd stretched the heel of a sock, in her lap and reached out with both hands.

"Inge, is that you? Little, naughty Inge with the cat eyes."

I didn't have a clue who she was. She chided me with a finger and cackled, "You got me into deep trouble when you stole my keys."

"Oh, my God, Louise?"

She nodded, "The same. After the Russians and your family left, this Pollack here asked me to marry him. He's been a good husband and I made sure everything stayed in perfect order just like your grandmother liked it. She was strict, but she taught me a lot."

"How did you know we were visiting Marienburg?"

"Malbork ... I still think of it as Marienburg too, for me it has never changed. When you bumped into the old man yesterday and asked about Ludwig Weber, he came to tell us. He is not all there," she tapped her head. "He ran all the way home and told us that visitors in town asked about Ludwig Weber."

"Who is he?"

"One of your uncle Peter's farm laborers. He just appeared one day in his tattered army uniform and stayed. He and I had ..."

she winked, "when he was young and handsome. I couldn't send him away ... Paradsky is a kind man."

Paradsky entered the kitchen with a tray holding a flowered china coffeepot and a delicious looking torte on a crystal cake platter. "Louise likes to bake. You like Schwartzwälder Torte?"

"Love it." Paul-Emile and I accepted a plate decorated with a lily of the valley design that matched the delicate, translucent porcelain cups, saucers and coffeepot. I stuck a fork full of the cake into my mouth and couldn't bring myself to swallow for I wanted to savor the delicious creamy filling, the cherries and the light fluffy cake. "Mmm, Louise, this is wonderful, the best I have ever eaten."

Paradsky and Louise beamed when I asked for another small slice.

"You recognize the china?" Louise said.

I shook my head.

"Your uncle and aunt's. Everything," she waved her arm, "belonged to them. You want something, just ask."

I hugged her. "Thank you, you are very kind." I wondered for a moment if the question on my tongue would offend them. No, they seemed comfortable with living here with someone else's possessions. And it had been such a long time since the war ended.

"I've read," I said, "that at first the Russians destroyed everything they came across. How were you able to convince them otherwise?"

They looked at each other then Louise said, "Paradsky moved me to your uncle's house when I went into labor. He buried all your uncle's and aunts prized possessions in the garden. I'd just given birth to our daughter when the Russians arrived. We were lucky. The officer with the soldiers loved babies and decided to billet with us in your uncle's house so he could enjoy the baby. He told us his wife was pregnant when he saw her last. He sat for hours holding our Silvy. As long as he stayed we were fairly secure. When he had to move on, he left his adjutant with us to keep the baby safe."

"Where is your daughter now?" I asked.

Louise wiped her eyes. "In heaven we hope. The adjutant could not stay. The winter of 46 - 47 was as harsh as the one at the end of the war. We had no food, no milk." She shrugged, "We did our best ... so many died."

Paradsky lit his pipe, Paul-Emile joined him and I lit a cigarette. Louise took up her darning again. After she wove the thread back and forth a few times, she said, "I saved a couple of boxes of books from the old house. It had to be demolished because of the artillery damage. You want to have a look? I also have a picture of your horses, the two you stole." She smiled.

I blushed. "We didn't steal them, we borrowed them. Amsel died and Donner ... we gave him his freedom. I often think about him and wish I knew what happened to him."

"He was a smart horse," Paul-Emile said, "he found a good home, I am convinced of that."

"Paradsky," Louise said, "go get the boxes with the books and the picture. What happened to you two when you ran off ... are you married now?"

"I want to marry her," Paul-Emile said, "but she won't have me."

"She always was stubborn. Maybe you have to spank her." Louise lifted an eyebrow.

We laughed.

Paradsky wheezed and puffed when he returned with a box under each arm and set them on a chair. He handed me the picture of Donner and Amsel. "You want?"

I studied the picture, then gave him a peck on the cheek and dabbed at my tears.

"Why are you crying?" Louise asked.

"I'm not sure. I loved them ... thank you, thank you." I clutched the picture to my chest. "You don't mind if I keep this?" I asked Paul-Emile.

"It belongs to you. After all who am I?"

"My prince?"

"Paradsky will take you back to the hotel now," Louise said, "I don't want him out too late. We want you to come back tomorrow. I'll fix a meal you will never forget and then you can look through the boxes and Paradsky will play for you."

The rising full moon made everything look white and cold. I thought about the day so long ago, when we Tessensdorfers returned from a visit to the Damrau relatives in the wedding coach drawn by four horses. We stole a huge pumpkin from a snowy field that night. It was the only time I ever rode in the coach. I wondered what had happened to it.

Before I left Paul-Emile to return to my room, I said, "I am glad you brought me here after all. Can you imagine, Louise, the maid, now lady of the manor."

"I don't suppose her life has been easy though, she looks a lot older than she really is. Life under communism was difficult especially for the farmers west of the former Poland whose holdings had been turned into collective farms. Wonder what happened to Louise and Paradsky during that time."

"Louise said that I was the first to visit."

"Well, can you imagine how your aunts would feel to see everything under someone else's control? You didn't have the ties they and your cousins have to their birth place."

"I often think about this. When you come right down to it, I don't belong anywhere, not really. Sometimes I'm sad about being unable to come home to my roots even though I know they are right here. But this isn't home either any longer. My mother's family arrived in this area in the sixteen hundreds and now...."

"That's a long time."

"She had to trace her German ancestry to at least 1800 in order to qualify as a bonafide Aryan during Hitler's regime. During her research she traced her family as far as sixteen hundred. They came from Holland and were canal builders ... all this land was under water back then."

"Whatever happened to your Grandmother Slavitsky?"

"She, my aunt and cousins left Danzig sometime in 1947.

Mother told me that my uncle disappeared from the face of the earth while returning to his unit. Someone from the army came looking for him at home. All Aunt Karen could tell them was that he climbed on his bike, waved goodbye and peddled off. He simply disappeared. I never saw Aunt Karen and the boys again.

"Omchen visited us shortly before we left for Canada. She told us that once the Russians entered Danzig, pillage, murder and rape became part of their daily lives. Young girls of twelve and old women of eighty, nuns, nurses, no one was spared. Many of the inhabitants committed suicide. The men were rounded up and shipped to concentration camps or to Siberia where many perished."

"Yes, I read about the Russians' despicable behavior," Paul-Emile said. "Many of my countrymen suffered at their hands during that time. That we were allies and prisoners of war and had suffered like them under the Germans didn't mean anything to them, a man was a man. Many Frenchmen died."

I sighed. We were going in circles. The Germans raped, killed and pillaged during the war, the Russians raped, killed and pillaged during and after the war, as did the French and the Americans. The British were a bit more reserved.

I opened my mouth to tell him what I was thinking then decided against opening that can of worms. Instead I said, "We didn't ask Omchen if she suffered indignities and she didn't volunteer, but her tears told her story. I saw her again when Kane, Magda and I visited her in Germany. She died soon afterward."

"She was a nice lady. Are you going to tell me about Canada?"

I wasn't sleepy and thought of Hamdi. Was he going to forgive me for spending this time with Paul-Emile? All of a sudden I had this terrible hollow sensation in the pit of my stomach. What if he didn't? I pushed an easy chair close to the radiator, pulled a blanket off the bed and draped it over my shoulders.

Paul-Emile drew up a corner of the featherbed, "Climb in, I'll warm you up ... inside and out." He grinned.

I stared at him and wondered what had come over me. I felt attracted to him, but I didn't love him. I shivered and said to divert his attention, "Do you want to hear about Canada?"

"I want to know everything about you." He dropped the corner of the featherbed, propped a couple of pillows behind his head and pulled the duvet all the way up to his chin.

<u>Chapter Thirteen</u>

The room was chilly. I tucked my foot under my bum to warm it and debated briefly whether I should join Paul-Emile in bed. But I knew that would raise all sorts of issues and stayed in my chair.

"I should probably start when your lovely papa took me back to my parents." I took a sip of vodka and glared at Paul-Emile. "You can't possibly imagine how much I loathed you and your family for taking away the life I had grown accustomed to."

Paul-Emile started to say something, but I held up my hand. "If you want to know about me, just listen. Nothing much happened. I went to school. German dictation was difficult, I had a lot of catching-up to do. English was even harder, only in French and algebra I excelled."

I mused, "I had a crush on the farmer's son downstairs. He was eighteen. My job was to fetch our daily ration of fresh milk from their kitchen every evening. I would sit at the top of the stairs and wait for him to come out of their living room. When he did, I bounded down the stairs and headed for the kitchen and our jug of milk which cost ten pennies. At first nothing happened. After a while he began to notice me and it became a game we played.

"One evening he kissed me in the dark kitchen. He tasted of sausage." I laughed. "Henceforth we would meet in the horse stable so we could kiss. Sometimes when a stable hand came inside for some reason, he would blind him with his flashlight while I ran away. During the day he ignored me. The whole affair was most unsatisfying.

"We, in our area, had not suffered too much from food shortages during the war, but after the occupation, life changed drastically. The German social, physical and financial system collapsed. Now everyone had to fend for themselves.

"When I returned from France, the farm house was still full of refugees. They lodged in every spare room. One of my aunts and her girlfriend, refugees from East Prussia, lived in a grain storage room they'd fixed up for themselves. Grandmother arrived from Tessensdorf in 1947 and moved in with my parents.

"Grandmother took one room for herself. Edward slept on the living room sofa and I had to sleep in the same bed with my parents. Horrible. Especially one night when I overheard them whispering. Father was angry and accused mother of cheating on him with one of my girlfriends' father, while he, Father, was singing with the men's choir. At first she denied it, then admitted to kissing. 'What's so horrible about kissing?' She asked.

" 'I'll never trust you again,' he said.

"I cried myself to sleep that night trying hard not to make a sound so they wouldn't know I'd heard. I cursed my mother and you, Paul-Emile, for allowing all this to happen to me. You were both guilty of betrayal."

"You are being unfair," Paul-Emile said. "It was because of your actions that you were taken back to Germany. I had nothing to do with it."

"It doesn't matter now. Life was more interesting in the village than I expected. One night a man left his hand behind when he and his colleagues tried to break into the stable to steal chickens, pigs and cows. Because of previous break-ins, my father and three men who also worked on the farm, took turns keeping watch at night inside the barn. The thieves used some kind of a saw to remove the lock. When one of them stuck his hand into the hole to open the latch from the inside, one of the men inside the barn swung an axe. The thieves never returned.

"Hunger plagued millions of people after the war. I too was hungry all the time. In the fall when the trees hung full of pears, apples and cherries many creatures, including me, feasted at the guest table of nature.

"In 1950 my parents talked about leaving Germany for good. I was ecstatic. 'Where are we going,' I asked them. 'Paraguay,' Mother said. I didn't have a clue where that was.

"Why on earth did they want to go there?"

"Lots of Germans. I don't know. Then came my father's pain. One day walking home from school I said to my cousin Hilde who had also moved in with us for a while, 'I'd drink my own urine if I knew it would take away his pain.'

" 'Yuck.'

" 'Yes, I would,' I said, 'I can't stand his agony, his crying and moaning. Shouldn't a man have more control?'

" 'When it hurts, it hurts, whether you are a man, a woman or a child.'

"I nodded, 'Pain is pain. I hate to go home.'

" 'Because of him?'

"I nodded again. But we had to go home. The next day when we returned from school he was gone. My mother was gone too. Hilde and I looked at each other. He died.

" 'Maybe he died,' Hilde said.

"She'd seen a lot of death when the Russians came to Tessensdorf. Quiet, the flat was so quiet until my brother ran in with his knee socks around his ankles.

" 'He's in the hospital,' he said.

"My father almost did die, then doctors finally removed his gallstones and gallbladder and he recovered. Because of this our immigration application for Paraguay was denied.

"I was crestfallen. Mother however, was not one to admit defeat. Canada was her next destination. Being a born Mennonite, she had no compunction about contacting the Mennonite Church in Hannover. They put her in contact with Canadian Immigration Authorities. They denied her application because of my father's recent illness. My tenacious mother, however, I don't know what drove her, made and was granted an appointment with the Canadian Consul.

"His name happened to be Weber, her maiden name. They

discovered they were distantly related. He promised to find her a Mennonite family in Canada who would sponsor us despite my father's recent illness. He came through. We boarded the Beaverbrae on December 6th, 1951."

"In the middle of winter, what a dangerous undertaking."

"Why?"

"Because," Paul-Emile said with a grin, "during the winter the North Atlantic is populated with ship-devouring sea monsters. Sailors for centuries have always dreaded the Atlantic's abrupt weather changes."

"Weather changes I believe, but ship-devouring sea monsters?" I laughed. "Never heard that before. You are right though, it proved to be dangerous, hurricane and all. The Beaverbrae was a Canadian freighter, no first class accommodations on her. The smell of fresh paint hit us when we boarded. Red and white was the decor of the railings, the bulkheads, the metal staircases, everything riveted down was red and white. She could accommodate up to seven hundred fifty people in her hold. The men and boys lodged forward and the women, babies and girls aft.

"Part of the cargo hold had been divided into curtained sections each containing three, three tiered berths. Everybody scrambled to find the best spot. I secured a top berth next to the bulkhead, Mother's was underneath mine. Edward, ten years old, stayed with my father.

"We'd agreed to meet on deck as soon as we were situated, to wave goodbye to my aunt who'd come along to see us off. The freighter undocked late afternoon leaving my aunt, who still stood on the wharf waving her handkerchief and everything we were familiar with, behind. We were underway toward an uncertain prospect for a new life."

"You didn't know where you were going other than Canada?"

"My parents probably knew, I didn't have a clue. Thank God I was no longer afraid to travel by ship. I'd decided that this was one adventure I was going to take full advantage of, enjoy to the fullest of my ability. Of course, having met Andreas, who was four or five years older, during our screening process and again when we waited for embarkation, made it all the more enticing.

"You, Paul-Emile, I relegated to the deepest crevice of my cerebral cortex. Andreas and I went for long walks, and whenever we found ourselves alone, he kissed me. Unfortunately, once aboard, that wasn't so easy. People and screaming, wailing children appeared to occupy every corner of the ship.

"Already the next morning the North Sea showed its nasty disposition by buffeting our freighter with strong winds and a swelling, angry sea. Soon the first passengers became seasick. I suffered from a bit of queasiness myself when I left the dining hall with its bolted down red and white metal tables and benches. I headed straight for the deck and bent over the rail with the others. Nothing came up. I only gagged and gagged, while others spewed over the side.

"I returned to the dining room because I hadn't been able to eat the blue, hard boiled eggs they'd served for breakfast. The kitchen was closed. I was undecided what to do next. Then a cute steward, with huge black eyes, a bit on the pudgy side and somewhat too short for my taste, approached me and said he'd bring me some bread.

"He spoke in English. I didn't understand what he said. I tried him in French, and sure enough he understood what I said, but when he answered me in French, I barely knew what he was talking about."

"Was he French Canadian?"

"Yes, I found out later when he locked me into the linen closet. It's funny now, it wasn't exactly funny then. I am jumping ahead of myself.

"That first evening after a full day at sea, someone shouted to come look at the White Cliffs of Dover. Across the channel blinked the lights of Calais. By the next morning we'd sailed into the North Atlantic. Peter, the steward, always stood at the entrance to the dining hall. I am unsure whether this was his job or what. Every time we met we smiled at each other.

"Our passage through the North Sea had been rough. Once we hit the Atlantic, rough was a mild term. Gigantic waves bombarded us from all angles. My mind was now totally occupied with suppressing the constant nausea that boiled in my stomach. I didn't even smile at the cute, young man. He stopped me and told me to lie on my bunk, to move with the ship and nibble on dry bread. He brought me several slices of their revolting, tasteless, sodden white bread and I followed his instructions.

"Surprisingly the next day, even though the waves grew, I felt a lot better. When I saw him again, I thanked him. While making my way back to my berth, I had to cling to the red railing to keep from running down the slope. He walked next to me for a short distance then stopped in front of a door. He pulled out a key chain, unlocked the door, stepped inside and waved to me to follow."

"Inge, that was dangerous."

"I was already bored to tears. I'd read the one book, 'Forever Amber' I'd brought with me, several times already, wishing I could have a romance just like Amber. And all of a sudden something was about to happen. I followed him inside like a lamb. My heart sat in my mouth, yet I didn't have a thought about any type of consequences.

"He'd taken me to a linen closet, stuffed with brilliant white sheets and towels. He pulled a bunch of sheets off the shelf, spread them on the floor, sat down and patted the place beside him.

"Amber's wantonness flashed before my eyes. His full smiling lips were alluring. I sat beside him and we kissed. Our tongues ran a marathon and I was unstoppable. I wonder what would have happened if he had tried to go beyond kissing."

His eyes blazing, Paul-Emile sat up in bed. "You behaved like a hussy."

I rose, with my fists balled, strode to the bed and glared down at him. "Don't you call me names you, you...."

In a way he was right, but I had been so starved for love, someone to hug me, to kiss me, to cuddle me. I sighed, returned to my chair and continued as if nothing had happened. "After a while he looked at his watch and said we'd have to go. He unlocked the door and stuck his head out. The coast was clear and I slipped out. I returned to my bunk and hid my smarting lips behind my earmarked paperback."

"You were lucky he didn't take advantage of you. Maybe I can take advantage of you now, would you allow it? Come here my sweet little hussy." He held out his arms.

I ignored him. "The next day the wind howled and rime covered the portholes, the railings and the deck and nobody was allowed topside. The freighter had turned into a toy the heaving sea tossed about without mercy. Mother arranged for my brother to stay with us because Father said hell in the forward hold was a mild description.

"Now that nobody could use the sea as a depository any longer, conditions became rather nightmarish. Not enough heads, buckets or what have you. So when Peter puckered his lips, I was ready to leave the stench behind me and followed him into the linen closet."

"Silence. The sound and misery of the retching humanity aboard did not penetrate the steel door. He prepared the sheets then took off his shirt. I looked at his bulging muscles, how fabulously exciting to be held in those arms. "

"You took your shirt off too?"

"Well ... why not? I was wearing a pullover. When he saw I wasn't wearing a bra, I didn't own one yet, he was surprised and told me I should wear a bra. What difference did it make whether I was wearing a bra or not, but I decided to ask Mother when we landed in Canada to buy me one."

"So what did he do next?"

"He embraced me and our naked chests met and it felt wonderful and we kissed. I was ready to swoon when he kissed my breasts."

"What happened then?"

"Nothing. Now it seems comical, back then I was a bit scared. Peter looked at his watch and said he'd have to go. He pulled on his shirt, peeked out the door, looked at me and shook his head. He stepped into the passageway and locked the door behind him."

"He locked you in the linen closet."

"Yes. I slipped on my pullover. My main worry of the moment concerned the other stewards. How was I going to explain my presence. I waited and waited and became angrier by the minute. Time stood still. The ship rolled. I braced myself against the steel shelves. What if the ship sank? I cried, because I knew I was going to drown there all by myself.

"If I banged on the door and screamed for someone to let me out everybody would be aware of my misdeed. Retribution. I pulled all the folded linen and towels I could reach off the shelves, threw them on the floor and messed them up. Suddenly a key turned in the lock. I slipped behind the door.

" 'Inge?' He said he was sorry but had to work. I slipped out into the passage and that was the end of my shipboard romance."

"He didn't invite you into the linen closet again?"

"Of course he did, but I didn't fancy being locked in again. I now concentrated on the fellow I'd met ashore instead. However, he'd met a girl a little older than me and wasn't interested any longer. By that time though nobody had any romantic notions. The weather deteriorated by the hour and so did conditions aboard.

"Luggage stored beneath the bottom berths slid along the steel deck first into one corner, then came smashing back into the other. It took all my strength to hold onto my berth to keep from sliding through the end slat. Anyone afoot was unable to stop their downhill plunge and slid with great force into the end of the iron passageway.

"People, some stunned, some bleeding, some with head injuries, tried to pull themselves up by the handrails, only to plummet down the sharp incline in the opposite direction. Some lay crumpled in a heap and pleaded for help. Others spewed green bile where they lay and at the same time tried to protect their heads and limbs from our suitcases, now lethal weapons.

"Mothers and children screamed, some groaned and blubbered, others prayed. Some curled up in their berths in fetal positions and didn't get up for days. The stench of vomit overwhelmed my senses, my mouth watered and my stomach lurched. I swallowed and swallowed again, I didn't want to become seasick. I gnawed on the dry bread I kept on my bunk, and chewed the same crust until it disintegrated.

"Sailors tried their best to assist, but they too had to hold to the handrails to keep from becoming a casualty by the rolling and pitching freighter. Someone shook me lightly. I groaned. Peter's face appeared next to mine. 'Come with me,' he said.

" 'Where are you going?' Mother said with a worried frown.

"I scrutinized her tired face for a moment. With one arm she tightly clasped my brother who heaved over the side of the bunk into a pail she held for him. I asked Peter in French. All he said was 'Up,' and pointed his chin. I gave her one last cursory look and followed Peter out of purgatory, up a ladder, to the third deck just underneath the wheelhouse.

"We'd entered a sort of salon. At least twenty or so young Germans sat and stood talking and laughing. My acquaintance Andreas was among them. This was a new world entirely. Although the ship still did acrobatics, the violence I'd experienced below was missing. Peter just left me there and disappeared through one of the several doors leading off the salon.

"Andreas walked over, 'You have an admirer I see.'

"I blushed but didn't say anything. 'Fraternizing with the help is strictly forbidden. I hope you remember that lecture.'

" 'Of course. What are you suggesting.'

" 'Just make sure you don't end up behind one of those doors ... crew quarters.'

"I turned away from him, walked to the large porthole and stared into a bottomless void. Without warning a sea monster, with its menacing tentacles and white foaming eyes slammed with all the strength it could muster over the bow. It spewed against the porthole with frothy patches of dense, white streaks and its mountainous, overhanging crests obscured all views.

"Afraid the monster was reaching for me, I stepped back, braced myself and watched from a distance as the shock-like, heavy sea, goaded on by banshee winds, blinding snow and sleet encompassed the ship and its living cargo. Once the ship reached the crest, it crashed with sickening speed into a deep gorge below. Andreas stood, legs spread wide, next to me. 'Quite a spectacle isn't it, are you scared?'

"I swallowed the bile that rose in my gullet.

" 'Force twelve winds,' he said, 'do you know what that means?'

"I shook my head and watched with awe the mountains and valleys outside.

" 'Hurricane,' he said. 'They expect it to last a while. The officers of this ship post the weather conditions for the crew every so often on that board.' He pointed. 'I've heard that we are either standing still or going backward.'

"Someone shouted, 'Iceberg!'

"Everyone crowded together at the window as we passed a towering cliff in the distance. It quickly disappeared in the mist. A fata morgana? As if this wasn't already enough excitement, they had to create more.

"Suddenly the ship lay on its side. We tumbled over each other and crashed into the opposite wall. My heart sat in my mouth and for the first time I silently prayed to God not to let me die. I tried to hide my tears and my fear and huddled against a door when without warning, we slid across the floor into the opposite direction. I banged my head against one of the bolted down chairs.

"Andreas crawled over, 'Are you hurt?' I pushed him away."

"You were terrified but wouldn't admit it." Paul-Emile said.

"I was petrified. All I could think about was the *Gustloff.*

Fate had finally caught up with me after all. When time came for the evening meal, we were told to leave the deck.

"The dining room was practically empty and the crew was still cleaning up the smashed dishes. A steward offered me two boiled eggs and bread which I took with me to my berth. Mother smiled when I returned. I offered her an egg and a slice of bread, she just shook her head. I told her she and Edward would feel better if they chewed on the bread, both declined.

"The ship continued to roll and pitch. Since I couldn't do anything about that, I pulled the blanket over my head, chewed on the bread and tried to shut out the moaning and retching. The next morning we woke to a gently, heaving sea and porpoises frolicking alongside the ship.

"We were all still alive. I promised God I would be very, very good. No more sinning or wicked thoughts or acts."

"Were you good?" Paul-Emile smiled.

"As good as I could possibly be. The rest of the trip was fairly uneventful except they ran out of food. It could probably have been quite disastrous if every single passenger had come looking for something to eat during mealtimes, but the majority were so sick they probably didn't even think about food. All they served were blue, hard boiled eggs, morning noon and night. Better than nothing.

"Seventeen days after we left Germany, we spied land on December 23rd. Despite the bitter cold, everyone who could, hurried on deck to get a glimpse of our new home. To our chagrin, we didn't enter the harbor but anchored way out for the approaching night. Several small boats came alongside to take off the sickest and wounded passengers.

"We had a wonderful surprise that evening. A hot meal, fresh fruit and hot chocolate for everyone interested. The next morning a harbor pilot boarded together with immigration authorities. Near noon, they served us another wonderful meal. Shortly after the freighter's engines hummed once more and we sailed slowly toward the wharf of St. Johns, New Brunswick.

"That same evening we sat in the train taking us to our future. If my parents knew, they never said a word about our ultimate destination. I don't think they had a clue as to our timetable. We traveled across Quebec, then Ontario where many people said goodbye and left the train. Only a few families remained to share the almost empty train heading west.

"We huffed on the windows to clear the ice. Except for an occasional signal lamp, or a light in a window, I didn't see much in the whirling white world outside. Mother sang Christmas songs, but I couldn't join in because I had laryngitis. We tried to sleep on the hard wooden benches. Would this ever end?

"Then something different. Christmas trees decorated with colorful electric lights glittered cheerfully at each small railway station we passed. Life existed after all in this vast country. We came to Winnipeg, Manitoba and had to get off the train. In the overheated railway station a man and a woman greeted us in German. We piled into their car and they drove us to their apartment. They served us a delicious dinner of cabbage rolls, potatoes and lots of gravy. Then they took us back to the railway station and our trip continued, this time on a local train. Six hours later we arrived in Saskatoon, Saskatchewan. We transferred to another train and arrived in Terrance, fifty miles north of Saskatoon, on the evening of December 26th.

"The brother of our host family was waiting and drove us to his home where his wife served us a belated Christmas dinner and gave each of us a small bible. A couple of hours later he drove us to our final destination three miles away.

"Snow five feet high lined the narrow, plowed road. He stopped in front of a large house. Wow, that was very nice. But then he took us to another smaller two-story house about fifty yards away. He opened the front door and we filed into a large black hole that felt like a freezer. Only seconds later a dim light coming from a ceiling fixture guided us into a living room. The man touched a match to kindling in the old-fashioned wood-burning stove. He rubbed his hands together and waved at the round dining table loaded with groceries. 'You have enough food and soon it'll be warm. I'll see you tomorrow.' "

"Did he speak German?" Paul-Emile asked.

"His wife too. When he'd gone we looked at each other, unsure whether to laugh or cry. We peeked into another room, a bedroom with a double bed, sheets, blankets and pillows. I wondered where my brother and I were going to sleep. Where was the bathroom? We stood near the stove still in our coats, scarves and gloves. Edward walked over to the table. 'Look at all this food, I wonder what's in that big box.'

"I read 'Cornflakes'. Not a clue. He tore the top and the inside bag open, plucked out a few flakes. Odd. We each stuck one in our mouth and chewed. Awful. We made faces and laughed.

"We opened one box after the other, butter, coffee, bread, horrible white gummy bread, cocoa, sugar, milk. Butter, all that wonderful butter. I took a slice of bread and cut off a piece of the hard butter. I adored bread and lots of butter and took a big bite, chewed, then spit it out. Pure salt. It took us weeks to get used to the salty butter.

"Mother heated milk and fixed cocoa. While the room warmed we discussed our sleeping arrangements for the night and looked for a toilet. There didn't seem to be one.

" 'Maybe it's outside,' mother said.

"We checked in the entrance hall and found a cubicle containing a bench with a hole and a pail underneath. Voilà, the toilet. I wrinkled my nose. My God, we were going backward rather than forward. This was disgusting."

"That must have been a shock. Who emptied the bucket?"

"Mother of course. Mother and Father brought in the bedding from the bedroom and laid it next to the stove and that's where we slept that first night. Knowing her, she probably fed the fire all night long. Toward morning she must have fallen into an exhausted sleep because when we awoke, the room had turned into an icebox again and the windows were covered with frost.

"Talk about cold and snow ... what had we gotten ourselves

into. It was all your fault I was even there."

"Don't be juvenile. You had to stay?"

"Of course we had to stay. My parents had indentured themselves for one year to work off the fare.

"But that didn't hold true for me. I was free to come and go. I left that godforsaken farm the first opportunity that presented itself. Although I guess it wasn't really godforsaken, for we had to attend church every Wednesday evening as well as Sunday mornings and evenings. Services were conducted in German. My father was Catholic and my mother had converted to Catholicism when they married. Here we were Mennonites and these Mennonites were no ordinary Mennonites. They called themselves Brothern Mennonites, a devout group indeed.

"For a time we had the farm all to ourselves. The other closest homesteads were three miles away in every direction. The man who owned our farm, a man in his fifties, was on his honeymoon in California. We didn't meet him until sometime in February. He'd married a woman twenty years his junior. I thought that rather odd at the time. But later, when I discovered Kane was eighteen years older than I, I didn't blink twice.

"In the meantime someone decided my brother and I needed to go to school. We had to walk one and a half miles to a small schoolhouse that housed one teacher and about twenty students, first through eighth grade in a single room. The kids behaved very well toward us, true Christians they were. Although we tried to make the best of our situation it was difficult to feel at home, especially with the unknown language.

"I knew a lot of English words, my brother almost none, but I had difficulty putting sentences together and the pronunciation was a real tongue twister. When it came to algebra or math in general I knew more than the teacher. I hated the school, but stuck it out until the summer of 1952. Learning how to speak English was my primary goal.

"The farmer's wife, a nice lady, knew I was bored and suggested I look in the newspaper to see what I could find to do for the summer. I saw an ad for 'companion to doctor's wife', and with the farmer's wife's help, I composed a letter. Two weeks later I received a reply and was invited to come to Saskatoon to present myself.

"Now you will probably gloat, because I'm going to say something nice about the Diderots. Living with your family in Paris had definitely been an asset. I put my best foot forward and knew I came across as reserved, quiet, sophisticated, with good manners."

"You quiet and reserved?" Paul-Emile laughed.

"Be quiet. They loved me and I loved them, especially their house, and I never looked back. I spent the summer with them at their cottage on a lake a hundred-fifty miles north of Saskatoon. The gateway to the north they called it, because all roads ended there.

"When we returned to Saskatoon I asked if I could stay with them and go to school. They agreed. Everything was peachy, except I was sixteen going on seventeen and had been kissed. I was dying to have a boyfriend, but they didn't allow any friends. So on Sundays I pretended to attend the Mennonite church, but roamed the city instead. The Gordons were Episcopalian."

"So, did you ever find a boyfriend? When did you have your first sexual experience? Or am I prying?"

"Are we talking orgasm or intercourse?"

He stared at me obviously surprised at my bluntness. "Don't they usually go together?"

"Not necessarily."

"So, are you going to tell me?"

"I'll come to that in a bit. I stayed with the doctor's family for a year. The best year of my education including Paris. I have to give your parents some credit. I call my stay with the Gordons my finishing school. Mrs. Gordon had been a teacher at one time and was adamant that I write each new word three times on a small kitchen blackboard. She taught me how to cook, bake and clean house. I watched her entertain and be a gracious hostess. Nothing escaped me.

"They had a beautiful grand piano with lots of sheet music and shelves filled with books such as Zola, Boccaccio, Balzac, Dostoevsky, Nabocov etc., I read them all. I didn't understand the meaning of a lot of the words, but that didn't deter me. I understood the gist of the stories and had a dictionary close at hand.

"Part of their basement was outfitted as an entertainment room with a billiard table, a dartboard, a phonograph and stacks and stacks of classical records. At first I spent hours sorting and dusting, when everything was in order, I had designed my own perfect little world. While I played billiards or darts, I sang at the top of my voice without disturbing anyone. I sang in Italian, in French, in German. My repertoire encompassed all the major arias, be it for soprano or tenor, I loved them all. The only thing I didn't have was a friend to share my domain with. The Gordons didn't want strangers in their house.

"School was difficult, but I managed to get promoted. When the Gordons asked me to spend the next summer with them at their lake-side cottage I was undecided. I'd met a girl named Marge at school who made a suggestion so way out, that I was intrigued and mulled it over for several days. Should I or shouldn't I?"

"What did you get into next?"

"I became a migrant worker."

"I'm not familiar with that term."

"I wasn't either at the time. I learned a lot, a new life, different people, a culture all unto their own.

" 'One of my sisters lives in British Columbia,' Marge said, 'not far from a huge strawberry farm. I picked strawberries last summer and made lots of money, well, maybe not a lot, but enough to buy a few new dresses and shoes. Why don't you come along? I'll take you to the employment agency, they are always looking for pickers. They pay for your round trip ticket if you stay to the end of the season.'

"The doctor and his wife gave me forty-five dollars spending money every month. I asked her, 'Can I make more than forty-five dollars a month?'

" 'That's peanuts, of course you can, lots of money.'

"My parents by then had fulfilled their obligations to the farmer and had moved to the small town of Terrance.

"I don't know what possessed me, I should have stayed in Saskatoon. It seemed as if the devil stood next to me and taunted me into this intermezzo comprised of new temptations, mischief and adventures. I wrote my parents a note telling them that I was leaving the Gordons and was going berry picking in British Columbia. By the time they could protest, Marge and I were on the train heading for Vancouver."

I finished the last of my vodka. "I'm going to sleep. Please don't disturb me."

"I want to hear about your orgasm," Paul-Emile said.

"What if I don't want to tell you?"

"Come on, finish, get it off your chest, maybe you'll feel better."

I poured myself a dram of vodka and sat on the other bed. "Perhaps you are right for once. I've never talked about this before." My feet were freezing. I slipped under the covers and settled a pillow behind my back.

Chapter Fourteen

"On the train we met four girls our age who were also going berry picking. They told us their parents depended upon them to earn money. I was intrigued. Even though they spoke fluent English, I noticed immediately that it was not correct.

"Marge elbowed me in the ribs and giggled. 'White trash.'

" 'What does that mean?'

" 'They are poor, really poor,' she whispered.

" 'So, what's wrong with that,' I whispered back. 'We are poor too. Aren't we going out there to make money?'

"She gave me a weird look. 'I'm staying with my sister. I'm doing this as a fun thing. If I don't want to pick I don't have to ... they have to. And you, Inge, you have to too, you signed the papers promising to fulfill an obligation.'

" 'You didn't?'

" 'No, my sisters are paying my way.'

"I mulled this over for a while. She deceived me. No big deal, I would manage, I always did. I asked the girls if they'd picked berries before.

" 'For the last two years,' one of them said.

" 'What is it like?'

" 'Ass-busting.'

"I looked at Marge who shook with laughter. 'What does she mean?'

" 'You bust your ass, that's what.'

" 'You work all day,' the girl said, 'and when night come, you crawl into bed and you don't wake until the sun come up and then you work all day and then you crawl into bed....'

" 'Where do you sleep?'

" 'Four to a room, we'd ask you to sleep with us but only four to a room. We find you a good roomie. We know who is nice and who is not so nice.' "

"Had you ever been completely on your own before where you had to totally rely upon yourself?" Paul-Emile asked.

"Not really, I always had somebody. I must say I was a bit concerned but I was also curious. My friend Marge had a smirk on her face which I would dearly have liked to wipe off with the flat of my hand. Then it crossed my mind, I may need her and her sister.

"One of the girls said, 'You bring your cook pots? You need them cook pots if you wanna eat.'

" 'Nobody told me about that.' This was getting more interesting by the minute. The flat prairie outside the window disappeared slowly and was replaced by hills, then mountains and the train traveled slower and slower and after a while we stopped.

" 'We are in Banff, that's Lake Louise.' Marge pointed.

"A huge hotel sat nestled on the side of the mountain overlooking the lake. I wondered what would happen if I stepped off the train and just stayed. I could get a job at the beautiful hotel.

" 'I know what yas thinking,' One of the girls said, 'you want me to tell ya? Cause I had the same idea.'

" 'It is very beautiful here.'

" 'One reason I don't mind this trip. I can dream, can't I?'

"When we reached Vancouver, a bus waited to take us to Chilliwack. In Chilliwack Marge waved goodbye and slid into the front seat of her sister's car. She shouted, 'Happy picking. I'll probably see you in a few days.'

"A truck took us five girls to the strawberry farm. The other pickers greeted my companions warmly. They introduced me as their new friend and we shook hands. What a motley group."

"Totally out of your element." Paul-Emile said.

"From Schiaparelli to this." I bit my lip. I was getting angrier by the minute with the man lying in the other bed. I closed my eyes and thought about those miserable days.

"Are you asleep?" Paul-Emile said.

"The girls explained to the others that I was new to all this. Then one of the four girls, Elsa, I'd traveled with said, 'I better room with her, she needs protection.' She took my hand and led me into one of the small rooms in a bunkhouse. It was furnished with a pair of bunk beds, a small table by the window and two wooden kitchen chairs. I swallowed hard and felt like crying. I pulled myself together and told myself, you wanted adventure.

"The next morning everybody rose early and headed for the cookhouse. I followed them and watched as they brewed coffee, opened boxes of cereal, loaves of bread and spread it with butter and jam. I didn't have any food. They were busy and didn't seem to notice when I retreated. I walked back to my room and sat by the window. I was starving. Strawberries, flashed like a neon light almost blinding me with anticipation. Fat, juicy, red strawberries. I wiped away a tear and watched and waited.

"After a while the cookhouse emptied and everybody congregated around a man distributing baskets. I followed them to a nearby field and watched them pick and pick. The first five or six plump juicy strawberries ended up in my mouth – delicious. I picked a few and dropped them into my basket then stood to straighten my back. The pickers scrambled to a narrow path, emptied their baskets and hurried back to the rows of strawberries. They didn't look up again until their baskets were full.

"By the time I'd picked one basket they were already on their third. I had to speed up."

"What did you do about food?" Paul-Emile said.

"Someone gave me a sandwich for lunch. After we knocked off work, Elsa accompanied me to a nearby store. I was dead tired and sunburned. I'd brought two books, but was too tired to even read a single page. Elsa told me the more berries I picked the more money I'd make. So I tried to get my act together over the next few days.

"I was never so glad to see Saturday, payday, come so I could rest my aching back. I can't remember what I got paid, but enough to buy groceries for the next few days. I bought milk, bread and butter and lettuce, that, together with the strawberries, was my diet for the next week. On Sunday Marge invited me to her sister's house for dinner. I quickly forgave her all her sins.

"At the beginning of the second week a young man, with his legs spread wide, stood watching us. He had an amused smile on his lips. Elsa who picked next to me mumbled, 'That arrogant prick.'

" 'Who is he?'

" 'The owner's son. Thinks he's really something.'

" 'Why do you think he is watching us?'

" 'Probably looking us over, trying to find a softy who'll play with him.'

" 'What do you mean?'

" 'You know, screw.'

"I wasn't familiar with that word. I stood and regarded him with cold speculation. He smiled. I arched my back, then went back to work. When my basket was full I went to empty it. He walked over, 'What's your name?'

" 'Inge.'

" 'Inge, that's different. Inge, can you drive a car and do you have a license?'

I smiled. My brain worked a mile a minute. I licked my dry lips. 'Of course I can drive a car, it's easy.'

" 'Do you mind helping me out? We'll only be about an hour.'

"An hour away from that – I would do anything, almost.

" 'Now, if you don't mind,' he said.

"I brushed off my hands, dropped my basket and followed him to his car. I looked back at the workers. The girls I had befriended watched as we walked away. I told him I had to clean up before I touched his car. After I'd washed, combed my hair and changed into a clean pair of shorts and shirt, I strolled out to the car.

" 'I lied,' I said. 'I don't have a license and I haven't learned how to drive yet. But I couldn't pick one more berry. My back is broken.'

" 'My name is Frank. Inge, I've never heard that name before ... let's go for a hamburger and a milkshake. I'll drive.'

"All at once life became more interesting. When I wasn't making much money I confronted Frank. 'You take me away from my job every time you want me to accompany you. I think it's only fair that you reimburse me for my time.'

" 'Okay, but this is our secret.'

" 'Of course.'

"He was fun. He took me to Vancouver to see the Inkspots. He took me to Bellingham to visit the Barnum and Bailey Circus and fishing in the Pacific Ocean. We went roller skating and visited Harrison Hot Springs. He fed me. I lost all the new friends I'd made the first week."

"What did he want in return for his generosity?" Paul-Emile asked.

"A listener. Does that surprise you?"

"That's all?"

"Well, he cried, and I felt sorry for him and I kissed him and he kissed me back. He was starving, but that's all, we just kissed. His Mormon wife of only a year had left him and was living with another man and his four wives. I'd never heard about the Mormons. He explained it all and cried some more. I hated to see a grown man cry like that."

"How old was he?"

"Twenty-four. The pickers wanted me to relate all the details of my trips, but I was vague. They all hated him. I am not at all sure why, because he was really quite nice although a bit whiny."

"After a month and a half of all this I had enough of strawberries and Frank. I told Marge I was quitting. She said, 'How are you going to get home?'

"I told her I would tell the employment office that I had to get home because my mother was sick and I had to go back to school. Frank gave me a note releasing me from my obligations. I spent a few days with Marge at her sister's, then Frank drove me to Vancouver and I took the train back home.

"Mother and my brother were happy to see me. Father called me a tramp. That didn't bother me much, because I knew what I was and what I was not.

"That fall, at the beginning of my senior year, I dated a couple of older boys. They had only one objective ... to conquer the new girl in town, but I would not relinquish what they most desired.

"At school I joined the track and field team. I was a good runner and a running long jumper. I beat everybody and was selected to represent the school at the track meet in the northern part of the province. I ran the fifty and the one hundred yard dash.

"At our school I'd run against anyone they told me to run against and when I won, that was it, but at the North-Central meet I had to run heats. I couldn't figure out why they kept calling my name to run again and again, when I'd won my races. When I had to do the running long jump my muscles cramped. Agony, I had to stop participating.

"My parents had allowed me take their car to the meet fifty miles away. The school principal promised to pay for the gas and warned me not to pick up any hitchhikers. On the way home I gave the pole vaulter from our school a ride, after all, he had placed first, why should he have to walk and hitchhike if I had room in the car.

"My legs ached so badly, I decided to go see the Hungarian doctor, my mother, a nurse, worked for and raved about. He was sympathetic and interested and wanted to hear all about the races. After he'd listened to my story, he told me to rest. He gave me a few muscle relaxers and told me to come and see him if ever I had a problem.

"When I returned to school a few days later, I presented the principal with my five dollar gas bill. He refused to pay because I'd disobeyed his orders. Now, five dollars doesn't sound like much, but my parents had no money to spare and they'd lent me the car under the conditions I pay for the gas. I did have the ninety dollars I'd saved from my berry picking days, but that was my treasure trove and I wasn't about to spend it on gas.

"When he refused to pay, I lost my cool. My temper, mostly kept in check, exploded and the whole school heard me submit him to my slander and accusations of treachery. He expelled me. I was shocked."

"What did you do?"

"I complained to the school board. They promised to look into the matter. He'd also recently expelled one other student in the twelfth grade."

"Then what?"

"I decided to wait a month and see what happened. The school board dragged its feet. With great reluctance I decided to kowtow and apologized to the principal. I desperately wanted to graduate. He turned red in the face and told me to get out of his office.

"Several students came to me that day and said they wished they had the guts to tell him off, that he was a tyrant and had kicked several seniors out of school over the years. I smiled, nodded and felt like a pariah. My first priority now was to get a job. But I discovered this was almost impossible in that small town. As if he'd spread the word, nobody wanted to hire me. So I read my school books and tried to keep up on my own just in case a miracle happened.

"Earlier that year, in the Spring, the Public Health Service examined everyone at our school for tuberculosis. In October, shortly before my eighteenth birthday, my parents received a letter from our Hungarian doctor, saying he needed to do a follow-up x-ray, because he'd found a suspicious looking spot on my left lung.

"I presented myself at his office and though he didn't touch me, he examined me thoroughly with and without his x-ray machine. A week or so later he asked me to return for a repeat x-ray.

"I was sure there was nothing wrong with me and it crossed my mind that he probably just wanted to look at me. Other than that, I didn't take any further notice of the situation. Later that month a howling wind blew the huge pregnant snowflakes almost parallel to the ground. I'd done some shopping for Mother and huddled in my parka as I trudged along the street wishing I were home already, when a car stopped next to me. It was the good doctor. He asked if I wanted a lift, he'd take me to wherever I was going. Of course I accepted, I was so cold. True to his word he took me straight home.

"A few days later he stopped next to me in a brand-new Chrysler. He stuck his head out of the window, 'Can I give you a lift?' He opened the passenger door.

"The sun shone that day and the temperature hovered just above freezing. The first snow of the season was melting. I looked at my shoes and wiggled my toes. They were numb and wet. I looked around to see if anyone was watching, not a soul in sight, so I slipped in next to him.

"The heater blasted hot air and soon I felt quite defrosted. When the powerful vehicle surged forward I relaxed against the door and looked at the man. He had a round face with slightly bulging blue eyes. His mustache was neatly trimmed and a halo of brown hair surrounded his bald dome. He was a husky man of medium build, probably in his mid forties. Now he smiled at me and that made him wonderfully attractive.

"He asked if I'd like to see a movie with him in Saskatoon. I studied him. Wrong, wrong, but – I'd love to ride to Saskatoon in this nice, new-smelling car, fifty miles in pure luxury. I told him with a smile that I must ask my mother for permission. I figured he'd probably back-pedal on his invitation. However that didn't seem to perturb him a bit.

" 'If your mother agrees, be on this corner,' he pointed, 'at four o'clock tomorrow afternoon.' He stopped the car and I got out.

"Don't laugh. I did ask Mother. She said he was a nice man and agreed I could go. I truly expected her to say no and was surprised when she said yes. I still can't understand what she was thinking that day, definitely not what I was thinking. Of course I hadn't told her about his bizarre behavior in the doctor's office. I never told her much about myself.

"We met as agreed on the designated street corner. I enjoyed the fifty mile ride in his new car. We sang to the music on the radio. He was a charming conversationalist and when we arrived in Saskatoon he suggested we watch television instead of going to a movie. He took me to a motel. I'd never been to a motel before and wasn't familiar with that word. I soon found out what it meant.

"He registered us at the front office and climbed back into the car. 'We are all set.' He drove around the corner and parked in front of a door.

" 'Come on, my dear.' He unlocked the door and ushered me into the room.

"Of course I knew he had mischief on his mind."

"And you went anyway," Paul-Emile interrupted.

"I was curious and wondered what would develop. Are you sure you are up to this?"

"Is it juicy?" Paul-Emile said licking his lips.

"That depends. I think it's kind of funny and maybe a little bit tragic."

"Why tragic?"

"Because it should have been someone I loved who initiated me into this new stage of my life. Of course if I'd been a prude this might never have happened. I blame it on Inge's little evil devils that are always hovering.

"Okay, here goes. I stood in the middle of the L-shaped room furnished with a small sofa, a rectangular cocktail table in front and an easy chair on either side. A small television sat on a table. On the other side of the room stood a double bed with bedside tables and lamps on either side. I felt slightly uneasy and wasn't quite sure what to do next.

" 'Sit down,' he urged, 'take off your jacket.'

"He helped me off with my jacket and scarf, laid them on the arm of the sofa and turned on the television. I sat on the edge of the sofa and stared at the black and white screen. An orchestra played classical music. I told myself, relax, let the evening take its course.

If he goes overboard, I'll handle it then.

" 'I am going to fix us a drink.' The doctor said.

"He had been a perfect gentleman so far. He handed me a drink. I sniffed, odorless. 'What is in this glass?'

" 'Vodka and tonic. Cheers my dear, as they say here.' He lifted his glass and drank.

"I took a little sip, enjoyed the taste and took another.

" 'Wow, take it easy my child.' "

"He seduced you." Paul-Emile said.

"Shh." I chuckled. "I sat on the sofa and concentrated on the musicians on the television screen. Watching television was still quite a novelty for me, for we certainly didn't have one at home. He sat next to me, very close. I smelled his aftershave lotion. I stared at the screen for I was afraid to look at him.

"He took me by the shoulders and turned me toward him. His moustache twitched and I almost laughed. He gave me a predatory look, leaned closer and kissed my lips. When I didn't protest, he gathered me in his arms and kissed me with a passion I had never encountered before. This man was an expert. Hmm, I liked it, liked it, very much." I looked at Paul-Emile and smiled.

"Needing to breathe, I pushed him away. I took a sip from my glass and to gain time I asked stupidly, 'Doctor, are you by any chance a gypsy?'

"He smiled and looked deep into my eyes. 'My dear little girl, the gypsy blood runs hot in my veins. I am full of passion, but my wife doesn't appreciate me. I want to love you, make love to you in a way you have never experienced before. Dear Inge, will you let me?'

"Before I could answer, he jumped up, grabbed me by the arms and twirled me around the room to the tango playing on the television. He bent me over backward and kissed my lips. His leg pressed into me; he slid me up and down his leg; we dipped and we kissed; and he picked me up and danced with me cradled in his arms. He slid me down his chest, he pulled me up again. He was so strong and wild.

"I couldn't stop laughing. Soon we were sweating and out of breath and the tango came to an end. We slumped onto the couch, stretched out our legs, looked at each other and laughed.

" 'That deserves another drink,' he said. He walked to the table and busied himself with the bottles. 'Servus, skoal, cheers *meine liebe* Inge. Here is to a beautiful evening.'

"By then I felt so lazy and relaxed and clinked glasses with him. We took a sip. The melody of a waltz came from the television. He pulled me into his arms again, held me tight and moved slowly to the music. I felt his erection against my belly, but didn't move away. He held me tighter and moaned. He stepped away from me and we danced once more.

"He pulled me close again and now we just swayed. He sighed, lifted my chin with a finger and kissed me lightly. He handed me my glass and I took a sip. The room was warm. I sipped again. We danced. I put my drink on the table.

" 'Drink *mein Liebling*,' he said, 'wonderful things are still to come.'

"I took a small sip. He whirled me past the fuzzy television screen until I felt dizzy and begged him to stop. We sat on the couch. He unbuttoned the back of my red dress. After he'd nibbled on my earlobe and gave me goose bumps, he pulled the dress over my head. I didn't protest. I felt so mellow and very expectant.

"He unhooked my brassiere, cupped my breasts and kissed them. I wondered if he could hear my hammering heart. He took off his shirt and clasped me tight against his hairy chest. He held me away from him and kissed my breasts again. I watched him with bated breath fascinated by his enthusiasm and wondered what he would do next.

"He murmured between kisses, 'Don't worry my sweet little girl, nothing will happen to you. I just want to kiss you and give you pleasure.'

"He carried me to the bed. The smooth, cool sheets felt luxurious after the rough upholstery of the sofa. He undressed. I'd never seen a naked man before. His erect penis pointed threateningly at me and I shrank away.

" 'Shh, my child,' he murmured, 'don't worry, he has nothing to do with you.'

" 'You promise?'

" 'Yes. Lie down please. I just want to kiss you.'

"And he did; and to my utter consternation, rippling waves of intense pleasure surged through my body and I didn't have a clue of what was happening to me. I tried to pull away, but he held me and devoured me with a passion that left me weak and gasping for air."

"*Sacré bleu!*" Paul-Emile whispered.

I smiled. "Was this what sex was all about? He allowed me to pull away. I leaned on my elbows and glared at him, shocked at my excitement and the thrill he roused in me.

"He asked with a little smile, 'You never experienced this before?'

"I shook my head.

" 'You are how old?'

" 'I am almost eighteen.'

" 'Now you know what to expect when a man makes love to you.' He smiled.

" 'What do you get out of this?'

" 'Pleasure. I usually prefer younger girls, but since this is your first time ... it was indeed a pleasure.'

"I frowned, 'Since you are a doctor I guess I can discuss this with you. Why do I have the impression that all this is very wrong?'

" 'Did you enjoy my ministrations?'

" 'Yes....' I hesitated, 'But I am also confused. I've never had sex before and now I think I have ... I feel violated.'

" 'Inge, I only kissed you, no reason to feel violated. You will probably thank me one day. There is neither right nor wrong only thinking it is, makes it so. You are afraid of your own passion. You were climaxing, the ultimate gift a man can give a woman. Don't be frightened of your sensations.'

"I mulled that over for a while, then rose, grabbed my clothes and walked into the bathroom. After we were dressed we left. We didn't speak for a long time. He glanced at me now and then and smiled."

"Then what," Paul-Emile asked softly, "surely you didn't ride together for fifty miles and not speak or do anything else?"

"I think I shocked him when I told him to drive me to the Gordon's house. 'Why?' he asked.

" 'Because,' I told him, 'I don't want to get sick all over your fancy new car.' My head was full of fuzz balls and my stomach was churning.

"All the lights were out in their house. I got out of his car, walked around to the back and waited a couple of minutes. When I looked, his car was gone.

"Of course I knew I couldn't ring the bell. Instead I walked to a café I knew of and drank a couple of cups of coffee. Feeling much revived, I walked across the Saskatchewan River Bridge and headed for the railway station. Half frozen, I entered the blissfully warm waiting room. I needed money to get home, so I called a fellow I had dated a few times when he was home on holidays. He wasn't happy my rousting him out of bed, but he came and took me to a small hotel near the railway station, paid for my room and gave me five more dollars to take the train home the next day.

"Did you see the doctor again?"

"I avoided him like a field of nettles."

"Why?"

"I was ashamed of what I allowed him to do. Over the years I occasionally thought about that man. One part of me said that I should have taken full advantage of him, after all what was wrong with kissing? The other part of me said I should have reported him to the police."

"What would that have accomplished?"

"Justice. He preyed on young girls. Shortly after this little interlude, or maybe it was a big one, because those delicious sensations he elicited, made me want to experience everything about sex."

"Did you?"

"My dear nosy Paul-Emile. According to your housekeeper Emma I would know when I met the right man and that hadn't happened yet."

I threw back the covers and jumped out of bed. "My feet are clods of ice, I'm going to my room and take a shower. Goodnight Paul-Emile."

I was surprised he didn't protest. While I was toweling myself dry I promised myself to be nice to him, at least until the end of our journey.

Chapter Fifteen

Mid-morning Paradsky picked us up in his sleigh again.
The sun sparkled in the cloudless sky as we moved silently over the
snow-covered road. I pointed to the left, "What happened to the
cemetery?"

"Gone. Louise kept the graves nice for many years, then they
came, took away the headstones and plowed everything over." He
shook his head. "Who knows how they think?"

When we arrived, the aroma of baking filled the house. I
peeked into the oven. Paradsky and Paul-Emile sat at the kitchen
table and lit their pipes.

"You like poppy-seed cream filling?" Louise asked.

"How did you guess? My favorite." I asked her if I could
help but she shooed me away and proceeded to methodically open
one jar after the other. "Who else is coming?"

"Nobody, why?" Her fingers moved swiftly and efficiently
filling one crystal bowl or plate after the other.

"This is all for the four of us?"

"Paradsky has a big appetite. You like Sljivovica?" Without
waiting for an answer she filled four one ounce shot glasses, called
Schnapspfeiflen, with the clear plum brandy. She slid two of the
glasses in the men's direction, raised hers and said, "*Na zdrowie, do
dna.*" (To your health to the bottom of the glass.)

She offered me the plate with the pickled herring. I took a
piece and popped it into my mouth. Off and on I'd buy a jar at the
supermarket but this was home-made and delicious. We nibbled on
the small blinis topped with sour cream, the pickled cucumbers,
pickled wild mushrooms, sausage, ham, rye bread and cheese. To
hell with my diet, this I was going to enjoy. Soon we sipped on a

glass of vodka and before long I felt so relaxed that I could have stayed there nibbling forever.

Paradsky however wanted to shoot billiards. So we did that. He was good, but I was better. That frustrated him to no end and he invited Paul-Emile to take my place. Paul-Emile was good but Paradsky was better. We laughed a lot and after a while Louise came and asked if we minded eating in the kitchen. We all agreed that would be a splendid place.

Paradsky took us on a tour of the house. It hadn't changed much, everything shone and smelled of wax. He took us outside and showed us his barns. "The old ones burned, all new."

"What happened to the windmill?"

"One day it just lay in the garden, big mess."

Louise called us in for a late lunch. We were still full from the *zakaski* (nibbles) but the stuffed cabbage rolls in a tomato cream sauce and potatoes looked too delicious to pass up. As we ate, Paradsky made sure our jiggers of vodka remained filled and every so often he'd say '*Na zdrowie*' and drained his glass.

I just barely touched my lips to the brim and saw Paul-Emile do the same, because I knew if I followed Louise and Paradsky's indulgence I'd soon pass out. After I'd helped with the dishes, I rummaged through the books Louise had saved from the old house where my mother was born. I found three with her name inscribed inside and decided to take them to her. I kept two for myself and browsed through the others, wishing I could take them all.

Freshly brewed coffee wafted through the house. Louise set out her pastries and poured, and Paradsky pulled a harmonica out of his pocket. As soon as he began to play he coughed, but he soon recovered and continued with a couple of sad melodies. When he finished he asked Paul-Emile, "You remember?"

Paul-Emile nodded, "I remember. Now I want to hear your happy songs."

And Paradsky played mazurkas and German folk songs. Louise and I sang lustily along; then he played excerpts from Smetana's 'The Moldau' and I cried, unashamed of my tears.

I had come full circle, now I could go on with my life.

Louise placed a hand on my shaking shoulder, "You are sad. Does Paradsky make you sad with his music? He is such a sentimental man, when he plays he ignores the rest of the world. I miss him already, for I know one day soon he will leave me. I hope and pray I will go before him for without his music life is not worth living." She sat in her rocker and wiped her nose with a corner of her apron.

When we returned to our hotel, Paul-Emile poured me a vodka, sat on the chair by the window and lit his pipe. "Are you going to tell me what happened next? Did they allow you to return to school?"

"No. But I received a letter from my friend Marge. She was living with her other sister in Winnipeg now and invited me to visit her. We'll get a job, she wrote. I checked with the school board, they hadn't come to a decision. I showed my parents Marge's letter and told them I was leaving. I might be back, again, I might not.

"They didn't say much and I had the sneaking suspicion they were quite glad to be rid of me. So I packed my suitcase and one of my flames, whom I really, really liked drove me to Saskatoon. A six hour train ride later I arrived in Winnipeg. I tried to contact Marge at the telephone number she'd sent me. It was the wrong number and I didn't know her sister's last name.

"I sat on a bench in the railway station and contemplated my next move. A lady sat next to me. We started talking and when I told her what had happened, she said, 'You can share my room at the YWCA. It'll cost you only two dollars a night.'

"I asked her what YWCA stood for."

"What does it mean?" Paul-Emile said.

"It stands for Young Women's Christian Association. When she said Christian, I immediately agreed to go with her for something associated with Christian couldn't be at all bad. She was sincere. The next day she took me to a German restaurant and convinced the owner to hire me as a waitress."

"You a waitress?" Paul-Emile laughed.

"What's so funny. I figured at least I would get one good meal a day. But being a waitress was harder than I had ever imagined. I could never keep the orders straight. The lady, I never knew her name, also took me to a boarding house where I rented a room for five dollars a month. Can you believe that? It was just a cubbyhole in the basement, but it was warm and several girls shared other rooms down there so I wasn't lonely.

"I wrote my parents where I was and what I was doing and asked them to write me when they had news from the school board. I never saw Marge again. About three months later, I received a letter from my mother informing me they were moving to Miami, Florida to take care of a great aunt I didn't know I had. I never heard from the school board."

"Did you date at all during this time?"

"I am glad you asked. Shortly after I started my job, a customer, an elderly German, I am talking sixties or early seventies, invited me to go see the movie 'Wintertime', starring Sonja Henie. When I hesitated, you never know about these old men, he offered to pay my way. I thought it over for a moment then decided I could handle him if he tried something funny. Since I was watching my pennies and hadn't even once gone to a movie, I loved those ice skating extravaganzas, I decided to take a chance. After the movie he suggested we go to a restaurant, called Little Europe, for a coffee. Up to that point he'd behaved like a gentleman, so I agreed.

"When we entered the restaurant, several customers hailed the old fellow and said they'd been waiting for him, where had he been? 'Entertaining this young lady. Max,' he shouted, 'give her a coffee and a piece of cake.'

"He took off his coat and hung it on a coatrack, then sat at the piano and played melodies from some of my favorite operettas, The Dollar Princess, The Bird Handler, the Count of Luxemburg and Der Zarewitsch and The Land of Smiles. I knew them all. When everyone sang along, I did too. My voice soared and I forgot I was among strangers. Max, the owner of the restaurant, sat next to me and listened to me sing. When the pianist stopped playing, Max said, 'I want you in my next production.'

"I asked him in English, 'What production?'

"He smiled and laid his hand on my arm, 'We speak only German here.'

"I stared at the six purple numbers tattooed on the inside of his forearm. He watched me for a moment then smoothed down his rolled-up shirt sleeve.

" 'We are in the process of casting for Die Fledermaus. I want you to take the part of Prince Orlovsky. Are you familiar with the operetta?'

" 'Of course, who isn't? I sang Adele's Laughing Song for a school program once, but I'm afraid that's the extent of my public performance. Does your maestro at the piano have a name?'

" 'His name is Benno, didn't he introduce himself?'

"I walked over to the piano and hummed, '*Wenn ich mit andern sitz . . .* (When I sit with others...).' He smiled, nodded and played the introduction.

"I'd always wanted to do this and here I was a stranger. Benno played the introduction once more. My heart almost sat in my throat. I took a deep breath and sang. It wasn't long, just twelve or fifteen lines. The acoustics in the room were horrible. When I finished, they applauded. Max stood and raised his hands in the air, clapped and shouted, 'Brava, brava.'

"I smiled and gave a mock bow. I had to think of you, Paul-Emile. You always insisted I was an actress. I proved it that night, because it wasn't really me that whole evening but someone else. Just a couple of hours earlier I didn't have a friend in the world and had been lonely and now here was this man shouting brava."

"Did you sing more that evening?"

"Someone brought me a laced cup of coffee, I took a sip, and another. I raised the cup and said, 'Cheers,' and downed it. I asked Benno to play 'Adele's Laughing Song'. The rum in the coffee set my vocal chords to vibrating and I sang and laughed and they loved me. They asked me to sing again but I said no. Max led me to his and his wife's and their intimate friends' table next to the kitchen and someone placed a second laced cup in front of me.

"Then a young man walked into the restaurant and sat at our table. Max introduced him, 'Kurt will take you home tonight,' he said. He turned to his wife and winked, 'The perfect couple, what do you think?'

"She nodded, smiled, and returned to the kitchen. Kurt and I studied each other. He asked me where I came from. I waved my hand, 'Here and there.' I was enjoying myself. Kurt was a good-looking blond. When he offered to drive me home I declined."

"Why? How did you get home?"

"My dear, they tried to orchestrate everything. I couldn't allow that. Besides, I decided to play the mysterious stranger. I thanked Benno for the wonderful evening then walked home. It took me over an hour.

"That winter in Winnipeg things turned nasty in more ways than one. I lost my job because the factory across the street from the restaurant where I worked closed. They didn't need me any longer. I'd saved a little money but of course I needed to work and didn't have a clue how to go about finding another job.

"While I walked home that last day, snow blew in my face and the biting wind howled as I entered the intersection of Portage and Main Street. Talk about Chicago being the windy city, Winnipeg wins hands down. I bent almost double, my calves tingled, my nose dripped, and my fingers had turned white and painful.

"Someone honked a horn. A red convertible coasted slowly next to the sidewalk keeping up with my fast pace. I frowned, and lengthened my stride. A man said, 'Climb in, I'll take you where you're going.'

"I squinted at him. He wore a coat with a fur collar. What could happen here in the middle of the city. I was so bloody miserable and depressed that I decided to take the chance. I climbed in and warmth engulfed me. 'Where do you want to go?'

"I gave him my address. He asked me what I was doing out in this terrible weather. I told him I was coming from work for the last time. Did I have any prospects. I shook my head. We rode in silence for a while, then he banged his hand on the steering wheel. 'Across the street from my work is a dry-cleaning company, they are always looking for someone. Why don't you try them tomorrow? I'll show you where, it's not far from your address.'

"Now that I was warm, I felt embarrassed that I'd allowed myself to be picked up. And as if he'd read my thoughts, he said, 'You are lucky I am an honorable man. You should be careful whom you accept a ride from.'

"I glanced at him and really saw him for the first time. He was young and handsome, a small man, clean cut, with warm brown eyes. I nodded, 'You are absolutely right. I have never done this before, but I felt so miserable and alone. You can let me out now. I can walk the rest of the way.'

"He stopped the car. I opened the door and was about to slide out, 'You don't have to worry about me,' he said, 'don't you want me to show you the dry-cleaning company?'

"A job, I did need a job, so I closed the door again and he drove on.

" 'By the way, my name is Bruce.'

"I didn't say anything. We drove in silence for a while, then he stopped and pointed at a large building I'd passed before. 'That's it. I work in the middle building across the street.'

"I read, 'Ebbla Movie Productions'. Just five minutes later we arrived in front of the house I lived in. 'Let me just quickly show you a street not far from here,' he said, 'where you could rent a nice room for a reasonable price.'

"I looked at the house more closely, it did look rather shabby. When he took me home again, he asked for my name and phone number and I obliged. The next day I presented myself at the dry-cleaning establishment. A lady asked me about my skills. I told her, 'I speak German and French and am quite good at math, I play the piano, love to read, am honest and willing to learn, other than that, none.'

"She tried to hide a smile. 'Well that's honest enough. I have an opening sorting punch cards. If you do a good job maybe we can train you as a computer operator.'

"I didn't have a clue what she was talking about. I thanked her and accepted the job to start the next day. Even though I dreaded going outside again, I jogged to the street Bruce had suggested I check out for rooms to let. Huge old trees lined the street on both sides and old, two and three story mansions sat in small gardens. They'd seen better days but were still elegant and attractive.

"I saw a sign in a front window, 'Room To Let' and decided to check it out. A chubby, elderly lady answered the doorbell. I asked about the room; she invited me in and took me upstairs. I loved the small, wall-papered room appointed with heavy, old furniture and a sofa that doubled as a bed. It reminded me of my grandmother's house.

" 'How much?'

" 'Twelve dollars a month.'

"I had to have that room even if it meant scrimping on food. 'I'll take it. I'll bring you the money tomorrow.'

" 'No cooking in your room. You'll have to share a bathroom with the sisters upstairs, oh yes, no men allowed.'

"I nodded, 'I can live with that.' We shook hands.

"I felt so exhilarated about my new life that I decided to take the bus to the Little Europe Restaurant. Max greeted me like I was family and asked where I'd been, they'd been looking for me. I told him I'd been busy, then noticed I was the only customer. 'You are open?'

" 'Yes, but it's early, our patrons don't usually arrive until six or seven. What can I bring you ... how about a Schnitzel?'

" 'I'm afraid a Schnitzel is beyond my budget. How about a cup of coffee?'

" 'How about a Schnitzel on the house?'

" 'Are you sure? I am kind of hungry.'

"He disappeared in the kitchen, I heard him talk to his wife Erna. When he returned he sat next to me. I couldn't help but stare at the numbers on his arm again. He watched me. I was about to ask him when he said, 'You have never seen these before?'

"I shook my head.

" 'You were in Germany during the war?' I nodded. Then he told me about the numbers on his arm, his wife's arm and his son's. I wept and was ashamed to be a German. He comforted me and told me he didn't think about those times any longer. All he cared about now was to make music, be happy and make others happy. 'Will you be my Prince Orlovsky?'

"I sniffled, gave him a weak smile and promised I'd be his Prince. He rubbed his hands together, 'Good, good, wait here.' He came back momentarily with a huge Schnitzel, mashed potatoes and gravy and Prince Orlovsky's libretto. 'You are already familiar with the music so we are in business. Rehearsal starts on Saturday at one o'clock, just come here and I'll introduce you to the rest of the cast.'

"After I'd finished the delicious meal, I thanked him and his wife and pulled on my coat. He asked me to stay, but I had things to think about and told him I'd see him on Saturday. 'One o'clock.' I waved and walked out into the cold."

"He shocked you." Paul-Emile said.

"To the core. At first I could hardly believe him. Max spoke for over an hour about things I didn't have a clue; his brothers, his sisters, his parents, his wife's parents, her siblings, all gassed. They were Jews from Vienna, entertainers, musicians ... whom had they ever hurt?

"I was mortified. How could any human being treat another in this manner? The more I dwelled on what Max told me, the more I felt as responsible as the ones who had committed this outrage. Until my talk with Max, I'd often felt the victim. I often thought, why did we have to suffer so many hardships? Why did so many people have to die? Why did everyone try to kill us? My parents never said a word about all this, but I am not at all sure whether I asked. They simply didn't talk about it. They shed no tears, voiced no recriminations, didn't moan about lost possessions, just quiet acceptance.

"For the first time I knew with certainty that terrible

atrocities had happened during the war. When the Russians, Poles, Czechs, Romanians and Bulgarians finally were in the position to take their revenge in those terrible months in 1945, they turned their hatred against their German conquerors. Without discrimination they heaped untold hardships and death on the defenseless German refugees consisting mostly of women, children, the old and frail. And now I knew why.

"On my way home that day I stopped at a library, checked out books and read, one after the other until I knew the truth. I wept and felt ashamed. The next time I saw Max, I said, 'How can you forgive us?'

"With a smile on his lined face and his warm, brown eyes twinkling he said, 'I am alive child.' "

My voice choked with emotion.

"Inge, this all happened so long ago." Paul-Emile rose and tried to embrace me.

I walked to the window and stared into the darkness. He too had suffered at the hands of the Germans. I turned slowly. He sat on the bed holding his cold pipe in his cupped hand. We stared at each other for a long moment, then I said softly, "Your mother convinced you I was evil, a bad seed, not worthy of your love."

"Mother is dead now, so is my father. I loved them."

"Of course. I understand. Better now, than I did when I was fourteen."

I walked into the bathroom, sat on the closed lid of the commode and tried to get my emotions under control. I was determined Paul-Emile should never see my tears again. I flushed the toilet, washed my hands and returned to the room.

"How was the rehearsal?"

I sighed and hoped Max was finally resting in peace. "The rehearsal. Fun ... it was lots of fun. Everybody was nice and wanted to know all about me. But I played the mystery lady and kept them guessing. Of course that didn't sit too well with some. I put on some airs and threw in a little French, two young men fawned over me. Two young ladies glared daggers at me. I laughed and sang. This once I would perform in German, I didn't come to Canada to be with Germans."

"You never spoke English?"

"Not when I was with that bunch. You've heard of Little Italy, this was Little Germany. Over the months I came to detest their living in the past. Many of these people who came to the restaurant, German and Austrian jews, some gentiles like me, White Russians, Poles and Hungarians still lived in an atmosphere of suffering with an unsalvageable loss of their former way of life.

"Most were artists, musicians, composers, poets and writers. I didn't want to sink into their kind of helpless desolation. They seemed to be waiting for something to happen. I couldn't understand why they didn't integrate. Only my loneliness had drawn me to these forlorn souls who lamented and yearned for those days when they didn't need to converse in broken English. I asked a few, why don't you go back if you miss everything so much. They shrugged ...what was there to go back to.

"I met a young German woman at the dry-cleaning place who'd been in Canada five years and couldn't speak English.

"We held the dress rehearsal in the theater to be used for our performances. Someone clapped in the mostly empty row of seats after I sang my part. When we finished, two young men I'd never seen before congratulated me. One said, 'We'd like to take you out, but you'll have to choose. I like opera, my best friend likes country music.'

"I said with a mischievous smile, 'What makes you think I'll go out with either one of you?' I wanted to go because they were Canadians. 'I am going to have a bite to eat, if you'd like to keep me company?'

" 'Both of us?'

" 'Why not, then I don't have to choose.' I laughed. Kurt my German admirer walked over and asked in German if I was ready, they were all going to eat. I linked arms with my two new friends, 'Not today, thank you.'

"We stopped at a drive-in restaurant and one of the men

asked me if I'd like a beer. Sounded great, I agreed. When I took a sip I almost spit it out, it tasted like medicine. 'What on earth is this?' I asked.

" 'Root beer,' he said and laughed.

"Did you ever drink root beer before Paul-Emile? I'll always remember that day because this was my first root beer and my first hamburger. Obviously life consisted of more than Wiener Schnitzel."

"Did you finally choose one of the fellows?"

"No. Even though they treated me tactfully, one of them was the son of the owner of the theater we were using for our performances. I didn't trust them."

"Whatever happened to the guy who steered you to the job at the dry-cleaning factory?"

"I moved, remember? He didn't know exactly where to. But I did run into him one other time in front of his place of business. He tried to talk to me but I ignored him and pretended I had never seen him before."

"Why did you do that? He helped you."

"I couldn't forgive myself for allowing him to pick me up like common trash. I was ashamed of what he must think of me."

"Inge, Inge, I bet he didn't think that way at all."

"Maybe not, but I'll tell you a little secret my dear. I didn't trust any man and it was because of you, Paul-Emile. I hold you responsible for my miserable teenage years."

"Now you are being dramatic again." He poured himself a dram of vodka, downed it and lay on the bed.

I stood over him, glared, and pointed my finger at his face. "Ever since I was six years old I adored and trusted you. Then you deserted me. When you rejected my love, I thought maybe something was wrong with me. Maybe I wasn't pretty enough or smart enough. And when the farmer's son didn't even kiss me on our one and only real date, I knew something was wrong for sure. So, after that I decided not to allow anyone close, that way I wouldn't be rejected."

"You haven't changed much, *ma petite*." Paul-Emile laughed. "That's why I adore you now like I did back then."

"Lies, all lies." I stretched out on the other bed and closed my eyes, wishing it were tomorrow and I could go home never to see this man again.

"Did you have sex?"

"I wanted to, but I was afraid what it would do to my reputation. Of course this fellow Kurt, one of the cast, really tried to get me into bed. I laughed and asked him, 'Do you really want to go to bed with a prince?' This made him laugh too. He didn't proposition me again."

"How did your operetta turn out?"

"It was a hit. We filled the theater in Winnipeg three times and were asked to perform in various smaller towns. I enjoyed the applause and was surprised at my own audacity. Having to dress in men's clothing gave me an anonymity and daring that surprised even me and I played the role to the hilt. Max was already talking about our next production, but I wasn't at all sure I wanted to continue within this German community. Even though I spoke English at work, I felt I was being sucked into something I didn't want to be part of.

"I declined Max's offer for a part in Der Rosenkavalier and stayed away from all Germans, including the restaurant, a favorite hangout by then. I missed them dreadfully. Instead, I worked overtime. They asked and I always said yes, one way of staying out of trouble and making more money.

"Mother wrote the occasional letter glamorizing Miami and its environs. I decided when I'd saved one hundred and fifty dollars I'd join them in Miami. That time came in December 1956. I boarded a bus and said *adieu* to Canada.

"I found a job as a bank teller almost immediately. A few months later I met Kane and my life changed forever. I gave him my heart, my soul and my body."

"He must have been some man." Paul-Emile smiled.

"He was that. One in a million. I will miss him as long as I live."

The next day we drove to Warsaw. I called Stephanie and informed her of my arrival time in Miami. "Oh boy," she said, "I can't wait to hear all about it."

"About what?"

"Your trip of course."

Paul-Emile looked grim. "So you are just going to take off. The past days don't mean anything to you."

"They were interesting and served a purpose I suppose, but I promised to be home for Christmas. The girls expect a tree and the trimmings that go along with the season. I can't disappoint them. You, my dear," I patted his cheek, "are a big boy. Of course you can come along if you want to," I said it teasingly, hoping he wouldn't accept.

"And watch Hamdi's mournful face? No thanks, I have my pride."

We waited for our respective flights in silence for a while. "Inge, when will I see you again?"

"Maybe soon, maybe never. I can't predict the future."

"What does that mean?"

"I'll see what happens when I see Hamdi. My heart will make the decision."

"You are going to sleep with him?"

"Paul-Emile, you ask too many questions."

They announced my flight. I gave him a buss on the cheek. Paul-Emile accompanied me to the door of the jet-way. After the attendant took my ticket I quickly removed my coat and fur hat and pressed them into Paul-Emile's hands. While he stared dumbly at the coat, I scurried down the jet-way. Halfway to the plane I turned, stepped aside to let the other people pass and shouted. "A present for your wife." I blew him a kiss and shortly after boarded the plane.

When I sat in my seat I regretted my behavior. I had been mean but I was sure the coat had cost him a pretty penny – better not to have to be obligated in any way. Freedom meant everything. I would write him a nice letter and apologize, I was sure he would forgive me. I pulled one of the books I'd retrieved from the boxes out of my carry-on, buckled myself in, and waited for the plane to take off.

I was glad when the flight attendant began to close the hatch and the seat next to me was still empty. Then I noticed a small commotion at the door. Shortly after Paul-Emile strode into the compartment and sat beside me. He laid the coat and the hat across my safety-belted lap. "You forgot this." The plane taxied toward the runway. "I've never been to Miami, it's high time."

I opened my mouth to say something then closed it and stroked the beautiful fur instead. After the plane hummed away at thirty thousand plus feet I stole a look at him. He sat motionless with his eyes closed. I saw his eyelids flicker and decided he was laughing. But perhaps it had been an illusion, because he didn't open them again until the flight attendant asked if I wanted a pre-dinner cocktail. I ordered a vodka martini. "Give him one too please, no, better make it a double because he'll need it when I get through with him."

She smiled. "You are acquainted with this gentlemen? He is very persuasive."

"He keeps pestering me to marry him."

"He is a good-looking man."

I elbowed Paul-Emile in the ribs. "You can stop laughing, you ... you...."

He twisted in his seat and planted his lips on mine. "Inge ... shut up! Now, we can either have a pleasant nine hour trip or a feuding one. If you don't want to sit with me I can move. I see lots of empty seats in the back of the plane, probably much safer if it crashes."

Choking with tears and confusion I said, "Oh Paul-Emile, I am fond of you, but Hamdi loves me, and I love him.... You and I met by chance ... why don't you leave it at that?"

"Very fond of me ... that is not the same as I love you." He pressed my hand where it lay in my lap. "I want to live with you...."

"Too late, let it be." I laid my head against the back of my seat and closed my eyes. Without opening them I said softly, "Love develops slowly. I adored and loved you once long ago. Maybe it wasn't true love. I was so young."

"You and your two men. You will have to decide. I'm not going to play along with your menage en trois thing. You have to chose."

"You have a wife. How can you possibly make demands on me?"

"You want me to leave you alone?" He made as if to get up. "I'll see if they open the hatch for me, I'll jump out and that will solve everything." He cocked an eyebrow.

I peeked at him. "You would kill yourself for me?"

"Not for you, for me. My whole life has been one disappointment after the other."

"Poor Paul-Emile." I smiled, patted his hand and wondered if he was serious.

When we landed in New York I called my house in Miami. Hamdi answered. I asked him if he minded if I brought Paul-Emile along to spend the holidays. He hesitated only a split second, "I'll find him a hotel room."

Magda, Dena, Stephanie and Hamdi awaited us when Paul-Emile and I entered the reception area at the Miami Airport. I saw them before they saw me. They talked and smiled among each other and craned their necks. I pointed, "There they are," and quickened my steps.

The girls embraced me. Out of the corner of my eye I saw Hamdi shake hands with Paul-Emile. Hamdi said, "I am glad you are here Paul-Emile. I have a proposal for you."

"Something interesting I hope?"

"I'll fill you in later. Inge, habibi." Hamdi wrapped me into his arms and kissed me hard on the mouth.

I introduced the girls to Paul-Emile. They politely shook hands, then Stephanie relieved me of the fur coat and hat.

"Gorgeous." She slipped into it and donned the hat and

paraded in front of us in her flip-flops.

"A real fashion plate." Dena chuckled. "Did he give it to you?"

I nodded and worried how all this would end. They'd come in two cars. Stephanie in Kane's old silver Corvette and Magda in my 1983 chocolate brown XJ6. The girls had scolded me about my extravagance, but the car was something I'd wanted forever. I told Magda to move over and stepped on the gas. The men sat in the back and chatted amicably about Hamdi's latest project at Tel al Amarna. They had finally received funding for excavation of Pharaoh Akhnaton's workers' villages.

Magda leaned close and whispered, "What did you bring him for?"

"Sh, not now."

When we arrived home, I was surprised to see a Christmas tree already decorated. Red balls of different textures, red crystals of various shapes and sizes, red hearts made of beads and sequins, red ribbons and a red glistening star on the top. It looked gorgeous.

The mantle also was swathed with red potted poinsettias, red blooming Kalanchoe, ivy, ferns, long needled pine and red candles. They'd festooned the stair rail with garlands and more red ornaments. The whole downstairs gleamed and shimmered in red, green and gold. "You like it?" Magda asked. "Aunt Julia's idea. Red stands for love she says. Roses will arrive on the day of the party. She and Uncle Arthur are absolutely wonderful."

Stephanie, who had beaten us to the house, leaned against the doorframe to the living room. "Magda, stop gushing for a moment." She fixed her green eyes on mine and flicked her chin in the direction of Paul-Emile. "Where'd you pick him up, Mommy?"

"Not so loud," Dena said, "that's Mommy's new interest. I told you about him."

"Did you have to bring him now? What will Albert say when I introduce your two lovers to him. This family is disgraceful." Magda dabbed at her tears.

I hugged her and kissed her on both cheeks. "Darling, you

don't have to tell him they are my lovers, for Pete's sake, what's come over you. You are getting to be so conservative. Are you really serious about this fellow? Do you think he'll fit into our family? After all, we aren't quite typical." I poured myself a shot of brandy and ambled into the music room to join Paul-Emile and Hamdi. The girls followed close behind.

"So these are your precious daughters," Paul-Emile said. "Beautiful like their mother and talented, but I hope not so stubborn. Your mother is a stubborn woman, even when she was a little girl she was stubborn. She stomped her feet until she had her way." He sat at the piano, played and sang, 'La donna è mobile' (Woman is fickle).

We applauded when he finished. "Monsieur Diderot," Dena said, "you have a great voice. Did you ever perform?"

"*Mon Dieu*, no. My mother was the opera singer. I guess I inherited a tiny bit of her talent. My interest though is strictly Egyptology."

"I can see this Christmas is going to be exceptional." Stephanie turned to the girls, "I am going to have to do a little more shopping, you guys want to come?"

They left us and in seconds Hamdi, Paul-Emile and I were alone silently contemplating each other. Paul-Emile slowly closed the piano lid and walked to the window.

"They can't wait to discuss all this. Inge, habibi, I am glad you brought Paul-Emile along, at least I have something else to talk about than golf. Stephanie has described her last few games shot by shot. If I didn't love her so much, I would have told her long ago to shut up."

Paul-Emile turned, "Inge didn't bring me. I brought myself, an uninvited guest. Just say the word and I am gone."

"Oh no," Hamdi said, "please stay. This is going to be a most interesting Christmas. Magda is presenting her young man. His parents are coming too. The girls have engaged a caterer so everything is under control. I've arranged for Paul-Emile to stay at the Sonesta Hotel on Key Biscayne. Unfortunately," he spread his arms, "we are full up here in this house."

I blushed. I'd never seen Hamdi so authoritative – very attractive. I took a sip of brandy and tried to hide my confusion. "What do you think, Inge?"

The Sonesta Hotel, where I became pregnant with Stephanie. I looked Hamdi straight in the eye. "Perfect."

Chapter Sixteen

Paul-Emile insisted on renting a car. "This way I can come and go as I please. After all, I am an uninvited guest."

"Do you have to dwell on that?"

He pecked my cheek. "May I call on you tomorrow?"

"We'll be about, you might want to telephone first though. Be sure to hold Saturday evening open. We are having a party and you are invited."

"I'll give you a call," Hamdi said. "Maybe we can get together after you've rested."

"Any time *mon ami*."

After we left Paul-Emile to his own devices, Hamdi said, "Let's go for a walk. I haven't been to the lighthouse for many years."

A stiff, cool breeze blew off the ocean. I zipped my jacket and knotted a kerchief over my head. We walked in silence for a while, then Hamdi said, "Are you in love with him?"

"No. I was maybe a little bit at the beginning but not now." I squinted at him. "He asked me to marry him."

Hamdi stooped, picked up a small stone and pitched it into the water trying to make it skip. "I could never do that. Kane could. So, what are you going to do?"

I took off my sandals and tested the water. "He has a wife ... I told him no."

"Then why is he here?"

"He hopes to persuade me." I picked up a plug of seaweed and examined it closely.

"Are you going to be persuaded?"

"No."

"What did you do in Warsaw? Inge ... look at me."

"What is this, an interrogation?" I dropped the seaweed. We exchanged glances and I saw his pain. Feeling guilty I said, "He took me to the old homestead. Darling, I'm freezing, let's go back. I'll tell you about it later."

"Is he a good lover?"

I stopped walking, "What kind of a question is that."

He clutched my shoulders. I'd never seen him so angry. "Inge, I'll fight for you."

"I'm sorry for going off with him. I love you, you don't have to fight for me. I've always been yours."

"Why did you sleep with this man?"

I kicked at the sand with my toes. Should I tell him that I had wanted to at one point? He waited patiently for my answer. I pressed his hand to my cheek.

"Darling Hamdi, don't be jealous. I did want to sleep with him. It sometimes seems that the little devils that lurk inside me rear their ugly heads and try to overwhelm me with temptations. I resisted because I knew if I succumbed, I would never be able to look you in the eye. So let's not dwell on it any longer. I am through with him." I laughed, stood on my toes and kissed his lips. "I'm really quite proud of myself."

Hamdi stopped walking and held me tight. "I love you habibi, always and forever. He took my hand and looked deep into my eyes. "Whenever I see you, sound fails, my tongue falters, thin fire steals through my limbs, an inner roar, and darkness shrouds my ears and eyes'." He smiled. "Thus Catullus translated Sappho."

Tenderness filled my heart to overflowing for this gentle man. Content, I smiled and watched the raucously screaming gulls fly overhead toward the darkening sky streaked with soundless lightning. We drove in comfortable intimacy for a while then I said, "I value my independence."

Hamdi remained silent.

"Sometimes I get terribly depressed."

"Recently?"

"Yes."

"Because he is in love with you?"

I straightened my arms on the steering wheel and arched my back. "In a way it's rather charming, it makes a woman come alive knowing someone desires her."

"I desire you ... have from the moment we met." We looked at each other and smiled.

"Yes, but this is different somehow."

"I have grown stale?"

"You know that's not true." Maybe he was right. Oh how I wished Kane were still alive, nothing like this would have happened, or would it?

Heavy thunder rumbled overhead and when we arrived at the house, the rain knocked with soft fingers on the windows. The girls were waiting for us. I'd barely hung up my jacket when they bombarded me with questions.

"What did you do in Warsaw and Marrakech come on give."

I led the way into the living room and sank into one of Kane's comfortable old leather armchairs. Hamdi lowered his long frame into the other. The girls sat at our feet. I told them about Paradsky and Louise, the snake charmer, and the man who told a small story. I told them of Paul-Emile buying the fur coat and hat on the black market.

"I shall write everything down in detail."

"How long will that take?" Magda asked.

"If I start at the time I met your daddy and of course Uncle Hamdi and write about all our adventures together...."

Hamdi cleared his throat. He had a twinkle in his eyes as he gave me a roguish sidelong glance. I paused. He was right, I couldn't possibly write about *all* our adventures.

The girls looked first at Hamdi then at me. "I smell a conspiracy between the two of you," Stephanie said. She rose, sat on Hamdi's chair arm and kissed the top of his head. "Are they immoral adventures or what?"

I waved at her with an airy gesture and continued, "... and

you growing up ... it'll probably take a while."

"Your childhood, we want to hear every little detail. Dena teased us with tidbits. It isn't fair she knows more than we do." Magda punched Dena lightly on the arm, "We want to know everything, at least as much as she does."

"Yeah, all of it," Stephanie said. "Or are you showing favoritism after all these years?"

Dena and I exchanged glances. "You know I have never done that and shall never do so. Dena just happened to be handy when I felt like talking. I promise, you too shall know everything. Now tell me about the party. Who is coming?"

Magda brightened. "We invited Albert, his sister, mother and father. They live in Boca Raton. Grandma and Grandpa, Uncle Edward and Aunt Amanda, Uncle Arthur and Aunt Julia are coming too. (Arthur and Julia Morgan were my best friends and Magda's godparents.) That's it. Isn't the Christmas tree gorgeous? Aunt Julia and I bought it at Macy's."

"And who is paying for all this?"

"Oh, you don't have to worry. Uncle Arthur said this was part of my engagement present."

"Engagement ... I thought this was just a get-to-know-each-other party."

"Albert asked me to marry him and I said yes."

"Magda, I haven't even met the man yet, how can you say yes? What if I can't stand him?"

"Mommy, don't be difficult. Don't you trust my judgement? Besides, you haven't been home much lately."

"Hamdi, please bring me a brandy and a cigarette ... this is all most upsetting." I wiped at my tears.

Hamdi smiled and walked to the teak bar in a corner of the room. Magda knelt in front of me. "Mommy, don't worry. I am a big girl and love him. He's kind and he loves me."

"You could have introduced him to us before, at least then I could have grown accustomed to him slowly ... oh, this is all just too much for me, after this long trip and everything." I sobbed into my handkerchief totally out of control. The girls hugged me and tried to calm me. I couldn't stop crying. Of course I knew it was more than just Magda getting engaged. I lit my cigarette with shaking fingers and took a big gulp of brandy.

"I think your mother is tired," Hamdi said. "Come on, I'll draw a bath for you, you'll feel better." He stretched out his hand and pulled me out of the chair.

When the bath was ready, he left and gently closed the door behind him. He was right, I felt much better. I slipped on a beaded *gallabieh* and unpacked my suitcase. When I came across Donner and Amsel's picture, I immediately looked for a place to hang them. I decided across from my bed where I could see them first thing every morning would be lovely. I'd just finished unpacking, when the girls knocked and asked to come in.

They sat on my bed and of course saw the new picture on the wall. "Beautiful horses," Stephanie said, "the photograph looks old. Did you buy it?"

"No, Paradsky and Louise gave it to me. They are beautiful, aren't they? Where is Hamdi?"

"He went to talk to Monsieur Diderot," Stephanie said.

"Now?"

"It's still early. Are you feeling better Mommy?" The concern in Dena's voice made me teary-eyed again.

"Dena told us a little about Monsieur Diderot," Stephanie said. "What do you have to add? Are you in love with him?"

"Stephanie! We are old friends, that's it. He'd never been to Miami."

"Cut the crap. You spent nearly two weeks with him. Don't tell me you didn't do anything I wouldn't do."

Dena and Magda laughed. "Look who's talking," Magda said, "you have a man on each finger. You're as busy entertaining as you are playing golf. I have also noticed that the greens are surrounded with admirers when you putt. Mommy, has your statuesque daughter told you that she has been offered a modeling contract? Golf clothes to start with, I think this is the beginning of a new career."

"Golf is my game to fame, but it'll be fun. So what else is new? Look at Dena, her dressing rooms are filled with flowers. Are you ever going to get married?"

"Haven't met the right one yet."

Magda ordered pizza. When it arrived, we continued to sit on my bed and munched and chatted about every-day little things. After a while they kissed me good night and I knew they hoped I'd be more forth-coming about Paul-Emile in the morning. I wanted to bare my soul to them, for they were my best friends, but there are certain things a mother does definitely not discuss with her daughters.

Our house smelled of roses, pine needles, of cider and cinnamon and hot buttered rum. The girls had done a magnificent job, so had the caterers and we were now awaiting the arrival of the soon to be new addition to our family. Magda, with her dark brown eyes, auburn, shoulder length, curly hair and red dress looked radiant and festive.

Dena wore a long, straight, black skirt and a red Victorian-style silk and lace blouse with a high collar and long sleeves. Stephanie had poured herself into a silver lamé, sleeveless jumpsuit with scooped neckline back and front. She'd piled her black, wavy hair on top of her head and wore ruby bangle earrings that came to her shoulders.

"What are you trying to prove?" Magda said. Then she looked at me. "Hey, Mommy, where did you get that dress?"

I turned in a circle. "You like it?" The black, knee-length velveteen skirt swished round my legs.

"By God, you look stunning," Stephanie said, "love the top."

The snug, long sleeves and the fitted bodice with a halter choke neckline was made of a gossamer beaded lace. My back was bare.

"This is great. Magda, your *fiancé* will realize right from the start what kind of a family he is marrying into. Our clothes say it all."

Dena and I laughed and Hamdi gave Stephanie a kiss on the cheek. "You all look beautiful. I am so proud of you." I squeezed his hand, so glad to see him happy and content.

When the bell rang, we gathered around Hamdi while he opened the front door. Arthur and Julia Morgan and my brother Edward and his wife Amanda, their arms loaded with Christmas presents, pushed into the house.

"Is everything in order, the caterers, flowers, drinks?" Julia asked. "I want this to be perfect."

I hugged and thanked her. My parents arrived and then the long awaited guests of honor. Albert, his sister Susan, and Walter and Doris Blacksmith filled the doorway with boisterous enthusiasm. Burley, bald Walter with a beer belly, Doris matronly, beautifully coiffured, Susan, a young Doris with gleaming white teeth and a million dollar smile and Albert. He was the one I wanted to get a peek at.

Walter stuck out his pudgy hand and crushed mine in his, "So glad to meet you."

I backed up and tried to extricate my hand. It appeared as if he'd forgotten he was holding it. His gaze was fixed on Hamdi and Stephanie both tall, willowy and bronze-skinned. I tugged and after I regained my hand welcomed them to our home. Magda took Albert's arm and led him into the living room. We followed and she introduced us.

He was slender, about five ten and wore horn-rimmed glasses. I looked him up and down and bet with myself that he had skinny legs. He had a quiet, stern face and the single patch of gray that streaked his thick blond hair gave him a certain distinction. I met his slightly startled gray eyes with a friendly smile and held out my hand.

"Hello Albert, I am so glad to meet you. Magda should have brought you around ages ago, but it's never too late, is it?"

He stammered, "Um ... pleased to meet you." We shook hands.

"Magda," I said, "why don't you introduce everybody to each other. I hear the doorbell."

A beaming Paul-Emile with a huge, beautiful poinsettia in his arms stood before me. He kissed my cheeks and whispered, "I love you." I grimaced, set the plant on the entrance hall table and preceded him into the living room.

Magda was about to introduce Hamdi and Stephanie to the Blacksmiths when Stephanie interrupted and stretched out her hand. "Hi, I am Stephanie, Magda's baby sister. This is my father, Dr. Hamdi Gamal." They shook hands with the Blacksmiths."

Mr. Blacksmith ogled Stephanie from top to bottom and licked his lips. He raised his eyebrows when he spied me standing next to Paul-Emile and frowned.

Hamdi smiled. He said something to Stephanie. Her brilliant teeth glittered like pearls on a brown velvet cushion when she nodded and smiled back at him. I wondered what those two were up to. I introduced Paul-Emile to Mr. Blacksmith and left him with them.

Dena had taken Doris and Susan under her wing and when the two women exclaimed about the masks on the walls and the Louis XV furniture, Dena said, "We are a rather diverse family, as you will discover."

Hamdi busied himself preparing drinks, and Julia whispered in my ear, "Who is that handsome man?" I apologized and introduced Paul-Emile to Arthur and Julia. Julia said, "Inge attracts the most interesting men. Years ago it was Hamdi and now you, Monsieur Diderot. Of course we must remember her husband Kane. I couldn't much like him, but he certainly was good-looking."

I smiled and hugged her. "Paul-Emile and I met when I was a little girl. Then we lost touch and didn't see each other again until recently when I went on that dig in the Libyan Desert with Hamdi. What a surprise. So I invited him to join us for Christmas. Don't you just love the way life manifests itself? It's all so exciting. I wonder if Albert will ask me for Magda's hand in marriage? How shall I answer him, should I give my consent? What do you think of him?"

"So many questions." Julia laughed.

"Mercurial Inge," Paul-Emile said.

Julia gave him a perplexed look. "We haven't spoken a word to Albert, wait, here comes Magda now towing her puppy after her ... I'll tell you later."

"Don't give him a hard time, be kind." Arthur said.

Mother chatted with Albert and Magda during the buffet dinner. My father sat close and listened. Good, that would get Albert used to her German accent and her gushy personality. Hamdi and Paul-Emile were getting real chummy. I wasn't sure what to make of that. Stephanie chatted with Walter Blacksmith. I hoped she wouldn't say something offensive. I never knew what spouted out of her mouth.

My sister-in-law Amanda and my brother Edward had a lively discussion with Julia and Arthur. I decided to join Dena, Doris and Susan to see what they had to say to each other.

Doris asked about our unusual decor. I said, "Didn't Magda tell you about our travels and interests?"

"We never met your daughter before tonight," Doris said. "Of course Albert filled us in but no, we have very little information about your family."

"Well, we are even, because Magda never once mentioned you either. How long have our children been seeing each other?"

"Albert told us he met Magda in one of the classes he teaches ... I think in his economic geography class. He came home all excited saying he met someone who showed real enthusiasm for his chosen field and that he was planning to ask her out. After this he didn't have much to say, but I saw he was happier than he had ever been before. When I asked him about his girl, he said she was the greatest. I asked him to bring her home so we could meet her, but something always interfered. Magda is beautiful and we love her name."

She turned to Dena, "Is your name Boag also?"

Dena stared at her as did I. Dena said, "Of course, so is Stephanie's, we are all Boags, including Mommy."

"But, but ..." she sputtered, "didn't Stephanie say her father's name was Gamal, that dark gentleman over there with the accent." She pointed her chin.

Dena said with a serious face, "That is her father, however her last name is Boag."

I patted Doris's hand. "My dear, it may sound somewhat confusing right now. After we get better acquainted you'll find it all makes perfect sense."

Walter Blacksmith walked over, "Mrs. Gamal, I mean Inge, your youngest daughter is quite the charmer. We talked about golf a bit, my game you understand. Is your daughter a good golfer?"

"My last name is Boag ... but it doesn't really matter, one is as good as the other. Walter, do you follow the LPGA tournaments at all?"

"Why should I do that? I am of the opinion golf should be confined to the men's arena. Women just clutter our courses and interfere with our tee-times."

"Oh, you are one of those."

"Do you play Inge?"

"Now and then."

"If you were a man I'd invite you for a game sometimes...." He spread his hands.

"It's all right Walter. I expect you like to win. I certainly wouldn't want to upset you."

"Madam, I am a thirteen handicapper ... should really be an eight. I've had some bad luck lately."

I felt a hand on my shoulder and looked at Hamdi who shook his head. However, I couldn't resist. "Walter, you wouldn't stand a chance playing with me, even though I'd have to give you eight shots at least and Stephanie ... why, she'd have to give you all thirteen."

Walter turned red. Fortunately he controlled himself and took a sip of coffee. I said, "Do you need a brandy?"

"Wouldn't mind. Make it a double."

I left him to contemplate his double Napoleon and picked my

way toward Magda and Albert. I saw Julia had cornered Paul-Emile. I smiled and silently wished him good luck. I said to Magda and Albert, "Shall we go into the sitting room for a little chat?"

I sat next to Albert. "So, you met in class. I thought students were not to fraternize with the instructors, or is that old-fashioned now?"

Albert turned as red as the balls on our tree. "I asked him out to dinner," Magda said. "I learned that from you, Dena and Stephanie. You have to go after what you want. I wanted him, so I asked him. You can't live in this house all these years and not learn something about how things are done."

I clapped my hands. "Brava darling, you did the right thing." I hoped her effort was worthwhile. "And now you want to get married. Do you have anything to say to me, Mr. Albert Blacksmith?"

"Mommy!"

"Mrs. Boag, I very much want to marry Magda and I hope you will give us your blessing."

"Albert, this is very difficult for me. When Magda was born I made her a promise. And as nearly as I can recollect it went something like this: 'You shall have a happy childhood and I will be there to guide you. You are a living part of me, and I shall love you forever'. Of course I fully realize that Magda is now an adult and makes her own decisions. However, to me she will always be my little girl, and my maternal instincts are as fierce now as they were when she was small. I shall not interfere of course, but ... shall we disregard the 'but' for now ... I think you probably are quite cognizant of what I mean."

"Mother, you don't have to threaten Albert."

"You know the old cliché, forewarned is forearmed. I absolutely hate to give her up, but I also realize I must."

"Mommy, are you finished?"

"Darling, I am finished ... I am sorry." I dabbed at the corner of my eye with my handkerchief. "I wish your daddy were here to welcome Albert into our family."

She rose from the sofa. "I'll get Uncle Hamdi."

"Please." I patted Albert's hand. "Be patient, we are a close-knit family."

"Mrs. Boag, I just want to marry Magda, I don't plan to keep her from you."

"Of course. I am sorry I am making a big fuss."

When Magda returned with Hamdi she said, "I told him that you are having a hard time giving your blessing."

Hamdi stretched out his hand, "Welcome to the family Albert."

"Of course," I blew my nose noisily, "welcome Albert."

Magda kissed me. "Boy, I'm sure glad this is over." She reached for Albert's hand, "Let's tell the others."

Hamdi said after they left, "Why did you make all that fuss? This was just a formality after all."

"I know, but I am not sure I can stand a son-in-law with skinny legs."

"What makes you think he does?" Hamdi laughed.

"He strikes me that way." We left the sitting room and joined the others.

Walter boomed, "Time for pictures."

We posed, everyone said 'please' and when Walter had exhausted us with his enthusiasm, Stephanie said, "How about a little concert? Hey Mommy," she whispered, "let's knock'm dead. Let's do Offenbach's Barcarolle."

She clapped her hands, "Dena, Magda, stations, Mommy...."

Dena on her violin and Magda on the piano played the introduction. Dena nodded and I sang the role of Nicklausse. Stephanie, singing the part of Giullietta joined me and we harmonized.

When we finished the beautiful duet Hamdi applauded. The others followed suit and everybody crowded around the piano. Stephanie once more whispered to Magda and Dena and on a nod they played, and we all sang with gusto, including Hamdi, Julia and Arthur, 'I'll give you a daisy a day dear'. We'd been singing this song ever since Magda learned to play it on the piano.

The Blacksmiths sat on the sofa their amused smiles frozen on their faces. I wondered if they had second thoughts about this marriage. After our little impromptu concert Hamdi took my hand and led me to Kane's chair. Paul-Emile fiddled with his pipe. Walter Blacksmith mumbled about returning home. Stephanie, bored once more, threw a golf ball from one hand to the other. I wondered whom she'd pick to marry, probably a race car driver or something outlandish like that.

After our guests except Paul-Emile left, we all sat at the dining table and played poker for a while with just the necessary conversation. Then Magda said she'd pass. She added, "Mommy was a real pill today. I've never seen her act this way before. What on earth came over you?"

"*Pardon Mademoiselle,*" Paul-Emile said, "your mother was not going to relinquish you without at least a little fight. She has quite a bit of drama in her. She should have gone on the stage."

"You were great Mommy," Stephanie said. "Magda, that Blacksmith family is going to give you grief, mark my words. I hope the son is less of a bigot than the father."

"What about Daddy," Dena said, "he swore he'd never play golf with Mommy." She laughed.

"They live in Boca and we'll live in Gainesville," Magda said, "not exactly a hop skip and a jump. Don't worry, I can handle them."

Paul-Emile folded his hand and rose. "Inge, this day will remain a highlight of my trip to Miami. Thank you for inviting me."

I accompanied him to the door and wished him a safe trip back to the hotel. Suddenly he pulled me out on the front steps, shut the door with his foot and embraced and kissed me. Just as quickly he let me go and whispered, "I will not allow you to sleep with Hamdi. I won't allow it." He turned and strode to his car.

I slipped back into the house, ran upstairs to my bedroom and sat in front of my vanity mirror. I'd just uncapped my lipstick when I saw Hamdi standing in the doorway. "What are you going to do, Inge?"

I looked at him in the mirror and for once felt speechless. I was all of a sudden very tired. "Please tell the girls I've gone to bed, I am exhausted, all these people...."

He closed the door and I was alone.

I took a hot shower, read for a while, but couldn't fall asleep. I pulled on my negligee, slipped downstairs and poured myself a small brandy. Kane's leather chair enveloped me with cool comfort and I thought about the two men in my life. Why was everything so problematic? When I was young I had to make these tortuous decisions whether to make love or not to make love. Was I good or bad giving in to my passions? And now at forty-nine, I still had to think about this dilemma – why not just love them both? Wicked Inge, quite wicked. Suddenly I wished Paul-Emile didn't exist and besides, who was he to order me about?

I stubbed out my cigarette, took the ashtray into the kitchen and threw the butt down the disposal. After pouring myself another dram of Napoleon, I slowly walked back upstairs. I paused for a moment in front of Hamdi's door then gently pushed down the handle and entered his room. He lay in bed with his head propped on a pillow against the headboard. I removed the book lying on his chest, took off his glasses, switched off the light and climbed in next to him. I lay quietly on the edge of the bed, it had been a long time.

For some reason everyone rose early the next morning. After we'd finished breakfast, Hamdi said he'd have to make a few calls and withdrew to the sitting room. He emerged an hour later. "I've made arrangements to fly back to Cairo because they need me at one of the digs. They came across something strange and the Minister of Antiquities wants me to look over the Brits's shoulders. I have reservations for this afternoon."

"What about Christmas," Stephanie whined.

"Sorry habib (darling), this is important. By the way, Paul-Emile is coming with me, so the trip won't be boring. He said he would be by in a little while."

While he said this he looked straight at me, smiled and winked. I opened my mouth to protest then shut it again, for I had nothing to protest. Last night had bound us together once more and he hadn't been the least bit stale. For the first time I could remember he was taking control, he'd never done that before. Of course since Kane's death he'd never had a rival either, and Kane was after all Kane. Kane had controlled everything.

"Monsieur Diderot agreed to go?" Stephanie asked.

"He is as dedicated to his work as I am," Hamdi said and smiled. "Egyptology, his one and only love, he told me so himself. When I find out what's going on I'll phone you. I have to pack." He strode out of the room with a spring in his step.

"I'll help you," Stephanie said. She squeezed my shoulders, leaned over and whispered, "I'll keep him busy."

I blushed at her insinuations. She probably considered this just an amusing occurrence. She didn't feel threatened. I kissed her cheek. "Don't you love your father?"

"Of course I love him and so do you. I'm not worried. But everybody ought to have a little excitement in their life. Ever since Daddy Kane died you've been moping. Now you have color in your cheeks again. You are almost back from mourning and I think you have Monsieur Diderot to thank for that. So I don't mind helping with a little hanky panky."

Hanky panky, if she only knew what a prude her mother had become. She stood tall and lithe in front of me and placed her hands on my shoulders. "Daddy Kane was the most exciting man I've ever known." Her eyes brimmed with tears. "I have doubts I'll ever find a man like him."

We held each other, commiserating at our loss and pain. She pushed me away and gave a timid little smile. "Wow, I'm glad I got that off my chest. Don't worry, Hamdi loves you, he'll forgive you anything." She was already backing out of the room, slammed the door and was gone.

I looked after her. She'd adored Kane and he her. Stephanie, Stephanie, what would have happened if he hadn't died? I squared my drooping shoulders and tried to think of something pleasant, but nothing came to mind.

When I had to think or was upset I did one of two things, I played the piano like a demon or worked in the garden like a demon, no weed was safe from me during one of my moods. I opted for the garden. I didn't find much to do. I watered a little, clipped a few dry branches and almost screamed when someone tapped me on the shoulder.

"Your Hamdi has it all planned," Paul-Emile said. "You must have given him encouragement. Did you sleep with him?"

"That, Monsieur, is none of your business."

"I will not allow my mistress to have a lover. You are either mine or we must part. I will not tolerate your cheating." He'd clasped both my arms and shook me. "You knew me before you knew him. Did he ever protect you from danger of any kind? Did he risk his life for you? Did he go hungry and sleepless for you? What do you have to say to this, Madame?"

I brushed his hands off my arms and stepped away from him. "You did not risk your life for me. When were you ever really in danger? You have no claim on me and calling me your mistress makes me laugh." I chuckled. "Mistress indeed. Paul-Emile you've become a pompous *âne*."

"Must I prove myself to you? What do you want me to do?"

I turned on the hose nozzle and watered my newly planted tubabuia. He watched the spray of water hit the mulch. I said, "I've discovered over the years that the easiest thing about saying goodbye always is to simply go. So go now and forget about me."

He shook his head as if waking from a dream and studied me with a wrinkled brow. "Forget about you, when I just found you? I will start divorce proceedings."

"Divorce would be pointless since I don't plan to marry again. I already told you that."

"Inge, you cannot play with me this way."

"I am not playing. I never encouraged you. Besides, you are trying to dominate me and I won't allow it." I looked at him pensively and wondered, had his war experiences left him with a diminished sense of self esteem after all. Where was his pride?

He threw up his hands and stalked out of the garden. I had to smile, Frenchmen and their arrogance. Paul-Emile started to annoy me.

We saw them off at the airport. I was almost glad to see them go. Men could so complicate one's life. When Paul-Emile embraced me he stuck something down the back of my dress. I nearly laughed, kissed his cheek and stepped back. Hamdi too embraced me, then with deliberate solemnity pulled my amber bug beads out of his pocket and placed them around his neck.

Stephanie clapped. "Look Mommy, he still wears your bugs after all these years." She turned to Paul-Emile, "It's their personal signal, ever since I can remember, that he will love her forever. Once she almost kept them, just for a minute or two. We all screamed at her to give it back and she did."

Paul-Emile watched with a thin smile as the girls kissed Hamdi and told him they loved him. After they shook Paul-Emile's hand, Hamdi said, "I guess we better get going, old man."

I felt a little bit sorry for Paul-Emile. But Hamdi was coming out of his shell and seemed to have finally overcome Kane's lifelong domination of him. He had taken control of his destiny. I found that attractive. We waved, and they were gone.

"Mommy," Dena said, "shall I retrieve Monsieur Diderot's note out of your dress?" I blushed as she fished for the note. "Aha, got it. Shall I read it to you?" She waved the envelope in front me.

Stephanie grabbed it, "Here, let me see it." She sniffed, "Pipe tobacco, quite pleasant. I've never met a man who smoked a pipe. Shall I open it?"

Magda tore it out of Stephanie's fingers and gave it to me. "You are so juvenile at times, will you ever grow up?"

"Come on," I said, "we are free, no responsibilities. I love you more than words can express and to celebrate I'll treat you to dinner and drinks at...."

"Joe's," they screeched. We linked arms and headed for the

exit.

After the girls said good-night and I had done my evening toilette, I made myself comfortable in the big golden four-poster and slit Paul-Emile's envelope open with my ivory letter opener. I pulled out the small piece of paper. It read: Expect you Easter Sunday, Oriental Hotel, Bangkok. PE. I mused at his terse note and shook my head wondering how I could discourage his adoration.

Someone knocked on the door. Stephanie peeked in, behind her stood Magda and Dena. "May we come in?"

Smiling, I waved them in. "So what does the note say?" Stephanie said. They sat on the bed and waited.

"Darlings, you are too nosy for your own good. So you don't have to snoop while I am out, I am informing you that I ate the note. If I get indigestion it's all because you can't mind your own business. You get my drift?"

"You're always inquisitive about what we are up to," Magda said, "so why can't we do the same?"

"Because you are my children and I am your mother, that's why."

"You want to play poker?" Dena asked.

I pulled on my robe and followed them downstairs. After Christmas Magda returned to Gainesville, Dena prepared for her upcoming concert tour and Stephanie played her first golf tournament of the season. After Dena left, I had the house to myself and wondered what I would do until Easter. I called Stephanie and asked if I could follow her for a while. She was happy to have me share her triumphs and defeats.

I called Hamdi twice but couldn't reach him. Of course I knew, when he burrowed around in the field he didn't think about anything other than what lay under the sand. Not a word from Paul Emile. I felt restless and left Stephanie to her own devices.

When I returned home I bought myself a computer. My brother initiated me into its use and then I sat down to write my story. Before I knew it, I'd filled page after page. Easter neared and I knew I was definitely not going to Bangkok.

Chapter Seventeen

A few days later Hamdi called from Cairo. "Habib, Paul-Emile had an accident. He asked for you. Can you come?"

I sat down. The veil shrouding my senses for the past four years suddenly disappeared, and I heard Kane shout for help.

"Habib, are you there?"

No, Hamdi would never do such a thing. They had been boyhood friends – lovers. No, Hamdi wouldn't. What a horrible thought, go away, please go away. I tried to shut off my brain.

"Hamdi?"

"Paul-Emile broke both ankles, it's nothing much. But since he asked for you, I thought I better tell you."

" Where did he fall?"

"At Tuna El-Gebel, in the catacombs."

My mind flashed back to when Kane, Hamdi and I visited them many years ago. "Inge? answer me."

"Where is he now?"

"In Minya with Uncle Tewfik." He laughed. "The twins are taking good care of him, don't worry. Are you coming? I certainly would love to see you."

"I'll be there as soon as I can make arrangements."

After we'd hung up I called Uncle Tewfik in Minya. In Egypt many of the telephones have this peculiar double burr when there is an overseas call. Uncle Tewfik picked up on the third burr. I identified myself. It had been a good four and a half years since I last spoke to him, although I did write the occasional letter.

Uncle Tewfik said he was happy to hear my voice. Not to worry, the Frenchman had only broken both ankles when he fell into a crevice. Oh my God – into a crevice.

"Where is the Frenchman now?"

"Sitting in a wheelchair in our spare bedroom. My twins are taking good care of him. He is special to you?"

"He is a childhood friend. We just recently reconnected. Is it possible to speak to him?"

"Hold on, I'll get him."

"Inge." Paul-Emile cleared his throat. "Hamdi's Uncle Tewfik is a splendid man with the most beautiful companions and sweet little children. I am in good hands. Sorry to bother you, but it would be nice if you could hold my hand while I recuperate."

"Was it an accident?"

"Probably."

"What does that mean?"

"Nothing. Are you coming?"

"I'll be there." I hung up before he could say anything else. Hamdi wouldn't – no never – he was gentle, I loved and trusted him. Paul-Emile fell and was seriously injured, Kane fell to his death – no, Hamdi had nothing to do with that. I grappled with my shadowy suspicions all the way to Cairo.

Hamdi awaited me at the airport. He smiled when he saw me, pulled me into his arms and kissed my cheeks. If he noticed that I didn't respond, he gave no hint. He hefted my suitcase and led the way to the exit.

"I'll get the car."

"I'll walk with you. I need to stretch my legs."

When I sat next to him, he said, "Inge, habibi, the love of my life, you are angry. Why are you angry with me?"

I laid my hand lightly over his on the steering wheel. "I am not angry, just confused. What happened?"

"Are you blaming me for his accident?"

"What happened?"

"He wanted to visit the catacombs, so I took him to Hermopolis then to Tuna El-Gebel."

"I am aware of all that."

"Paul-Emile, you probably realize, is an inquisitive person.

He wanted to examine everything. I warned him of hidden passages and pits ... to stay in the main gallery. He peered into a side passage leading off the main gallery and directed his flashlight along the aisle partially blocked by fallen rocks. Without saying a word he scrambled over the rubble. I followed him, warning to be careful.

"He shone his flashlight at the ceiling. It looked okay. Then he swung it in a circle and gasped. The light wavered, he took several steps backward, gave a shout and disappeared. I called his name and asked him if he was all right. He groaned and said he thought his ankles were broken. I told him I'd go for help."

"He saw something that spooked him."

Hamdi gave me a sidelong glance, then pressed his thin lips together and stared straight ahead.

"You saw it too? What did you see?"

"Nothing. I didn't see anything." He gave me an annoyed look. "When I reached the front entrance, I sent the guide to Mallawi to bring a stretcher and more help. We had a hard time getting Paul-Emile out of the crevasse ... he'll be okay ... you don't have to worry."

I crossed my arms over my chest, leaned forward and looked at him. "You may as well tell me, because if you don't, Paul-Emile surley will."

"I doubt it."

I couldn't get another word out of him. He took me to his beautiful old house near the Giza pyramids.

"I prepared your room, hope you like it."

I admired the sparsely furnished rectangular entrance hall with marble floors. Sconces on the walls illuminated the high beamed ceiling encircled with a crown molding hand-painted with beautiful Arabic calligraphy. Nothing much had changed here since I first visited this house some ten years earlier.

The living room, with its twenty-foot domed ceiling and skylight in its middle, was crowded with antique furniture, paintings, books and artifacts. I sat on the Louis XV sofa, upholstered in silvery silk with tiny gold specks, and thought briefly of Hamdi's wife who died in childbirth and left Hamdi this house in her will.

"The whole house has electricity now, you want to see?"

I followed Hamdi through a maze of rooms, then up a staircase tiled with beautiful Islamic designs. On the roof a bar, tables and chairs had been set up. Below us twinkled the lights of Giza and Cairo and to our left loomed the mighty pyramid of Cheops.

"So where do you want me to sleep, in your *haramlik*? Did you wire the women's rooms too?"

"Everything. You want to see?"

"Why not." We walked downstairs to the second floor and into a charming airy room with cool marble floors and two large *mashrabeya* windows, one overlooked the courtyard, the other the street.

He opened one of the bedroom doors and led me inside. "I decorated this room just for you, you like it?"

My mouth fell open when I saw the mirrored walls, the golden four poster bed, the chandeliers on either side, and the black and gold decor of the curtains and the bedspread. I turned and stared at Hamdi who smiled.

"You recognize it?"

"Of course I recognize the decor. What is the idea?"

"We were happy in that room. I had visions...."

"Hamdi, that was twenty-seven years ago." I embraced him. "Darling, you are such a sentimentalist and full of love, and I ... I have all these horrible suspicious thoughts about you. I don't know what comes over me sometimes."

"Inge, habibi, I love you so much. My heart aches when I see you with that man."

That instance I knew I had to tell him what dwelled on my mind. I had to give him an opportunity to defend himself.

"Come, let me show you the other harem rooms. They are for the girls, each one is decorated in her favorite color."

He loved us, he was incapable of being mean. We returned to the living room. I poured myself a small brandy, sat on one of the gold chairs and lit a cigarette.

"Hamdi, what I am about to say may upset you, but if I don't clear the air I will always have doubts. Please forgive me."

He sat opposite me and waited.

"I am upset about Paul-Emile. What I don't understand is that you allowed him to lead the way. You knew that could be dangerous. It brings back strong memories."

"Are you talking about Kane?"

"Yes."

"What does his death have to do with Paul-Emile's fall? Inge, you were present ... you hold me responsible for Kane's death?" He snatched my ivory cigarette holder from between my fingers, stubbed out the cigarette, knelt in front of me, placed his hands on the arms of my chair and scrutinized me. His face was stern, his eyes hard. I drew away from him, never having seen him this fierce.

All of a sudden his expression changed, the stern lines vanished and a half smile returned to his lips. "I have loved you as no man ever did, not even Kane, and as no man ever will. If you like you can blame me and I'll shift the blame to my ancestors."

I couldn't help but laugh. "To Sennofer that ancient rascal?"

Hamdi didn't laugh. He removed my amber necklace from around his neck and let each bead slip slowly through his fingers. A faint smile crossed his lips. "I've fingered each bead a thousand times and have identified the insects. Do you want to hear what they are?"

I winced and tried to bite back tears. What had I done?

"No, it doesn't matter." He held out the amber and gold necklace, "Take it ... the time has come for us to part. You don't trust me and if you don't trust me you can't love me. For the children's sake, I hope we can be civil to each other." He sank onto the settee, slumped forward and cradled his head in his hands.

When I had myself under control I said, "Hamdi, I don't want my necklace back. I want more than civility between us. I need you and rely upon you. But you don't seem to see me as a whole person, a person with a history that started way before we met. Paul-Emile was an important factor in my life. Now that I found him again, an old affection for him has resurfaced."

I sat next to him on the settee and hugged him. "I think when you married you were unconsciously punishing me, because you knew I loved Kane more than I did you. You knew that deep in your heart."

He nodded slowly.

"You pledged your undying devotion, yet you also physically removed yourself from that pledge. I was angry at first, but after a while, in all honesty, I was relieved.

"Your marriage to Kamala signified an end to the way I felt about you, and I slowly weaned my heart away from you. Darling, Hamdi, I do love you. I told Paul-Emile that you are my comfort and I couldn't imagine life without you. But if that must be...."

His hand was firm and steady when he touched mine. And when he spoke, his voice calmed me and I saw honesty in his eyes. I knew now that he understood me, knew of my doubts and fears and was sincere in his sympathy.

"I can tell you are attracted to him ... Inge, I won't share you with Paul-Emile."

"I can't figure it out myself. All I am aware of is, that when I first recognized him and we'd talked, I was suddenly very young again and I liked that. I could tell, for him too the years fell away. We had experienced a tremendous trauma together and this bonded us and still does. Here was someone who knew me when I was a child.

"I'd almost forgotten how precocious and difficult I was and how much my mother must have suffered when she couldn't find me. I never thought much about this. Later, when I met Kane ... love at first sight, darling, everlasting, an unknown up to that point, so involuntary, forbidden, exciting.... When he declared his love for me, I was delirious with joy, but also suspicious. Why did he love me? Up to that point I'd always fought everything and was at odds with authority, teachers, parents. I cloaked myself in an aloofness that kept most people at a distance. If I kept my defenses up I wouldn't get hurt was my motto.

"When Kane pursued me and asked me to marry him, I suddenly deflated like a balloon. Somebody loved me. Kane loved me. I also soon realized he had been astute enough to recognize my insecurity and took advantage of the vulnerability that lurked underneath my steely exterior. But to me all that mattered was that somebody loved me.

"Paul-Emile's desertion became a thing of the past and I had pushed him out of my mind. I'd found my new love. Darling Hamdi, can you understand now that the Inge who married Kane, and the wanton Inge who allowed you to love her, is not the same Inge of today? After all these years I've finally discovered who I truly am. I am strong now and will live and love as I see fit. If you can't accept this we must say goodbye."

He nodded, kissed my cheek and said with a faint smile. "Sometimes you remind me of the heroine in a stormy romance, and other times I see smoke streaming from your eyes as if your impulses overwhelm you with their power."

I laughed. "My mother had stronger words ... she saw murder. I think I have mellowed over the years, what do you think?"

"Don't mellow too much, I wouldn't know what to do with a pliable Inge." He smiled his regal smile and said almost sadly, "I think I was born to live and dig in the sand and be alone. You want to go to the Mena House now?"

His brown eyes twinkled. I felt as if I was standing at the edge of a high precipice and a strong gale was sweeping me clean of fears and doubts, freeing me from the blunders and follies of my past. I smiled. "Maybe I'll try out your new bed after all."

Chapter Eighteen

The next day Hamdi and I drove to Minya. We made small talk but didn't touch on the person I knew lingered on his mind as well as mine. After a while he asked, "When did you see each other last?"

"I was fourteen and had murder in my heart." I laughed. "Not really. Who knows what would have happened if I'd gotten a hold of our Luger and Paul-Emile at the same time?"

"You had a Luger?"

"We, hm, found it." I wondered what had happened to that gun, I must ask Paul-Emile. I hurried on with my story. "I lived with the Diderots four and a half years, then they sent me back to my parents. That nearly blew my mind ... from luxury to ... well, I can't exactly say poverty, because that would be incorrect. But we certainly had no standing in the community and no money to spare.

"Our apartment building in Hannover had been declared unsafe so we had to move. My parents were considered displaced persons in the village of about three hundred people who'd lived there forever. Mother milked cows and hoed weeds in the fields of the farmer in whose house we lived. Father drove the tractor and plowed and did whatever one does with a tractor. Later they built themselves a kiosk and sold newspapers and magazines.

"Edward was a caring little brother and helped me adjust to my new surroundings. He asked a lot of questions, and I told him things I had never talked about before to anyone. I figured after a while he wouldn't think about it anymore."

"How old was he?"

"Eight. He was probably my life saver. He listened without prejudice or criticism, completely nonjudgmental. I'd acquired a bit of an accent in France and the kids in the village taunted me and gave me a hard time at first. After a while of course they got used to me.

"My Aunt Gretchen, you've heard me talk about her before, enrolled me immediately in a private school three kilometers from our village. I was their star pupil when it came to French lessons.

"In a way I fit in quite nicely thanks to living with the Diderots. They had insisted on refining my manners and behavior, and had managed to teach me to be ladylike. But now I rebelled. I felt like kicking everyone in the shin. I harbored much anger, and my impulsive, jubilant and expressive nature frequently took over. I frequently ran into trouble with my teachers and people in authority in general.

"Unfortunately for me, most of the students at that school had more money than I did. That really irked me, because living with the Diderots the matter of money never arose. But here money was absolutely crucial to gain any sort of status. The teachers knew who could bring them baskets filled with sausage, fresh butter, fruit and vegetables and who could not. Favoritism ... you wouldn't believe the bowing and scraping."

"You never, all these years we've known each other, talked about your childhood."

"You never asked." I tapped his arm lightly. "I was really quite unhappy at the school. I did make friends with two girls from my village who attended the same school. We became friends. I always thought of myself more cosmopolitan. When I asked them if they'd ever kissed a boy, they just shook their heads."

"And you had."

"Of course. I'd been a gay Parisienne, ready and dying for more than a kiss."

"He kissed you?"

"Just twice, just little kisses. Of course I didn't have to reveal that to them. I made a big deal out of it and described how delicious it felt. They envied me and sighed. They envied me even more when my parents decided to emigrate to Canada."

"Weren't you tired of moving, always starting anew?"

"Darling, you know the German expression 'Wanderlust'. We are born eternal searchers. Even when we are grown we try to shake off the fetters of life. Although I haven't told you the whole story, I call my escapade with Paul-Emile youthful courage, for I had no thought of death even though I had encountered it many times."

"When will I hear about these youthful escapades?"

"When we are old and decrepit and have nothing else to talk about." I kissed his cheek and he smiled. He never pushed for more than I was willing to give. "Hamdi darling, this is all so boring I don't really want to talk about this anymore. What did you find at Amarna?"

Uncle Tewfik's gray hair shocked me when we arrived in Minya. He was in his early seventies, so this was a natural phenomenon. His protégées, the twins, now in their mid-thirties, surrounded by five beautiful, rambunctious children, greeted us with hugs and kisses and happy chatter. Uncle Tewfik introduced each of his children. They stretched out their hands and said, "How do you do."

I hugged them and repeated their names.

"The twins wanted them to be just like your daughters," Uncle Tewfik said, "so of course that included teaching them English. They are quite good at it, if I may say so. They are a little shy, wait until tomorrow."

I gave the tittering twins another hug. Paul-Emile sat in a wheelchair with both legs in a cast up to his knees. I leaned over and gave him a kiss on each cheek, while Hamdi greeted him with a slight inclination of his supple figure and a cool smile.

The children danced around Hamdi when he returned to his car to retrieve a big box of chocolates. Paul-Emile looked after Hamdi with a frown on his face. Amused at the men's antics I said to Uncle Tewfik, "This looks like a happy house. Do you ever get a rest?"

"I built myself a room you Americans call a den. Nobody is allowed to disturb me there. Fortunately they are respectful of most of my wishes. I love them, and when you love your children they are easily forgiven for their trespasses."

"I agree."

One of the twins raised my arm and held it against hers. We laughed and I thought back to our first meeting when we compared skins, mine so white and theirs so black.

They'd prepared a feast which we topped off with Hamdi's delicious pralines. Paul-Emile patted his stomach and complained about too much good care.

"I am giving the children French lessons. Their accents are better than mine."

The children objected, but I knew Egyptians had a natural ear for languages and believed him. Hamdi had made reservations for us at the Nefertiti Hotel. When we readied to leave, Paul-Emile rolled his wheelchair next to me and pinched my behind. I jumped and felt like punching him in the nose.

He hissed, "Are you?"

I tweaked his nose and stuck out my chin, "That's for me to know and you not to find out. Sweet dreams."

"What kind of an answer is that? You trying to make me angry?"

"I love it when you get angry, but unfortunately you are unwell right now. Save your anger for another time."

When I sat in Hamdi's Rover, I waved, blew him a kiss and smiled.

"You love him, I can see you love him."

"No you can't. You are talking yourself into something that you don't know anything about. Don't waste your time on guessing games. I expect a martini from you tonight, hope you brought the fixings."

"Your room or mine?"

"In the lobby."

"Habibi, tell me about you and Paul-Emile, so I may understand."

Yes, perhaps this was the time. "All right, my room, but..."

I waved a finger at him, "you better behave yourself." We linked arms and walked to my room.

He fixed us a drink, made himself comfortable on the bed, while I sat on a chair and told him an abbreviated version about when I was a little girl.

When I finished, I yawned. "What do you think now?"

"Did you ever tell Kane?"

"No, he never asked."

Hamdi nodded. "Why did you love Kane?"

"Because he loved me. He didn't want to love me, but he couldn't help himself."

Hamdi chuckled softly. "Kane told me. He was quite shocked by his weakness."

When I yawned again he said, "Are you ready for bed?" He rose to go.

"Please stay until I'm asleep."

I took a shower, climbed into bed, snuggled into my pillow and smiled.

"What are you smiling about?"

"You sitting next to my bed gives me a wonderful sense of comfort."

I rose early the next morning and walked across the street to the mist shrouded Nile. No wind, no sound broke the solitude, not an object moved. After sunrise, a rift in the mist revealed the wonderful blue sky. I felt a hand on my shoulder and turned. Hamdi handed me a cup of steaming coffee that tasted like hot chocolate. I had yet to find out exactly how the Egyptians managed this flavor, was it cardamom and sweet condensed milk? I sipped slowly, gazed across the river and remembered my first trip to Minya.

Hamdi, as if reading my mind said, "You have come in a circle since Kane found you."

"I wonder what will happen next."

We returned to the hotel and sat down to breakfast. Hamdi said after he'd taken a of sip of coffee, "I contacted Paul-Emile's wife."

"What did you do that for? Are you trying to make trouble?" He squeezed a few drops of lime onto his *fool* (mashed fava beans), added a teaspoon of cumin, a dash of salt, pepper and oil and mixed it slowly. "Wouldn't you want to be notified if your husband had an accident?"

I stuck my fork in his fool and tasted. "Perfect, fix some for me too please. Well, of course, but his situation is different. They aren't close."

"She sounded very concerned."

"She did?" I nibbled on the Vienna sausage.

"She's coming to pick him up."

My head shot up. "You are kidding." I looked with distaste at the Vienna sausage on my fork. "Why can't they serve real breakfast sausage?" I stuck the last of the sausage in my mouth and chewed. "Paul-Emile said she didn't care what happened to him."

"How do you know he's telling the truth?"

"You are still jealous."

"Of course I'm jealous. He's trying to steal you away from me, so I have to do everything in my power to prevent that."

I walked to the buffet. After I'd helped myself and filled a plate with the delicious Ismailia melon for Hamdi, I returned to the table.

"Well, what do you have to say?" Hamdi looked at me scowling, then forked a piece of his melon, chewed and waited.

"Say about what?"

"Don't play dumb."

I bowed my head, slowly cut the melon into bite-size pieces and didn't respond.

He sighed. "She's coming on Friday."

"Two days from now."

"I promised to meet her at the airport."

"Did you tell Paul-Emile?"

"I thought we would surprise him." He smiled. How about you, will you play along? Then you will be sure if he told you the truth."

"That's dirty dealing." I popped another piece of melon into my mouth.

He shrugged, "All is fair in this game we call love."

"I have to think about that."

Afterward we drove to Uncle Tewfik's house. The blue sky had disappeared and a light wind rustled the leaves in the garden. Paul-Emile sat in his wheelchair under a huge, blooming jacaranda tree in a field of blue, bell-like flowers and was surrounded by brown children who recited the numbers in French.

"*Un, deux, trois*," they shouted.

I kissed his cheek. Suddenly a gust of wind blew the flowers across the sparse grass. The children scrambled after them and tried to catch them as they floated in the air. Uncle Tewfik greeted us then looked at the sky.

"I think we are in for a blow."

The sky grew browner and the sun had almost disappeared. The twins collected the children who ran before them into the house and Hamdi pushed Paul-Emile onto the veranda. The fern-like, feathery leaves of the jacaranda tree fluttered like hummingbird wings. A flower shower followed. We shut the door and watched and waited.

As the sea in a great hurricane rages against the land, so now the desert raged into Minya. Every palm, every tree, every rill and every house became the victim of its wrath. Along the tunnel of mimosa trees lining the street it went like a foaming tide through the town and roared out again into the desert sea. The wind shifted and it returned eddying sand at the corner of buildings, beating at our doors and windows while we watched with awe at its ferocity.

I sat with the three men for a while and listened to the howling wind, then excused myself and walked into the kitchen. The twins and their children sat at a table nibbling on dates and drawing pictures. I studied each drawing, tousled their hair and praised them. One of the twins handed me an envelope. Curious, I opened it and found a note written in Arabic. I pondered the girl thoughtfully.

"*Min* (from) Samia?"

She nodded. I thanked her and tucked the envelope into my trouser pocket. I couldn't read Arabic and decided to wait until I saw Dena or Stephanie, who could read it to me. A few days, weeks, didn't really matter, it had already been four and a half years since Samia's death. I wondered what Samia had to tell me.

My heart beat faster – what if she accused Hamdi? I pulled the note out of my pocket again, unfolded it and studied the beautiful script. If I hadn't come to Minya, I would probably never have received the note.

A tan colored sky still loomed overhead and the air smelled dusty, but the wind had settled into a dead calm. I decided to go for a walk and soon reached the Nile. A small beach jutted out into the muddy water. Tall, elegant date palms sprouted like giant soldiers out of the sand. Squealing children already splashed in the shallow water. One woman clanged aluminum cook pots against the rocks while she scrubbed them, and another slapped clothes across a large stone, causing sudsy bubbles to billow into the air.

I sat on a small sandy rise and watched the scene. Samia had been Stephanie's nanny and Hamdi's distant cousin. Had she planned mischief with this note? Why had she written it in Arabic and not in English? She knew I'd need a translator. What if she accused Hamdi? No, she'd loved Hamdi. What else could it be? An apology?

All of a sudden babbling, brown little children surrounded me. I never came to Egypt without a treat in my tote-bag. Their chatter and laughter escalated when I withdrew small packets of M&Ms. They danced on their naked feet, showed their white teeth and opened their mouth wide to pop in another of the coveted chocolate candies.

They became bold and shouted, "*Aktar, aktar*, more, more," pushed at each other and tried to peek into my bag.

I showed them the empty paper bag, "*Halas, halas*, finished, *yalla*, go away."

They raced toward the water and with great strides, exuberant screams and leaps, the boys jumped back into the water.

I rose, brushed the sand off my slacks and walked slowly back to Uncle Tewfik's house.

Dawn the next morning came like a tired pilgrim after the *hadj*, dark, pale and faint. Fog lay like a sodden blanket thick and impenetrable and the eaves and trees dripped with moisture. We played with the children waiting for the fog to lift. Later Uncle Tewfik and Hamdi lifted Paul-Emile into the Rover and we said good-bye.

We installed Paul-Emile at the Nile Hilton. I took an adjoining room. Hamdi understood, or said he did, the need for me to be close, for Paul-Emile was unable to fend for himself. After Hamdi left, I helped Paul-Emile unpack his toiletries and his suitcase. I retrieved a bottle of cognac from my suitcase, poured us each a shot and lit a cigarette.

"What happened?"

"Carelessness," he said, "I didn't watch where I was going. All of a sudden, bam, the ground disappeared."

I watched him closely. "What spooked you?"

He turned red. "What are you talking about?" He fumbled for his pipe in his *gallabieh* pocket and stuck it between his teeth.

"Hamdi saw something."

"Did he tell you that?"

"He won't say. Are you going to tell me?"

He sighed, "Simple carelessness. I am at your mercy, you can do anything you want with me."

I cracked my lips in a faint smile. "See you." I waved and returned to my room.

Chapter Nineteen

Paul-Emile called me on the phone a couple of hours later and begged me to keep him company. I laid aside my notebook and went to his room. He'd propped himself against the headboard. "Here I lie, lucky to be alive, and you have no sympathy for me. A mistress should be sympathetic."

"Well, my dear, as you recall, I told you already I am not your mistress and don't intend to be. Our rendezvous turned into a pleasant interlude. You are a charming man Paul-Emile."

He patted the sofa next to him. "At least allow me to hold your hand like you did when you were a child."

I pulled a chair next to the sofa and sat down. "I keep thinking about your wife. Poor woman, she has my pity."

"You seem to be fixated on my wife. I can live without her. Why are you so cold toward me? I thought when we met, at last here is someone who'll understand me. Inge loved me once, she'll love me again. But now, as I lie here, I have recognized that one can't lock up the wind. You'll always be mercurial, you are not made to stay with anyone."

"That's not true. What do you know about me really? I told you about some of my escapades when I was young. Sometimes though, adventures get tedious as a daily faire. What I didn't tell you about was my loneliness. On Sundays I used to stand on the sidewalk and watch families leave the church. They held hands, they laughed, hugged and chatted. I wanted to be part of them. Alas, I was only an invisible onlooker. Alone, empty nights ... forget it, it is long past. I had Kane and now I have Hamdi."

A spasm of irritation crossed his face. "Now you have no fears?"

"No, I haven't any fears left."

Paul-Emile smiled. There seemed tenderness, irony and a shadow of sadness in his smile. "Love isn't always carefree is it?"

"I've discovered since we met that it is smart not to look back too much, one can't return to the past. It's like falling off a cliff, or like a poppy field's destruction after a hailstorm, nothing remains constant."

"Why don't you marry Hamdi if you are so much in love with him?" Paul-Emile broke into an ironical laugh. "You know, in a way I feel sorry for you."

"For me? I am perfectly happy. Hamdi too is perfectly happy as long as he knows I love him. We don't need to marry. Why don't you divorce your wife and find a good woman? Not me ... you'd have a heart attack every day if you lived with me. I am unpredictable, fond of doing my own thing.

"Tell me about your wife. You said she was haughty ... is she big, small, thin, fat; is she a brunette, a blond, a redhead; did you ever love her?"

"She's big and fat and a brunette. No, I never loved her ... I'll take that back. At first I did because she mothered me and felt sorry for me. When she became pregnant, she hated her size and complained constantly. After that we just grew apart. I really don't want to talk about her. She is immaterial ... we have nothing in common except a son."

"Have you always been faithful?"

"Always ... unfortunately."

"Only the dead are always faithful."

He stared at me. "The dead...."

"Yes, they are the only ones who have that capability."

He laughed. "Perhaps you are right."

Restless, I walked across the room a couple of times then sat on a chair by the window.

"You know," he said, "I've always admired your walk, even as a little girl, you looked as if you had a basket of flowers on your head, except when you ran, you ran like a boy. I am glad we are together now. Ever since we met again, surprisingly the time we were apart vanished like an early morning fog."

"It did? I am glad. Not for me. When your parents sent me back to mine, I waited for you to come to me. When two years passed and you didn't come, call, or write, and when I wasn't good enough for the farmer's son downstairs, I began to have doubts about myself, my worthiness. I also perceived that my parents weren't particularly fond of me. Sure I was head-strong and at times difficult, but I was at a difficult age.

"From then on I dressed myself in an iron armor and told myself, who needs them? I can stand on my own two feet. And on the subject of men ... I knew they just wanted one thing, namely to satisfy themselves. Consequently I became aloof, hard to approach and suspicious. That made me even more lonely. Therefore, since it suits my mood, I consider myself a product of your actions. It all started with you because I loved and trusted you."

"You hold all this against me because I didn't succumb to your charms ... or better yet, your planned seduction?"

"You didn't love me any longer, tell the truth."

"Damn, I hate lying here totally helpless and having to listen to your blabbering." He took a deep breath and let it out slowly. "Okay, I shall tell you the absolute truth. I loved you, but you overwhelmed me with your needs. I wasn't ready to take on any responsibilities. I wanted to play, and going away to school allowed me to be a young boy again, with my parents looking out for my interests. Even though I felt deep affection for you, I also secretly wished you had returned to your parents when first given the opportunity.

"I immersed myself in my studies, made friends, socialized and tried not to think about the past. When my parents caught us together and took me to Switzerland and sent you to Germany, I sighed with relief and felt free at last. But I did love you, only not the way you wanted me to love you. I did really send you postcards. It made me feel less guilty for deserting you."

I nodded. "So you do have a conscience, admirable ... then

you met little Inge again. And you decided to take advantage and introduce a little excitement into your climacteric years ... a little diversion from a routine that has grown stale over the years." I laughed. "You tried to use me ... again ... well, come to think of it, I guess I used you too."

I clapped. "Bravo Paul-Emile, we deserve each other." I frowned, "It almost cost me my relationship with Hamdi. That's unforgivable. But my dear, I will be honest and admit I enjoyed this intermezzo. You plucked me from my doldrums after Kane's death. Now what do you want to do? Do you want to get married?" I asked with a straight face.

He gulped, "I ... I ... can we just go on as before? Perhaps eventually you'll discover that you still love me after all and we'll consummate our relationship."

"Don't bet on it. I see you've withdrawn your marriage offer."

"Are you angry?"

"My dear, I'm not a bit vindictive. It's not part of my nature. Tell me truthfully though, what would your wife say if she found out you were having an affair?"

"I told you, she doesn't care."

"Does she have more money than you do?"

He raised an eyebrow and grimaced. "Lots more. What do you have in mind?"

"Archaeologists don't make much money, at least that's what Hamdi always told me. Does she hold your purse strings as well as Camille's?"

"That, my little, nosy Inge, is none of your business. Hand me those crutches please."

I handed him the crutches. I had hit a sore spot and smiled. "Paul-Emile, you are a fraud, but a loveable fraud." I kissed his cheek and was just straightening out when someone knocked. I opened the door to Hamdi.

"Am I interrupting anything?"

Paul-Emile chuckled, "Inge is using me like a cleansing

machine, and when she is through with me she won't remember me for another thirty years."

Hamdi smiled. "Have you told him about Kane and me?"

"Darling, Kane and you are none of his business, although I did ask him if he'd ever been with a man. That raised the good Paul-Emile's eyebrows." I laughed.

Hamdi smiled and kissed my hand.

"I bought a computer and am writing my memoirs. What do you think of that?"

Paul-Emile chuckled. "Our Inge is planning mischief. What do you think, Hamdi?"

"Our Inge...." Hamdi fingered the amber beads at his neck. "I've arranged for dinner to be served in your suite. Inge and I will keep you company, after that unfortunately we'll have to leave. I promised Kane's uncle we'd stop by for a visit."

"Of course, another of Inge's Cairo connection." Paul-Emile said.

After dinner was served, I took a sip of the white wine. "Have you ever looked at the face of a living ibis or a baboon? I mean, really examined them?"

The men looked at me and smiled as I continued. "The ancient Egyptians thought that the grave facial expressions of these creatures suggested thoughtfulness. Do you think they look thoughtful? Well, I guess it doesn't matter what you or I think. What does count is what the Egyptians thought. Of course that brings us to Toth, the god of learning and wisdom, the inventor of writing, the vizier and official scribe of the afterworld."

"And Toth was symbolized sometimes as an ibis and sometimes as a baboon." Paul-Emile said.

"Ah, to have been an ibis or a baboon, or a crocodile or a cat. These darlings led pampered lives of luxury in the temples while they were alive and when they died, they were honored by mummification. This was not enough though. The Egyptians built catacombs for these darling departed as well. I remember marveling at all the crowded galleries, nooks and crannies and wondered what else beside the mummies lurked in those dark mouths yawning at us. What was it the two of you saw down in that off-shoot gallery?"

Paul-Emile looked at Hamdi then stared at his plate and took a bite of the stewed chicken.

"Thanks for the history lesson, habibi. However I must disappoint you. I didn't see anything special. Did you Paul-Emile?"

Paul-Emile sighed inaudibly and shook his head. "No, nothing, just a lot of debris from the crumbling walls and ceiling."

I licked my finger. "Do you think anything lives there besides the mummies, mice, rats and snakes? May I have some more of the cucumber salad please, it's delicious."

Hamdi handed me the bowl.

Beads of perspiration formed on Paul-Emile's forehead. He pushed his plate away.

Hamdi rose from his chair. "My dear friend, I've arranged for an orderly from the Anglo-American Hospital to stay with you tonight and tomorrow night if you wish."

He looked at his watch then opened the door and called to someone. He introduced the young man as Ali, who smiled and bowed. "He's at your service, as long as you need him."

I suppressed a laugh, rose from my chair and reached for my purse. I kissed Paul-Emile's cheek and told him I'd see him in the morning.

With a dark smoldering look he said in a dry tone, "Enjoy your visit with your relatives."

Hamdi took hold of my elbow and led me out into the hall. I was about to open my mouth when Hamdi shushed me and walked briskly to the elevator. Once on the elevator I said, "You are getting to be as commanding as Kane used to be."

"He was a good teacher, but he never allowed me to exert myself." He smiled.

"Are we really going to Uncle Youssef's now?"

"I told them we were coming."

The clan was waiting for us. I was kissed a hundred times and it didn't seem at all like four and a half years since I last saw them. We chatted late into the night and I was ready for bed when we said good bye.

Kane's cousin Zaya hugged me. "I've missed you so much, can't you stay longer? I have so much to tell you."

I hugged her back and was about to climb into the car when she said, "Did Hamdi tell you about the giant cobra he saw?"

"Where, when? No, he didn't say anything."

"See, there is much that has happened. Please stay a few days longer?"

"Where did you hear about the snake?"

"Uncle Tewfik's twins, the delightful creatures they are, know everything that goes on, so sometimes we chat on the phone. It takes away the boredom. They told me about the Frenchman staying at their house." She pinched my arm lightly and giggled. "They think he is your lover."

"The snake, Zaya."

"What?"

"The snake."

"Oh. One of the twins, I can never keep them straight, said the men from Malawi had to kill a giant cobra before they could get the Frenchman out of the pit. Why are you so interested what kind of a snake it was, does it matter?"

"No, not really. I'll tell you what, after the Frenchman leaves, we'll have tea and talk. I am bushed." I kissed and hugged her, then climbed into Hamdi's car.

When he drove off I said, "Zaya told me you saw a giant cobra in the catacomb."

"Where did she hear that story?"

"From Uncle Tewfik's twins."

"They exaggerated. It was nothing, just a small asp."

"Is that what spooked Paul-Emile. Did he warn you?"

"Of course habibi. He shouted, 'Snake', everybody heard him."

"Everybody. There were just the two of you. Are you telling the truth?"

"Do you want to come to my house now? What do you want to do?"

"You are evading me. I think I'd better go back to the hotel. After Paul-Emile leaves, I'll stay a few days with you."

Once back in the hotel room, Hamdi poured me a small cognac. I was wide awake again. "I want to talk about the snake."

"I don't." Hamdi gave me a stern look.

There was more to that snake than met the eye and I would find out. I excused myself and did my toilette, put on a nightgown and climbed onto the bed. "Kiss me Hamdi."

Chapter Twenty

The next morning Paul-Emile rang early and asked me to breakfast with him. When we sat opposite each other sipping coffee, he said, "Did Hamdi stay the night?"

I gave him an amused glance. "Hamdi and I have known each other a long time. We are like an old married couple. We don't need to spend the night together to enjoy each other's company."

"I'm sorry. I have never been involved with a woman who has a lover. This is a new experience. I am not sure how to handle it."

"Are you talking about your wife or a mistress?"

He blushed. "I don't have mistresses."

"Why do you have a flat on the Left Bank?"

"To get away from my wife naturally."

I rose and told him I needed to get ready for my luncheon date with my friend Fayza whom I met years ago when I lived in West Africa. "See you this afternoon."

"West Africa, you lived...."

"Monrovia, Liberia ... I'll tell you about that adventure some other time."

Shortly after I returned to my hotel room about three in the afternoon, Hamdi rang to say that he was heading to the airport to pick up Paul-Emile's wife. He'd be back in two or three hours. "Maybe you could keep Paul-Emile company until we arrive."

"Absolutely darling, I do want to see his face. What if he is telling the truth?"

I ordered tea and while I sipped I wrote ideas for my story in my notebook. The telephone rang, I ignored it. Soon it stopped. I lay on my bed and thought about Paul-Emile. He was becoming a bit clingy, that I couldn't stand.

Kane had always gone his own way. At first it had bothered me. But once I felt secure in our marriage and the children came along, I attributed his roving to his super abundant vitality. I looked at my watch, time to shower.

After I did my toilette, I dressed carefully, perfumed myself, fluffed my hair and blotted my lipstick. I knocked on Paul-Emile's door and entered his suite. He gave me a wry look.

"Ah, Madame can spare a few moments for this cripple."

"Are you feeling sorry for yourself?"

Ali came out of the bedroom. "Thank you Ali for taking care of Monsieur, I'll take over now. If we need you again I'll send word."

After Ali left, Paul-Emile said. "It's a pity things are the way they are between us. When I met you again I imagined you as my happiness pill, my cloud of happiness. Suddenly my life was precious again, expectant, full of dreams. Recently, when I slept, I felt your breath on my face, but when I woke you were further away than the stars in the sky."

I laughed softly.

Paul-Emile frowned, "You don't take what I say seriously, do you?"

"You should have told me this years ago. Now tell me about the snake."

"If you'd only give me a chance ... a few weeks. I'll make it up to you ... come to Paris." He reached for my hand.

"The snake, Paul-Emile."

He looked confused, "What snake...."

"The one you didn't tell Hamdi about when he tried to help you after you fell."

"I ... I did warn him...."

A knock on the door interrupted his reply. Paul-Emile sighed. She was small in stature with a well-preserved figure, clad in a snug-fitting red, knee-length, long sleeved, silk dress. She had abundant, short gray, wavy hair and her eyes, the color of husked chestnuts, sparkled as she practically exploded into the room on her red stiletto heels. Her light step gave an impression of youth. She flung herself at Paul-Emile's chest.

Paul-Emile cringed and shrunk into himself. Before he could say a word, she broke into rapid French then covered his ears with her hands and rained kisses on his face.

"*Mon amour, mon amour, mon pauvre amour*, are you in pain?"

I noticed her delicate, but somewhat aging hands, the backs of which were covered with freckle-like spots. Paul-Emile glowered at me and his mouth tightened in a stubborn line. When he seemed to have himself under control he said in English, "Celeste, Celeste, contain yourself, we are not alone."

Hamdi had followed her into the room and behind Hamdi stood a waif of a girl holding a valise. As if Celeste saw me for the first time she said, "*Enchanter, enchanter*, your secretary I presume? And Dr. Hamdi, a charming man. Ah, *mon pauvre enfant*, how I have worried about you since Dr. Hamdi called."

She turned to me. "I missed him so. He has never left me for so long before. Little trips, yes, but...." She dabbed delicately at her eyes with her lace handkerchief. "He is so frail and needs nurturing. Ever since the war ... the Boche ... that awful child...." She turned to Paul-Emile, "Celeste is here now, she will take care of you."

Paul-Emile's lips pursed with suppressed fury as Celeste dabbed at the lipstick on his face with her handkerchief. She waved the girl with the valise closer and spoke in French. The girl dug in the bag and withdrew a small bottle. She handed it to Celeste who unscrewed the top, took a whiff and made a face. She wafted it back and forth under her husband's nose who tried to get away. He managed to push her aside and struggled to a sitting position. His neck veins stood out in livid ridges as he shouted at her to leave him alone.

"Now don't excite yourself," she said, "you know it's bad for your health." She turned to us with a slight smile on her lips. "He is so heroic, so brave ... Matilde, I think a massage, your wonderful hands will soothe and relax him."

"Inge, give me those damn crutches."

Trying to hide a smile I handed Paul-Emile his crutches. He shoved the cocktail table aside and pushed himself off the sofa, hobbled into the bedroom and slammed the door.

Celeste looked lost and small as she stood in the middle of the room with her face buried in her hands. Her body shook as she lowered herself into one of the armchairs. With tears brimming in her eyes, she forced a smile on her trembling lips.

"I love him so much. He is my life. Every time he leaves me I am afraid I'll never see him again ... he is my life."

I felt a little sorry for her. "Surely Madame you are used to him going on excavations. After all, that is his work."

She had herself under control again. "I am not talking about *les excavation archéologie*, Camille always accompanies Paul-Emile on those. We have to watch him because he tried to commit suicide several times." She frowned, "Did my husband call you Inge?"

"That is my name." Suicide, my God, no wonder she was so concerned. Maybe that's why he said he'd been let out of prison. The prison of self-destructive tendencies. All of a sudden I understood his pain.

"You are not the child he rescued from the war ... no, it can't be. He told me she was dead." She glowered at me.

"Madame calm yourself, your husband was as surprised as you were when he hired me and found my name was Inge. A coincidence, for it reminded him also of the same child."

I turned to Hamdi. "Dr. Gamal, I think Madame and Matilde will take good care of Monsieur Diderot." To her I said, "If Monsieur needs me, please tell him to call me at Dr. Gamal's residence. He has the number. I shall just quickly inform Monsieur of my departure."

I knocked on the bedroom door.

"What do you want?"

"It's me, Inge, Monsieur. I came to say good bye."

"Come in." He sat bent forward on the bed with his forehead

resting on his palm. I whispered his name. His slumped shoulders straightened as he studied me with a stony expression.

I stepped into the room, shut the door behind me, and sat next to him on the bed. I took hold of his hand and stroked it. Poor Paul-Emile, so fragile after all and I had shown him little sympathy. When he'd told me in Marrakesh that he felt he'd escaped from prison, had he referred to his depression? Had our meeting lifted him out of his psychic pain? If so, how could I leave him like this?

As if hypnotized, he stared at my stroking fingers. His voice sounded dull and distant when he said, "I had a lot of problems adjusting when we returned to Paris. You were so carefree and happy, I envied and almost hated you at times. After all, your people were responsible for my misery and stolen youth. My parents sent me to a psychiatrist. After months of therapy she asked me to marry her."

"Celeste?"

"Yes."

"She is older than you?"

"Ten years. She's controlled my life by making me dependent upon her. I despise her. When you and I met so fortuitously, I felt suddenly jubilant, reckless and free. Whereas the sky was always gray before, our meeting showed me it was also blue and I saw the sun, its rays and felt their warmth. My life changed in an instant and I had hopes for the future.

"My prison walls melted like snow and I gloried in my new self, strong, independent. I gloried in my new free will, without direction, pure joy and happiness. I was foolish to ask you to marry me, but I wondered what it would be like. I realize of course that I can't desert Celeste at this stage in her life, it was just a transient dream. I am sorry."

I knelt before him and grasped his face between my hands. "I think our short time together has healed many wounds we've carried with us since childhood. Now we have cleansed ourselves and we can go on. We are not old yet. You've shown by your actions that you can be a free spirit. You are no longer dependent on

Celeste's ministrations and you know, as long as you see the sun brilliant and warm you can do anything you wish. I declare you cured of what ailed you." I kissed his lips lightly. "Call me if you ever need me and I'll come."

"Inge, I do love you and always did."

I said nothing. I squeezed his hand then rose and without looking back returned to the sitting room. Hamdi and Celeste watched me closely as I picked up my purse. I stretched out my hand to Celeste, "It's been a pleasure to meet you. I wish you both the best."

When Hamdi and I stood in the elevator he said, "You are finished with him now?"

"I am finished with him."

A happy smile spread over his face. He took my elbow and led me to his car. "My house?"

"Let's try that gold bed of yours, shall we? And after we'll call the girls."

"And after that I am going to take you on a Mediterranean cruise. First stop Beirut, second stop Latakia, agreed?"

"Agreed." I pulled Samia's letter out of my purse, tore it into a hundred small pieces and let them fly one by one out of the window.

"What are you littering Cairo's streets with?"

"Oh, something to do with love and trust, habibi.

Epilogue

Cairo, 2004

While Hamdi and I sat on the roof of his house in Giza enjoying our ritual evening cocktail, Cairo resonated with hundreds of muezzins calling the faithful to evening prayer. Their melodious voices, each having selected his own pitch and tempo, sounded like a discordant symphony. Even though I had been coming to Cairo for over forty years and considered it my second home, I never ceased to be enchanted by the mysticism of this ancient land.

Hamdi unfolded his lanky frame from the wicker chair, leaned on the wall and looked at Cheop's illuminated pyramid. "Habibi, when will you live with me forever? I am thinking about retiring. My bones ache and creak when I crawl around our excavations. Always we find something new, sometimes I think we've just begun. When I'm a hundred we will still be digging for treasures."

I joined him at the wall. He placed his arm across my shoulders and hugged me. "I still love you more than life."

I stood on my toes and kissed his lips. "Don't be greedy. I am already spending most of my time with you. Magda complains that I neglect my grand parenting duties and Dena and Stephanie say they are lonely when they come home and find the house empty. You could always move in with me."

"Ah, habibi, I still have so much to do here. Do you ever hear from Paul-Emile?"

"Once a year for the last twenty years. He sends me a birthday card and two dozen red roses, otherwise we have no contact. He still claims to love me, does that surprise you?"

"Maybe you were too hard on him."

"I thought you were pleased that I cut the cord."

"Yes, but I felt a bit sorry for him. I think he loved you."

The telephone interrupted my reply. Hamdi whispered, "It's Camille Diderot." He handed me his cell phone.

I listened. "I'll leave tomorrow." I handed Hamdi his phone. "Paul-Emile is ill. His wife recently died. Camille thinks I can cheer him up."

"You must go of course."

"Could you make the arrangements, please?"

Camille Diderot and to my surprise Dena awaited me at Charles De Gaulle Airport.

"What are you doing here?"

She kissed me. "Ever since Camille sat in the front row at the Sydney Opera House as he'd promised when we first met, we've been seeing each other off and on over the years. He keeps asking me to marry him."

"And you never said a word. Since when have we been keeping secrets from each other?"

"Oh Mommy, don't frown, it's no secret really. It's just that Camille no longer empties out the flower shops every few weeks, a sign he's ready to settle down." She linked arms with Camille and gave him a quick kiss.

"Madame, do you remember our trip to Siwa Oasis?"

"Of course. You said you were smitten."

Dena and Camille laughed.

"And so was I," she said. "It's just that we both have been so busy, but now ... how is Uncle Hamdi, and Stephanie ... haven't heard from her for ages."

I stared at them. Camille resembled his father so much it was eery. "Fine, fine, he's thinking of retiring. Stephanie is in Dubai playing, as always, to win. After her victory at the Ladies Open last year she's finally concentrating more on men. Hope she finds someone soon before it's too late to have babies."

"I hope so too."

"How is Paul-Emile?"

"Apathetic," Camille said, "he's lost his will to live since my mother died suddenly four weeks ago."

"I am sorry for your loss."

"She was eighty-seven, still strong, willful and domineering. Then one day he found her dead in bed."

"How horrible."

"He's been depressed for years," Dena said, "but now we are really worried about him. We thought maybe you could snap him out of it."

"Is he aware I am coming?"

"We told him." Camille said.

When I entered the Diderot apartment, I almost gasped, for nothing had changed. I walked slowly through the rooms and entered the kitchen, almost expecting Emma to sit at the kitchen table drinking a cup of tea. Instead it was Paul-Emile sitting at the table twirling his pipe. I stood for a moment watching him. He turned his head in my direction and regarded me. Then he slowly laid down his pipe, put his head on his arms on the table and wept.

I massaged his thin, quivering shoulders, pressed my tear-stained cheek against his head and mumbled soothing words. When he had himself under control, he whispered, "I killed her." He looked up at me.

I smiled, not believing a word.

Paul-Emile's head sank despondently onto his chest once more, he passed his hand over his face. "I administered her medication every morning and night. Sometimes she counted the pills, other times she just emptied the small salt cellar I used and washed them down with her coffee. That fateful morning I distracted her by showing her an article in 'Psychology Today' I knew she'd be interested in. With my heart in my throat I gave her seven of her time-release morphine capsules. She swallowed them absentmindedly ... without looking ... trusting me ... only interested in the article on behavior modification for those afflicted with dementia. When she asked to be helped back to bed I obliged. She never woke up." His voice had grown hoarse.

I gave him a glass of water.

"She made my life miserable and when she refused to allow Camille to marry Dena because she was your daughter, I knew I had to free us of her." He groped for my hand. "Inge, what must I do now?"

I stared at him in disbelief. Not wanting to add to his pain, I said calmly, "Nothing. It'll be our secret."

He shook his head. "It's my turn now, but I don't have the courage."

He stuck his hand into his jacket pocket. I expected to see a gun in his hand, but he withdrew a small blue pouch instead.

"Your diamonds. I'm sorry I kept them so long." He handed me the pouch.

I opened the draw string and shook them onto my palm. "They are rather small, aren't they?"

"A carat each I think."

I leaned over and kissed his cheek. "Thank you Paul-Emile, I'd almost forgotten about them. Whatever happened to the Luger?"

He fiddled with his pipe. "I threw it into the Seine when Camille was born."

"It's dangerous to keep a gun in a house with children."

"Inge, please ask Camille and Dena to join us, I have something to say to all of you."

"You sound so morose." I rose and hugged him. "You should be happy. We can plan for a wedding now, no more obstacles."

He looked at me with tears glistening in the corner of his eyes. "Our wedding?"

I smiled. "No silly, Camille's and Dena's."

"What about us?"

"I guess we'll be sort of family after they marry." I tried to sound cheerful. "We'll celebrate all the holidays together." I bent forward and tried to coax a smile.

"And Hamdi?"

"Hamdi?" I asked surprised. "Why, Hamdi will be there too

of course."

He nodded, "Of course. Please ask the children to join us."

Their music floated through the apartment, Camille at the piano and Dena playing her violin. I silently entered the music room, lowered myself onto a chair and waited for them to finish.

Suddenly a gun shot rendered us motionless.

I jumped up and followed by Camille and Dena ran into the kitchen. Camille extracted a note Paul-Emile clutched in his lifeless left hand. He straightened and glanced at it, then silently handed me the note.

Paul-Emile had written in French. My little Inge. Peace is at hand. I honestly loved you from the first moment we met. Over the years I often scolded myself, you were a fool Paul-Emile to allow others to take over your responsibilities. But it was the easy way out. And now my love, finally, the years of yearning and loneliness are about to come to an end. Thank you for coming and allowing me to gaze upon you once more. The gate to freedom is about to open. Love my son as your own, that's all I ask of you now. Till we meet again, your Paul-Emile.

The End

Select Bibliography

Thorwald, Juergen, 'Defeat In The East'. Ballantine Books 1951

Zacharias, Rainer, 'Neues Marienburger Heimatbuch'. Verlag Wendt Groll GMBH, 49 Herford 1967

Knopp, Guido, 'Die grosse Flucht'. Ullstein Verlag 2002

Ertel, Manfred, 'A Legacy of Dead German Children'. Spiegel Online International 2005